£2.49

Mind Games & Ministers

Chris

First Printed Edition, Chris L. Longden, 2014

Published in partnership with Seed to Deed Ltd

Chris L. Longden

Mind Games & Ministers

IN MEMORY OF EMMA PRIEST:

24 Oct 1972 – 9 Dec 2013

Best friend, wife, sister, Godmother. Expert on drinking tea, on doing good by stealth. On laughing. And on loving life.

Acknowledgements:

Nurture & Never-ending Story: Ian, Ruby and Gregory Agnew

Nature & Nurture: Yvonne and Brian Longden, Steven, Rozina, Eesaa and Yaaseen Longden/Chaudry

Editor: Laura Ripper

Editorial Support: Leonora Rustamova and Tim E Taylor

The Champions: Ian and Helen Stubbs, Kay and Colin Fitter, Simon Byrne, Gina Parker, Lori Gimelshteyn, Melanie Leveque & the Fawcetts, Naomi Baker, Liz Sykes, Helena Thornton, Anthony Nealy, Charlotte Dawn O'Connor, Willemien le Roux, Helen Vale, Octavia Leigh, Jacinta and David Heydecker, Sarette Strauss, Lisa Haworth, Steph Chamberlain, Alison Rayner, Lesley Elliott, Ilana Alix, Margaret Edwards, Nina Cooper, Stuart Vallantine, Hanzina Vries, Brian Snell, the Lorna Young Foundation crew, DOL lasses and all of the Holmfirth Writers Group

*(**Note to reader:** a key to explaining the chapter titles can be found at the end of the book)*

About The Author

Chris Longden was born, and grew up, in Tameside, Greater Manchester, UK.

Her career has focussed on social housing and community development. She lived in Namibia, southern Africa for several years, where she gave birth to her first child whilst working with the Kalahari 'San' bushmen. She wrote and edited two books on the lives of the San.

Chris now lives with her family in west Yorkshire, where she manages the Lorna Young Foundation and is a founding partner of Not Just a Trading Company.

Chris occasionally writes at her 'funnylass' blog and always welcomes followers. But only if they have a marvellous sense of humour and appreciate fine coffee, political and social commentary. And budgies …

http://funnylass.wordpress.com

Prologue 1

FRIGG IN HELL: ONE YEAR AGO – IN SEPTEMBER

It took approximately five seconds for me to lose them from my line of sight. Just ten of my longest strides, swinging round the corner, and then they were gone. Twenty yards away, over the road, the number 308 bus to Huddersfield was shuddering out carbon monoxide as a random collection of passengers waited to board.

If I could make it across the road without looking over my shoulder. Concentrate on scrabbling together the correct bus fare. Ignore the burgeoning gravity of the situation.

Then I could be at London King's Cross by 3 p.m. and on the Eurostar by 5 p.m. France by 8 p.m. Passport already conveniently in handbag. Funny, that.

Even now, even in the midst of this unhinged act, my mind was a whirl of timing and computations. But calculating the logistics of international escape, the perusal of timetables and the possibilities of self-catering apartments in Brittany would at least prove to be exotic, more tantalising preoccupations than the usual drudgery. The never-ending conveyor belt. A ceaseless procession of bags, books, shoes, dinner money, nursery fees, medicines, nappies and crappy plastic toys that Grandma always insists on buying.

The burden of domestic dross is bad enough when two of you have to share it. But on your own? It's frigging hell.

So I waited for a pause in the never-ending stream of the A616 traffic. The 'Car is King' world. Self-obsessed drivers, oblivious to pedestrians teetering on the kerb. Not a road for the dyspraxic sorts, this one.

I smiled wryly. Now wouldn't that be fortuitous? To end up getting squished by a car instead. Our local headlines would proclaim "Mother of Two Tragically Killed in Tourist Town – Leaves Orphans". The word "Mother". It could be so powerful; so evocative.

So suffocating.

But in the end, I didn't cross the road.

It wasn't, however, the thought of little Matthew, clad in a thin fleece and shivering in his pushchair, that changed my mind. No. The hasty retreat was effected by less obvious maternal manipulations.

Imagine this, Rachael.

A forty-eight-inch TV screen. A crappy day time chat show For Real People and Their Problems.

Cut to an excited looking audience. Cut to my daughter, Lydia. Of how she might end up looking, at the age of sixteen. Slouched on a studio chair, clad in black with a smearing of purple-noir eye make-up. Wearing a sullen and slack-jawed expression. The sleazy chat show host now rolling up his verbal sleeves for the inevitable sparring.

"So, Lydia. When you were five years old, your mother, Rachael here, abandoned you and your little brother Matthew. Leaving you outside a cafe. That must have been devastating!"

Cut to appalled facial expressions of the audience. Lydia responds:

"Totally. An' it were that café from that Last Of The Summer Wine *TV programme. An' she left us next to that life-sized Compo the Tramp dummy. Me and our Matt have had, like, this phobia of wellies ever since."*

Cut to me. Having gained some sixty pounds. Having lost two front teeth. Three inches of black roots showing. Rachael burned-out blondeness. About to launch a whining defence of how difficult it had been, trying to bring up two kids on your own…

I plummeted back down to reality.

No.

I stepped back from the kerb.

I would not be embarking upon the Eurotunnel escape route. Mummy might well be a God-awful mummy, but at least she will be there to fight her corner when the children hit their even-arsier teenage years and no doubt decide to accuse her of physical, mental and emotional neglect.

Turning around, I scuttled back to the little buggers. They couldn't have been on their own for more than a couple of minutes. I had left them behind the queue for *The Last Of The Summer Wine* tour bus just next to the bacon-butty cafe. Before they entered my field of vision, I heard a Lydia-lamentation:

"Mummy!"

I stopped at the corner of the charity shop, my cheek hovering millimetres from the chilly brickwork. A voyeuristic curiosity. Wanting to see how they felt about my absence. Lydia was flapping those perpetually mitten-clad hands. A perfect picture of despair. Matthew was clenching the sides of his pushchair and leaning forward. Copying his sister's exhortations, but with a lusty bellow and a twist of the west Yorkshire accent:

"MUUUH-MEH!"

Toddler version of the haka. An overwhelming waft of scorched bacon and eggs wasn't helping to dampen the testosterone overdrive. Matthew was not thinking "Mummy's buggered off somewhere and I'm well naffed off about the prospect of orphanhood!"

Nah. Matthew wanted a bacon butty.

Similarly, Lydia wasn't really distressed. She had conjured up her best am-dram posturing and was about to yell again when an older couple - a pair of walkers - adorned in matching yellow Gore-Tex, stopped.

"Have you lost your mummy, lovey?"

Lydia ignored the woman, wiping snail-trails from her nose onto her coat sleeves and commenced this time with the "MUH-MEEEH!" version of my name. Matthew, distracted by the man's Nordic walking pole, grabbed it and attempted to bite it. The man resisted and yanked the stick back. Matthew yelled incomprehensible insults at him. One of the customers seated at the outside cafe tables winced at a waitress.

"Bluh-deee 'ell! 'Ee's got a set of lungs on 'im!"

Unluckily for them, Matthew had inherited his father's booming intonations.

Yellow-clad lady tried again.

"Is your mummy in the cafe? Shall we go and look for her?" She tried to take Lydia's hand, but Lydia yanked it away, as if the woman's touch had burned her. Small brown curls shook out a furious declaration.

"If you get lost you must always stand in one place and shout for your mummy! You don't ever go anywhere with a stranger!" Liddy raised her voice up another notch. "Because strangers might look nice on the outside. But they're all evil on the inside! And you're one of those evil strangers. And you want to steal me!"

The pleasant chatter from the cafe tables and the Summer Wine tour bus queue ceased. Customers were staring at the drama. My offspring were certainly giving the usual brass band or Morris dancers you got appearing in Holmfirth market square a damned good run for their money.

I decided to stop the lingering and a-wavering behaviour. I made a beeline towards the children.

Gore-Tex lady was looking a tad upset. Obviously not used to being outed as one of Satan's minions in a very public place. Attempting to reassure Lydia that, no, she was actually a nice person. But Matthew was grabbing at the woman's walking pole. He won his prize this time, swinging it above his head in triumph. But managing to whack his sister in the face in the process.

It took five minutes to stop Lydia's nose from bleeding and to soothe the trauma with a packet of Smarties. I put on my 'smiley, bubbly, coping with life's little foibles' face and tried to exit with some grace. Adopting a hollow claim that I had "just nipped around the corner to look for my little boy's fluffy bunny – he must have dropped it somewhere", I attempted to usher the children ahead of me. But my cleverly constructed image floundered. Countered by Lydia.

"What fluffy bunny, Mummy? Matthew doesn't have a fluffy bunny! He doesn't have a bunny that's fluffy. He's got a green panda. But that's in his pushchair with him. And a panda isn't a bunny, is it? Which bunny do you mean?"

The cappuccino crew could now see me for the child-abandoning harridan that I truly was. Yeah. Cheers for that, Lydia.

"Sssh!" I hissed at her. "Come on!" Yanking her by the collar of her jacket. Perhaps I tugged too hard. But months of sleep-deprivation ladled with lashings of shame are not the best ingredients for parental patience and all things apple pie. The collar-dragging only gave her licence to burst into choking tears again.

"But Mummy. Don't be mean! I thought you'd gone and left us. Just like Daddy did!"

I stopped pulling her.

A scramble, a jumble of fear must have been brewing in that little head of hers. Despite my assumptions that she hadn't missed me for the two minutes that I had fled from them. I softened my voice.

"Oh, Liddy. Come here. You daft thing." Folding my arms about her. She oozed Smartie-streaked snot and tears into my hair, her little body racked with sobs. Matthew though, didn't want to be left out of the drama. He took the opportunity to herald a word that I had never heard from this child before.

"Da-deee! Da-deee!" I did my best to ignore that latest little development.

"Lydia, sweetie – Liddy!" I crouched down to face her. Holding her at arm's length.

"Liddy – listen. I'm not going anywhere. And your daddy didn't leave us, you know!" The latte-lovers were still staring nonchalantly at their afternoon's entertainment. At this clapped-out thirty-eight-year-old mother of two. Whose husband must have just recently deserted her. Probably for a classier, more tanned and toned younger model, despite her public denials to the contrary.

"Lydia – your daddy still loves you. He always will. We've talked about this before, haven't we?" Lydia's sobbing escalated into a high-pitched, wolfish howl. She gnawed at those red woolly mittens, telling me:

"I know, I know that really. But he's still gone 'n' left us. Hasn't he? And I don't know what to do now!" She buried her soggy face into my neck.

The people at the cafe averted their gazes. Carried on with previous conversations. Embarrassed. Or bored. Perhaps hoping that a random accordion player or an itinerant folk dancer might turn up, for a much-needed change of scene.

Ignoring the audience, I engaged my brain in some serious mental pummelling. I should have known. Should have bloody well known. Lydia was a little girl with an uncanny ability to read between the lines. She had seen me rip open the oh-so-casual-looking white envelope that had popped through our letterbox those few weeks ago. She must have witnessed the look of horror on my face. And even when I thought that she was safely tucked up in bed and away from the adult world, it turned out that she had overheard those telephone conversations. "Who were you shouting at last night? About them getting married and you not knowing about it, Mummy?"

Yes. Lydia would have been able to sense just how desperate I had been feeling recently. She would have soaked up the escalating depression after the initial, overriding horror. My girl would have known just how close I had come to actually getting onto that bus and scarpering from them both.

So my hug for her was forceful. Transmission via osmosis. No 'child-appropriate' language for this little situation.

Please believe me, Liddy. My maternal shortcomings may be all too apparent these days. But I'm going nowhere. You can trust me on that one …

(Still, lady. Don't you ever – and I mean ever – make me do that shitty daytime TV chat show thing. Because then, I really will sod off and disown the pair of you …)

Prologue 2

KERES ON THE ROOF: 20 MONTHS AGO – IN JANUARY

The wind is whipping, whooping about the building. Perhaps this strange howling is coming from an unwanted mythical being, curling itself around the spire of the chapel. And maybe I'm beginning to believe in the luck of the gods.

Meaning that there'll be a group of vengeful creatures up there. Having a field day of it all. Icing themselves to the slates. Waiting for the inevitable fall of snow some hours later. Then leaping off and landing upon the next poor, unfortunate sod to be in the wrong place, at the wrong time.

Lydia is clinging to my dad. He has carried her from our house to cortege car, then from Daimler to departure point. No one can prise her away from Grandad today. But Grandad isn't as hard-wearing as he used to be. He'll be in agony with his bad back by this afternoon.

I feel bad about this. I should have been the one to clutch her wee five-year-old flesh 'n' bones to my own vastly receding bosom, throughout this day. But I'm not too steady on my feet right now. Bit lightheaded. Tablets from the doc.

"We can't rely on our Rachael to get it all done properly. She's a bit off her head at the moment, Terry ... she's talking a right load of tosh," I heard my mother saying to my dad the week before. And Dad replying, "Well. She always talked a load of tosh, love. And right now, I reckon that she can probably be forgiven for talking even more crap than she normally does."

And it's funny, because today I've been thinking a lot about clothes. Most unlike me. Tripping along behind the coffin, I wonder if I should have rifled through our loft. Resurrected my bike leathers. Hardly funeral wear, of course. But definitely warmer. And somehow more appropriate. Adam would have taken one glance at me shivering in the pew here, at me in my daft dark blouse, skirt and opaque tights and would have said:

"Ha! Rach. You look like Miss Prudeypants of Prudesville in that get-up."

He would have preferred the smell of linseed and leather, as opposed to Lily of the Sodding Valley, which mother insisted on squirting onto me earlier. Cheers for that, Mum.

Something is missing. My eyes flick from left to right. Where is the Whiffy Boy? Oh, yes. I remember now. Matthew is at the childminder's. Too cold for a toddler to be to-ing and fro-ing in these kind of temperatures.

And Matthew wouldn't be able to remember this day, anyway. We all said that when we were talking about The Children.

Lydia is unbearably quiet. She chews at the new red mittens that Adam's mum bought her yesterday. Her tiny globe-eyes peering through sodden wool at the rows of people behind her. Scanning them all, politely perched on their clenched buttocks. And those who are lurking, standing up at the back of the congregation. She has probably never seen so many grown-ups in one place.

I only glance around once, but I can instantly pick out Shaun's towering form. Head and shoulders above all the others. Although, of course, I knew that he was there anyway, before I could see him. I can always tell. My legs feel the adrenaline before my eyes can clock the sight.

And then I hear Big Jim, over in the next aisle. Out of hospital now. Managed to get him here in time. Jim is on crutches. Is sobbing. Must be a bugger trying to blow your nose when you can barely move your legs or arms properly.

The minister ends his sermon. But I'm not really listening. He's been wittering on about Adam's love for bikes, rock music, his family and his gadgets. And all that's fine. The minister is a good chap. Your ultra-

liberal sort. Warm heart, big smile. Lots of wriggle room for a slightly different approach. To life. And to death.

So we're having a quickie-funeral at the crem itself. I didn't want any unnecessary fannying around from church to crem and back home again. I can't be doing with all those stupid, twatty up-yourself cars. It might be a rite of passage for some – but for Adam it would have been a "bloody great big waste of money".

So, yeah. Everything has gone the way that I – that Adam – would have wanted it to go. The wishes of the dearly departed and all that. Not that we ever seriously discussed this kind of thing with each other. Dying was something that Adam didn't waste a minute thinking about.

Dying was an irrelevance.

And now comes the irreverence. A very personal, discreet oh-so-sinful grinful. My mother has no idea about this. She is going to be appalled. "Not appropriate, Terry," she'll say to my dad afterwards.

I might have been operating in la-la land over the last couple of weeks, but I had managed to instruct the funeral director about certain requirements. That the wooden box containing the body of my husband should move along to the music. In style. Our style.

As the minister gives the signal, the velvet curtains twitch. And the conveyor belt – that dark, flat tongue starts-up and beckons my beloved to another form of existence.

A gentle mechanical humming can be heard. Ready now. And the sound system kicks in. The coffin judders forward.

Those dust-blighted, velvet curtains open. I see several people on either side of me jump at the Shock of the Rock.And it's Adam's favourite. His own request.

"If I kick the bucket before you do, Rach – I want to go out to AC/DC's 'Highway To Hell'."

And I'm laughing and I'm crying.

I'm laughing and I'm crying.

Chapter 1

PANDORA ON THE DOORSTEP: REAL TIME

"I'm piggin' sick of this Indian summer malarkey. I'm sweatin' bloody cobs, I am," the bulky and perspiring man installed behind the counter at Mottram Post Office had felt the need to tell me. But after waggling the collar of his shirt in order to emphasise his sogginess, he had been surprisingly helpful in providing the directions to the constituency home. Apparently, I was "too blonde and too good-looking to be a terrorist," or to be any other kind of random nutter who might have ambitions to blow up an innocent politician. So he didn't mind telling me where the fella lived. Providing that I convey a message from Post Office Man to the Right Honourable Michael Chiswick to "get his lot to do something to sort out all the bloody immigrants here. And all the dog muck. Ruining our country, those sort of things are."

I managed to keep my gob shut. For once.

Two minutes later I had found the cottage and parked my tiny about-town car outside. I was enjoying the fact that for the first time in over twenty months I was not accompanied by two small people. So, no one to argue with over whether the use of seat-belts was some kind of odd whim that Mummy liked to inflict on them out of sheer malice.

I half expected to see some sort of bodyguard-type person hanging around. I knew that government ministers usually had some kind of protection. But perhaps the weekend beefcakes had been culled in the latest round of government spending cuts. Maybe these days they were only herded out for public events. I grabbed the parcel from the cool-box again and locked my car. It was a sweet-looking cottage, for sure.

Morning glory going a bit wild, but that added to its charm. A snug-looking little home, tucked well behind the railway line. Away from prying eyes.

Somebody had invested quite a bit of money in the front door. Top-notch security model, by the looks of it. But crafted to look olde-worlde, with stained glass and a brass fish-shaped door knocker. I gave it a tentative rap. Then waited a minute. Must be no one home. I decided that Michael Chiswick would be doing the usual thing that his social class got up to at the weekends. Punting down the Cherwell, sipping Pimms, no doubt. Shooting pheasants (or peasants?) Or maybe he was halfway through some seedy session with a high-class whore in Kensington. A bit of bottom-spanking of a Saturday afternoon. I was about to turn and leave, but then the door opened. The man himself.

"Why, hello there!"

A cheery greeting. He seemed to recognise me, but looked slightly puzzled. Probably not expecting the woman who hung out with battered ladies to be prancing about on his doorstep. He was wearing a stained T-shirt (the stain appearing to be something like oil) accompanied by a pair of long shorts. And carrying a screwdriver.

This was a stupid idea, Rachael. Should've just dumped the damned parcel at his constituency office or something.

"Look, I'm sorry to bother you at the weekend," I began, "only the women at Sisters' Space forgot to give you their thankyou gift when you came to visit us at the centre the other week. The publicity's already been helping us with early sales. Even before we've actually opened the shop and cafe."

"That's good to hear! We aim to please. It's excellent stuff – what you're doing there."

"So, anyway. Here's the gift that they made. I said I'd drop it off. I live just over the tops – in Holme village. I'm not a constituent of yours, but my parents are. Down the road in Stalybridge."

Too much information, Rachael. Like he gives a toss.

But he beamed at me, and then at the parcel. I wasn't sure whether it was Politician-Smile or Genuine Smile.

"How very kind of you all. It's got to be chocolate, right?"

I nodded. "Yes. So pop it into your fridge straight away or it's going to melt pretty fast in this heat. I've had it in a cool-box while I drove here. I don't have air con in my car. Well. I don't have the flashiest of cars. As you can see. But we decided to put more than the usual amount of chocolate into your gift pack. So you probably shouldn't eat all of that yourself. Maybe you could give some to your mother or something?"

I stopped in horror.

Advice to the Minister for Communities on the refrigeration of foodstuff? Excuses about owning a farty little car? Assumptions about his private life? And – oh, God – his mother is probably dead or something. A hideous skiing accident. Or the result of a malfunctioning stairlift in her Georgian mansion perhaps …

And now he was frowning. And patting his stomach. Looking up at me. Brows furrowed.

"Are you saying that I need to lose some weight?"

I gave up all pretences of polite, professional chit-chat now. I semi-panicked, free-wheeling into:

"Well, come to mention it, Michael, you have been giving Eric Pickles a bit of a run for his money these days …" I sniggered. Quite the wit.

But he didn't seem to be sharing the joke. In fact, he looked rather taken aback.

Faux pas. Michael Chiswick won't be used to sarcastic bints from Stalybridge. The females that he will be more familiar with, will no doubt be your fawning types. No. Having the mickey taken out of Michael by the opposite sex would not be the done thing.

I half-flung the parcel towards him.

"That was a joke. Obviously. I mean, you're probably the fittest minister in the Cabinet. Well, I don't mean 'fit' in the northern sense of the word. That people would fancy you or anything. I mean – you look like you enjoy a good workout. Pumping your iron, or whatever they call it."

He simply looked at me. Quite amazing, unusual clearest-grey eyes. He hadn't taken the parcel from me. I gabbled on.

"Oh, God. Look. Just ignore me. I'd better be off."

My cheeks were tingling. And not from UVA/UVB over-exposure. He was leaning against the door frame now, fiddling with the end of the fish's tail on the door knocker. After a short silence he gave me his considered response.

"Your pedicure choices are interesting."

I looked down at my sandals. That morning I had yielded to Lydia's demands to get the nail varnish out ("you never do girly things with me!"). Consequently, my toenails were various shades of electric blue, magenta and fluorescent green. Classy. Plus a home-made 'tattoo' that she had lovingly scrawled onto my foot in order to complete our pampering session. In felt-tip. *Mummy Smelz.*

"Clearly not a trend that's reached London yet," I tossed my head. Holding the gift towards him still (please take the sodding parcel).

"Certainly not something that I've seen the ladies of Chelsea wearing recently." He took the parcel at last and gestured towards his mucky T-shirt.

"Still, as you can see, I'm not one to talk about style. Been messing with my bike all morning." He gestured to a Triumph parked at the side of the house. A bloody bike. My thoughts began to drift. But his voice called me back to planet earth.

"Listen. I've just made some coffee. Do you want some? It's the finest Oromo Ethiopian stuff."

Trepidation.

I blamed Lydia for all this. This caution. Her stranger-danger obsession must be infectious. Yesterday I had overheard her trying to drill it into her three-year-old brother.

"And, Matthew, you should always make sure that a grown-up knows where you are. And who you are with. Even though you're a stinky bum and no one would want to murder or kidnap you anyway!"

So I told my mind to cut the crap. Just accept the offer of a brew. I nodded. "But only if you're not a serial killer. Because no one knows where I am."

"Strictly speaking, I'm not a serial killer. I don't do it regularly enough to qualify for the accolade."

He beckoned me to follow him into the house, calling over his shoulder, "Leave the front door open. It's stifling today, isn't it?"

I followed him down the hallway, under a low ceiling, original beams exposed. Probably late eighteenth century, like a dozen or so other cottages in Mottram. Just before the end of the passage I paused to peer at a framed photograph on the wall. Four men, all grinning manically at the camera. Tanned and sporty looking. Michael was on the far left. His hairline had barely changed since the photo had been taken, but these days silver rivalled the auburn. The men were padded out in identical black skiing jackets, goggles and other protective paraphernalia. White-capped mountains in the background. Ha. I had been right about his family. Wealthy skiing sorts, no doubt.

My thoughts were interrupted by the crunch of gravel at the cottage gates. Craning their necks to see past the open door were two children. A boy and a girl. Aged about twelve. Both astride bikes and both out of breath.

"Hey, Missus – Missus!"

I moved back outside. The girl had a chubby face and bright pink cheeks, splashed with freckles. She was bubbling over with High Drama.

"There's a fingy – a disaster! Can you come and 'elp?"

Michael was behind me now.

"What's the problem?"

The boy had two jagged front teeth. A bit accident-prone, no doubt, giving him a cheeky pre-pubescent vampire look. He gabbled,

"It's that old lady – she's gone an' 'ad a flood!"

"Which old lady?"

"You know – the mad old one round the corner. With the dodgy cat. Come on!" They manoeuvred their bikes back around. I glanced at Michael.

"Probably nothing," I said. "But I'll go and take a look."

"I'll come with you," he answered, rubbing his hands together. "I've not got much else on the agenda for this afternoon. So, let's go and see whatever it is that Freckles and Fang are on about!"

After locking the front door, we both broke into a run down the hill after the speeding pedal-kids. I was glad that I had chosen a sturdy bra that day. Not wanting to be afflicted with Jogger's Black Eye. I called over to Michael.

"Freckles and Fang, you said. Do you know those two, then?"

"No idea. Don't know any neighbours, I'm afraid. Made the names up. Don't tell anyone though. It'd be 'Minister Insults Chavvy Children' all over Twitter, before you know it."

The children dumped their bikes on a communal lawn outside some former council-owned maisonettes at the bottom of the hill. They vanished inside. The front door of one flat was wide open. Water was trickling out and over the threshold.

"Hello?" I called, as I approached the front door. No answer. I slipped my sandals off and Michael followed, kicking his scruffy Tevas onto the lawn. The water wasn't too cold, but the sensation of sodden carpet on my toes was most unpleasant. I swished my way into an old-fashioned but smart-looking little home. Now a watery mess. Freckles and Fang were balancing on the furniture. Standing on sofas in wet trainers was clearly something that these children didn't consider to be a discourtesy. Water was pouring down the walls and dripping in rivulets from the ceiling.

A memory uncorked itself. Bobbed to the surface.

This maisonette's layout was exactly the same as the one that Shaun and I had carried out some late-night surveillance at. Over in Manchester. Well over a decade ago now.

The police had been hard-pressed on time and officers available. Told us that if we wanted to get the drug-pushers evicted – and convicted – it would be quickest to catch them on camera ourselves. As usual there were more than a dozen empty properties in that part of Whalley Range and there happened to be one, a void – exactly opposite to where the dealers were living.

And Shaun and I had performed more than a bit of discreet surveillance on the druggies that night.

I remembered it had been hard, rough stuff. Up against the wall of Bedroom Number One.

I remembered that at one point Shaun had knocked over the tripod that the video camera was balanced on.

I remembered thinking, "It used to be gentle, but now it's frantic. Frenetic. But maybe this is just us? Me and Shaun. How it will always be."

I didn't understand why, then. I probably thought, "Better this than nothing."

Brought back to reality with a bang. Or rather, a squelchy farting sound. Clearly a speciality of Fang's, who was squeezing his wet palms together and chuckling away at his ingenuity as he bobbed up and down on the sofa. Delighted to have an audience to present the catastrophe to, he chanted, "He's gone upstairs. The man what lives here. To the flat above. Where the woman what's flooded it lives. An' he's goin' mental at 'er! He —"

I interrupted him.

"Has anyone switched the electricity off? Or the water?"

"Dunno!" they chimed in unison. Fang added, "Woah! Maybe there'll be a massive explosion an' we'll all get killed!"

The girl continued.

"We only just found it, like, five minutes ago. We saw the old bloke what lives 'ere get back from town on the bus. He went in his house – in

’ere – and saw all the water. And then he came runnin’ out and was bangin’ on ’er door. Then he went into ’er place an’ started totally freakin’ out at ’er. The weirdy old lady.”

“He’s goin’ loop-the-friggin’-loop at ’er!” Fang agreed. “Can you ’ear ’im up there?”

I turned to Michael. “I’ll go up to the next flat. See if they’ve made things safe up there. You stay here with these two. Find some pans in the kitchen or something. Start bailing out.”

I squished back outside and found the entrance to the upstairs flat. The door was wide open and I could hear shouting. Water was gently flowing down the poor-quality stairs carpet. No point in trying to announce my arrival. They probably wouldn’t be able to hear me above the yelling.

As I reached the top of the stairs, the stench hit me. A combination of soggy, mildewed material, accompanied by ‘animal pong’. And something else more acrid. Urine. Great.

Now, I would never describe my own home as being on the right side of ‘clean’. It contained plenty of kiddy-generated muckiness. But my house wasn’t crawling dirty. And my home wasn’t sofa-sticks-to-your-arse minging. This place was, however. And this smell was considerably worse than the ‘social-housing whiff’ that you sometimes encounter in rented properties at the lower end of the market – that sickly concoction of sweat, dirt, stale air, mould and damp. Here was good old-fashioned Filth. Here was years of grime and neglect.

The flat belonged to an elderly woman. In her early nineties by the looks of it. Sitting in a wing-backed armchair and clad in a mauve, badly stained polyester dress. She had wild, candy-flossed white hair and crumpled skin the colour of an old, yellowed elastic band. Like me, she had bare feet. But unlike me she seemed to be enjoying the experience, attempting to swish the soggy carpet beneath her toes. The TV was blaring out some dreadful daytime quiz show at maximum volume and standing opposite her, hands on hips and puce with rage, was her neighbour. Stout and seventy-something, with tufts of white hair springing from everywhere except from his head. He acknowledged my presence by jabbing his finger at the armchair-lady.

“The bloody silly cow’s gone and wrecked my house! Left a tap on in her kitchen! I told the council to move her, God knows how many times!

I've told 'em that Miss Simpson is bloody doolally and they want to sort her out. But did they take any notice? Oh, no! It's all about civil liberties these days. Even if they're off their trolley, like she is!" His trousers were soaked, almost up to the knees.

I spoke quietly, trying to take the edge off his anger.

"Have you made the place safe? Turned the stopcock off? We need to turn off the electrics, too."

He shook his head. "Yes. No. I should have done. I turned the tap off. Should've thought about the others. She bloody hasn't moved from her sodding chair. Stupid old bat!"

"I'll do it. Tell me where they are."

He gestured to the tiny room next door.

The kitchen stank. Flies free-wheeling around an overflowing bin. Rubbish ready to float in the water. Whether the flood had been caused by a running tap or a blocked sink, the situation hadn't been helped by several dozen half-empty tins of cat food on the counter, which covered the kitchen work surface, and filled the sink. Those, along with a similar number of empty HP sauce bottles and what seemed to be hundreds of empty cellophane wrappers for Supasave currant teacakes.

Interesting dietary habits.

Nestled on a sideboard stacked with yellowing newspapers was the lady's object of affection. A mackerel-rippled and lardy old cat. One closed-up eye, and its nose scored with scars. It shifted when I moved towards it, starting to hiss and arch its back. I ignored the horrid furball and managed to locate the stopcock under the sink and the fuse box in another cupboard, turning off the electrics.

Back in the living room, things were considerably quieter now that the TV had been silenced. The man's yelling seemed to have petered out. He was wheezing away, though. Shuddering breaths of fury. I asked him his name ("Bridges. Jim Bridges.") and whether he had reported the flood yet.

He raised his palms aloft now, shaking them in despair.

"I've tried! I don't know who I'm bloody ringing. It's all answering machines or call centres. It's a Saturday so no one gives a bloody damn! We bought our place off the council years ago. And they're sayin' I have to sort it out my bloody self! I don't know what … the wife used to do all that stuff. And she only died a couple of months ago …" He broke off in a half-sob, rubbing his bald head.

Poor bloke. I turned to the old lady.

"So, did you buy your flat off the council too, Miss Simpson?"

She shrieked at me in a loud monotone. Hard of hearing – certainly (if the volume of the TV had been anything to go by). Not wearing her hearing aids – probably.

"I'm having a little paddle!"

And then she launched into a chorus of 'Oh, I do like to be beside the seaside'.

Mr Bridges laughed bitterly.

"Does she buggery! She's still council. Or New Banks Housing Association or whatever it's called since the council sold their houses off. She's a tenant. I'm a what? A leaseholder. And I've told 'em I don't know how many times that she's lost her marbles. She in't fit to be on her own …" He was talking himself into a frenzy again, so I broke in.

"Look. Let me call them for you. I work in housing – with the housing people. You go back downstairs. Get your kitchen pans out, and get those kids downstairs to help you to start getting rid of some of the water. And there's a bloke down there too – send him back up here, will you? And get your own leccy and water switched off. OK?"

He paused for a second, but seemed to realise that he had very few other options (other than murdering his neighbour) and stomp-squelched off downstairs. I turned to the old lady. She was still merrily paddling away and informed me, "It really is a little bit like being at the seaside today."

"But, Miss Simpson," I attempted at the top of my voice, "you'll end up with a chill. I mean, my feet are cold and I've only been here for five minutes. You must have been sitting like this for ages!"

“What’s that? I prefer Scarborough myself. Well, Blackpool was a trifle too common for my liking. Full of Scousers and the Scottish, you know. Probably still is. They never go home, those sorts.”

“But we need to get your flat safe and dry for you again, Miss Simpson. Do you have a relative or a friend? Someone who you can stay with for a little while until we get everything sorted out here?”

“What’s that?!” she shrieked again. Followed by the opening lines of ‘Liverpool Lou’. I groaned inwardly. This was going to be difficult. Uncomfortably similar to dealing with my own, illogically-reasoning small children. But, obviously, a lot more distressing. Because at least with kids you can hope that one day the wee varmints might begin to make more sense to you.

Miss Simpson’s home could have made a small fortune as a set for a 1970s or 80s TV series. Well, if it had been cleaner, perhaps. I desperately scanned the living room for photographs of any friends or relatives. The only pictures on the walls were of the Royal Family. And I doubted whether Prince Harry’s recently acquired philanthropic backbone would involve him offering to parachute into the Peak District in order to rescue smelly old ladies from their watery abodes.

High-pitched voices from the stairwell declared the arrival of Freckles and Fang, followed by Michael. Miss Simpson looked up, ceasing her warbling. Suddenly becoming more animated.

“Ooh – you’re that one off the television, aren’t you?” Rheumy eyes fixed on her new visitor. Michael nodded warmly, exuding senior politician status (despite the shorts and oily T-shirt).

“Well, you may call me Mary. And I must say, that it’s an absolute privilege to finally meet you in person!” Miss Simpson shrieked, her voice adopting a much more refined accent now. “Some people are just born to read the news. They have the breeding. A bit like that Trevor McDonald. A proper gentleman. And he’s actually black, that chappie is. He really is! You really wouldn’t know it though, if you closed your eyes and just listened to him.”

Michael smiled indulgently. Fang and Freckles looked at each other, then back at Michael. All wide-eyed. The same beleaguered expression. I could see now that the children were twins. Yes. Very twinnishly-alike.

"Hey, Mister – are you famous then? Do you really read the news? Which channel? Is it Sky?"

Michael neatly side-stepped the question.

"Well, my job does have a bit to do with the news," he admitted. "But let's focus on this good lady here. What are we going to do to help her get out of this mess?" He looked at me, raising his eyebrows.

"Well. That's why I wanted you up here, Michael. My mobile is in my car. I need to borrow yours."

He sighed. "And there was I, thinking that the call for me upstairs could be for something a little more fanciful." He reached into the pocket of his shorts and was about to pass me his phone, but with a flick of my head I saw what Fang was up to and instead of taking the mobile, I ended up leaping towards the boy, yelling, "Oi!" at the little critter.

"Hey! Gerroff! Friggin' 'ell!" the kid blurted back at me. He had been incredibly quick off the mark and was attempting to sneak a photo of Michael using his own phone. I whipped the mobile out of his trigger-happy hands and stabbed a finger at him.

"No photos! This is not your school playground – this is someone's house!"

"Give it us back! I only wanted a photo to show me mates. Check out if 'e really is famous!"

He squinted at Michael with fierce concentration. As if, if he stared hard enough, the relevant episode of *X Factor* or *Hollyoaks* might come flooding back to him. Fame in Fang's eyes probably didn't lend itself to editorials in *The Guardian* or a grilling on *Newsnight*.

I handed him his phone back. "Tough. Now just behave yourself, won't you? And anyway, you two should be back downstairs. With your pans. Helping Mr Bridges to bail out. Go on!"

I pointed to the door and the boy scowled at me, muttering something like "Stroppy mare" as they slouched back downstairs. I turned to Michael. He was beaming that blinding grin at me again.

"Blimey. You are indeed a dark horse. Even if somewhat stroppy.

Emergency services, bossy teacher, bodyguard and PR person all rolled into one. Would you like a job?"

I reminded Michael that I wasn't a wealthy relative of his and therefore I didn't possess the right credentials to work for him.

He sighed. "You really shouldn't believe everything that you read in the papers, you know." He handed me his phone, which had been tucked somewhere into his shorts. It felt pleasantly warm to the touch.

A fleeting – surprisingly lustful – thought crossed my mind. I shook it away. Bit of a sidewinder, that.

While I fiddled with his phone, Michael informed me that the twins – whose names were Tia and Tyler – hadn't been particularly interested in helping Mr Bridges to bail out his property. Tia had been more intent on telling Michael that she liked to call their social landlord 'New Wanks'. And Tyler had been experimenting to find out whether the wallpaper was easier to "rip off in one big peel now that it's all piss-wet through". Apparently, Mr Bridges had objected to this and had threatened to hit Tyler on the head with his Ken Hom wok.

"So as a bit of an incentive, I've offered them a tenner if they knuckle down and do a decent job of assisting Mr Bridges properly."

I wondered whether Mr Bridges would end up voting for Michael at the next election, as a result of his help. Probably not, if the faded BNP flyer in the chap's front window was anything to go by. And anyway, Mr Bridges seemed completely oblivious to the fact that a senior government minister had been helping him out of his soggy situation.

Chapter 2

PANDORA PROPS UP POSEIDON

As I fiddled with the internet on Michael's phone, Miss Simpson persisted with her tuneless wailing. It was 'My ain folk' now.

Michael whispered to me. "You know, she really should be in specialist – sheltered –housing or something. I've never understood why old people don't ask for more help. It's there for them, after all. Britain has an amazing welfare state in comparison to most other developed countries. I'm proud of how hard I've fought to keep it. People really should make the most of it!"

I looked up from the phone. His lips were pursed. Genuinely baffled. I smiled, blankly. Then politely resumed my button-pressing. Talk about naïve, I thought. Or maybe, he was a bit dim after all. Perhaps he truly believed that someone like Miss Simpson would be able to ask for help. Still. You don't get to be a senior politician unless you talk crap from time to time.

"Right," I told him. "I'm calling New Banks – the housing association – now. Going to try and get an electrician out to make things safe. Then social services. And some temporary rehousing help for Miss Simpson."

Michael put his hands on his hips. I think it was meant to be the Senior Minister Pulling Rank With Small Blonde Bossy Lady thing, but it looked slightly out of kilter, given his day-glow shorts and the oil stained T-shirt.

"Look. I'll just call up my PS – that's my private secretary …"

Yeah, I know what a PS is, thanks, Michael.

"We could get the number of the person in charge at New Banks. Or the director of communities for Medlock Council, or whoever. And I could be on to them in a jiffy."

No. I don't think so, Michael. (And the director of communities at the council is absolutely the last individual I want to be in touch with right now)

So I quickly replied. "No. Let's not go pulling your government strings and whatnot. Have some faith in the marvels of our glorious welfare state! We'll go via the housing association call centre. Then you can listen to just how seamless your communities infrastructure is."

I grinned at him. He narrowed his eyes. I had been right the first time. This was a man not used to – or at ease with – having the piss taken out of him.

To demonstrate just how this kind of thing did (or didn't) work, I decided to put the call onto speakerphone. At first, the New Banks employees manning the weekend call centre were most helpful in meeting my expectations. They dropped the call twice. On the third attempt, we actually managed to speak to each other and they agreed to send out an electrician.

But dealing with Miss Simpson's situation proved to be trickier when I called Medlock Council itself. I explained to their call centre staff that I needed some speedy assistance from social services, but they insisted on speaking to Miss Simpson herself. So I let them listen to a verse of 'The gypsy rover'. They eventually got the message. Next I asked for the contact details of an emergency duty social worker, but was told, "We can't give out numbers to the public. And due to budget cuts they're very short-staffed over the weekends. So you might not get a call back for a few hours."

Tell me something I don't know.

I turned back to Michael.

"Time to circumvent the system, I think. But let's do it my way, not yours," I added, with a wink. (Pride comes before a fall.)

As the manager of Sisters' Space, I had access to Medlock Council's intranet for housing employees. So it was easy to track down Linda

Beveridge's mobile number.

After several rings, the call was answered.

"Linda, it's Rachael. Rachael Russell, here."

The Linda-gushing began in those familiar throaty tones.

"Rachael! How are you coping these days? Are the kiddies okay? I've been meaning to call you for ages! Oh, and guess who I bumped into the other day at the town hall? Shaun. Shaun Elliot! And I was thinking – it's been ten years. Ten! Since we were all working together at Manchester."

(Oh, bloody hell, Linda. Put a sock in it, won't you?)

"So here's me and Jake, working together again. But for New Banks Housing now! And with funny old Martyn ending up as our boss! But housing is so incestuous, isn't it? And then Shaun Elliot trucks up as the new head man for Medlock Council! Done even better for himself than Martyn! Of course, you can imagine Martyn's face when he heard the news, because Shaun always had the good looks and the height, didn't he? And …"

(Linda! For God's sake!)

I tried to look for the volume button on the phone but Michael would have heard every word even if it hadn't been on speakerphone. Linda had a loud voice. And she never stopped talking. It used to drive Shaun crazy when we all worked in the same estate office for Manchester City Council. His room was next door to hers, and he would often jump up and slam his office door to shut out the sounds of her wanton advice and excessive emoting. Linda never noticed, though. Hide of an elephant.

"Anyway. Yes. I saw Shaun the other day. Mr Very Important Person found time for a quick chat. He was asking whether I'd seen you recently, since you stopped your London policy to-ing and fro-ing job and instead … now that you're running Medlock's women's centre. Because there's a job going at the town hall that you might be interested in, he said. I told him to give you a tinkle and ask you himself. Mind you, I always reckoned that Shaun was a bit keen on you. I was —"

"Linda," I had to interrupt the machine-gun mouth. The woman had no idea about that particular chapter of history. Hardly anyone did, in fact. But she still needed shutting up, as we were on speakerphone. I glanced over to Michael. He was peering out of the open window. Watching the pan-handling out of the front door below.

"Sorry, I've got to be quick here, Linda. Big problem. Elderly lady. Very vulnerable. Flooded homes. Can you tell me who's on standby homelessness this weekend for you lot at New Wanks – I mean, New Banks?"

Thankfully, she took the hint. A few seconds later she was back on the line and by a strange quirk of fate, it turned out that Jake Bamber was the employee assigned to standby. I grabbed a broken pencil from Miss Simpson's sideboard and scribbled his number down.

"This is all quite interesting after all," Michael called to me from where he was leaning on the window sill. "How the system appears not to be working." I wasn't sure if he was being sarcastic or not. I couldn't see his face. But he added, "So do leave the speakerphone on, won't you?"

I glowered at his back, and then turned to Miss Simpson, shouting, "Do you think you could keep the singing down a bit, Miss Simpson? The minister here wants to use you as a social experiment and we're finding it difficult to concentrate." But she ignored me, launching into the fourth verse of 'Scarborough Fair'.

Jake Bamber sounded sluggish.

"Yeah?" he mumbled. Not sounding at all like he was earning his overtime rate for prompt and punchy out-of-office hours emergency homelessness advice.

"It's me, Rachael," I announced, and began to gabble out the situation to him. He cleared his throat, now answering me in velvety tones.

"All right. Stop there. First of all, I'll forgive you for dumping me – the love of your life – for a life of domestic dross with your two ankle-biters instead. But do hang on a minute, Rachael. Because I've got a particularly gorgeous piece of arse right here in bed with me right now. Sound asleep in bo-bo land." I heard him shuffle out of the bedsheets.

It was now Saturday afternoon. (These people without kids.)

"Right." I heard the flick of his lighter. "Bit hung-over here. So try to speak quietly, poppet. And do turn the old lady off, if that's her singing sea shanties in the background."

I sketched out the circumstances to him.

"OK, Rachael. Correct protocol – due to financial constraints – is for me to ring around all of the B & Bs in Medlock. Find the cheapest ones with current vacancies. But it would be quicker to get the old dear over to Brenda Kray's at Lancaster House Hostel on Brindleford. It's the nearest place. Even though it's out of the Medlock area and in Manchester's boundary. I'm pretty sure that Brenda's got a couple of rooms there right now. If you want me to back it all for you, though, you'd need to convince me that she's vulnerable."

"Oh, Jake, of course she's bloody vulnerable. You've just heard her singing! She's paddling away, too."

"Right. Fine. I'm convinced. So. Get her over to Lancaster House. And a certain Shaun Elliot, who's now in charge of the homeless side of things for Medlock Council, will just have to cough up the cost of a more expensive stay in Manchester. Now, there's a bloke who's sold out to become one of those faceless cogs in the wheels of capitalism."

(Oh, God. Don't let Jake start wittering on about this now).

"That's ace, Jake. I'll get her over there, pronto. Ta, mate."

"Fab. Off you trot. I'll get Martyn Pointer to throw his weight behind it for us, too. Alright, he's always been a bit of an old woman. And a bit too religious for my liking. But he's not bad as far as the bosses go. Plus, he enjoys anything that leads to a bit of argy-bargy with Shaun Elliot, which can only be a good thing in my book."

"OK. Bye, then." But Jake was on a roll now.

"And whilst we're on the subject, you wouldn't believe how much shit Shaun has created in just the couple of months that he's been heading up half of Medlock Council. Redundancies all over the place. I'm run ragged with all the union stuff I'm doing. Plus, I'll never forgive him after what he did to my Rachael. Oh, I know you'll say that it was years ago now but … management! Never sleep with the bastards!"

Speakerphone horror at the forefront of my mind, I cut in as fast as I could.

"Jake, I've got to —"

"Oh, by the way. I loved your pic in the papers."

"What?"

"With that Chiswick minister bloke. Him helping to promote your Sisters' Space thing. Stunning photo of you as always, poppet. But what's with the Tory boy? He's not bad-looking actually, but it's not like you to be hanging round with the smarmy bourgeoisie —"

"Oi!" Michael's head snapped round, glaring at the phone. "I'm not a Tory!"

"Who was tha …?"

"Right! See you then – and thanks, Jake!" I rabbited, prodding the 'Off' button on the phone and handing it back to Michael. He tucked it into his shorts, incredulous, "What a ridiculous thing to say, for God's sake. I'm a member of the Fabian Society."

"Well, Jake's a member of the Socialist Workers' Party. And they don't see a lot of difference between your Fabians and your Tories. But then I'm sure you know all that." Michael rubbed his chin thoughtfully before replying. A growth of stubble there. The weekend look, perhaps.

"And here's me thinking that the hardcore Marxist sorts had died out with the dinosaurs. But, of course. That explains it."

"What?"

"His other prehistoric beliefs. Referring to the woman he presumably picked up last night as his 'piece of arse'. Very enlightened, I must say."

I burst out laughing.

"He's gay, Michael! Jake's gay. And his humour is very tongue in cheek!"

Michael huffed, and I couldn't resist adding, "But at last, I've met someone with an even more defective gaydar than mine."

Now it was time to get Miss Simpson packing. I asked Michael to manoeuvre the old lady out of the chair, while I sorted out an overnight bag for her, embarking upon the Hunt for Great and Greying Knickers in her faded and filthy bedroom. After locating various items of clothing (hoping to God that those were HP sauce stains) I squirreled them into a couple of carrier bags. Michael had – rather impressively – managed to get Miss Simpson down the stairs and out of her house, and a few minutes later, a New Banks-dispatched electrician arrived and was making the place safe. As we were busily evicting the evil cat, an inquisitive neighbour from a few doors down pitched up. Michael persuaded her to feed the thing for the next few days, promising the woman, "I can assure you that the state will remunerate you for any feline expenses incurred." The neighbour's eyes lit up. I envisaged that a few receipts for fresh salmon and perhaps even lobster would be dropped off next week at Michael's constituency office in Stalybridge.

We locked up Miss Simpson's flat and I went to check on Mr Bridges and the twins. The latter were squeezing sponges into pans and debating whether Mr Bridges would end up committing suicide over his recent misfortune, with Tia murmuring,

"Hey, Ty – if you drowned yourself in a pan of water, would it be better, d'ya think? Than slashin' your wrists? Hurt less, I mean."

"Dunno. Worst thing would be having to saw your own head off or something like in that film we were watching the other night."

Mr Bridges' daughter arrived now, courtesy of the 346 bus from Droylsden to rescue her father from his aquatic disaster. Michael moved Miss Simpson over to a low garden wall and settled her onto it. The sun was still blazing fiercely, but she had insisted that he tie a rain-mac headscarf over her head – "just in case". Michael turned to me.

"Right. Next move. Cars. Yours? Mine? I don't think that Miss S would bear up well on the back of my motorbike."

His words took me aback. A very generous offer, of course. But completely out of the question.

"I don't think so. Surely it wouldn't be … professional. For you. It's a bit … well, it's a bit 'involved', isn't it?"

He pulled a face. "Christ! She's a neighbour!"

"Yeah. And one that you didn't know existed until an hour or so ago."

"Admittedly. Point taken. But I'm a great believer in practising what one preaches. I'm forever making speeches about neighbourliness and responsibility. I'm the Minister for Communities and despite all that, it's rare that I get the chance to —"

"Engage in a bit of cheap voyeurism," I finished his sentence for him.

He folded his arms and stared at me.

"Very funny. Look. I'll go and get my car."

"Michael – please don't think that I'm being awkward about all of this. But this place. This area that I'm taking her to – where the hostel is. Well, it's a bit rough. Inner-city Manchester. It won't be like when you normally get to visit housing estates and they wheel out cute face-painted kids for the minister and expect you to get all giddy about the new shitty rabbit hutches that pass for social housing these days. And. Well. Your car. What is it that you drive?"

"My own car? A Prius. Toyota Prius."

"Quite. A Prius. A Prius that wouldn't last two minutes there."

He nodded slowly.

"I do get what you're saying, Rachael. But very little fazes me, you know. You obviously don't know about my previous career. The military. Before I went into politics. Lots of action. Afghanistan, Iraq, Kuwait, Bosnia. All over the place, really. So, if any of the civvies start getting rough with me, I can easily take them out. With a John Prescott!" He pretended to punch the gable end of the garden wall.

"Very macho," I sighed, thinking to myself that the likes of Michael Chiswick would hardly be some kind of Squaddie, now, would he? More like a Sandhurst officer.

I was glad that he wasn't aware of my previous CND affiliations. Although my membership had lapsed a couple of years ago, it wasn't really the time or the place to start debating just war and pacifism. But Michael was determined.

"So, yah-boos to your scare-mongering. I'm off to get my car. And," he added, more quietly, "I do realise that Miss S is a bit … pongy, but never fear. We can always open the windows."

"Michael," I shook my head again, "if we had to use either of our cars, it would be mine. Because it already smells of wee. Although that's because of my youngest child, not because of me – I hasten to add. But it won't be your car. Or mine. Because – look. We're pretty much jumping here."

"I'm sorry?" he stopped in his tracks, looking baffled. "We're jumping?"

"Fleas," I hissed. "Her whole flat is infested. That bloody cat. The dirt. Lots of little visitors that neither of us would want in our cars. Laying eggs. New Wanks – I mean Banks – will have to fumigate her flat. And both of us will need to de-louse before we get home."

"Oh. I didn't see anything. I haven't been bitten. I don't think …" he murmured. He started to peer closely at his T-shirt. It made him go slightly cross-eyed. In a rather fetching way. Then he involuntarily started scratching the back of his neck, realised what he was doing, and started to laugh.

"So. Leave me with sorting her out," I told him. "I'll get a taxi to take us. It'll cost a bob or two, but the council will pay it back."

"Right; well." Hands on hips, he pondered his response. Then came to a conclusion.

"OK. You're probably right. I guess I'll just go on home now and have a good scrub with the old loofah. Leave you to it, then." He shrugged. Then turned to go.

Tiny pinpricks of sweat had formed above my top lip. I tasted the salt with the tip of my tongue and then wiped the moisture away with the back of my hand. As I did so a soft September breeze brushed itself across my face. That was something to be grateful for at least, on such a muggy afternoon.

"Bye," I called out. "And thanks for all of your help." Disappointment expertly disguised, I crouched down to retrieve Miss Simpson's slippers. She had kicked them off onto the pavement.

Bloody politicians. Full of the talk. Let everyone else do the dirty work. I'd worked with them for long enough to know what a bunch of self-obsessed, egotistical …

But now, here came his voice again. Close by.

"Er. Hello. Rachael?"

I was squatting on my haunches with the slippers. Wincing up at the sun and trying to fix them onto her feet. Michael must have turned back round again, quickly. He had stooped down next to me. His face only inches away from mine.

"I was kidding." He moved to take one of the scruffy slippers from me. His fingers delayed (deliberately?) against mine. Crouching at Miss Simpson's calloused and mottled feet, I was doing my best not to look at her curling yellow toenails. So I was forced to look right into his eyes. That almost transparent – translucent – glassy grey.

"I was joking," he repeated.

"Were you?" I grumbled. "I really couldn't tell. Maybe you and the rest of the Cabinet need some extra training sessions. A short course on 'How to be really witty' …"

He prodded me in the stomach with his forefinger. Unprepared, I toppled over, landing in an undignified sprawl on the pavement.

"Hey! You rotten sod!" Appalled at the frivolity of his action.

I brushed down my cut-off jeans as he fastened Miss Simpson's slippers onto her feet, "Ah, if you can't take it, Ms Russell, don't dole it out, I say. And by the way, you've got very weak ankles. They'd never let you in the army with your lack of balance."

"Huh. I'm too mentally well-balanced to be allowed to serve in the armed forces actually. But I still think that you're just nosey … that you want to witness the misery of the Great Unwashed."

Michael muttered under his breath and I caught the phrase "leftie reactionary feminist", which instantly cheered me up. At least he had grasped my own politics quite quickly.

But then he held the phone out to me. "So call the damned taxi," he commanded. "And I'm coming too. Whether you like it or not."

Michael went to say goodbye to Mr Bridges and his daughter, while I listened to Miss Simpson warbling 'Sloop John B' for a few minutes and then he returned, "Bit of another crisis now. Poor chap very nearly had a heart attack when his daughter asked him if he'd remembered to renew the household insurance cover. Apparently 'the wife did all that'."

"Oh, God. Did he? Remember to renew it, I mean?"

"They're not sure. Going to look for the paperwork." He dropped his voice now, so that Miss Simpson couldn't hear. "I did suggest to Mr Bridges' daughter that if her father wasn't covered, perhaps they could think about the small claims court. But then she launched into a diatribe about 'my' government preventing ordinary people like her family from accessing Legal Aid."

"Hah! She's a sharp one. So she recognised you, then?"

"Seems so. But honestly. Talk about silliness. Forgetting to renew something as important as your insurance. I mean …"

(Ah, yes. What kind of a silly person would do that kind of thing? The sort with different priorities from the rest of us. Who is too busy. Or distracted. The kind of silly person who doesn't really contemplate the future or mortality …

I mean, fucking hell, Adam. How hard was it for you to have done the odd bit of paperwork from time to time? Why did the boring stuff, the admin stuff, always have to fall to me?

(But no. Enough of that. Enough anger at Adam.)

The pip-pip of a car horn heralded the arrival of Top Car Taxis. Tyler and Tia had reached their boredom threshold in terms of helping Mr Bridges and had already mounted their bikes, heading back to their own New-Wanks-owned home. A couple of minutes later, Mr Bridges' daughter emerged from the maisonette and held out Tyler's phone to me. He had left it behind in the living room. I tucked it into my bra for safe-keeping, planning to deliver it to him later on when I collected my car from Michael's.

Michael steered Miss Simpson into the front seat. She smiled, chirruping "Oh, look! A sheep!" every few seconds in between her strange bursts of musical regalia. We wound our way past the fields and farms that made up a sizeable chunk of Michael's constituency, speeding through the prettier parts of the Pennines and into the more urban areas. And then further on, towards inner-city fallout. Fairly soon I could see the four dreary tower blocks marking the boundary of the Brindleford estate. Brindleford always reminded me of those early, heady days in housing. When the adrenaline side of working on the estates could become addictive.

As could some of your colleagues.

My right breast suddenly vibrated and burst forth with some crappy pop-music ringtone.

"Damn!" I muttered, as I swatted my bra – trying to shut it up. "Don't let me forget later – to find out where Tyler lives and to drop it off."

"Oh, I can do that," said Michael, breezily.

"I wouldn't, if I were you. You saw what Tyler was like. Imagine the headline. 'Minister Nicks My Mobile Phone'."

"Christ, yes. And 'the bastard also promised to pay me a tenner and then forgot!'"

Chapter 3

ERIS AND ARES – GOING AT IT

The taxi driver told us that his name was Ali. He was the chatty but wary sort. His shift-wearied eyes glanced at us through the rear-view mirror as he raced his vehicle across red-bricked backstreets, swinging around corners to avoid imaginary queues of traffic. When I asked him to take us to Brindleford, he had replied:

"You sure you vannago right there? I mean, right into the estate? It's not a nice place, that one."

"Please. I know Brindleford well. I used to manage the estate for Manchester council. A few years ago now."

"Aah – you listen to Ali, now!" the taxi driver said, shaking his head. "It's ten times vorse on there than it vas, even two year ago! Me brother-in-law got knifed on there last year. He were just doin' a Saturday night pick-up. And this guy called him a filthy Paki. Just 'cause he vouldn't have none of the bloke's 'Oh sorry mate ah'm three pound short, innit'. So it all kicked off big time. Ended up gettin' stabbed, innit!"

From the front seat, Miss Simpson stopped her ditty for a minute and chipped in with, "Scurrilous peasants! The lot of them!"

"Well, I've never heard of the place," Michael whispered across to me. "And all right, my constituency doesn't extend into the Manchester boundary per se. But we're only a few miles off. And I am the Minister for Communities, after all. It can't really be all that bad, can it? If I've never heard of it. And I don't live so far away myself."

I snorted in a most unladylike manner. "'Fraid so. Brindleford might never have had a riot, or a government inquiry. But surely your civil servants have briefed you on your deprivation indices and your super output areas? Brindleford ranks as god-awful in terms of poverty and crime."

"Well, yes; of course. But I simply don't recall the name ever cropping up."

"Interesting. Well, when I was managing the Brindleford estate, the police always said that it was a hell of a lot more violent … harder to police, than nearby Moss Side. Which no doubt, you'll have heard of."

I paused. Receiving a piercing gaze from him. Perhaps he was trying to fathom out whether I was an undercover member of the opposition or not. But he sighed.

"I'm sorry to say, Rachael, that if it's not *actually* in my constituency, or on the national map with some kind of a big news hoo-ha, I probably wouldn't know about it. It's a funny old life, being an MP. Being a minister. Especially if your patch is in the North. You're in London during the week, doing the Commons stuff, and then you're racing to and from the constituency. Or stuck on the West Coast line while engineers fiddle with the signals. At the weekends I'm at the mercy of Graham the Griper and his like at the constituency office in Stalybridge …" He shook his head. "I should have pushed harder for one of the south-east constituencies. I really should have."

My hackles rose. "Well, look on the bright side. Maybe at the next general election they'll find you some pretty, leafy suburb in the depths of the south where the nearest troubled council estate or whatever is some fifty miles away. And where the biggest social issue that the local MP has to face is whether any of the villages qualify for Britain's Best Hanging Basket of the Year."

He held his hands up.

"Sorry, sorry. I didn't mean to come across as so self-pitying. In comparison to a lot of people and their jobs, I've probably got very little to complain about. And I'm always eager to learn more about people and places that I'm unfamiliar with. Which is why I wanted to tag along with you to see what happens with Miss Simpson. Call it middle-class voyeurism if you will. As you did before."

"I used the term 'cheap voyeurism', if I remember correctly. And anyway, never mind the ABs. When it comes to your own particular social strata, I reckon that the phrase 'upper-class voyeurism' might be more accurate."

Again, I wondered if I had overstepped the mark, as a slight pause lingered in the air. But then he did that public-schoolboy guffaw thing. Meaning that perhaps he wasn't the sort to take himself too seriously, after all. Good. I couldn't bring myself to play the brown-nosing ministers game these days. So maybe I could semi-forgive him for chortling along like Boris Johnson.

"Fine! Fine! Whatever. I know that you think I'm oh so green. That I've never lived life on the edge. But don't judge a book by its cover. I've seen a bit of action in my time, you know."

"So you said," I conceded. "But let's not go trying to compare action in Afghanistan with murder in Manchester."

Miss Simpson broke into a rendition of 'Frankie and Johnny'.

Two minutes later we arrived in Brindleford. There were hardly any cars driving around the estate. Perhaps because of the sweltering heat of the day. Perhaps not. Ali bipped his horn at two youths who deliberately stopped in the middle of the road when they saw the taxi approaching. He had to swerve to avoid them, gesticulating at the pair ("You're crazy!") They mouthed the standard 'eff-off' response. The roads on Brindleford were littered with bricks, and although Ali had his air con cranked up high, a shimmering heat haze hung over the tarmac. The road glittered with glass, pockmarked by beer cans. Graffiti adorned fences, gable ends and even lamp posts. Ali slowed down now, avoiding the more obvious piles of broken glass. Michael perused the graffiti as we passed it.

"This Kiera sounds like a popular girl." Several different tags claimed carnal knowledge of her.

"Must run in the family," I added, because the next fence panel noted that Kiera wasn't as talented as her mother. We both erupted into childish sniggers as the taxi reached the end of the road and the final panel culminated in an accusation against Kiera's dad and the family dog.

I shook my head, attempting sobriety. “You know. We’re both sitting here, laughing, but people living here can get stabbed over much less than this kind of thing. I once had to transfer an entire family – seven people – from Brindleford over to council properties in Sheffield. The result of a dispute over parking. Thanks to the attitude of their next door neighbours. A family called the Murrays – or the Mad Murrays. The Murrays always went the extra-mile on anti-social behaviour. They liked their vendettas. They were more of a gang really. And what they did to their next door neighbour’s teenage lad … a Murray classic. Broke three of the kid’s fingers by holding him down and hammering them with a mallet. Just because he parked his car in ‘the wrong place’. Not that the police could ever prove it …”

Michael grimaced as I continued.

“And it was the mother – Michelle Murray – who wielded the mallet on the lad.”

“Charming lady,” he replied. “But then, you get unsavoury sorts everywhere, don’t you? Wherever you live in the world.”

I shrugged, and gestured to the streets outside. “No. Places like Brindleford shouldn’t be seen as some kind of microcosmic example of the good and bad of human nature. They’re more a product of organisational ineptitude. Places that grew to become nightmarish communities to live in – and directly because of government policy on the Right to Buy. Unemployment increasing. The gap between rich and poor widening. And also because central government allowed a load of talentless fat-cat local bureaucrats on massive salaries to head up all the urban regeneration and the housing organisations …”

(And now Shaun is one of them. Oh, the irony).

Shaun, who used to scorn all things senior management. Shaun, who, after a particularly drunken Christmas Party one year, pissed into a plant pot containing our chief executive’s prize Orchid.

But Michael just held his hands up and smiled vacantly. “Well, Rachael. You have an interesting theory there. And some contentious opinions. But I’m sure that if we had the time, we would be able to find some points of commonality …”

I sighed, inwardly. Classic politician’s evasive tactics. He looked away and checked his phone for messages. Dismissing The Ranting Bride Of Trotsky. Ever so politely.

Ali slowed the car down again and glanced back at me for direction. I waved him ahead.

"Lancaster House."

"Ah, yeah! Know where you mean! Place for people in trouble. Bit secret – innit?"

Strictly speaking, the building was the local authority's hostel for people who were temporarily homeless. But Ali's take on it was fair enough. And Lancaster House did try to keep a low profile on the estate. Plenty of Brindleford residents needed to feel superior to your undesirable homeless sorts.

Ali's cab pulled up outside Lancaster House, causing Miss Simpson to pipe up with:

"So we're off to the Dinky-Doos then? Happy Valley in Llandudno?"

No sign of any seaside variety shows, however. Just a bleak, monolithic landscape of more-than-usually-neglected social housing.

Michael helped her out of the car and I took her arm, motioning her towards the front door of Lancaster House. But then I realised my mistake.

"Sod. No purse. What am I like? I've left it in my car." Michael brought his wallet out from his shorts, brushing away my thanks with a shake of his head. He handed a twenty-pound note to Ali, so I told the taxi driver, "We're going to need a receipt. But also – would you mind waiting for us until we've dropped this lady off? We won't be long. And we'll pay you extra for the wait."

Ali looked doubtful. He shook his head. "Ting is, Miss," he gestured outside of his window, "I don't know any other drivers what'd be crazy enough to be hanging round here, innit? I mean, not on a Saturday afternoon. They're already drinkin' by midday here. I mean, if I'm sittin' here I might get me vindows bricked in or some nutter havin' a go – like what happened with me brother-in-law, innit? And I'll be getting me other calls …"

I began to chew my lip, wondering if there was anyone I could call on to pop over to the Brindleford estate and give us a lift home. Not likely. My parents weren't even comfortable with the twenty-minute drive over the border from Stalybridge to my house in Holme (no doubt terrified of being hijacked on the Saddleworth moors by a marauding Yorkshire infidel).

But Michael made a move. He took his watch off and handed it through the open window to Ali. I glimpsed a flash of royalty. He had tucked another twenty-pound note next to it.

"Keep the money, regardless. And the watch as a deposit. Until we get back."

Ali peered at the watch, taking it from Michael. Ali beamed. Ali was impressed.

"Hey, mister. Nice vatch. Rolex, innit?"

"No. It's a Breitling," Michael replied. "So it's worth a bit."

And the rest.

"And I hope that it assures you we'll be back here soon. And that I do have more than enough to be able to pay your fare for the wait. And for your taxi windows, should they get bricked in. Although I doubt very much that that would happen."

Our taxi driver had been convinced. He nodded slowly, but gestured to the prayer beads dangling down from his rear-view mirror.

"But you knows … I'm a good Muslim. So I don't need a vatch to be trusting you all." He tried to pass the watch back to Michael through the open window, but Michael just flapped a hand at him, striding off to catch up with Miss Simpson, who had shuffled on ahead of us. I moved off after them both and called back to Ali.

"Just hang onto it for us. It's probably safer with you than it is on his wrist in the middle of Brindleford, anyway!"

I caught up with Michael, who murmured, "Hmm. Now who's building a reputation for the place?"

He shielded his eyes from the sun as he glanced up and down the road, nearly tripping over a dead fox that was hanging off the kerb. It already had a bit of a maggot infestation, by the looks of it.

Lancaster House was a 1980s red-bricked, narrow-windowed monstrosity, forged on the cheap. There was no signage, because of that need to foster an element of discretion. And if you weren't already familiar with the place, it was easy to assume that it was just another cluster of social-housing flats. Its attempt at ambiguity however, was somewhat hampered by the fact that someone had added graffiti in enormous letters on its gable end, which misspelled:

'Dos House Scum'.

I glanced up at the building, vivid memories returning to me. Days before promotions, performance indicators and catering to the whims of Whitehall policy-makers. Brindleford was one of the first patches I had managed as a housing officer. Lancaster House's resident warden, Brenda Kray, had been there some eleven years ago and was still at the helm today. I had spoken with Brenda a few times recently in relation to women from Sisters' Space who needed a hostel place, but I hadn't been inside Lancaster House for some years. I wondered if the building would still contain that suffocating stench of unwashed clothing and microwave meals. A fragrance that never left the place, despite Brenda's use of bleach and disinfectant bordering on OCD.

As Michael and I escorted Miss Simpson towards the building's porch, from behind us came a sudden burst of squeals, yelps and the sound of running feet. A young woman, wearing a miniscule strappy top, a pair of jeans and sandals, sprinted past us. Her hair was dripping wet. Over her shoulder she held a squalling infant wrapped in a towel, and alongside her dashed two boys. The younger one – about the same age as Lydia – had braided, African hair. The other boy – probably about ten – had a blonde number-one cut. The woman threw herself towards Lancaster House's intercom and jabbed the buttons desperately. Without waiting for a response, she shrieked:

"Let us in! It's Dawn. Dawn Hibbert! Brenda said we could come 'ere anytime if 'e starts kickin' off!"

The intercom hissed impotent static back at her. She booted the door. Hard. The older boy followed her lead. The baby sicked up a milky substance down the mother's back, over her Betty Boo tattoo. This Woman Called Dawn still had soapsuds in her hair. And underneath her skimpy vest (declaring 'Goodtime Girl!') she was braless. The top clung to her in embarrassing, damp patches.

I gestured to Michael. Keep an eye on Miss Simpson.

"You all right?" I asked the woman. Her face moved away from the intercom. Decorated with a swollen lip and a deep red mark, indicating the bruises to come. She was attractive, although her face was currently contorted by a snarl.

"Do I fuckin' look it?" Turning her back on me, she began to thump at the door with one fist. The browner, younger boy pulled a face at me. Div. The blue-eyed, blonde kid began to attack the brickwork of Lancaster House with a red pen-knife.

But I was less concerned about their bluntness and more mindful of the baby. She was a small tot, perhaps only nine or ten months old and she clearly wasn't enjoying being subject to her mother's attempt at battering down the door of the hostel. She had begun to embark upon a hysterical ik, ik, ik-ing noise. Looking like she was going to puke again.

"Come on – hey – don't do that to the door," I directed at them all. "It's a proper security door, that one is. Booting it won't get you in any faster!"

Dawn glared at me. Chin back, as she narrowed her eyes. So I adopted the 'I can be as arsey as you but don't want to be right now' stance. Arms folded. Braving it out. Pretending not to care that one of her youngsters might try to stab me right there and then. They probably wouldn't have done, of course. But you can never be too sure when kids are excited or angry and in possession of short, stabby things.

The intercom crackled, interrupting the stand-off. A young man's wheedling voice:

"Me mum's not here. Come back later."

The woman smacked the metal panel with her hand and shrieked, "Fucksake!" Her youngest son now began pounding the door with his pristine trainers. I tried again.

"Look. Pack it in with trying to kick the door down, eh? I work with Lancaster House. I can get you in quicker. Just shift out of the way a minute." I gestured for the woman to move aside and then pointed at Miss Simpson. "I need to get this lady in here, too."

Dawn turned to face me again with frantic eyes. For a second I thought that she was going to give me a Mancunian pow slap. Smack me one. But then she seemed to think better of it as she glanced over at the pathetic, bedraggled form of Miss Simpson, who had hobbled away from the disturbance and who had parked herself against a low wall a few feet away. Michael was hovering now. Looking unsure. Perhaps wondering whether he should act as guardian angel to the elderly lady or interfere with the family in crisis.

"Fine! Whatever!" the woman growled, her nostrils flaring. "Just tell that dickhead – Neal – that Dawn Hibbert's out here with two little 'uns and a baby. And if we don't get inside in the next thirty seconds, Vinnie Murray'll be here an' will be kickin' the shit out of us! And then me …? I'll be gettin' someone to kick the shit out of Neal Kray!"

I took over the intercom. Pressing the intercom button down, I held it for nearly ten seconds, until I heard the same nonchalant male, teenage voice answer:

"Yeah? I told you. She's not in!"

I, too, knew Neal. Of old. And I wasn't putting up with any teenage twattiness right now.

"Neal. Its Rachael Russell here. From Sisters' Space – the women's centre in Medlock. I need to speak to your mother. We need access urgently."

There was a pause and then a drawn-out, "You'll have to wait. Me mum's gone shopping. She'll be back in bit."

Click.

Little git. A girl's giggle in the background. So, Neal had a friend over did he? Which might explain why he was being even more of an awkward sod than usual. And sure, the entire country was enjoying a glorious late summer, but Miss Simpson had been soggy for quite a long time as far as I could tell, so I was fretting about the whole pneumonia thing. And now there was this woman – Dawn – and her kids. And whatever – whoever – it was she was running away from. The baby began whining again. A low crescendo rising to a piercing howl.

"She's starvin'!" Dawn began to tell me as she jiggled the infant. "She's not had her dinner. And she's got no nappy on, neither. As me and her were havin' a bath together when he started on me." The small hand-towel wrapped around the baby was already sodden around her little bum.

"So, I've got to get her some friggin' nappies! Brenda didn't have any in, last time." She looked frantically down the road again. Then across it, to the seedy '24/7 Open All Hours' shop. Which didn't actually appear to be open at all, due to the fact that its metal shutters were down. But that was the way of Brindleford. Unless you wanted to be constantly forking out for new panes of glass, you kept your shutters down. Michael offered some advice.

"Look. Why don't you nip across to the shop and get whatever you need – pronto – and we'll look after the children for you?"

"Jesus!" The woman shot back. "You're not from round here with a voice like that, are you? But no. Not being funny, like, but how do I know you're not some kind of paedo? Leavin' me kids with you … And anyway … shit. No time."

She cast furtive eyes up the road again. Her youngest boy added, "And you've not got yer purse on yer, Mum."

"Fucksake, yeah."

Michael tried again. "Look. I've got some cash on me. I seem to be making a habit of bailing ladies out today." He took his wallet out and Dawn looked pathetically grateful at the offer, but she was jumpier than ever. Jiggling the baby up and down again.

"Look. It'd be better if you went over to the shop – instead of me," she said to Michael. "'Cause if I go … once he gets his bike out the lock-up and started up, he'll be here any second. He knows I'll be headed for Lancaster House. An' knowin' my luck he'll end up rippin' me head off in the middle of the fuckin' corner shop."

I nodded at Michael. He looked unsure and began to say, "But I don't like leaving you all here – if the person who has just done this to you is about to arrive —"

I interrupted them.

"To be honest, Michael, if the person who's done this does pitch up … having another fella here probably won't help matters. Blokes in a mood don't like having other men around on the scene … Yeah?"

I looked to Dawn. She nodded. Michael wavered. My turn to issue commands now.

"Michael – please go to the shop. If it does kick off here, you can be back in a second. Tell him what you want," I instructed the woman.

A quick smile from her now. And then back to a pretty pout.

"Oh, ta. I'll pay you back. Size four nappies. Whatever brand. Don't care." Michael sighed and then nodded, breaking into a jog across the road. She gabbled after him:

"And baby food. Jars. Whatever's sweet." A pause. She called out:

"And a pack of ten Superkings …" Michael nodded without looking back as he skirted the bricks littering the middle of the road.

"Oi!" she suddenly remembered something else. Bellowed over to him.

"And some Tampax. Super size!" The magical 'Tampax' word rebounded starkly across the estate. Sending her two sons into eruptions of boy-giggles. Despite the gravity of the situation, I smirked. (Bet no one had ever bawled that at him from across the Commons lobby.) Michael, however, simply raised his hand in acknowledgement to us without turning around. Mr Cool.

But the scale of Dawn's voice had changed now, sliding into a high pitch.

"He's comin'! He's comin'!" Five sets of eyes stared furtively down the main road. A buzz in the distance. Dawn moved back to the door; started pounding at it. Yelling, "Just let us in, you nobhead!"

The tiny figure of a man astride a motorcycle appeared around the corner. Moving towards us at breakneck speed.

"Come on! Just open the door! Come on!" She pounded harder. Genuine terror.

Desperate measures were needed. Pressing the button down on the intercom once more, I was met with an exasperated, "What? I told yer, she's —"

I cut him off with a rapid verbal warning.

"Look, Neal. I know your mother very well. And you also know me, Neal." (Best Headmistress approach. Mix it up with a bit of Annoying Salesperson On the Phone Technique, i.e. over-familiarisation via use of your victim's Christian name.) "And I know several things about you. Especially one particular thing … from some eleven years ago. And I'm sure that you wouldn't want me to start shouting across the whole of the estate about what happened to you at your seventh birthday party, hey, Neal?"

Dawn's face seemed to have aged suddenly. Etched with fear. The motorbike had arrived now. It attempted to screech to a halt on the main road, some fifty yards away from us. But the driver lost control. The bike mounted the kerb and skidded on the grass embankment, delivering an ominous crunch. Its owner – this Vinnie guy – had managed to dismount before being dragged under the bike. He staggered upright and looked at us all. And then back at the bike. Get Dawn? Or check bike. He chose the latter. It bought us another five seconds.

The Seventh Birthday Party Threat had worked. The miracle occurred. The buzzer sounded and the door-lock clicked open. Dawn shoved open the door and her family scrambled through it. I gestured frantically to Miss Simpson, trying to get her up and off the wall in time to make an escape. My elderly friend however, simply smiled vacantly at me, shook her head and then commenced with a chorus of 'I Could Have Danced All Night'.

My Fair Lady was not sodding budging right now.

So the door slammed shut behind them, just as the man left his bike and sprinted up the path. He charged the door with his shoulder. It withstood the force. Then he let loose a string of obscenities about Dawn and directed, "Fuckin' bitch!" at me, pounding on the door with his fists.

I had already moved over to Miss Simpson and together we watched him working himself up into a frenzy. He was bare-chested, wearing baggy tracksuit bottoms, and his arms and hands were covered with tattoos. His cheek, too. One that I recognised – a gang tattoo from east Manchester. He shouted. He ranted. He swore. I couldn't make most of it out, but it finally ended with, "And now me bike's totally screwed – and it's all 'cause of you Dawn – you stupid fuckin' cunt!"

Anxious about the effect that this might be having on Miss Simpson, I put my arm about her shoulders (moving back slightly at the overwhelming whiff of Eau d'Urine). She didn't seem to be remotely alarmed, though. In fact, she appeared to be quite content about the unusual occurrences unfolding before her. And who could blame her? It was probably more exciting than her Saturday tea-time telly.

Chapter 4

POOR OLD PEGASUS

The entry doors of Lancaster House had been designed with the most violent people in mind. They could withstand the onslaught of this pillock, Vinnie. And then the penny dropped. Dawn had mentioned his surname, too. Murray. Vinnie was certainly acting like every member of the Murray family that I had ever had the pleasure to know.

Bloody typical of my luck, I thought. Turning up at the hostel at exactly the same time as a trailer for a Murray Almost-Massacre. I hoped that Dawn would call the police, now that she was safely inside. I doubted whether Neal would have either the wherewithal or the inclination to think of it.

But now – finally – Vinnie seemed to be slowing down on the physical side of things.

"Fuckin' bitch!" He kicked the door, hard. And then, yelped, "Shit!" as he grabbed at his toes. His footwear consisted of some kind of gangsta slipper-trainer type thing. Clearly not as hard-wearing as he had hoped it would be. I tried not to smirk. Hoping that the bastard had broken several toes.

He half-hopped away from the hostel door. From a few houses away someone's pet pooch was going crazy. A booming bark. Doberman, probably. And then a metal clang, the sound of a shutter being pulled down. The launderette next to the 24/7 reacting to the sounds of a one-man battle outside. But Vinnie was taking a break from the action now. He was standing on one leg and nursing his toes, as he squinted into the sun and peered up at Lancaster House. Scanning the front of the building for faces at windows and muttering to himself, he decided that he had could cope with the self-inflicted pain and placed his foot back onto the ground, taking a battered packet of cigarettes from his tracksuit pocket and lighting one.

Michael arrived back on the scene. Crossing the road and juggling his purchases. He called out to me, acting remarkably casually for someone who must have heard the commotion.

"They've run out of plastic bags, I'm afraid." He nodded down at his rather eclectic shopping combo.

I stalked past Vinnie and met Michael on the path, attempting to stop him from proceeding any further towards Lancashire House, by speaking in a low voice.

"Michael, this guy is a fruit cake. The sort who would headbutt you even for smiling at him in the wrong way. You already saw the state of that woman – Dawn. What he did to her. And now he's just gone and damaged his precious motorbike," I gestured to where it lay abandoned on the verge, "so he's not in the best of moods. And here comes you. Some bloke carrying nappies for his baby and Tampax for his girlfriend. It won't look good to him."

"Gosh, no. I suppose it won't."

"So just give me two minutes to figure out how I can get Miss Simpson past him and into the hostel. And then we'll be in the taxi and heading home. OK?"

But Michael just shoved his purchases into my hands and then whispered back.

"Don't worry, Blackadder. I have a cunning plan!"

I sighed. The man was so unbelievably out of his depth here.

Vinnie had ceased the aggro-action now. Rooted to the spot and inhaling deeply from his cigarette, like a starving infant sucking milk from the teat of a bottle. I felt a sudden craving for a ciggie myself, now. Ridiculous. After all these years.

The change in his behaviour was a little bit disconcerting. Only twenty seconds earlier he had been trying to kick the door down. Threatening to kill Dawn. And here he was now. Almost motionless. The only movements were from his hand and his eyes as he continued to glare at the windows of Lancaster House and then flick his gaze back to us. Cigarette to mouth, and back again. Mr Bad was doing his best to stare us out as we approached him. A challenge. Arms folded.

He wasn't a big bloke in terms of height, but he was stocky. The obligatory male Manchester summer wear – the bare chest as soon as the calendar reaches April, the baggy bottoms – pointed to the fact that he liked to work out. He had the abs. And he was good-looking in your hard-man sort of way. A number-one haircut and a flattened nose indicated that he might have some experience of the boxing ring. Perhaps Vinnie wasn't solely content with smacking the female of the species around for sport. He was mixed-race – Afro-Caribbean, by the looks of it – and had a three-inch-long scar running from one corner of his eye to the edge of his lip. Plus the gang tattoo on the other cheek, of course. And now with fresh scratch marks down one side of his face. Dawn must have fought back.

Quite the gent, indeed.

I ignored the attempts at non-combative intimidation and strode towards where he now stood, blocking the door. He chose to develop a hacking cough, snorting hard and then grebbing upon the ground. A globule of phlegm landed just centimetres from my right sandal. Yes, he was a charmer, this one. Well and truly.

Finally, he deigned to speak to me.

"So who the fuck are you, then? Some other nosey mate of hers, what she's not told me about?"

His eyes were glazed over now, as he gave me the once-over. Giving me the 'I'm so cool 'n' scary that I don't even register hostility' performance. And it was the eyes that drew my interest. The pupils were dilated. He was sweating heavily, too. It was a hot day, for sure, but Vinnie's entire torso was dripping wet. Such perspiration-affliction meant one of two things to me. Either he was going through an early menopause or the bloke was 'on' something. I reckoned the latter.

I caught the sound of a baby's wail inside Lancaster House. Poor mite needed her dinner. Cue Vinnie noticing what I was carrying. He jerked his head towards the baby food, nappies, Tampax and cigarettes.

“You helpin’ her out? You’re best keep your friggin’ nose out of it all. You’ve no idea what that bitch is fuckin’ like.”

I kept my voice cool and steady. Sidestep the accusations. Avoid any arguments.

“This is the first time I’ve ever met Dawn. I’m actually here because I’m looking after this elderly lady. And your behaviour is frightening her.”

I gestured to Miss Simpson, still perched on the wall. She was staring directly at Vinnie and looking (rather unhelpfully) not at all scared.

“So please, can you try to calm it all down a bit? Because, as you can see, she’s very frail. And she desperately needs to get into this place.”

He took a step closer to me now. Jaw clenched. Trying to be as menacing as possible.

“I said – you’re best not helpin’ that fuckin’ slag!” He jabbed the lit cigarette perilously close to my face. But I stood my ground.

Until this point, Michael had been standing next to Miss Simpson. But as Vinnie’s actions became more testy, he stepped forward. I felt a twinge of panic. Michael would be the sort to try to do the gallant thing. And someone like Vinnie would be looking for an excuse to kick off again. Interfering posh bloke asking to have his face smashed in. Michael moved next to me. Placing a protective hand on my shoulder (which I didn’t particularly feel the need for, thank you very much), he spoke in low tones.

“Really. We're just here to help Miss Simpson. She’s just had to leave her home. We need her to get access to this place. Get her dried out.”

Vinnie looked over at Miss Simpson again. Plastic bags huddled to her bony chest. In response to his gaze, she took the opportunity to dislodge her false teeth with her jaw, protruding them from her mouth at him in a gesture of defiance. It looked rather freakish. Vinnie glanced back at us, frowning. But the aggression seemed to have melted away now.

“She a drinker, then?”

It took me a second to follow his logic. Michael's reference to ‘dried out' possessed different connotations for Vinnie.

I ignored him and moved over to Miss Simpson, taking her by the arm and musing that if Vinnie had more sympathy and interest in alcoholics than in his own young family, then maybe that was the best approach to getting the old lady safely inside.

Michael seemed to be having the same thoughts. He put his arm around Miss Simpson too, guiding her towards the front door. Vinnie seemed torn. Should he swing back into action, view this as a direct challenge? Or just let the do-gooders get on with their pitiful acts of benevolence? He spent a couple of seconds more, looking at Michael. Sizing him up. Michael had about five inches on Vinnie. For the first time it occurred to me how solidly Michael was built. "Like a tank!" my dad would have said. "And with real army posture!" my mother would have added. Funny how the politician tag had stopped me from noticing it before.

Vinnie's delayed mental processes seemed to be veering on the side of caution. Perhaps getting arsey with this particular fella wouldn't be such a good idea. Still, backing down wouldn't come easily to a man of Vinnie's character. So he decided to engage in a smattering of verbal provocation, instead.

"Right. So. What are you supposed to be, then? Some gay social worker or summat?"

But before Michael could respond, Miss Simpson sprang into action. Shaking her arms away from us and turning to face Vinnie, she held her plastic carrier bags aloft, like some geriatric Scales of Justice. Producing an eerie growl from the back of her throat. And then she dropped one of her bags to the floor.

Pointing her finger at her new opponent, she screeched, "You! You thunderous thug – you ought to be ashamed of yourself! You yellow-livered yobbo! You misogynistic miscreant! The wages of sin are death, remember? And now … now you're insulting a man of true saintliness! How dare you talk to the minister like that? He is a leader of our flock! He is a man of the News! He is the Minister of the Good News!"

Vinnie looked genuinely shocked at the outburst. Perhaps he hadn't come into contact with many demented pensioners. Especially ones who still had some fire in their belly, as Miss Simpson clearly did. I was also more than a little taken aback. Impressed, too.

Must remember that one. Misogynistic miscreant.

Vinnie began to sift words in his drug-addled brain for the correct reply, but she cut him off with, "Don't you deign to speak! You should be quaking in your boots before him! He has friends in high places and he would think nothing of smiting you – hip and thigh bones!"

Michael and I exchanged looks. Vinnie gawped at Miss Simpson. She stooped to pick up the plastic bag that she had dropped and moved towards Michael, nodding at him.

"Thank you, good minister." Taking Dawn's shopping from me and squirreling the goods into her plastic bags, she squared up to Vinnie and announced, in a frighteningly authoritarian voice. "Begone from the narrow gate!"

Vinnie did as he was instructed, stepping to one side. She pressed the buzzer on the intercom and as the teenage voice answered again, she commanded, "Young Neal – it's Mary Simpson here. Lady absconding from watery near-death. Discharging myself from duty. Bearing nappies for bairns. Kindly open sesame please."

I stalked past Vinnie and caught up with her. Over the intercom I could make out Dawn saying to Neal, "It's all right. It's only that old lady. You can let her in. Just hope the other two stop him from gettin' in." The door opened, Miss Simpson shuffled in and it quickly slammed shut behind her. Vinnie had made no attempt to barge past me, or to try and access the building. In fact, he seemed a little deflated; somewhat disorientated. The feeling was mutual. That little outburst had been the most lucid communication that we had experienced from her during the entire afternoon.

A few seconds of quiet, and then Vinnie turned to Michael, with a gruff mutter.

"Look, mate – sorry about … I didn't realise you were … you know. A minister. And that. Shit. I really need another cig …" He rummaged in his pocket and drew out his pack. Offered one to Michael. "Do yer want one? Shit – sorry for swearin'. I bet you're not a smoker, neither."

But Michael smiled at him. Then nodded.

"Well, I did kick it for a few years, actually. But I got back into it after service in Afghan. Stupid of me, really." This revelation startled Vinnie. He raised his eyebrows.

"Yer what?"

I grinned inwardly. Michael was a clever sod. Vinnie was intrigued.

"What do yer mean? Servin' … the Forces?"

Michael nodded. Not elaborating.

Vinnie continued: "Like ... What? Were yer some army chaplain or whatever?"

Michael pursed his lips, trying to give his best, his most honest, answer. (Unusual for a politician, that.) I was doing my best not to smirk. But Vinnie wasn't pausing to let Michael answer. Instead, he was rambling on, reflecting to himself.

"Best chaplain we ever had was in Northern Ireland. You'd have never known he were a God-botherer till you saw 'im in is collar an' shit. He was sound. But yeah … Shit! Can you believe this? I did Afghan too … Where else have you done?"

Vinnie offered the cigarette and proffered his lighter. Michael managed to avoid the direct question again. Instead, he flicked his head towards Vinnie's right arm, "Queen's Lancs tattoo, isn't it? You don't see many of those around."

The corners of Vinnie's mouth twitched. Chuffed to bits. Someone had recognised his badge of honour. And now his smile split into an enormous grin, parading a set of gold-flecked teeth. I wondered when his role-modelling of American gangstas had begun. But, hell. Whatever. Wonders never ceased. Michael had won the bugger over.

"Hey, my man! Not many brothers recognise that one!" Vinnie tipped his chin upwards. Proud. "Goddit done in 2006 after they disbanded the Queens. Used to get the piss taken out of me after I moved over to Sheffield an' transferred to the Rifles. Lanky-hating bastard Tykes, that lot were over there. Ha!"

A booming laugh. Funny man. Michael grinned along with him, and then stopped. Ceased the mirth.

"So. The Rifles. You must have seen quite a bit of action in Afghan?"

Vinnie nodded, a cloud passing over his face. He took a long drag of his cigarette and then flicked the ash away. Staring up at the brickwork of Lancaster House. "Yeah, man. Lost a lot, we did. A lot of the lads. Good soldiers."

I wasn't sure whether he was being overly dramatic or if the mention of fallen comrades really had affected his mood so quickly. Either way, the entire discussion was proving to have a very adverse effect on me, causing me to want to rush home and immediately renew my CND membership.

Time for my own exit, then. I decided to opt for the kind of distraction technique that I would normally employ with Matthew. Although this was less about a three year old sticking Jelly Tots up his nose and more about moving the attention of wife-beater away from wanting to intimidate his family.

"Here's an idea!" I interrupted. The conversation had now moved on to 'Operation Johnny Bastard Towel Head'. Or something along those lines. The two men looked over towards me.

I pointed towards Vinnie's fallen motorbike and widened my eyes at Michael. (Take the hint. Get him away from the door, please.) Vinnie glanced over to his machine – to his first love, lying on the faded grass.

"See! Not only do you two have the army in common, but Michael loves bikes nearly as much as he loves God. Go on, Michael – see if you can help him get it all fixed up nicely."

Michael was on board now, telling Vinnie, "Well, I'm not exactly a mechanic, but I have been doing them up for years. Come on. I'll take a look."

Vinnie was pathetically grateful. He now had a fellow bike-convert to tell his woes to. As they walked onto the grass, doing the dog-shit dance in order to reach the machine, Michael nodded sympathetically as Vinnie pointed out the damage. Even when Vinnie tried to bring the conversation back to "that stupid bitch's fault", Michael expertly deflected the discussion to all things bike. Free to try to get into the building myself now, I pressed the buzzer and waited for an answer. Futile, probably. Neal wouldn't be able to juggle the hasty arrival of Dawn and family and then a Miss Simpson sort. Multitasking wouldn't be his strong point.

So, as I waited I continued to watch Michael. Surprising myself as I realised that I was – quite unconsciously – smiling. These days, overhearing conversations about the merits of road bikes versus sports bikes always made my blood run cold. Yet here I was, watching Mr Politician dealing with someone like Vinnie. Both of them gushing over something that looked like an oil-smeared dead metal beetle lying on the faded grass. Smoking cigarettes and talking the kind militaristic gung-ho crap that I hated. Yes, here I was. Grinning at the Right Honourable Michael Chiswick. Admiring all this. People skills at their finest.

And then a voice called out.

"Rachael Russell! Long time no see, so it is!"

A scruffy old red Vauxhall Astra had pulled up not far from the spot where the men were poking about with the bike. Brenda Kray emerged. A well-rounded woman of fifty-five, with ruddy cheeks and mop of frizzy hair – Brenda looked every inch the stereotypical farmer's wife. But she was a Dubliner by birth and now a long-term Brindleford resident. With a murderous East End surname. Not really related to *those* Krays, of course, but she was happy to perpetuate the rumour. Every bit helps if you live on Brindleford.

I trotted over to her and helped to hoist overflowing shopping bags from the boot of her car, outlining the fact that in the space of the last half hour she had acquired five new residents. She wasn't too surprised, however, having immediately noticed Vinnie's presence. She pulled a face, "Jaysus. She never learns … that Dawn. Always ends up back with him. And he's a total scrote. He is, so he is."

I explained how I had happened to get entangled with the Miss Simpson scenario. And that I had enlisted the help of Jake Bamber, bringing the old lady to Lancaster House so as to avoid the Great Medlock B & B Ring Around. She nodded ferociously.

"Good. You know that I couldn't give a feck about their budgets. Whether it's New Banks' dosh or the council's. No worries, my love."

Then I told her – hoping that I didn't sound like a total grassbag – that Dawn and her family had barely made it into the hostel in time, thanks to Neal's ineptitude.

"The little shit. Not letting them in! Lazy fecker will have been sittin' watchin' the telly and stuffin' his face with biscuits, so he will! And if his so-called girlfriend is with him then you would have had no chance. She's got the manners of a monkey, that one."

By now we had reached the entrance. She noticed the door immediately.

"Oh, Jaysus! Would you look at it! Look at the damage! Cost a fortune! Oh, that Neal. He's feckin' for it, so he is." She placed her shopping bags on the paving stones, shaking her head. "So, how did you manage to get the little toe-rag to open it for you in the end?"

I smiled serenely and explained how the mere mention of Neal's seventh birthday party had quickly moved the state of affairs on. She snorted her best piggy-laugh.

"Oh! Ah, now, that would have spurred him on, of course. I had forgotten all about that, so I had!" Chuckling, she used the key to unlock the door and heaved her shopping bags inside, turning to gesture towards Michael with her thumb.

"And the chappie – man off the telly – there," she jerked her head towards Michael and Vinnie. "What the feck is he doing here?

Right on cue, Michael weaved his way over to us. The door to the hostel was still wide open. But by now, Vinnie had lost all interest in gaining access to the refuge and was pulling his bike upright. I introduced Michael to the warden as "a neighbour of Miss Simpson's". The concerned citizen nodded agreeably, "I've managed to persuade Vinnie to go home. But he won't leave his bike on the lawn. Says that someone will steal it. And. It seems to me that he's been drinking."

I nodded in agreement. "Yes. And the more hardcore stuff by the looks of it. Smack?"

Brenda pulled a face. "Oh, yes. Or crack. Whatever the hell the idiot can lay his hands on."

"So, because he shouldn't be driving," Michael continued, "I offered to take the bike back for him. I've had a tinker with it and it's rideable. And he says that he trusts me. What with me being a minister and all."

He shot me a cheeky grin. Very boyish. My heart engaged in a sudden kick-start. I shoved a mental stick into its spokes.

"No. Hang on a minute, Michael. What about insurance? His bike probably isn't covered. And what about a helmet?"

Back to Black. And a suffocating blanket of panic-sodden thoughts. Dragging me backwards. Heart frozen in horror when I opened the envelope that morning. An unbelievably formal and cruelly detached letter from the insurance company. It had taken several minutes for the realisation of what it meant for us to sink in ...

But Michael's voice was singing at me. Pulling me back to the present.

"Yes, I didn't like to ask him about insurance, really. But I'm covered for third party. And he told me it will only take a jiffy, so we can forget about the helmet for just a few seconds. He lives just round the corner from here. Anyway, what's life without a bit of a risk every now and then?"

I ignored his flippancy and focussed instead on the fact that somehow, I couldn't imagine Vinnie uttering an expression such as 'jiffy'.

"Well, that's all well and good, Michael. But what about your protection?" I offered. Aware that my voice was wavering slightly. "If you come off that thing in your shorts, without leathers, you'll really —"

Michael interrupted me and playfully pushed my shoulder. He spelled it out to me.

"I'll go slooowly!"

Turning to Brenda now, he cocked his head. "Has she always been such a worrier?"

He left us, jogging off to the bike and patiently observing Vinnie who gave him a cursory introduction to its marvels. Then, when he was finally permitted to mount it, he threw his leg over the seat, revved up and moved off, looking over to me and mouthing "*Slooowly*". Followed by a Cheshire cat grin. Vinnie cast a scowl at us over his shoulder and then loped off down the road after Michael. Brenda shook her head at me.

"Well, he's either an insensitive sod, my love, or he doesn't know much about you."

I tried to sound pragmatic. No need for the mother of all martyrs impersonation.

"No. Well I've only met him once before today. On a constituency visit to us at Sisters' Space. He knows nothing about me. Or my life. And actually … it might be best if neither of us mention the fact that he was here today. No one seems to recognise him. And Vinnie seems to think that he's some sort of posh vicar."

Brenda nodded, and then I remembered to tell her about Miss Simpson and our little infestation, questioning whether she would want me, as well as the pensioner, inside the building. Two potential flea-bags in residence. She gave me one of her looks.

"Rachael, most days of the week here I've got people riddled with bugs and the like. So I've got a sure-fire method of killing every feckin' creepy crawly known to man … but you mustn't ask me where I buy the stuff from. It's something only a few of us in the hostel de-lousing business know about. So you won't be finding it on any of the supermarket shelves, so you won't."

"Sounds a bit …"

"Illegal. So it is. But it kills the little bastards. Although I swear to God that me, our Donny and Neal have started glowing in the dark … been using the stuff for some ten years now. Bound to affect you one way or another. So, yes. You and your nice gentleman friend are welcome inside. Once he gets back from his mercy mission." She grinned at me, showing a missing molar and nudged my shoulder, teasing me. "And didn't I notice a bit of the old chemistry between you two there, just now?"

"Oh give over, Brenda. You should stop reading your Mills & Boons. Or have you graduated on to the *Fifty Shades of Grey* sort of things these days?"

She laughed. “Oh, I don’t do porn. I’m too old for all that fiddling about with your private parts, so I am. And speaking of which … let’s go and rescue Dawn and the others before Neal gets the superglue out.”

Chapter 5

SANCTUARY OF DELOS (OR THE DOSSHOUSE)

We encountered Neal at the top of the stairs. As a small child he had worked hard to develop a facial expression that perpetually conveyed the message 'Do I give a shit?' As a lanky adolescent, he had mastered the look. Although today the attitude was literal, because he was holding a dirty nappy at arm's length. Horror etched upon his face. No doubt wondering what on earth had happened to his lazy Saturday afternoon with girlfriend and scoffing Jammy Dodgers. Dawn must have been throwing her weight about with him. Her voice echoed down the corridor.

"Bleedin' 'ell, Neal! Don't be a thick twat! You just shove it in a plastic bag and tie it up. Dump it in the normal black bin. Typical innit? I knew that she'd shit in it as soon as I managed to get it on her. Little get!"

"But … God – it *stinks*!" he wheedled.

Dawn's elegant answer came hurtling back.

"Jesus Christ, it's only baby shit! I bet your room smells a lot worse than her arse does!" Eighteen-year-old Neal descended into three-year-old mode, making puppy-eyes at Brenda climbing the stairs towards him.

"Mum!" he groaned. "Can you do this?" Holding the dirty nappy towards her.

"I've got my hands full of shopping, Neal. In case you hadn't noticed. Act like the adult you keep telling me you are, for feck's sake! And then come and help me unpack the shopping before you get back to slobbering over whatsername in your bedroom!"

I left the shopping bags outside Brenda's family living quarters and made my way to the hostel end of Lancaster House and to the communal living area. The place still bore the hallmark scent of Cup a Soup, but today it was accompanied by a strong whiff of baby poo. Dawn's youngest was crawling around the chairs, looking a little happier for being fed and now clad in nappy number two. Brenda would have to try to sort out some baby clothes for her, though. Miss Simpson was sitting in a high-backed chair and the baby's two brothers were slumped in front of a TV. Neither of them took their eyes off the screen to register my presence. I was half-tempted to fetch them a bucket in order to catch their TV-slobber.

"You OK, boys?" I asked.

"Hrrghh," the older one replied.

The younger one chipped in with, "Well, at least they've got satellite here now. They didn't 'ave it last time we were 'ere. But the telly's shit. It's well tiny."

Neal peered in through the doorway, a packet of Jaffa cakes in his hands. No doubt already having managed to avoid helping his mother out. He paused to see what the boys were watching on the TV. The smaller child asked him, "Hey, Neal! Bet you've got a better telly in your room, haven't you?"

"Yeah."

"What size?"

"Forty-two inch."

"Cool. Can we come and watch yours, then?"

"'Kof!" said Neal, nonchalantly, as he left the room.

The younger boy took aim and fired at Neal's back with an imaginary gun. The older, fair-headed lad couldn't seem to remove his eyes from the screen, but mimicked the accents of the actors, drawling to himself:

"The man teeell mee to fook off; I keeell him." He drew a finger across his throat in a parody of mafia-style execution.

"Is this a Welsh film, then?" I asked.

"Eh?"

My attempts at humour were lost on blondie buzz-cut. His little brother continued to whinge on.

"That's so not fair! That's a load of bollocks, that is. Why do we 'ave to put up with shitty nob-sized TV? Cheap twats."

"Oi!" I raised my voice. They both looked at me now. "Mind your language!" One pair of lips curled, and the other tutted in disgust at my prudish attitude. Then their attention was turned back to the film, where a gunfight had erupted.

I tried again. "So. What are you two called? How old are you both?"

"He's Tony Soprano. An' I'm Scarface," the older boy commented.

Blam! Somebody else had been shot on the TV now. Hang on a minute … this was Saturday afternoon. Shouldn't we be viewing some kind of genteel whodunnit? Apparently not. And splat! Camera effect now showing crimson brain material oozing down the viewer's screen. No. This definitely wasn't *Midsomer Murders*. And I couldn't recall Miss Marple ever calling someone a 'stupid motherfucker' in between mouthfuls of her egg and cress sandwiches. The smaller boy now jerked his thumb towards Brenda's family's living quarters, where Neal had sloped off to.

"That Neal, eh? He wants to watch his step. Messin' with us. What'd our weapon of choice be then, Mace? I reckon we should use the Glock on 'im. Ha!"

"Yeah."

The younger one checked out my reaction with a gappy grin. He had caramel-coloured skin and collar-length hair, braided into cornrows. He was a cutie, all right. Squarely built and a real replica of his dad. Mini-Vinnie. His brother was taller and more sinewy, with that almost white-blonde hair. Different fathers, probably. Seeing that I wasn't impressed by his words, the smaller boy decided to reply to my question after all.

"Alright. Well, he's Mace and I'm West. I'm seven and he's ten."

I'd encountered plenty of kids called West before. But Mace was a new one on me. Why would anyone want to name a child after an anti-mugging tear-gas spray?

"Mace?" I asked the older brother. "That's an unusual name you've got there."

Mace looked at me as if I was an imbecile.

"Mace. For Ma-son. You know – Mason. I mean, that's like, hardly un-yoo-shu-wall. Got three of us in our year six at school."

"Oh. Right." I said. "I get you now."

Of course. So, maybe Mason had been named because Dawn was a highly skilled stonework artisan. And perhaps West had been christened for Vinnie's love of all things nautical and geographical.

Still, I could hardly talk. It wasn't like I had named Lydia after my love of Greek mythology or a romantic encounter on that particular Greek island. Nah. My Liddy had been named after The Muppets' performance of 'Lydia the Tattooed Lady' back in the 1970s. Classy chick, me.

"So what's your little sister's name?" I asked. The baby had raised herself onto her feet, wavering at Miss Simpson's chair and patting the old lady's papery knee with a podgy hand.

"Poppy-Rose," came the answer.

Perhaps a result of Vinnie and Dawn's shared enthusiasm for flora and horticulture.

I turned my attention to Miss Simpson, who seemed to be telling Poppy-Rose a story. It wasn't your usual fairy tale or Disney saga though. Something about the growing numbers of asylum seekers in the UK. She was reading from a copy of *News Of The Nation*, one of our country's more rabidly right-wing tabloids.

"What balderdash!" she exclaimed, rattling the newspaper. "What utter twaddle!"

A fleeting memory caused me to smile to myself. If Adam ever saw a copy of *News of the Nation* he would say to me, "Sad bastard rag. Wouldn't even wipe my arse on it." Miss Simpson would no doubt have been in agreement with my husband. And this was all very interesting. Since leaving her flat in Mottram, the elderly lady's communication skills seemed to be improving. I had been led to believe that it was the other way round with Alzheimer's – that moving someone from their home would cause further distress and confusion. But maybe Mary Simpson was a one-off. I hoped so.

A sudden movement from the corner of the room caught my eye. Dawn was leaning out of an open window. I hadn't noticed her there before. I walked over and touched her lightly on the shoulder. She looked back at me. Smiling apologetically and lop-sidedly, thanks to the swelling on her face.

"Oh. Hiya. Just having a quick smoke out the window. Friggin' needed one. Can't really go outside with 'im hangin' round, can I?" But before I could reply, Brenda marched into the kitchen.

"Now, you – Miss Fag Ash Lil. If you want to smoke, go and stand in the courtyard downstairs like everyone else has to do. You know damned well that it's secure out there. It's not like you haven't been here a million times before, so you have! And go to the freezer there and get some ice on that eye now. Silly girl!"

Dawn ignored her. Dropping her cigarette butt out of the window, she gave a low whistle and uttered, "Hey! It's the pigs! Who called them out, then?"

I scuttled over to the window to witness the Minister for Communities emerging from a police car.

Back at the front door, Michael was wiping perspiration from his brow with the back of his hand. He was accompanied by two police officers – one of them a handsome hunk in his mid-twenties, and the other even younger, his face pockmarked with acne. Michael might have been sweating somewhat, but he still managed to greet me with a confident smile, explaining, "Just a bit of a mix-up. Chaps here had to pull me over. Incorrect attire and all that. I've given them phone numbers for them to check out my ID."

The two police officers were busy, juggling various radios and phones between them. Michael whispered, "They seemed to think that I'm some kind of aristocratic drug-pusher. They've been rather snippy with me actually. But don't worry. Everything will be fine."

But it wasn't looking good. No, indeed. In fact, it was all going rather tits-up. On this, my first weekend ever without kids in tow, I had somehow ended up spending the day with a posh but socially curious senior politician, a demented and incontinent water-logged pensioner and an ex-squaddie psychotic wife-beater and his abused family. And now, on top of that, two coppers – one who turned out to be a bit of a smart-arse and the other a groveller.

The phrase, "Michael. I told you so. You daft sod" was on the tip of my tongue, but I managed to swallow it. We waited for several rather agonising minutes, and finally beefy-copper put his radio back into his pocket, turning back to us. Full of apologies. Looking ever so slightly paler now, under that glowing tan. The man had definitely caught a glimpse of his career in the force taking a sudden nosedive into the cack. Michael grinned.

"Smashing. So I came up squeaky clean with Scotland Yard, then? No formal warning even?" His eyes twinkled. He knew the answer, damned well.

"Not at all," said Mr Square-Jaw. "As you say, Sir – your actions were in the public interest … assisting with removing a violent man away from a domestic abuse scenario. I'm sure we can let this one go."

The younger officer was less experienced in the art of back-peddling, however. He gabbled, "But it's a tough job here? You know? Like, you can't believe what anyone on this estate tells you, you know?"

He had a rising inflection. And he used the 'like' rather too much as a vocalised pause. Two of my pet hates. And they reminded me of just how young he was. Perhaps a good seventeen years younger than me. The git.

The other officer stepped in again. Wanting to silence his wet-behind-the-ears colleague. "Yes, and the bike doesn't have insurance. So we'll be checking that out with the owner."

"No problem, chaps." Michael was all magnanimous mirth. "Bet you didn't think you'd end up having to call the prime minister's office direct today, though, did you?" His mannerisms had turned ever so slightly Boris Johnson again. Friendly buffoon. They both shook their heads. Chastened. But I couldn't resist my own sideswipe.

"Well, I think that the minister has been extremely reasonable in his reaction to you on all of this. I, for one, wouldn't have blamed him if he had decided to refer to you both as a 'pair of plebs' or —"

Michael cut me off with a dirty look.

"Quite. Thank you. Anyway, Rachael, I think that you'd better brief our friends here. About this case of domestic violence. That is your area of expertise, after all."

With the emphasis being on 'your'. As though he seemed to think that I couldn't deal with the odd officious copper. So I shook my head, correcting him. "Well, no. Not today, Michael. I'm not working. I'm just a bystander in the wrong place at the wrong time."

The older policeman, though, had the wit to realise that he might be able to do a further bit of damage limitation. "All the same, Madam, we would appreciate your professional view on the situation. Mr Chiswick did assure us that you're an expert on such matters."

I eyeballed Michael. He gave me an innocent shrug. I replied, "Well. If the minister wants to ladle on the charm, who am I to refuse? That's his area of expertise, after all." With the emphasis being on 'his'. I noted that Michael had cast his eyes to the heavens now. Ha.

So I spent a couple of minutes outlining my take on what had happened and told the boys in blue that it might be worth them checking out any outstanding injunctions against Vinnie Murray. Then I nodded towards Brenda, who was now hovering at the entrance to Lancaster House. After speaking to her, they disappeared upstairs to see if Dawn wanted to press charges against Vinnie. And Michael was busying himself with taking phone calls. His mobile had been chirruping non-stop during the last ten minutes. Brenda turned to me. Hands on hips. Squinting into the sun.

"Well, I'd best go and finish off sorting your old lady out. She's been asking for a toasted currant teacake. Speak to you Monday, no doubt." She began to close the door.

I called out, "You're a gem, Brenda. Snack preparation for inmates isn't in your job description, you know."

"Ha! Feckin' job description – load of bollocks, so it is."

And the door closed with heavy thud.

Finally, it was just the two of us again. Standing a couple of yards from a dead and very rancid fox. Next to the three-foot-high 'Dos House' graffiti.

"What time is it?" I wondered aloud. "I've lost all track of it since we got here and started having various mini-crises." There was no time-telling instrument on my wrist. Matthew had bitten through my watch strap the day before. (Strange child. Always biting things.) But Michael's phone told us that it was 5.30 p.m.

"Well now. Doesn't time fly when you're having fun?" Michael murmured. He put his hand between my shoulder blades, perhaps with the aim of propelling me into action. Perhaps not. Either way, I flinched. And then felt embarrassed at my sudden movement.

"Speaking of time," he added in a low voice, "come on, Jumpy. I think we need to go and retrieve a certain watch from a certain taxi driver."

Our taxi was parked around the corner from the hostel. And our driver was still in possession of the watch. Ali handed it back to Michael and stepped on the accelerator, barely giving us the chance to close the car doors. His eyes glanced at the rear-view mirror.

"Vat was it with the cops, hey? I saw you on that guy's bike. And then them bringin' you back in the cop car. Did they charge you, man?" Ali was thirsting for information. But Michael smiled enigmatically. The driver prattled on.

"Nice one. 'Cause I'm sittin' here thinkin', if they is pullin' him in … keep hold of the blingy for him, Ali-boy. Your cops round here like, would take it off you. And you is never going to see it again, innit!"

I gave Michael a knowing-nod. At least I had only indicated that the policemen were plebs. Ali's inference was much more slanderous. Michael just gave me That Look.

"Anyway. You's got to be havin' some friends in high places, eh? Friends the cops maybe don't vanna mess with, innit?" Ali also seemed to have got the impression that Michael was some kind of posh drugs baron.

We sped out of the estate and onto a B road, cutting through a long sliver of countryside and back over the Greater Manchester county division between Lancashire and Derbyshire. I mused on the Dawn scenario. There she was, trapped in your classic, abusive relationship cycle. Probably not even aware of the hows or the whys of it all. But despite that, she possessed an inner confidence, a sense of self that even years of therapy couldn't give to a person. Surely it was all about upbringing. All about where your own little life was created, where it began in the entire sweep of the social pecking order. I noticed it a lot in my current line of work – in the lower strata of society ("Who the fuck are they to talk down to us?") But I had also witnessed it at the higher end of the spectrum ("Of course I deserve to be well educated, rich and powerful. Goes without saying.")

And sure, I wouldn't want Dawn's life. Certainly not the Vinnie-baggage side of things. But I wouldn't have minded a bit of that internal self-possession. Or however your sociologists or psychologists referred to it.

(A woman like Dawn wouldn't give a toss about the correct way to behave. To live. To die. Or to grieve. Of the opinions of others and what they thought about you…)

Speaking of which.

"This being pulled over by the police stuff," I spoke in hushed tones to Michael. "Are you playing all of that down? I mean … Could it cause problems for you?" He shrugged.

"Probably not. But you can never accurately predict things in politics. Even tiny little incidences like we experienced today. It's a little bit like gambling. You can guess the likely outcome of aggregate actions. But that's as far as it goes." He turned towards me, wagging his finger.

"And anyway, shouldn't you be more worried about your own professional standing? It sounded like a certain person was bending the rules in order to get an old lady some help."

"No," I replied. "No 'bending' involved. Circumvention, perhaps. If you know how the system works, you can sometimes get it to work a bit faster for you."

"Rightio. So … if you hadn't been there, this afternoon. What would have happened to her? And to Mr Bridges?"

"Difficult to say. Mr Bridges was struggling, but he had his daughter, after all. He could have moved in with her for a bit."

"So, Miss Simpson?"

"Well. Mr Bridges was completely pissed off with her. As you saw. So even if he had wanted to help her …"

Michael finished my sentence: "The poor chap clearly didn't have a clue about who to contact."

"Exactly. Too many organisations involved. Those of us who have the joy of working in the social sector get confused enough ourselves. So, yes, Mary Simpson might well have ended up dying of hyperthermia overnight. These things aren't uncommon."

He smacked the palm of one hand with his fist. Exasperated.

"Maybe not. But they damned well should be! This is precisely why we needed to get the Social Care Bill through its reading. And the opposition bloody scuppered it yet again last week!"

"Well. That would have all been very nice for your lot, of course. But I doubt if it would have helped Miss Simpson today."

A noticeable judder of Michael's head, and a puckered brow. Switching cerebral channels to debating mode *a la* the Commons, perhaps.

"But, Rachael – think of all the Miss Simpsons of the future. We can improve things, streamline the system. Make things more seamless."

I pulled my face. "Oh, I can see that you've got noble intentions, Michael, but do you really think that civil servants will want to streamline themselves out of a job? Because that's what you're talking about, ultimately. Even if your bill gets through there'll be all kinds of seamlessness review groups and streamlining inquiries and cost-efficiency assessments…"

I stopped myself. Had I overstepped the mark? Been too glib about protocol with ministers? After all, you never know when you need a politician in your pocket to pull some strings for your battered ladies. So I decided to put the brakes on. Smooth over the wrinkles.

"Sorry, Michael. You probably think that I'm being very facetious."

But he just shook his head at me, "Well. I'd have to disagree with you on your rather tabloid-newspaper-sounding thoughts about our marvellous civil servants, of course. Lots of the poor devils are being streamlined, left, right and centre. But don't apologise for your honesty about things. That's what I miss about the army, actually. A bit of straight-talking does everyone the world of good. And one tends to forget that in politics. But anyway, Rachael. I have to say that you do show an appalling lack of faith in things —"

"Ha," I interrupted him, relieved that he was at least pretending that he didn't mind my offhand attitude, even if his private thoughts were that I was an opinionated gobshite. "I've got plenty of faith, Michael. But not in our archaic political system. In fact – and I know that it's hardly fashionable these days – I've probably got more faith in the existence of God than —"

"And I, on the other hand, have no faith in religious matters. Despite having had the best Catholic education in the UK, at Ampleforth College."

"Oh. Not Eton then? Surprised at that…" I rubbed my bare arms. Ali's air con had successfully transformed the car into a refrigerator on wheels. "Right, well. I've heard of Ampleforth, but I thought it was for very well-to-do Catholic lads who were hoping to enter the priesthood."

"Well, some of them were up for that. But not me. Although Vinnie clearly has me pinned down as a religious nut. Anyway – speaking of our newfound friends – will your women's centre end up helping Dawn out? I think that she'll be needing it, now more than ever."

"What makes you say that?"

"Well, when I took the bike back for him – just as the police pulled me over when I was nearly at the house, I saw these two white vans screeching away from outside of their place. Off at a cracking speed. Next thing, Vinnie arrives as the police are asking me questions. He goes inside and starts shouting. Apparently, everything had gone. Furniture. The lot."

"Oh, God. The bailiffs?"

"Maybe. Money owed to someone, that's what I was thinking. Vinnie ran straight back outside. 'Where's my bike?' Checking it's still there."

"Typical!" I spat.

Michael didn't reply now, although he kept eye contact with me, perhaps surprised at the venom in my voice.

"It would have been his bloody drug habit that caused it!" I continued. "So there he is, terrorising his family, causing them to lose everything that they own … and all he gives a shit about is his sodding motorbike! Bloody men!"

My head jerked ninety degrees away from him. Staring into the blinding sunshine outside. (Don't blink, Rachael.) We were now in a nondescript outgrowth of Stalybridge. An elderly man sporting a flat cap was standing at a zebra crossing with a bedraggled greyhound. The traffic wasn't stopping for him. But Ali waved man and dog across and then sped on towards Mottram. Our taxi driver's benevolence somehow took the edge off my outrage.

I looked down at my lap. Broken nails, dry hands, freckled fingers. Getting older, Rachael. Definitely.

"I'm sorry. You must really think that I'm a bit of a man-hater. Saying stuff like that."

"No. Not precisely. Rather more like a bike-hater, I would say." Michael answered quietly. "Perhaps also, a hater of men who beat up women. And if they have a bike and slap women about … Well. You'd probably like to crucify the bastards."

Perceptive.

"But anyway," Michael led on gently, "the furniture vanishing from house aspect. It might have made the police think that I was involved.

Part of some crew who were trying to extract payback from Vinnie."

I nodded, woodenly. I had been acting out the Ms Professional role all afternoon, but in one split second I had lost the plot. Erosion of the cool, coping veneer. Still, maybe the counselling sessions with Fran on Feelings (as I liked to refer to my bereavement counsellor) after Adam's death hadn't all been a complete waste of parking fees and additional nursery-hour costs. I was becoming a tad faster on running what Fran called those 'spot-check emotional inventories' these days.

I had been narked by the fact that someone like Michael could fall so easily into conversation with someone like Vinnie. Point of commonality between nice chap and utter twat? The love of motorbikes and all things male, military and macho. And at the end of the day, the bit that really got on my tits was this one – Bloke Choosing Bike Over Family.

I was about to apologise again, but Michael simply reached over and tapped my hand. No need to. And then he changed the subject.

"But anyway. Now you need to reveal that little secret to me. When you were chatting to the police before, Brenda mentioned that you had managed to get Dawn's family into the hostel by blackmailing her son. Something about a birthday party."

"Ah," I grinned, my mood brightening. "That was all about Neal's birthday party in the warden's flat at Lancashire House. About eleven years ago now. Back then, I was doing one of my first housing-officer jobs. Got landed with Brindleford. And one day I popped in to see Brenda about something, and there was this tea-time birthday party going on. Loads of little lads tripping out on excess E-numbers and sugar overload. Utter bedlam."

"Sounds like my idea of hell."

"Yeah. And halfway through it, Brenda had a new family turn up, out of the blue – an emergency admission. So she asked me if I could keep an eye on the boys while she sorted it out. The kids were all ready for their next party game. 'Pin the tail on the donkey'. But it turned out that there were no drawing pins for the tails. So I managed to find some superglue and I agreed with the boys that just a tiny smidgen on the paper 'tails' would work well enough if we were all very careful. Bit daft of me really, looking back. I didn't know about the lack of frontal cortex development in small children, back then."

"Is that your polite way of saying that children can be stupid and annoying little swines?"

"Ha. You don't sound too fond of children, Michael." He pulled his face.

"Well, Rachael, I might as well admit it. No. I can't stand the little buggers. Even when I was a child myself, I never really had much time for other kids. In my mind, until a human being can have a rational, adult conversation … well. They're not really worth bothering with. Oh, I'll do the kissing the babies stuff on the campaign trail and all of that. But quite frankly, small, slobbery creatures that either babble or talk inane drivel make me feel physically sick."

Well. Points for honesty, at least.

"But don't tell anyone I said that. It's hardly an acceptable view in today's child-centric society. The headline would be 'Minister Eats Babies for Breakfast' or something. Now. Continue with your story." I nodded.

"Right. Well, we carried on with the game, but in the middle of it Brenda called me out of the flat to ask me a question. Meanwhile, Neal – full of the typical birthday-boy bravado – had his turn with the blindfold. He decided it would be funny if he got his willy out. Waggling it around a bit. And he thought it would be hilarious to stick it up against the wall and demonstrate to his friends what a big tail for the donkey it could be."

A wide grin split Michael's face, revealing deep dimples in his cheeks. I hadn't noticed them before. I wanted to press my thumbs into them. But I resisted the urge.

"Well – he must have kept it there for a good ten seconds or so. And of course, globs of stray glue were all over the donkey picture. So it got stuck. Good and proper."

Michael erupted with laughter.

"Oh, bloody hell! What a scenario! You couldn't make that up, could you? But yes. Oh, yes. It rings so very true for a boy of that age!"

"That's right," I pointed my finger at him, "and don't tempt me to get all negative about the male of the species again."

Michael tried to compose himself, nodding sagely.

"Well, you, Ms Russell, might want to use this example as another battering ram for your feminist diatribes against us male oppressors, but look at it this way. Young fellows like Neal might be unappealing as a child, but it's chaps like him who grow up to be the great explorers and world leaders, you know."

I stared hard at him. Unimpressed by the logic.

"I beg to differ. Perhaps you'd be right if Neal had experienced the benefits of a public-school education. If he possessed the family connections, vast amounts of patronage and friends in the media … perhaps then he could have become your explorer and world leader type. Being led onwards and upwards by his Wonder Willy, no doubt. But Brenda reckons that he'll be lucky to ever get a job. He's been unemployed for two years now – since leaving school. Can't even get shortlisted for an interview. Though, knowing Neal, he probably isn't that bothered about trying to. Best thing that Brenda could do would be to kick him out. Make him stand on his own two feet."

My thoughts turned to Matthew. Of his incredible flashes of brilliance, his frighteningly astute pre-schooler intelligence. His ability to take apart an entire DVD player without being asked to. To melt a whole cache of Mummy's make-up down the side of the radiator. But of his sheer backwardness when it came to any attempt to wipe his own little arse, as long as muggins here was on scene to do it for him. My commonly reoccurring worries about The Future Of Matthew were interrupted by Ali.

"This it?"

We were crunching up the gravel hill that led to Michael's cottage.

"Yes. Home James and all of that." Michael replied. "And thank you for everything that you've done for us today." On top of the return fare – steep enough in itself – I noticed that Michael had added a more than significant tip. Ali looked astonished, but this quickly turned to bemusement, when I asked him to write me a receipt ("who'd have thought the Manchester Mafia keep an audit trail, innit?") As we got out of the taxi, he called to us.

"Glad we got out of that place alive, innit! Anyvays. Look after your lovely lady. Have a nice time. I'm off for me first Stalyvegas call!"

Then Ali headed back down the hill and out of Mottram. The depressing ambition of a Saturday night in Stalybridge. Picking up binge-drinking teenagers. Praying that none of them would chuck up in the back of his cab.

"Nice chap," commented Michael.

"Nice tip!" I added. "Would it be eligible for one of those controversial MP expenses claims? Or will you be submitting a claim to your Mancunian drugs baron overlord?"

"No to both," Michael answered, scratching his neck.

"Well," I replied. "I'll claim the fare back from the homeless section at Medlock Council. And I'll get you the cash from my car in a second. They wouldn't be able to cover the tip though. They're a bit strict about that kind of thing."

"Ah, not to worry about any of that," Michael said carelessly. "And I wouldn't normally tip that much. But don't you think that it was the least I could do? After he looked after my watch. And after we infected his taxi with fleas."

A sudden urge to itch my ankle.

"Oh. Oh, God – yes," I realised. "I'd completely forgotten about that. The fleas. Poor Ali!"

Chapter 6

DIONYSUS, THE AMPHORA AND A CRAP FROZEN PIZZA

It was time to head on home now, before any more bizarre scenarios could hurl themselves in my general direction. I stepped over to my car, "Right. I'll just get you the cash, Michael and then I'd best be off. Thanks for all your help with Miss Simpson."

"Stop!" he commanded. Raising his hand in the air like some twenty-first century version of the Green Cross Code man. Minus the silly outfit. "What on earth are you doing?"

"Going home." Pausing with my keys mid-air.

"Please don't take offence at this, Rachael. But after everything you advised me of previously … even from here I can see that the inside of your car looks like it would be prime real estate for a small colony of asylum-seeking fleas. Surely you'll need to de-louse?"

A neat line of lollipop sticks stuck to the rear windscreen were a dead giveaway; *this woman is not the best at keeping a clean vehicle.* And, in addition to the empty Monster Munch packets, squashed drink cartons, random raisins, my work files and the kids' ripped copies of *The Beano*, a pair of Lydia's knickers lay on display on the parcel shelf. Yes, I knew that they were clean, of course, but innocent members of the public wouldn't. Hopefully Michael hadn't noticed them.

Attempting to deflect attention from my pigsty of a car, I chirruped, "I'm impressed, Michael. You're learning!"

"And I'm itchy and need a good scrub," lobbing his reply right back at me. "And I suspect that you do too. Coming?"

I narrowed my eyes. Clarify, please.

He added, "I have a rather large shower cubicle."

I pursed my lips. Hoping that any such pouting might come across as more Brigitte Bardot than Hilda Ogden.

"In your dreams, Michael. And the size of some bloke's shower receptacle has never mattered to me. I'm a teeny-weeny caravan-sized cubicle sort of girl, myself. I don't go for show-off big top nozzles."

He laughed, "Well, you've rumbled me there. So, perhaps you'll be pleased that my cottage has an outside shower room. All very normal-sized. But with a deceptively, fiercely-pummelling shower-head."

"Sounds better."

"And all this means that we can both get clean without infesting my house. Or your car. And then I can lend you some clothes. Unless you'd prefer to drive home naked, of course."

I hesitated for a second. And then I seemed to catch Vicky's teasing voice – little sister cooing in my ear, circa 1989 – "Rachael is a frigid stiff!" I mentally poked her in the eye. And then shrugged. OK.

He gestured with his head, and I followed him around the side of the house and into a cottage garden. An explosion of colour – flowers, grasses, herbs and brambles. To me, the neglected and overgrown look had always had more appeal than manicured lawns and privet.

"But first, Rachael, would you mind having a quick look at this?" He pulled his T-shirt over his head, screwing it into a ball and lobbing it into the lavender bushes. The sudden half-nakedness made me feel as if I should avert my eyes, look away. But then, I've never been particularly good at fake modesty.

"A look at what?" I asked. He tried to reach a hand round to his lower back.

"This. Is it a bite? Or perhaps a very unattractive boil?"

His back was a soft golden colour, marred only by a scarlet spot. I peered closely, my nose just inches from his flesh.

"Definitely a bite. I've got a couple on my ankles." My eyes moved upwards. Drawn to the point between his shoulder blades. His skin was a different colour there. Less tawny, less texture. Smoother. Like the shiny inside of a pink seashell.

He murmured, "Excuse the hideous scars. They always put the girls off."

"You can barely seem them," I lied. "How did that happen?" He turned round and folded his arms across the auburn-silver hair on his chest. The posture made his biceps look quite impressive. I resisted the urge to pinch them and challenge him to an arm-wrestling competition.

"War wounds, of course!" Eyes wide, a tight little smile on his lips. No mirth in his eyes, although there was a glint of ochre. From tabby to tiger? But he was skilful at self-effacement. And it masked whatever it was that I had caught a glimpse of.

"Oh. From Afghanistan?"

"Not quite. I'll bore you with all that some other time, when I'm not itching my tits off. Right. When I'm done, I'll find you some spare clothes of mine and leave them outside the door for you."

The sound of running water accompanied my wait in the wild cottage garden. Bees, which should by rights have been on their last legs, were still bumbling about. A blackbird was fluttering in and out of the hedge at the end of the garden. He should have been bedding down and getting ready to nest at this time of the day. But this heat seemed to be messing with the heads of both man, lass, bird and beast.

I heard Michael call, "Shower's free, fleabag!"

Making my way into the shower room, I stripped off and was surprised to find Tyler's mobile phone still squished inside my bra for safe-keeping. I placed the phone on the side of the sink and then dropped my clothes out of the window, with the intention of bagging them up and taking them home with me. Then I showered, borrowing Michael's shampoo to wash my hair. I couldn't resist the urge to peek into the bathroom cabinet, but there was nothing of interest in there, though (no lady-things, no Viagra.) While I was drying myself on a non-fabric conditioned towel (single man?), Michael rapped on the door.

"Clothes outside!"

I paused for a few seconds, and then opened the door to find a pair of Bermuda shorts and a navy-blue T-shirt. I yanked the cord in tight around the shorts in order to keep them up. The top was baggy enough to hide any gratuitous nipple action, should that little embarrassment transpire. *Sans* knickers and *sans* bra. Not done that for a while.

I towel-dried my hair and then examined myself in the full-length mirror. For once, my legs were smooth, de-fuzzed and even had a bit of a tan, thanks to the unusual weather. The *Mummy Smelz* tattoo, thankfully, had been washed away.

I was hardly *Vogue* Model of the Year, though. But would *Vogue* model woman know what to do with a flea infestation, survivors of domestic abuse and demented, incontinent pensioners? I very much doubted it. And yet, despite my attempts at positive affirmations, I could still hear the siren song of the Emergency Make-Up Bag calling me.

Back at my car, the compressed heat boomed out at me. I scrabbled for the cosmetics bag in the glove compartment. Its contents were rather gooey, but they would do the trick. I gurned into my compact mirror and began some fast re-surfacing work.

Some things don't change.

Sixteen years ago. One of those all-nighters with Shaun. I told myself that we never really got any sleep anyway. So why bother with taking the make-up off? And so it was perfectly reasonable behaviour to sneak into the bathroom in the wee small hours. Amend the eyeliner and sluice on some more mascara.

I snapped the compact shut. Disgusted. That had not been Good Feminism back then, had it, Rachael? No. Reading Virginia Woolf while letting Shaun screw me over? One kind of cancelled the other one out, didn't it?

And neither was this. Prannying about in your car with the gloopy dregs of your war paint.

I wondered whether Jess wore make-up. Probably not. Saint Jess would possess both inner and outer natural illumination. Juggling her high-flying career in the charity world while ironing Shaun's shirts. Feeling equally fulfilled by digging wells for blind orphans in Benin as she would when carrying out all manner of domestic dross. Yeah, Shaun had always known which side his bread was buttered on. Jess would be the sort to listen attentively to his tales of underhand local authority dealings and changes to by-laws without recourse to fake snoring. Unlike yours truly.

But enough of that.

In a conscious decision to move from vanity to self-flagellation, I dragged one of the kids' metal nit combs through my hair. Bloody painful. Barnet sorted, I hastily removed Lydia's knickers from the parcel shelf and shoved them under the passenger seat. I grabbed my handbag and took out my phone. No messages about recalcitrant offspring antics. Champion.

Then I made my way to the back door of the cottage, weaving my way through a utility-room. A floor strewn with old editions of *The Guardian* and lovingly adorned with bits of metal and motorbike.

(Another pang. Best ignored.)

On entering the kitchen, the Aga caught my beady eye. There were few material possessions in life that I got giddy about, but here was one of them. An Aga was something that I'd always harboured a secret and shameful desire for. The epitome of idyllic, rural lifestyle. And yet all too impractical in my house. Matthew would have baked an entire box of Lego in such a contraption. Lydia would have bribed her brother to crawl into the small oven. And hey presto. Toasted Matthew for tea.

But the rest of Michael's kitchen was a far cry from the pages of *Country Life* magazine. A mess of stacked crockery, piles of clothes, towers of unopened letters and paperwork, books and newspapers. And this was all quite unlike his public persona. Because the man on the news was always Mr Neat, Urbane and In-Control. This place though – his home turf – was warm, wild and bohemian. I sank into a navy-blue sofa, a beaten-up old thing with faded coverlets and a technicolour throw draped over it.

Michael was wearing a faded Harvard T-shirt and a fresh pair of shorts. He stood next to the kitchen counter, wielding a bottle opener, and pointed the corkscrew at me.

"Blimey. Those shorts were far too small for me. Middle-age spread." He patted his not at all lardy stomach. "But they look very fetching on you. You look like Bobby Charlton playing in the '66 Cup Final. Especially with the bruises."

I flinched at his skills of observation. Yeah. I was definitely not *Vogue* Model Woman.

"Thanks for the compliment. The bruises are from a certain small child who's been trying to kneecap me with a lightsabre all week. In fact, tonight is the first time that my parents have offered to have both my kids for a sleepover. It's actually my first night off from getting attacked or harassed in, what – twenty months?"

"Crikey."

"Yes. It's a never-ending assault course with my two. Matthew's three and a half. He's at that age where he likes to bite or attack random people. And Lydia prefers the approach of slow mental torture."

"Hmm. They sound utterly charming. Makes me grateful that I'm allergic to anyone under the age of eighteen. But don't get comfy on the sofa. Outside with you. Let's catch the last rays while our pizza is cooking."

"Pizza?"

"Yes. I'm starving and you must be, too, after the day that we've both had. So, apologies for the cheap and cheerful cuisine. And I hope to dear God that you're not a veggie."

I shook my head, heaved myself up and did as I was told. Michael followed me back through the house, carrying an uncorked bottle of wine and two glasses.

"Good. Because I only hang out with carnivores. I live on frozen meat-feast pizzas when I'm back in the constituency. And I add generous, extra toppings of dead animal onto the shop-bought versions. So what with the wine obsession and the meat consumption, I'm anticipating that

I'll be developing gout fairly soon."

At the back of the house a dreamy, picture-postcard view of the darker crowns of the Peak District unfolded. Next to a boxed-off herb garden stood a wooden bench and a small cast-iron garden table. I perched on the bench while Michael tried to steady the legs of the table with a stone from the garden.

"You're very lucky to have this to wake up to, Michael. You can even see Kinder Scout from here. It's beautiful."

He nodded and looked up at me as he squatted underneath the table. "And property here is so incredibly cheaper than in London. Plus in terms of scenery, there's no comparison. The view from my Bloomsbury flat consists of fire escapes and dead pigeons. Mind you, I can see the top of the London Eye. If I stand on my toes."

I shot him a sceptical look. He raised himself back up and picked up the bottle and glasses from the stone flagging, placing them onto the now-steadier table.

"I don't think so, somehow," I told him. "I know your lot all too well. Your pied-á- terres. Your tables at The Ivy. I've spent plenty of time working with MPs and government in London. My first job after graduating was working for an MP. As well as doing a year with a senator in the States. And until pretty recently I was working as a policy advisor in Whitehall. So I've seen the kind of stuff you get up to in all your Commons bars. I'm all too familiar with your hard-luck stories."

"Really?" He looked slightly taken aback as he uncorked the wine bottle. "And here was me thinking that you'd only ever had experience of general thuggery in the domestic arena. Sounds like you've had an eclectic career to date, Ms Russell. I need to know more. But first of all … wine."

He started to fill one of the glasses.

"If that's for me – best not," I said. "Driving and all of that."

He ignored me.

"No. I've decided. You're going to have a rest. And some grub. And you're going to appreciate my wine. And that means at least one or two decent-sized glasses of it. And then we can taxi you back over the border. Where is it you said you lived? Holmfirth? Holmevale? Holmebridge?"

"Just Holme."

"Yes. That was it. Why is it that Yorkshire folk are so terribly unoriginal in their place names?"

I frowned. "But my car?"

"Easy. You could either taxi back over the hills again in the morning and collect it – taxi fares would be my treat, of course – or, I could even drive it over to your place for you tomorrow. Vinnie trusted me with his vehicle, after all."

"Yeah. And look how that ended up."

I chewed the inside of my lip. He could tell that I was feeling disconcerted. I heard a faint sigh.

"Sorry, Rachael. I know I'm very direct. Goes with the job. But think of it like this. I've already told you that I don't have any roots in this part of the world. I don't get visitors. Treat me as a charity case, if you like. Indulge me."

I picked up my phone. Half hoping for an emergency message from my mother in relation to the kids. Half hoping not.

But no message on phone. Dilemma.

"And you've already confessed to having a very rare night off. And this wine here – my wine – is rather special, you know."

"Well. I did notice the wine rack, Michael. It looked like it was about to collapse. You must be a bit of a connoisseur. Do you stamp on the grapes in your own back garden, then?"

The two glasses still stood, untouched. He picked one up, slowly twirling the stem between his fingers.

"Something like that. This one is a favourite. From my family estate in France."

I blinked hard. It took me a few seconds to realise that he wasn't actually joking. He noticed my reaction.

"Hum. That probably sounded a bit ostentatious, didn't it? It's only a piddling little place in southern France, really."

(Not at all, Michael! My family specialise in produce too. Next time I see you, I'll fetch you a bag of some of my dad's home-grown tomatoes from his Greenhouse Estate in Stalybridge. A whole four foot square on a rain-drenched patio, you know.)

"So please. Try it. Unless, of course … you have another reason why you can't stay and have a drink? Perhaps you jettisoned your kids for a Saturday night hot date or something?"

I shook my head. "No hot date."

Tabby-grey eyes fixed onto mine. I looked away.

"Oh, all right then," I said "Go on. Give us some of your cheapo plonk!"

He passed me the glass. It was classy, heady stuff. I told him that it had to be the best wine that I had ever tasted. He cocked his head.

"Thank you. Not exactly complemented by the crap frozen pizza, though. This burgundy goes best with a steak. And I should really have gone to the effort to make you a proper meal. I imagine that you don't get much time off from cooking and whatnot. Being on your own. With the kids, I mean."

A pause. Waiting for my reaction.

"Yes. It's non-stop, that's for sure," I volunteered as I looked down at my unkempt hands. One of my fingers still encircled in rings. Unpolished rings that were fast approaching the tarnished look.

"But I didn't realise the actual circumstances, Rachael."

Wine and the warmth of the evening sun in the garden. The dusky scent of herbs. The affability of it all had caught me off-guard. I sat up straight. Preparing for the inevitable.

(How will it play itself out? The end of all banter? A dead-ended exchange? Embarrassment? Apologies? Morbid curiosity? Or maybe even a quick change of subject – side-stepping the elephant in the room? All classics.)

But I was wrong. We had none of that. Michael moved to the overgrown herb garden and started ferreting about in it. Yanking out some deadwood. Unusually, though, he kept looking up at me. Most people were appalling at eye contact when they heard The News.

"So until Brenda at the hostel mentioned it … I had no idea that you had lost your husband. That's just … horrendous."

Blackened strands of vegetation in his hands. Shaking his head.

"It's a terrible thing," Half-crouching, combing through the mint and marjoram mini-forest.

"Being left on your own with the kids. Utterly dreadful. So," he turned and lobbed the weeds into the lavender bushes, "you can tell me to mind my own business. But I just wanted to say. That if I've been at all insensitive this afternoon. Or sounded like a complete prick. About anything. Well. I do apologise."

I raised my legs to my chest, hugging myself. Self-preservation via body language. But I quickly put my legs back down again. Not as a result of any impressive psychological insight, but because the shorts were rather wafty and I had suddenly remembered that I was knickerless.

"Well. If you mean the motorbike thing. Then, yes, I can get a bit … uptight about that kind of thing. But for God's sake, don't be tiptoeing around me. Behaviour like that completely does my head in." I sipped my wine. He listened.

"I hate the way that people fanny about. When you've been bereaved. Even people who were quite sensible previously can't deal with you, act normally around you anymore."

"Oh?"

"They get all freaked out. Yeah, you get the odd person who might cross the street in order to avoid you. Or who never even mentions it to you. But most folk seem to think that they have to act in a constantly morose manner around you. As though you'd somehow take offence if anyone else in the world were enjoying themselves. Everyone doing the eggshell walk for poor old you."

Michael stepped out of the herb garden now, plonking his backside onto the side of the boxed panel.

"And a lot of people seem to think that because your other half died in particular circumstances – for example, an illness, dangerous driving or whatever – that you'll want to start campaigning for that cause. As though you'll want to set up a new charity for stupid men who kill themselves riding motorbikes. Or something."

My words petered out. I looked away, across the valley. Evening lights of the little villages nestling along the looming peaks of Derbyshire were beginning to glow. I began again.

"The thing is. I've always been a campaigner. I've always tried to challenge injustice. So I'll never be lacking an outlet for changing the crappy things in society. Whether at home or overseas. And I don't feel the need to cause a big ruckus about our own particular … tragedy."

I swallowed. Not an adjective that I frequently used. Most of the time, I viewed losing Adam as simply a stupid, shitty dose of bad luck. Which could have so easily been avoided.

(Correction. Which Adam himself could so easily have avoided. But again, best not to think about that.)

Michael gulped some of his wine and stood up.

"OK, so you'd prefer me to be honest with you? No tiptoeing, you said."

"Please."

"Well. At the risk of sounding quite brutal here, I'm not too fond of burned pizza. So do you mind if I go and fetch it? I mean – we can wait if…"

Straight to the point again. I smiled. And he nodded. He wandered back to the house and soon emerged with pizza, plates and a box of cupcakes. I hadn't lost my appetite, despite the threat of meat overkill. Michael plonked himself on one of the cast-iron chairs, while I preferred to stay at a more discreet distance, perched on the wooden bench, as I ate. He tucked into his food, swallowing an enormous mouthful and wiping his mouth with the back of his hand. Hungry-man, lack of self-consciousness. (I had forgotten that. I missed that.)

"So, tell me. Does it get better over time?" he asked, adding quickly, "I don't mean losing your husband. Of course it doesn't. I mean – do you get better at it? Dealing with people's reactions. You know. People like me. Clumsy bastards who can't manage to say what they intend to!" He groaned and dropped his head towards the slice of pizza that was halfway to his mouth. His nose skimming the mozzarella.

"Oh, Michael – you're doing fine," I chuckled. "Just don't tiptoe. But to answer your question … no. It gets worse. I mean, I get worse at it. I get ruder to people. Because I hate the monotony. Whether it's someone at the bank and you're explaining the mortgage situation. Or something medical to do with the kids. Or a sales caller wanting to speak to your husband. Or when a parent at your kid's new school invites you 'both' to a barbecue …"

(Or the insurance people. No. Don't think about the insurance people. Shelve that one.)

"Yeah. It just gets tedious. And I'm genetically predisposed to using black humour when I'm naffed off. Which not everyone appreciates, of course. It can upset people."

"Oh, no," Michael carried on. "Forget the black humour. From having only known you for a short while, I would say that you would be far more likely to resort to sarcasm. Which everyone knows is —"

"I know, I know. The lowest form, and all that. And you're right. Adam was forever telling me that I deserved an Oscar in Sarcasm."

It felt good to say his name out loud.

Michael stood up to help himself to a fourth slice of pizza. "Christ, I'm hungry after today's escapades. But Rachael, if your attitude is working for you, who cares? Who cares what other people think of you? Why should you have to conform to some 'bereaved person' role? You come across as quite an opinionated person, who I wouldn't have thought would give a tinker's cuss what people think about her."

Nail-on-head moment.

"I don't know. But it does bother me. Despite the way that I might come across to others. When it comes to this subject, I guess I do care about how people perceive me to be reacting. Whether I'm absorbing myself in the pre-requisite grieving widow stuff."

I stopped talking. Conscience pricked by a not-so-romantic reminiscence.

The two of us in his car. Me and Shaun. In the car park next to Oldham Art Gallery. I glance out of the window and notice the car that has pulled up alongside us. My parents' next-door neighbour. Nosey Norman.

Please don't see us. Please don't judge me. I know, I know. It's too soon. Too soon after. But this is different. Shaun and I never fit the usual categories of...

"Well, I say that you really should disregard the views of other people. Surely what's most important … is you and your children? Have the three of you developed a sensible way of getting to grips with it all? If that doesn't sound too …"

I waved his concerns away with an arc of green pepper.

"It's hard to say. The kids are still so young. It happened twenty months ago now. So Lydia – she's six, soon to turn seven. And yeah, obviously – she does have very strong memories of her dad. Matthew was just off his second birthday. Doesn't remember anything. So you can read all the self-help books, get your bereavement counselling, join your internet support forums ..." I paused for a minute, trying to formulate the words. "But how we've been dealing with it? I don't think that we have. As a family, I mean. If that makes sense. It could hit the kids a lot harder in their teens. Who knows?"

"Yes," he nodded, licking a stray strand of mozzarella from his lips. "And different personalities react differently to trauma. Same for kids as for adults."

"And nothing is static. To begin with, Lydia didn't want to talk about losing her daddy at all. She would say to me, 'let's talk about something nice instead!' And now it's progressed to the opposite. Questions about God, what happens to dead bodies, will she have to go and live in an orphanage if I die? Can she have my dresses because I never bother to wear anything nice? That kind of thing." He smiled wryly.

"Interesting child."

"And as for Matthew? I can't have a sensible conversation with him unless it involves Spiderman or bottoms."

"Well, as you know, I've yet to have a sensible conversation with any child," he chimed. "Not that I've tried hard, if I'm honest. I just don't have the patience. Not even for my own nephew and nieces – who in my humble opinion are odious little brats, actually – so you already have my admiration for being capable of spawning and bringing up a child. Or two of them. But surely you aren't completely on your own? What about your friends, your family?"

"Oh, my parents have been great. They do as much as they can for us, but they don't exactly live around the corner from us. So I don't like to rely on them too much. And Adam's parents are lovely, but they're in Reading. My sister, Vicky, is in London. And then there's my best friend, Kate. She's always done her best to help, but she's got enough on her plate with having twins as well as being a teacher."

(And Shaun? Funny way of helping, that).

Michael suddenly reached across the table, snatching up a brightly coloured box.

"See. I've got cupcakes. Cheap and quick dessert. I know how to treat my guests well." He opened the box and shoved them at me. I declined. "Suit yourself." He put an entire cupcake in his mouth and chewed. A Matthew trick. Gannet.

I asked him, "Did Brenda tell you anything about the accident?"

He shook his head and swallowed. "No. Not at all. She didn't elaborate. I didn't ask."

No point in holding back now, Rachael. Go for it.

"Well, this is what happened. Adam was in South Africa with his best friend Jim."

"No," Michael held his hand up to stop me. "I'm all for not fannying around, as you like to put it. Not tiptoeing. But I don't want to be intrusive." He shook his head, licked chocolate crumbs from his lips and waved his hand in front of him. Giving me the choice to move on from the conversation.

"It's fine. Honestly. I've had to tell so many people now. The words themselves don't mean very much."

He bowed his head slightly. All right then. Continue.

"Adam and Jim were in South Africa. On holiday. The result of a competition that I entered, actually. Me and my OCD need to win once I've got my mind set on something. A supermarket competition. The more toilet rolls you bought, the more entries you were allowed. I went all out on the old bulk buys of the stuff. And I won a trip to South Africa for two. Only, of course, we had the kids so we couldn't go there together. So we decided that it made more sense if Adam went. With a friend. His mate Jim from the biking club. They were on day six of their holiday. The day before they were due to fly back home."

He nodded. I sipped more wine. I had been wrong when I told him I was used to telling this story. No. I was used to conveying the bare facts to people who didn't know me. The administrators and the bureaucrats. Not this sort of background information, this version of events. Fran on Feelings was the closest I had come to on this level of detail. And she was paid good money to listen to me witter on, so she didn't count.

"And then came that infamous knock on the door. A Sunday afternoon. Two uniformed police officers. I thought it was something to do with work. With Sisters' Space. Some case, maybe – kicking off. Lydia trotted over to the front door. Her usual chatty self. But then they asked me if there was someone who could watch the kids. And I knew then. I just knew it."

Chapter 7

TWO TALES OF THANATOS

The musical chimes of a clock drifted through the open window. Striking the hour. I let them finish.

"Jim and Adam were both motorbike crazy. So Jim had this idea of hiring a bike for their last day. Said he wanted to 'explore Africa the proper way'. Adam had wanted to go shark-cage diving. Apparently he had said to Jim, 'We can go biking any time. There aren't many sharks in Yorkshire are there?' But Jim got his way."

Michael was stroking his five o'clock shadow.

"So, at the end of a nice day they were finishing off their little bike tour at a nature reserve on Cape Point. A very twisty road. And one of those 'sharp bend' signs that you would have expected to be there. Well. It wasn't."

I twisted my fingers into strands of hair, feeling the dampness from the shower.

"Adam was driving. Jim was on the back. Both were sensible riders. They'd seen too many accidents not to take it seriously. They weren't complacent with their bikes."

I was chopping carrots for a casserole. Adam had commented, casually, 'Hey, remember that Shaun – that bloke you used to work with who's a member of the Manchester Biker Club? Apparently he had a really bad accident today along the Snake Pass.'

Heart a-skittering. Followed by a flare-up at my husband. Because for

Adam 'bad' meant that poor old Shaun had written his sexy superbike off. For Adam, Shaun's broken arm paled in comparison to the tragedy of smashing up a top of the range bike.

"They lost control on the corner that skirted the edge of a cliff. A sheer two-hundred-foot drop. Off Cape Point itself. Literally the end of the world. But Adam managed to do some kind of manoeuvre so that they fell onto a ledge. I know. It sounds crazy doesn't it? Like something from a film. But, well. Adam didn't make it. Jim survived, though. Broke a lot of bones."

"Bloody hell," came from Michael, who was now sitting on the edge of one of the cast-iron garden chairs.

"There was an investigation. Meaning that it was all a long and drawn-out process. Release and transportation of the body. Death certificates, disposal of body certificates. But the inquest said that it was 'accidental death'. And that he died instantly. Through head injuries. No bike fault. No problem with the road…" I paused. Michael had worked his way through the cupcakes and was toying with the remnants of the fifth in its paper case. He looked up.

"Christ. So … does that make you feel as though you got no real answers?"

"Yes. But that's okay. I can accept that it was a crazy, freakish thing to happen. Jim can't, though. He wanted answers. And he still feels responsible for pushing on the 'let's hire a bike' idea."

Michael muttered, shaking his head. "God. Poor bloke."

"Yes." I added, "And I tell him to get over it. Forget the whys and the wherefores. I tell him that Adam could just as easily have been killed by a shark if they had followed his own daft idea for a bit of testosterone-induced fun. I tell him that if he's going to use that kind of logic, shouldn't I also blame myself for my obsessive bulk buying of toilet roll?"

Michael smiled grimly. "Hmm. Can we call this 'Rachael-Logic'?"

"If you like. I just think that it's wasted energy to search for answers. To beat yourself up. It's about as sensible as feeling that some horrible God up there in the clouds has decided to smite you and yours because you think that his religion is a load of old tosh."

"So you're not a … believer, then? Before, in the taxi, you said that you placed more faith in God than in the political system."

"Yes. I am. Just to confuse you."

He pulled a face. "Explain."

"Well … I guess all I'm saying is that I don't go for traditional answers and crass sentimental responses to death anymore. Got rather too much of that after losing Adam, from people who seem to think that they've got a direct line to God. It strikes me as the height of arrogance to believe that if you pray hard enough you can somehow persuade a supernatural being to answer your petty little prayers. Or even the big cares and woes of the world."

His head nodded slightly as he continued to carve up small corners of chocolate with his thumbnail. I continued.

"So I'd still call myself a Christian, but I don't do the doctrines. The dogma. Any organisation that aims to control people's minds is something that I'll run like the wind from."

"Right. So you told me what you don't believe in. The negatives. But what do you put your faith in? The positives?"

"Hmm … Maybe just that 'love overcomes everything'. Even death. Even when life feels like utter shit. If you can hang on in there somehow. Yeah … it does."

I swallowed, aware of the fact that I was talking an awful lot. Becoming the conversation-hogger that I was always accusing Lydia of. But it felt good. So damned good to be having a discussion with another adult for once. Not about work. Not about kids. And not to a bereavement counsellor who was always glancing past me and at the clock on the wall.

"It's hardly intellectual theology, though, Michael. But going back to the day of the accident. I still have pockets of … memory-blanks. For example, only the other day I remembered just how horrible I was to the police." I shook my head at the recollection. "Get this. They arrived, broke the news to me and then I told them that they had to leave because

I had to take my children to a friend's birthday party and I was in a hurry."

I chuckled, darkly.

"Poor sods. They'd just had to do the worst part of their job … 'You're now a widow with two small children.' And there was me getting all bolshy in case we were late for sausage rolls at some random kid's party. They had to take my car keys off me in the end."

Michael turned his chair around. It screeched and grated on the flagstones. He threw one leg over, straddling it.

"Well, it's not really comparable to what you've been through. But I lost my dad when I was just nine. Cancer. He was dreadfully ill for two years."

"Really? Oh … that's awful."

"Yes. But I've got lots of lovely memories. Sailing, fishing, building a tree house. Before he got ill. But going back to what you were saying before – about your children's reactions. For a good three years after he died, I wouldn't talk about him. I would even walk out of a room if people mentioned him."

"Why do you think that was?"

"Not sure exactly. Embarrassment? That might sound strange … but I don't like to be pitied. Who does? And also, I think that I was angry. It messed up our perfect little family unit. We were well off. Lovely home in Buckinghamshire. The place in France, of course – oh, I'm not going for the whole poor-little-rich-boy sympathy vote here, by the way …" He glanced at me.

"I know."

"And my family were – are – quite liberal, in many ways. But we've always been 'mustn't grumble' sorts. And then there was my little sister. Dad died the day before her third birthday. So we just had to carry on as usual. Ponies, parties. Prepping her for the inevitable showjumping stuff. All that. You know. Your usual nice childhood pastimes."

(Hmm. Not really, Michael. We didn't even have the space for a rabbit hutch in our back yard in Stalybridge, never mind a pony. And unless you count the annual summer trip to the Dogs at Belle Vue as 'showjumping' …)

"No. I don't think that it's an easy thing for any child to express. And if you're a boy … perhaps even tougher."

He rose from his chair and stretched. A move that exposed his stomach – zigzagged with golden hair. I quickly cast my glance away.

Grief and lust. Sometimes the opposite sides of the same coin.

The light was waning now and there was a soft, heavy feel to the evening. Perhaps a thunderstorm brewing. Nature's way of dealing with too much humidity.

"Now," he said, "I suppose that this is the last thing I should be doing if I want to make it to fifty. Got three years to go, in case you were wondering." His words baffled me until I saw that he had drawn out a packet of cigarettes from his pocket, along with a lighter.

I had forgotten all about the Michael and Vinnie ciggie-moment. At the time I had even wondered if it had just been a Michael-ruse, a trick to loosen Vinnie up. Get him to feel the smoker's bond with the Very Reverend Michael Chiswick.

"Want one?" he asked me, offering the pack as he sat down next to me on the wooden bench.

"I'll have a drag," I conceded, telling him that I hadn't had a ciggie since a certain pregnancy test over eight years ago. But I ended up spluttering and wincing as the smoke hit the back of my throat and burned my lungs.

"Silly idea," I wheezed.

"Ah, well. Reckless Rachael, eh?"

There was a natural pause in our conversation as Michael inhaled, then exhaled. I sniffed at the air, the scent of lavender and herbs mingling in with the smoke. Musky stuff. Sexy stuff. Just add a whiff of Marmite and I would have thrown even more caution to the wind. I'm strange like that.

“I had a good time this afternoon,” he suddenly announced, tipping his head to one side. “I suppose I shouldn’t say that. You’ll end up reiterating that I’m some kind of cheap voyeur.”

“Nah,” I smiled. “You probably just enjoyed the front-line buzz. You get it with any job where you come face to face with members of the public who live lives a bit more on the edge than the rest of us. Housing. Social services. Police.”

“Hmm,” he considered this. “Perhaps. But maybe I’m missing active combat. And don’t laugh. I’m serious! War zones can be pretty unpredictable places, too. Talk about adrenaline rush …”

“I bet.”

Keep your gob shut about the CND membership, Rachael. There’s a time and a place.

“And everything we saw today. It’s making me ponder things a little bit more. Am I becoming too detached? I mean, I have my emails and letters filtered through to me. I have my ‘people’ to read reports for me. Is that really representing people? Meeting the odd constituent in the surgery?”

“It is a bit removed, I suppose.”

“I mean, sure – in theory – Michael Chiswick can influence things in Parliament, or in the Cabinet. And work to change policy. Push a bill through and all that. But … oh. I don’t know what I’m saying. I’m rambling on now” He took a drag on his cigarette and then continued.

“OK. Example. These local people’s forums we’ve been rolling out to every local authority area … the idea is for us to get poorer communities more effectively involved in local decision-making. And I hate to sound patronising, but … can you imagine the likes of Dawn and Vinnie embarking on a family outing to their local people’s forum? Expressing their views in a rational and coherent way?”

“Yes. You do sound patronising.”

“Apologies. Would it help instead, if I suggested that the government laid out a nice spread of KFC and cheap ciggies and booze in order to ensure that they turned up?”

"No. That would make you sound even more detached and pompous. And it would remind me why I decided to jump ship from doing any work for Whitehall. But anyway … excuse me for a minute. I do need to call a taxi."

No signal on my phone, though. Dratted Peak District and its hills.

"Oh, yes. Now you've reminded me what I wanted to ask you more about. Your Whitehall stuff. Before you ended up doing your local thing with the women's centre. Tell me how all that came about."

I switched my phone off. And then on again. Nothing. I sighed.

"Well, as you know, I started off as a housing officer on some of the toughest estates in Manchester. Then I moved into policy and more senior management stuff. I ended up specialising in anti-social behaviour and getting asked to represent northern social-housing issues for various Whitehall committees. So I was doing the Leeds to London shuffle at least once a week."

"You play it down, Rachael. You've got to be pretty good to be asked to sit on one of those committees."

"Yeah, right. They'll draft anyone in if they're from the regions. Whitehall likes to feel that it's got its clog-dancing and Lancashire hot-pot contingent fairly represented. But after having Lydia and having had six months away from commenting on inspection regimes and the like … well. I just couldn't face going back to it."

"So, becoming a mother helped you to see things differently?"

"Oh, no. Not in the way that you might be thinking," I corrected him. "None of that 'Now that I'm a mother everything else has fallen into perspective' crap."

(God, Rachael, don't get too honest about your disregard for traditional maternal-instincts here.)

"No. I definitely didn't want to be hanging out at mums' and toddlers' groups, chatting about organic biscuits and sleep patterns. But I also didn't want to be spending time with civil service fast-track graduate recruits who were more interested in their next dinner party in Islington than really improving the lives of ordinary people. So when I saw the job managing Sisters' Space … it made perfect sense."

A gentle question from Michael, "And I imagine after losing Adam … you felt that you'd made the right choice after all?"

"Yes. Ironically. At first, Adam wasn't best pleased about me going back to the front line. Managing a women's centre. It meant a drop in income for us. I'd been the main breadwinner. Adam was self-employed. Did IT consultancy, but the jobs could be irregular."

"Right."

"But it wasn't that, so much. Adam didn't like the danger element. Blokes hanging around Sisters' Space. Wanting to beat women up. Not something that I used to encounter very often at conferences in London, that's for sure."

"But he was OK with the job change in the end?"

"Oh, yeah. He saw how much happier I was. Much less of a ratty cow."

I shook my phone again. Nothing.

"And you can't argue with that. So now, of course, it means that I can be back home for the kids at a reasonable hour. Not stuck in London, doing overnighters."

"Well. It sounds like you made a sensible change, work-wise. For that particular time in your life." Michael looked up at the darkening sky. "Perhaps we should go inside. It's getting chillier."

The bottle of wine was empty now, but we took our half-full glasses with us, moving through the kitchen and into the lounge. A dapper little room, with an obviously expensive but tired-looking leather sofa, armchairs and two enormous bookcases that seemed to be groaning under the weight of reading material. ("All for show, of course.") There was an antique grandfather clock and the walls were adorned with paintings – seascapes and landscapes. I nestled myself into the sofa.

Michael sat in one of the armchairs, leg thrown over the armrest. It amused me to see him so casual, so at ease in his own home. He jiggled his leg and looked slightly puzzled.

"But don't you ever think, Rachael, seeing as though you care so much about injustice in society —"

"Ah, you were ruder before. You said that I was 'opinionated'."

"Whatever. Don't you think that you could really make a difference on a larger scale? I do think people like you should be leading, rather than making up the ranks."

"Oh, Michael. Didn't you listen to me just now? Career ladders. Not me! And just listen to your military imagery … that was such a politician sort of thing to come out with."

He raised his eyebrows. "But I am a politician! I don't know any other way to be! I'm programmed to grill people like this. Anyway," he held his hands up in surrender, "I take it that this means you won't be looking into the job that this Shaun character wanted to talk to you about?"

"I'm sorry?" Not sure if I had heard him correctly. And did his voice have a slight edge to it? His body language was oh-so-casual now, though. Stretching his arms above his head, I heard a bone crack and then he reached into his pocket for his own phone.

"Would you just look at this? The damned battery has died again. Time for a new model, I think. I'm sure the Cabinet Office can afford it."

"That reminds me. I really should order a taxi."

He reached over to a cupboard drawer, yanked out a phone charger and then knelt on the floor to plug it in, saying over his shoulder, "Look, I'm sorry if that sounded a bit … intrusive. It's just that this Shaun bloke ... his name seemed to come up quite a lot today. And every time it did, you sort of … flinched. Made me wonder. That's all. I notice people. It's part of my training. My vocation, if you like."

Try to change the subject, Rachael.

"Would that be your training for the priesthood? I mean, I still can't believe that Vinnie ended up thinking that you were that sort of a minister … not the brightest spark, was he?"

Leaving the phone plugged into the charger, he stepped over to the sofa and sat down next to me. It was a two-seater. He folded his hands in his lap and looked downwards. Smiling to himself with fake humility.

"Well. What can I say? Some of us are born to look innocent and devout. Spiritual, mystical qualities, et cetera …"

And then he moved his hand to rest on my left wrist. His forefinger stroked my forearm. Upwards. I stared at the grandfather clock opposite us.

Tick.

Stroking it downwards.

Tock.

"Rachael?"

"What?"

"You've got goose bumps. And it's not cold. In fact, it's still very warm in this room."

"I know. I've got Raynaud's disease. It's this blood-circulation thing, where you feel the cold more than your average person. But it's not really a disease. In fact, I don't know why they call it a disease, because you can't catch it and it makes me feel a bit like a leper when I …"

That talking-too-much-when-nervous thing. Again.

Pulling me gently towards him.

"You're a very strange lady."

"Well. You're a crap vicar."

His head dipped slightly and he moved his hand to my neck. Then, resting the palm of his hand on my hair, he pulled my mouth to his. He tasted warm, spicy.

Our kisses became deeper. Juicier.

Kissing someone for the first time.

Kissing someone for the last time.

We both moved now. Bodies clumsily trying to fit together more easily on the small sofa. Michael elbowed a cushion off and wrapped his other arm around my waist. Under my T-shirt. Stroking my bare, braless back. His stubble grinding into my chin.

And then the phone rang. Not mine. It sounded more like a landline phone in one of the other rooms.

I came up for air.

"Shouldn't you get that, Michael?"

(Purdah Calling Rachael?)

"Mmm. Perhaps." Eyelashes tinged with dark auburn. Looking down at my mouth. Moving in to touch my lips with his again.

"Shit!" He moved back suddenly. His face flicked away from mine. "Sorry! Yes! The landline!"

It continued to ring. As Michael seized the phone in the next room, my own mobile buzzed. A signal at last.

My mother had sent me a bizarrely constructed text message.

"Tried 2 fone Yur owse. But yur not In. Ope yur havin gud tyme aneewy. Kidz gud but Mat had dodgy tum & had acident so Grndad cros as poo al over conservetri..si yu tumrw.xmamx"

Michael's voice drifted along the corridor. He sounded agitated, but I could only hear the odd phrase.

"No – absolutely nothing to get … Oh, course … minimal risk … Yes … But these things happen …"

I gave up trying to listen and scrolled through some recent photographs I had taken. Quite a few were from Sisters' Space, of the women engaged in business-planning sessions for our new cafe and shop. But whether the photos were of women-at-flipchart, women-learning-latte-art or women-in-chocolate-workshops, every one of them had been ruined by Dee – one of our more abrasive characters at the centre – pulling what she liked to call her 'spazzer face'. I turned to my family photos instead. Rather too many with Matthew biting things. Hopefully he would grow out of that soon. And then Lydia with her pet stick insect Arthur, sitting on her forehead.

I felt sorry for Michael and his claim not to like small children. They might ruin your life in many ways, but at least things were never dull around them.

He returned to the room now, rubbing his forehead.

"Sorry about that," he said "Work. I switched the volume down on my mobile when we were talking before. And then the battery died. So they had to track me down on the landline instead."

I had noticed that when we had arrived back at the cottage – he had barely looked at his phone. I had just assumed that on a Saturday night, he was allowed to have a few hours off. Apparently not.

"Nothing bad?"

"Had to speak to a guy called Alex Hewlitt. Chap who leads the Guvnor's little Politbureau. Political appointment. Spin doctor. Complete twat. Having a pop at me for 'A near miss today, Michael, my friend …' He started off with bitching at me about the police and the bike thing on Brindleford. So … hang on. I do just need to double-check …" He moved over to the bay windows overlooking the front garden and peered through them.

"Good. Trevor's back."

"Trevor?" I asked. (His dog? His cat? A homeless old man outside? An imaginary friend?) He closed the curtains.

"Security chappie. One of the more annoying parts of my job at this current moment in time. That's what Alex Hewlitt was getting all arsey about. 'Where was your protection this afternoon? You can't afford to take risks.' As though Alex gives a shit if some random psychopath wants to stab me. It's the potential for the headlines and the scandal stuff that sends Alex into the hissy fits."

"Oh. So this Trevor … should he have been with you?"

"Well, Number Ten would prefer it that way. But every minister does have an element of choice about protection. And I don't particularly feel the need for it on a lazy Saturday. So I let Trevor have the afternoon off. He's from around here himself. And his dad is ill – last stages of cancer and in a hospice in Warrington. So I told Trevor to go and spend a few hours with him. The old fella seemed to be taking a turn for the worse. But Trevor's back now and in the Merc outside."

He picked up his phone.

"Ah, yes. Here we are. Trevor texted me half an hour ago. 'Here now. Dad doing better.' Ha! Ha ha ha!"

"What? He said 'Ha!'? About his dad being so ill?"

"No," Michael sniggered irreverently. "The laughter was mine. Trevor added something else. 'Good-looking lass.' Meaning you. How very northern of him."

"Oh. But when would he have seen me?"

"Well, he'll have had a nosey around for any bombs that you might have casually squirreled about your Fiat. And him checking out your vehicle would have brought your ID up. Photo…"

"What? He can access my photo? Is he MI5 or something?"

"Yes, of course he can. And he can access lots more, too." He perched next to me on the sofa now, hand on my knee. "And in terms of him profiling you, I think he'll have you down for a very disturbed person indeed. Driving a vehicle so appallingly littered with underwear and disembowelled toys. But to answer your other question, no. He isn't MI5. The bodyguard division are called 'specialist protection'. Those police, army, intelligence sorts – they all overlap. Anyway," he added, "Are we going to get on to human rights and protection of personal data now?"

"Nah," I replied. "Because I'll no doubt be accused of being opinionated again."

He ran his tongue over his teeth. Best not to reply.

"So wasn't that a bit of a risk, then? You having a gap with no security being around?"

He looked nonplussed.

"Well, there's rather a lot of talk about heightened security alerts at the moment. Hence me being stuck with overkill on protection. But in terms of Al Qaeda and the like, they'll hardly want to take out the man in charge of communities. Not when they've got your defence minister and the Home Secretary to go after. So personally, I think it's all rather a waste of public money. Having someone skulking around all the time."

I nodded in sympathy. But I didn't really have a similar point of reference (unless Matthew trailing after me to the toilet trilling, 'You having a wee or a poo, mummeh? Can I watch?' was a fair comparison.)

"But more importantly than the damned bodyguard issue, Alex needed to talk to me about some other stuff going on, on the domestic front. Meaning that I need to pop by and see the prime minister tomorrow afternoon. So, rather inconveniently I've got to get the earlier train back tomorrow morning now."

He touched my cheek gently, drawing his finger across it. But I moved my face away from him.

"Right. Well. You've got an early start. I might be best using your landline to order that taxi."

He folded his arms and looked intently at me.

"No. Stop talking about taxis, woman! I want you to stay. To stay over here, I mean. No taxi."

He put his hand on my upper arm. Trailed the fingers down to mine and then tried to pull me up off the sofa – wanting me to follow him. But I stayed put. Blood a-buzzing through my brain.

I shook my head. He let go of my hand, and his shoulders slumped as his smile faded.

"God. I'm sorry. I'm being incredibly selfish." He plonked himself back onto the sofa again. Hands clasped together, Head down.

"I'm being an absolute self-centred bastard, aren't I? I'm so used to … No. No excuses. I'm making gross assumptions, aren't I? Look. How about you just forget the taxi anyway, and choose a bed. I've got two spare rooms and it makes perfect sense."

"I can't." I shook my head again and began to rub my forehead. (Think carefully.)

His eyes flicked up at me. "I'm sorry. I shouldn't have …"

I cleared my throat. Trying to find the right words to say and holding my hand over my eyes, as if blinded by the sun. Lower thine eyes.

"No, Michael. It's just that … I made a sort of promise to myself. That I wouldn't get involved with anyone else. For a good few years. I have to think about the children. I can't do this. Do you know what I mean?"

He nodded, gently.

"Of course I do. So again. Please forgive me for jumping the gun there. It's just that I … . Well. I'm clearly attracted to you. I fancy you, of course. And I can only apologise if…"

I moved my hand away from my eyes and pressed a finger to his lips.

"You might be Mr Big Shot Politician, but you're rather gullible, aren't you?"

"What?" He frowned.

"That was a joke. Can't you tell?"

"No …" he paused. "So …"

I took my finger away from his lips and kissed him, then told him.

"I was being sarcastic …"

"Oh. Yes. That sarcasm thing of yours." He kissed me back. Tongue and teeth now. But then it was his turn to break away from me.

"Seriously though. Hang on. You did say earlier that you often had concerns about how other people perceived you. Whether you were going about things properly. Being widowed. The right way to do things."

"That's right," I said, clasping my fingers around his, "but I don't see anyone here that I need to gain the approval of. Do you? Is Trevor going to have a perv through the bay windows and grass me up to my mum?"

"No ..."

"Fine. Come on, then." This time it was me pulling him up from the sofa. "I thought you were eager to find me a bed to sleep in, Michael..."

Chapter 8

POST-HIMERUS, AND BATHTIME

He found me a bed. It was a little bit more luxurious than my usual horizontal hang-out. Goose-feather pillows. Expensive-looking sheets. No mushed-up lumps of play-doh stuck to the end of the bedpost ("*It's a baddie alien, Mummy!*") No empty snail shells from the garden under the pillow. No pink milkshake stains or stray Rice Krispies adorning the duvet cover. And even stranger (even better), it contained a very adult presence and that musky scent of herbs, smoke and Ralgex.

A watery sun spliced through the slats of the window blinds, striping itself across the bed. I caught the sound of church bells drifting down the valley from the Roman Catholic church. Early morning communion for the hardcore.

Michael turned over, and nudged my earlobe with his nose.

"Poor lamb – were you chilly? I see you managed to get the T-shirt back on."

"A little," I fibbed. I might be good for taking the lead in terms of bed choice and boudoir antics, but I had never been one for baring all. A long pause, and then Michael began to snooze against my neck again. The occasional half-snore.

I touched his hair, combing it lightly with my fingers. A full head of the stuff, despite the stress of his job. Reddish brown, shot through with silver strands. I watched his chest rise and fall. But the moment of intimacy evaporated as I realised that I had been sectioning his hair with my fingertips, in the same way that I always did with the kids when embarking upon the Great Nit Hunt. I was trying – but failing – to swallow the bubbles of laughter when I was saved by the sound of the fish door knocker.

Michael started, awake. Propped himself up on one arm and coughed.

"Who the hell can that be? It's Sunday morning, for God's sake. What time is it, anyway?" I looked over at the bedside clock; a rather grand brass affair. More antique than Argos.

"Seven thirty," he groaned, rolled over and plonked a kiss on the top of my exposed thigh. "Christ, my back aches like hell. I need some more Ralgex on it. You and your drowning old ladies…"

Naked, he padded to the door, grabbed a dressing gown from the back of a chair and made his way down the stairs. Another rap. The bedroom was directly above the front door, the window was open and I could hear a peculiar pinging sound. Accompanied by a squeaky voice.

"Hey! Pack it in, you daft twat!" *Ping!*

A short screech as Michael pulled back the bolts on the front door.

"Oh. Hello. What are you two doing here?" *Ping!*

I recognised Tia's voice now.

"Er, well. We called round yesterday when we realised he'd left his phone." *Ping!*

Now Tyler: "But you weren't in." *Ping!*

"An' it cost over eighty quid, it did, and us mum'll friggin' kill us if it's lost."

"Right," said Michael. Trying to collect his thoughts. *Ping!*

Tyler's voice again. "So can you just go an' ask 'er for it?" *Ping!*

Then a different male voice. Very bass. Hint of a West Indies accent.

"Oi! Stop throwing the gravel about, all right?"

Then Michael. "It's all right, Trevor. I know them." His voice was now directed at the twins. "But he's right. It's not only annoying, but you might hit my bike. Or a window." Tyler sniggered, lowering his voice to a growl.

"Down, Boy! Good Trevor." Tia erupted into giggles.

I heard Tyler again.

"Your bike's cool, though. Triumphs are well lush. You're mad not puttin' it in the garage. You'll 'ave it nicked. Us dad used to 'ave a bike before us mum banned it. An' then 'e left." A flatness in his voice. "'Cause she bans everything what's dead good."

"You're right," replied Michael. "I do normally lock it up in the garage, but I'm afraid that I forgot to last night."

"Well. You'd 'ave been a bit busy wouldn't you, eh?" From Tyler. A snort from his sister.

"So." Michael again. Trying to change the subject. "Your phone."

"We know she's 'ere," Tyler told him. "'Cause 'er crap car's over there."

There was a slight pause in the conversation. Then Michael responded.

"What makes you think that that isn't my car?"

"Because," from Tia now, "Trevor-Built-Like-A-Brick-Shithouse and your other bodyguard whatsitmen are always sat in a Merc. We always see you in it."

"Yeah," Tyler continued, "and anyway. We've seen the other car what you've got in your garage. The black Toyota Prius. I can't see you and your 'ard men heavvies going, 'Oooh, yeah, we'll have a Merc and a Prius and a Triumph and, like, for us fourth shit-hot ride we'll go for a banana-yellow Fiat Panda. What goes about as fast as an 'airdryer."

I stuffed the eiderdown in my mouth, trying to smother the laughter.

"That's quite an unfair assumption to be making," replied Michael. "Fiat Pandas are highly regarded for their eco-credentials."

"Eco-crewhat?" asked Tia.

“Anyways,” her brother countered, “we know it’s hers ’cause there was a pair of Disney Princess knickers on the parcel shelf. Unless they were yours.” They dissolved into fits of giggles again.

Michael decided it was time to get stern.

“Well, the owner of any vehicle parked on these premises is actually none of your business. Now. I’ll go and get your mobile. Wait here.”

I heard him close the front door, then a creak or two as he climbed the cottage stairs. He jogged over to me and flung himself onto the bed.

“Did you hear that?” he whispered. “They’re smart little devils, aren’t they?”

“Yes,” I replied. “And you were even cleverer to not actually lie to them about anything. And blinding them with your pompous grown-up speak.”

“I know!” he beamed. “I’m glad you noticed! That’s the prerogative of a politician, of course. So, where is the bloody mobile? Please tell me that you’ve still got it.”

“On the sink, in the outside bathroom. Don’t worry. I checked yesterday. There were no photos of you on Tyler’s phone.,” I whispered back. He kissed me hard on the mouth, and rubbed the top of my thigh. “I’ll be back and seeing to you – very shortly …”

A minute or so later I heard him at the front door.

“Here. Mind how you go. Oh. But, hang on.” There was a pause, and then Michael continued.

“Here you go. Ten pounds. For helping Mr Bridges and Miss Simpson out yesterday. ‘back at ya’ and all that.”

Tyler’s response was immediate and to the point.

“So, shouldn’t that, like, be a tenner each? ’Cause I mean … you goin’ off with me mobile caused me a right load of aggro.”

A ‘Sheesh’ from Michael. Then, “Wicked. Ta,” from Tia. I heard the click of the gate.

"Bye!" they shouted back at Michael. Then "Bye, Trevor, boy!" followed by a bark and a growl. And finally, Tyler hollering, "Bye to you, too, Miss Whats-yer-name. His bird upstairs. Enjoy yer shaggin' with 'im!"

Michael came back up the stairs and into the room, shaking his head. "Bloody disgraceful. They got twenty quid out of me in the end. I hate kids!"

"Well," I replied, "you told no lies. They told no lies. You should be impressed with their performance."

He jettisoned the dressing gown, crawled back onto the bed and began to kiss my neck.

"Never mind their performance; I'm more concerned with mine. I have to go to London now. And you being so irresistible … you're turning this into a very hard experience for me."

"Hey, Michael." His lips were on my shoulder blade now but I nudged him off and started to snigger. "Was that your new gangsta speak? That 'back at ya'? Is that the influence of Vinnie, your new best mate?"

"Oh, be quiet, you," he mumbled, tearing at my T-shirt. "We haven't got long left. I've got a train to catch. I've got that appointment with the prime minister this afternoon."

"Well, maybe you can remind him about those training sessions for Cabinet members, to improve your collective and individual senses of humour. And while you're at it, you might want to request a course on how to speak to your average twelve-year-old child."

"Shut up, smart-arse. Come here." I scuttled off the bed and towards the bathroom.

"Actually, I've got an idea, Michael. Let's multi-task. Do some effective time management. Have that shared shower you mentioned yesterday, after all."

An hour later and it was Michael's turn to take charge. "Destination Manchester city centre. Drive me to Piccadilly station," he told me. "Trevor will tail us. It'll buy me a bit more time with you." We left the cottage in a last-minute mild panic. Michael looked damp and crumpled, but respectable enough in a short-sleeved shirt and trousers.

He squeezed himself into the front seat of my car and peered through dust-encrusted windscreen and up at the sky, commenting, "I really thought that we were due a thunderstorm after all this humidity." The azure blue of the last few days had vanished, and only grey, muggy cloud lay ahead of us on the Hyde Road.

Even before we set off, I was mentally chastising myself for the state of the car. By the time we had reached Godley, Michael had discovered that a fluff-encrusted lollipop had stuck itself to his laptop bag. I was mortified.

"God, I'm so sorry! Bloody lollipops. They're great bribes, but when Matthew gets to the last bit, he either presses the sticks onto the window – as you can see – or if he's in a bad mood, he lobs them at me from the back seat." Michael shushed me.

"Stop apologising for your way of life. I've always liked dirty women."

"Good thing, too. Because right now, I'm feeling like a right old scrubber. Wearing another set of your cast-offs today. And I can't believe that you've lent me a Man United top. If my dad could see me in this, he'd be doing his nut!"

"But I thought you were from Manchester?"

"Precisely. True Mankys support Man City. My dad reckons that it's only the wealthy suburban sorts who aren't the real Manks – along with the posh people from down south who follow Man United."

"That's not what I've heard. Anyway, your violent prejudices against the Reds don't bother me. I'm a rugby man, myself and consequently, I don't have much time for the girly-game. Although in my line of work I do have to pretend to admire football. In fact, that very shirt you're wearing was actually a gift from the Manchester United chairman, Sir … oh, I can't remember the chap's name now …"

That made it even worse. Still, maybe I would never see Michael again and my dad could use it to dress the Guy Fawkes in. And we could get the kids to chuck it on a Stalybridge bonfire in a few weeks' time.

We were speeding through Hyde now and on to Denton, out of the semi-rural area and into the urban sprawl of Manchester proper.

"I think I'm going a bit too fast …" I fretted.

"Not to worry. If the bobbies give us any more trouble, Trevor can fish his blues and twos out. He likes to show off."

"So, this special protection malarkey. Which organisation decides who's the best person to protect you? I would have thought that your security blokes, the assassin-spotting experts, would have been your army sorts."

"Well, it's all semantics, really. MI5 assesses the initial risk and then the police and the military decide what kind of specialism is needed for each ministerial portfolio."

I glanced at the dashboard clock. "But I still don't understand why you're going by train. I thought ministers who get allocated government cars get driven to and from London."

"Sometimes. Depends on cost, constituency location, carbon footprint, whether there is an emergency, et cetera. Usually I go to London by train from Manchester. So once we get to the station, Trevor will abandon the car and one of his cronies will collect it and take it back to the fleet. Trevor will get the train and keep an eye on me. Then we pick up the next car at Euston."

We were zooming past the red-bricked terraces of inner-city Manchester now. The Sunday morning leftovers – the pizza boxes, kebab wrappers – tumbled along in the wind, pausing only to get stuck in the odd pile of Saturday-night vomit. A mangy brown moggy suddenly decided to play hara-kiri, dashing across the road in front of us. I stamped my foot down.

"Jee-sus!" Michael declared. "Christ on a bike! Good braking, girl!"

"Less of the blasphemy, please, Michael. I thought you were a devout Catholic boy." We had stopped at the traffic lights at Belle Vue. He pretended to mop his brow.

"Needs must." He looked over his shoulder at the Merc behind us. "Trevor's a sharp one. Good reflexes. Most people would have hit you, there. But anyway, I'm half-Jewish so I'm allowed to take the name of your so-called Messiah in vain."

"Really?" I inadvertently stalled the car.

He burst out laughing. "Didn't you notice my Jewish attributes last night?" he glanced over at me, grinning.

"Well, yes. I did. But it didn't seem polite to comment at the time." I started the car again and held my hand up to apologise to Trevor behind us. Sorry, Trev-Boy.

"My mother is Jewish. So according to Jewish law, I'm regarded as being fully Jewish. My father was Roman Catholic. There was a bit of a hoo-ha initially. But his parents got over it. Displaying prejudice against Jewish people wasn't exactly in accordance with their socialist principles and they were big chums from way back when, with Harold Wilson and his family, so they didn't want to appear to be hypocritical. Meaning that when I put in my appearance on planet earth, my mother's family got their own way and I got circumcised. And then, later on, Dad's family got their own way and I headed off for an Ampleforth education."

"Right. So didn't you get any hassle at school? Did no one hold you to be personally responsible for killing off our Lord and Saviour?"

"Ha, no. Nothing like that. They were all perfectly accommodating of the token Jew-boy. Although being far too exposed to religion at school does seem to have put me off it for life. Having said that, though, yesterday, when Vinnie mistook me for a man of God … it's been making me think long and hard about changing career direction. Perhaps I have a new calling."

"I can imagine. So next time you're at some state funeral or asked to do *Songs Of Praise*, I bet you'll be trotting out the God-speak with the rest of them. Anyway. You've got twelve minutes until your train. Go on!"

I had driven as close to the station as I could, stopping the car. He grabbed his bag and took two House of Commons embossed business cards and two pens out of its side pocket. Thrusting a pen and a card at me, he said, "Your number".

I scribbled it down and he did the same, adding a number to his card.

We swapped miniature cardboard rectangles.

"That's my personal mobile phone number, so you can get past the staff. I have to juggle a work and a personal number. But watch it, though. I can't guarantee that Big Brother or some dodgy journo isn't listening in, no matter what Leveson and the other deluded sorts tried to do."

I nodded. He leant over to kiss me. It lingered. We lingered. But I broke away and gripped the steering wheel with one hand.

"Michael, look. You shouldn't feel under any obligation to stay in touch. We had a great time. But we're both adults here, so I don't expect …"

He frowned, pushed a strand of hair back from my eye, tucking it behind my ear.

"Hey. None of that. Look …" His eyes flicked to the car park outside. "Trevor's already abandoned the Merc. He'll be here any second. But listen, Rachael. I don't do this kind of thing lightly. Of course I'll be seeing you again."

He noticed my silence and added, "That is … if you want to carry on with ..."

"Nice to be asked," I said, frostily. Still clenching the steering wheel. He looked at me, uncertain. I felt the corners of my mouth twitch. He grinned.

"Christ, I never know whether you're teasing me or being sarcastic. Now, come here!"

One more hard kiss on the mouth, and then he squeezed himself out of my car.

As I turned back onto the Hyde Road, there was an ominous rumble of thunder. Seconds later I glimpsed a flash of light from the city, behind me. Small spit-spots of rain began to plink onto my grimy windscreen.

I opened my car windows. In my book, the scent of wet pavement and damp earth after a hot spell very nearly beats the whiff of Marmite and Ralgex.

The rain only lasted for fifteen minutes and had petered out by t arrived back in Stalybridge, where I said farewell and many a tha to my parents. Or, more precisely, to my mother ("*Your dad's still hi in the allotment shed.*")

I bustled the children into the back of the car as Mum presented me with various carrier bags. The first contained a collection of Lydia's home-made buns (*"All made by me, Mum! Matthew was useless. All he did was lick the kitchen worktop."*) The second consisted of a selection of fresh soups made by mother (*"Well, I don't know how you can abide that packet soup, Rachael. It gives me the trots. Home-made is best. You just have to get yourself a little bit more organised."*) The third held a dozen paintings by Matthew-Picasso-On-Ritalin-Russell (*"He says that you never have time to make paintings with him at home..."*) and the fourth and largest bag was *"the ironing that I noticed last week at your house. I took it home with us and did it properly, because the children look scruffy enough at the best of times.")*

Driving home, I began to feel at a low ebb. Down. Double-down. It wasn't because of my mother's words. Yes, the woman should have a First Class Degree in Backhanded Remarks, but I was learning to live with it. So why the sudden drop in spirits? The children were happily listening to a Famous Five audio book, which allowed me some time to think. But I knew what it would be. Just the usual. Guilt. Which we all know is the most unproductive and negative of emotions. But, for me, a familiar old chum.

It was guilt. Guilt because I had enjoyed an entire twenty-four hours away from the children, without missing them at all. Guilt because I had just engaged in hot, sweaty sex with a bloke who I was taking a bit of a shine to. Guilt because of Adam, who, yes, might be operating on a different time and space continuum to the rest of us these days, but who was still my husband, the father of my children. And finally, the most illogical, most uncomfortable flush of feeling of all. Guilt because of Shaun. Not just because of what happened with him previously, but because I knew that he wouldn't like the idea of the Michael thing. About Rachael moving on.

All this was a crazy recipe for thinking. So I topped it all off with an additional sprinkling. Guilt because I'm shit at making soup and I can't be arsed to iron. The Rebellion Against Real Motherhood thought cheered me up and took the edge off the black clouds. Meanwhile, an ed on the back seat of the car over whether The Five y the dog to eat ice cream (*"He'll get diarrhoea and stery solving will be ruined by runny dog-poo"*) and girl or not.

shouting 'Boy' at me, but Mum, I say that she's a girl. She's a funny sort of girl, though, isn't she? More like a boy. There's a word … what is it? The word for a girl who acts like a boy?"

"I think it's 'butch', Lydia," came my offhand answer.

"Yes. OK. So, I'm going to be a butch girl just like George!"

That's the problem with being a lone parent. The kids just don't get the nuances of conversation in the same way that adults do.

A few hours later and we were engaged in the usual Sunday night bath and bedtime ritual. Lydia had quickly hopped out of the bath, claiming that she didn't want to share it with her brother (*"He wees in it. Even if he says he doesn't. And then he drinks the water. He's a disgusting little chimpy-chops."*) Wrapped in a towel, she had taken herself off to my bedroom to finish her school reading book. Matthew was howling as I tried to remove what looked like a lump of peanut butter cemented into one of his ears. Although it could well be a nasty case of ear wax discharge. We didn't keep peanut butter in our house. Still, he might have been exposed to some at my parents'. I sighed. Another small, but telling frustration. No other adult about to confer with on the "is it peanut butter or is it ear wax?" question.

Whilst rinsing Matthew's ear out, I smiled to myself. Imagining how Adam would have tackled this. He would have offered Lydia extra pocket money to taste the substance extracted from her brother's ear and to tell us what it was. At first she would have squealed in horror, but then her little brain would have started working overtime. A quick risk assessment of Daddy's proposal. The situation would end in Adam grabbing Lydia and tickling her until she threatened to wet her knickers. I would be droning on at him.

"Oh, Adam! Why do you always have to get them all giddy just before bedtime?"

Sometimes, conjuring up an amusing image of family life with Adam still in tow did the trick for me. But this time the smile only lasted a few seconds. As I rinsed the soapsuds from Matthew's hair, I also tried to flush away the unbearable sadness. That Adam had never had the chance to discover his little boy's personality. That his Matthew was, in fact, growing up to become the kind of lad who would quite happily experiment with eating random substances lodged in his ear, without any form of monetary bribery.

I turned away from my musings. Matthew finished his screeching fit and I hoisted him out of the bath, ruffled a towel round him and scooted him towards his own bedroom. I went to check on Lydia. She was lying on my bed in her bath towel with the alleged reading book cast to one side, and for some reason various bras of mine had been draped along the rumpled duvet. With one hand behind her head and the other clasping my mobile phone to her ear, she was chattering away. She registered my sudden presence and then waved me away with a gesture of irritation.

"I'm talking!" she hissed. A perfect impersonation of my most ferocious Satanic Mother voice, accompanied by a conspiratorial whisper into the phone.

"She's been such a moody-pants tonight. Oh, and guess what else? I'm stark naked under this towel! I am! I'm a naked baby! That's what we always called Matthew when he was a tiny baby in the bath. 'Naked bay-bee', we'd sing at him…"

I marched over to her, demanded the phone and pointed to her room. She skulked away.

"Hello?" presuming that it would be my mother or my sister. But it was a man's voice. Michael's.

"Ah, Rachael. At last!" Michael said. "I've been forced to participate in the most erudite discussion with your daughter. She tells me that she's 'nearly seven'. Going on seventy is more like it. Does she always talk that much?"

"Oh, God, Michael. Sorry. What's she been saying?"

"Nothing too dangerous. I asked to speak to you and told her that I was a friend from work. She told me that you were bathing a very revolting sibling called Matthew. Who 'drinks his own wee', apparently?

And that she was supposed to be doing her reading book from school but 'stories about fairies are so boring and for total spannerheads'. So she decided to try your bras on instead."

"Right."

"And then it was 'Do you know what some ladies do? They get their boobies sliced open in a special hospital and a doctor puts a balloon in each one, and sews it back up again. To make the boobies look bigger. So that men will like her more'."

"Oh dear. Sorry. That's my fault. Well, Kate's, too. My best friend. We were talking about implants, for some reason. Lydia overheard and wanted to know what they were. Kate decided it would be a good chance to educate her goddaughter on the power of the media and how women are increasingly being oppressed in terms of their appearance. And this turned into chit-chat in general about body fascism."

"Hm. This Kate sounds like a barrel of laughs."

"Ha – no. She's fab, is Kate. But she's got twin boys. And they're rather different to Lydia. Liddy hyperfocusses. And she ended up becoming rather too interested in terms of the physiological, rather than the socio-political impact. We tried to backpedal, but Lydia was asking us things like, 'What kind of a knife would they use? Could they use those crinkly craft scissors so that the lady could have a nice pattern on her boobs?' And then last week I caught her explaining breast-implant surgery to a little boy when we were in a shoe shop. She probably traumatised the lad for life …"

I tailed off, remembering that Michael was a man of rather loftier preoccupations when it came to the great scheme of things. A man who had only recently emerged from a meeting with the prime minister. A man who didn't seem to be too enamoured with the overall concept of children in general. And to whom I was now relating my hilarious exploits with a small child in Stalybridge Market's 'Shooz 2 Chooz'.

But he replied, "Oh, I doubt it. The lad would probably have just dismissed her as some daft little girl wittering on about a load of feminist-induced tosh."

"Hmm. Given your remarks there, should I take it that your meeting with the PM wasn't about him offering you the job of minister for the

Department of Women and Families?"

"Ha. Very good. But that would fill me with even more horror than if he'd asked me to head up the Department for Work and Pensions! Or God forbid, Transport."

Shrieking from next door. An ominous crash.

"Hang on a minute," I broke off, and threw the phone down. A squabble had broken out between a naked Matthew, who had dared to venture into Lydia's room and was trying to steal her 'box of precious things'.

I picked the phone back up and apologised to Michael, who replied, "Look, I'll call you back if it's a bad time."

"No, honestly. They're sorted now. I threatened them with muesli for breakfast. So tell me about this meeting. Did you get your knuckles rapped for losing Trevor yesterday? Was Alex the Twat there too?"

His laughter boomed down the phone line.

"Oh, I like that, Rachael! Yes. That's perfect. Alex the Twat. A name that suits him down to the ground. But actually, that wasn't why I was summoned. Have you caught the news today at all?"

"No. I try to avoid it when I can. Too depressing."

"Ah, well. The PM and Alex wanted to talk through a bit of a scandal that hit the papers this morning. Yesterday while we were on Brindleford, they had a tip-off. It's one of my junior ministers, Ben Hardy. He's been having an extra-marital affair. And *News Of The Nation* – well, I'm sure you know that they're the worst of the gutter press – have managed to procure some pictures. But it's even juicier than that. Turns out that Ben is gay. Fella has a wife and four kids and has been leading a double life."

"Oh. Oh, crap. Not good news for anyone, then?"

"No, not great. Of course, there have been similar precedents in government in terms of politicians being outed, so you'd think that we can ride the storm. But the prime minister is fretting about our ratings in the polls and the last thing we need is a sex scandal right now. So tomorrow morning I've got to get out there and do some damage limitation. Press conference at ten o'clock. Try to watch it if you can."

"Oh. Shame. I'll be at work."

"But I thought that you were in charge of the place?"

"I am. I suppose. But …" I paused. "Actually. I think I've seen quite enough of you for one week."

He chuckled. "Well, I definitely haven't seen enough of you … and I'm wondering if you wouldn't mind Skyping with me later and being a certain 'naked baby' under a towel?"

I was about to reply when Lydia came charging into the room to inform me, "Matthew has gone into the garden with no clothes on and says he's going to eat one of my pet woodlice 'cause he hates me!"

"Got to go, Michael," I said. "I have to liberate some garden insects from being devoured by *homo toddlerus*."

"Ah, Rachael. You're a woman always on a mercy mission. Let's speak tomorrow, eh? Goodnight."

Chapter 9

AMAZONS IN AGREEMENT

Any frivolous fantasies of checking out the news headlines in order to catch the Ben Hardy coverage were soon snuffed out, thanks to a bit of a spat over whether both kids had brushed their teeth that morning.

"Why should we bother?" my daughter groaned. "I mean, I'll be having toast at Breakfast Club in a minute. And Matthew's baby teeth will all fall out soon. What's the point? Who cares?"

Parcelling the kids into the car, I made the silly error of switching Radio 4 on. Matthew launched into a piercing screech.

"I hate that! I hate that!"

Accompanied by Lydia.

"Boooring! Put our Disney music on, Mummy. This is rubbish. Turn it off!"

It was only 7.30 a.m. and I was already kiddy-sick. Sure, wanting to listen to the news was hardly worth getting so het up about in the great scheme of things. But that wasn't the point. The point was that I couldn't remember the last time that I had been allowed to listen to grown-up stuff without a small person attempting to ruin it for me.

Matthew was parroting Lydia now: "Turnitoff!"

Peevishly, I hiked the volume up to an excruciating level. Trying to deafen them into submission. And then, after a quick side-glance, I turned it off altogether. At the traffic lights, the man in the car next to us was staring blankly at me. Perhaps wondering why I was attempting to inflict death by 'The Today Programme' on two small children. Now that silence reigned in the car, Lydia whispered to her brother (not-so-quietly), "She's the meanest mummy in the world, isn't she, Matthew? Like that nasty old bag Miss Hannigan in *Annie*."

I yelled at her.

"For God's sake, Lydia! Can't you just put a sock in it for once?"

Yes, I know that my positive parenting manual would have advised me to ignore the more trivial backchat, but there had been far too many *Annie* allusions of late. The most recent one had occurred when I was buying a bottle of wine in the local Co-op. For the benefit of random shoppers, Lydia had declared in her most am-dram voice across the aisles, "Uh-oh. Mummy's buying beer again! She's just like Miss Hannigan!" And then she proceeded to inform the girl at the checkout, "Our house is as dirty as an old orphanage, you know. And it's full of children locked in the cellar!"

So that morning I gladly deposited Lydia at Breakfast Club (where I was reminded of outstanding fees for last term) and moved on. I happily left child number two at his nursery (where I was politely asked, "Could you return the spare underpants that Matthew had to borrow?") And I finally made a beeline for Medlock, experiencing a twinge of remorse for the fact that heading to a workplace full of women who had been attacked by brutal men seemed a much more cheery prospect than having to look after my own children day in and day out.

I switched the radio on again, but by now I had missed any news coverage involving Michael.

After arriving at Sisters' Space, I swiped my card through our security system. It wasn't a bad little techno-contraption given that we survived on a shoestring, and the door-entry system buzzed me into the centre. As I hung my coat up, Gillian, our most senior case worker, cornered me. Not usually the nervy sort, my shaven-headed deputy was a tad tetchy today. Telling me that she had heard on the jungle drums that there were rumours of even more funding cuts across the Greater Manchester local authorities. I spoke to her in the kind of language that she understood best, ladling on the sympathy.

"Nah. Get a grip, Gillian. I've heard nothing. Go take a chill pill. I need to get the staffing schedules sorted."

Three women had been hanging around outside the centre when it opened its doors to the public at 9 a.m. Each had been a visitor to Sisters' Space in the past, but all had experienced fresh assaults over the weekend and we were usually their first port of call. Less than a third of women experiencing domestic violence report it to the police. Believe me, I know my facts on this kind of thing. Can rattle it off in my sleep (and frequently do – Adam once left the marital bed for a night because I kept shouting "Mitigating circumstances – my arse!" in the wee small hours.) And today, none of these particular women – Jade, Gemma and Jean – had been in touch with the bizzies. Probably because they knew that very few reported cases actually lead to a charge being made against the perpetrator (seven per cent, in fact.)

All this meant that trying to get a woman to officially log an attack often felt like a waste of time to the staff at Sisters' Space. Of course, nudging women to seriously weigh up the pros and cons of going for the legal jugular was something that we felt obliged to do. But often it made more sense to focus our energies on going all out with the support needed to extract them from the abusive cycle of a destructive relationship pattern.

So I've never minded delivering any form of rant that touches on the fact that one-third of local authority areas in England still offer no service for women experiencing domestic violence. This was one of the statistics that I immediately flagged up to Michael on our very first encounter. Michael Chiswick happened to be a government minister, but he was also the constituency MP for Sisters' Space and we wanted to tap him for some support with our new cafe and chocolate shop initiative. I'd never met him before and Gillian had been the one to liaise with his local constituency office in order to arrange the visit to the centre a few Fridays ago in mid-August.

"Is that so?" was Michael's response to the beginnings of my spiel about the pathetic lack of help available for women across the country. "But don't you think that walk-in GP surgeries or the family support centres would be better placed to provide the advice that women need? I mean, one-stop shops are the government's preferred approach, you know. Rather than having to shell out for yet another service and all the

accompanying overheads."

The notorious Dee, one of our gobbier service users at Sisters' Space, had been standing alongside Gillian and me as we were discussing this with Michael. I caught Gillian rolling her eyes at Michael's response. Dee just yawned, displaying silver fillings. Now, I hadn't expected the minister for communities to be out there with pom-poms and performing high kicks in celebration of domestic abuse services across the land, but he could have sounded a bit less obstructive. Following on from his previous comments, Michael then asked me whether our service would refuse to help men who were victims of domestic abuse at the hands of female partners. The kind of stuff that I was used to being challenged about. But irritating, nonetheless.

Gillian's eyes were now on the ceiling. She had already written Michael off as some kind of upper-class, anti-women politician (and I noticed at this point that she had deliberately pinned her 'Lezzer and Proud' badge to her lapel in preparation for his visit). Dee was behaving in an even more unhelpful manner. Pulling that horrible 'spazzer' face of hers behind Michael's back while rubbing her eyes, fingers encircled in those gold sovereign rings that looked more like knuckle-dusters. The police were forever telling me that Dee 'gave as good as she got'. I didn't have an opinion on that, but today her eyes were looking rather manic and I reckoned that she had been necking the Tammies again. Dee was a wild card, all right. And she didn't like politicians (well – who does?)

"So, would you then?" he had prompted. "Help a man who had been attacked by a woman?"

I had done my best to disregard the body language of Dee and Gill, answering, "No, we wouldn't. Even if he was bleeding to death and shouting, 'Help me! Help me!' through the intercom. We'd just ignore him."

Michael's eyes had widened in surprise. I'd seen him on the TV and in the newspaper plenty of times, but I had to concede that he was certainly better looking in real life. There was something about him that reminded me of the actor, Basil Rathbone. Albeit in technicolour and without the deerstalker and pipe (perhaps worryingly, I've always had a thing for actors who play Sherlock Holmes). But in real life, cut glass upper class accents have never done it for me. And of course, there I was again – blundering away with my usual smart-arse responses. Almost immediately I realised that I had probably overstepped the mark. He wouldn't be used to such off-the-cuff remarks from one of his constituency workhorses.

"Sorry," I had replied. "But I often get asked that sort of thing. And it upsets me that people might think that we'd turn a blind eye to anyone in need. Just because of policies or statistics. Of course we'd help a man if he was genuinely suffering from domestic abuse. So long as we weren't compromising the needs of the female service users."

Dee's gruff tones then joined in the conversation, directed at Michael.

"She gets a bit touchy, does our Rachael. You're lucky that she didn't smack you one for asking her such a stupid question. Eh, Rach?"

Thanks for that, Dee.

I had spent over an hour that afternoon trying to convince Michael that Sisters' Space was more than just a council-contracted service, shoving a few leaflets at women. Yes, we held the contract with Medlock Council and did the bog-standard advice stuff, but our women's centre went the extra mile with counselling, courses and working closely with other agencies like the police and social services. Yet, to provide all of these services, we needed far more money than the paltry amount that the council gave us under our agreement with them. Meaning that we relied on a small army of volunteers. And on a certain Rachael Russell spending hideous amounts of time on fundraising.

Still, that was what made the work so attractive for me. Surrounded by people who genuinely believed in what they were doing. And despite my inability to rein in the sarcasm with him, Michael had impressed me. He seemed to like our approach, remembered people's names and ate lots of our chocolate. And after the visit I was pleased that his 'people' had followed through with the goods – providing large amounts of publicity for us, which had led to a backlog of early orders for the chocolate.

Lydia had been enamoured too, by the fact that a photograph of her mother had featured in the Manchester Evening News. *She had cut it out and stuck it on our fridge, pointing it out to any visitors with a "Ta-da! Mummy is famous!" (My dad was less impressed, however, telling me, "Can't be doing with that Chiswick bloke. He's a slimy git.")*

Other than the Gillian-wobble, Monday morning began in the usual way. I spent half an hour plotting out our staffing schedules and assigning time slots to existing cases for resettlement and support workers, counsellors and specialist court advocates. And then I headed for a quick brew and to check that Jade, Gemma and Jean had received a quick needs assessment before they joined in with the survivors' support group later on in the day. Fellow survivors were often more helpful in urging someone to break the cycle of abuse than authority figures or perceived do-gooders like ourselves.

The three women were in our kitchen-lounge, making drinks for themselves. Jean had come straight to Sisters' Space after being discharged from A & E. She had a split lip and stitches through one of her eyebrows, having informed the hospital staff that she had fallen over one of her grandchildren's toys. As you do, at 2 a.m. on a Monday morning. She was a frequent visitor to A & E, so they wouldn't have bought her story, and anyway, she didn't have any grandchildren. As I walked into the kitchen area, the TV was blaring and Jean was holding a cold compress to her forehead and complaining, "There's nowt on but shite. For people what have nowt better to do. Me – I'm normally doin' me shift at The Samaritans at this time of a Monday."

I glanced at her. Wondering if she was taking the piss. Apparently not. Her gaze was fixed to the screen.

"What's on?" I asked. Apparently, it was something called 'Cash in the Trash'.

"Never heard of it," I remarked.

Jean commented, "It's bloody awful. Where the presenters go through the rubbish bins of, like, rich and famous people in Hollywood and in London and that. An' they nab all their shitty cast-off crap, an' they do it up and then sell it for a mint. To some brainless pranny what's impressed by stuff like that. But I wouldn't be rummaging through anyone's bins if you paid me! I wouldn't. Bloody losers, bloody twonks."

I poured myself a cup of filter coffee and then looked at my watch. Just gone ten. I reckoned that Michael's press conference would be underway by now so I asked the women if they would mind if I watched the news. Jean picked up the remote control and handed it to me. We seemed to be just in time. The BBC news reader told us:

"And following yesterday's exposure of a gay extra-marital affair involving government minister Ben Hardy, we are now going live to the Department for Communities, where the senior minister for communities – and Ben Hardy's boss – Michael Chiswick, has just arrived in order to speak to the press."

The picture moved to Eland House, a modern fusion of glass and steel; a building close to London's Victoria station. A place all too familiar to me. The news reporter took up the story.

"And as you can see, there is a bit of a media frenzy here at Eland House. This is the first time since becoming minister for communities that Michael Chiswick has had to face any form of controversy in relation to his department. In fact, you could say that until this point it's all been pretty much plain sailing for him as senior – but here is the minister himself."

The camera moved to the right and Michael came into view. He was smiling, wearing a short-sleeved shirt. No tie. Carrying a cup of coffee. That Breitling gleamed on his wrist.

I moved my fingers to my lips, hiding the grin as a sudden memory of Saturday night came back to me. The watch had snagged my hair during one particular moment of passion and I'd stopped what I was doing to tell him that I wished some bugger on the estate had nicked the damned thing off him after all. "Be quiet," he had murmured, "It's rude to talk with your mouth full."

I shielded my smirk with my own cup of coffee. Michael was nodding at the throng of cameras, bodies and waving microphones that were being held back by officials.

He began with, "I want to start by reassuring the public that despite the headlines over the weekend, it's business as usual here at the Department of Communities. Insofar as the private life of a junior government minister is concerned, I will be treating the situation as I would with any other member of the team. Offering full advice and any necessary support."

A blonde, female journalist with an unusually low-cut bright yellow suit and a massive amount of cleavage on display was standing right at the front of the band of reporters. She attempted to interrupt Michael but he held up his hand, speaking sharply.

"Let me finish."

Jade blurted out, "Jesus wept! Look at the tits on her! Bet *she's* not used to getting short shrift like that from a bloke. Mind you," she prattled, "he's probably gay, that one. Most of that lot are."

Jade was nineteen. She was tall and large-framed and favoured the Goth look – pallid, white foundation and lashings of black across the eyes and the lips. No physical injuries, from what I could see, but often the make-up can hide it. Certainly the clothes can. Gemma was petite and in her early twenties. She reminded me of a pixie. Perhaps it was the lime-green hair. She came to Sisters' Space every couple of months with an assault of one kind or another. The last time she'd been with us, her fiancé had been trying to coax her to set a date for the wedding. By kicking her in the kidneys. She always seemed to float back to him, though. Today she was perched next to Jade, sporting a plaster cast on her wrist.

She curled her lip and commented, "She's a right one, she is. Simone Whatsername. Shaw. She's got that column in *News of the Nation* and she does that gossip show on one of the Freeview channels. She's full of it. Did some documentary where she had her tits made bigger an' they filmed it all. The whole thing. Blood an' guts. Reckons being slit open and having eight pounds of plastic shoved into you and sewn back up means you're in charge of your life. But, like – how wrong can you be? I mean, alls she's doin' is gettin' men to wank over her."

I looked at Gemma. I wondered whether she had encountered Lydia in a shoe shop recently. Or at least possessed a similar fascination with breast augmentation. Either way, I appreciated her take on things. She carried on.

"An' all she ever writes or talks about is bitchin' about other people. She just slags anyone and everyone off. Can't stand her. Stupid friggin' cow."

Less PC, of course, but Gemma seemed to be more familiar with the likes of Simone Shaw than I was.

Michael was now concluding.

"And I want to finish by saying that, both the prime minister and I have been appalled by some of the regressive tactics that the media have employed in order to cover this issue. It's as if the Leveson Inquiry never took place!" Here, he paused for a split second and deliberately looked at Simone Shaw.

"And as well as the gross intrusion of individuals' personal lives, some of the rhetoric used during reporting has bordered on the homophobic. I would like to remind everyone in the media," he nodded towards the group in front of him, "that there is a young family involved in this situation. Please respect their feelings. Additionally, if it comes to light that any illegal means were used in generating the information gathered then I'm sure that the parties involved will look towards the regulatory recourse."

He turned away to face members of his staff behind him, indicating the end of his address. A chorus of voices jostling to put questions to him erupted.

"Minister! Shouldn't you …"

"Mr Chiswick, don't you think that …"

He held up his hand again.

"All right. OK. Just a few questions."

The first was from a BBC political correspondent, a reporter with ridiculously geeky looking spectacles. Not the 'I'm so uncool that I'm cool' look, but the truly nerdy-speccy-four-eyes look.

"Mr Chiswick – an obvious question. Will you be asking Mr Hardy to go? What does the prime minister really think about all this?"

"That's two questions, Justin. Bit unfair on the others," Michael quipped. The reporter smiled back. (It pays to be nice to a Beeb man.)

"Anyway. 'No' to your first one. And as for the second, the prime minister's take on the situation is exactly the same as mine."

More calls from the other reporters for recognition. Next up was a rather chiselled-looking man with a mid-Atlantic American accent. He said, "Interesting to hear your allegations about homophobia, Mr Chiswick. So, are you saying that you feel the press would have dealt with this situation differently if the individuals involved were engaged in a heterosexual relationship?"

"No, I'm not saying that," Michael shot back. "But what I am saying is that some sections of the media have been using terminology – employing language – that I and many others feel to be extremely derogatory to the gay community."

Another voice called from the back.

"Does that mean *you*, Mr Chiswick? Are you personally offended by homophobic language?"

"Absolutely!" He fought back "Why wouldn't I be?"

Jean was leaning against one of the kitchen cupboards, mug of tea in hand. She motioned at the TV and commented, "Hmm. That were an obvious dig at him. Tryin' to say that he must be gay himself. Bit out of order, that. Whether he is, or isn't."

I had just taken a swig of my coffee. It went down the wrong way and I started spluttering. Jean held a finger to her lips, shushing me. She was enjoying this Michael And The Media Show. But Jade had started to whine and fret about the fact that she was missing her favourite morning quiz show ('House-proud and Horny'.) Jean gave her a filthy look. We carried on watching. Michael was moving away from the cameras when Simone Shaw in the sickly yellow suit appeared, blocking his retreat into Eland House. Jutting herself forward and challenging him. Breasts like twin torpedoes. She spoke into her own microphone.

"Mr Chiswick, you're blaming the press as per usual, but if it wasn't for us," she motioned to the rest of the media crowd, "the public wouldn't have a clue about the adultery and lies of a government minister. How many more members of your government are leading immoral and deceitful lifestyles, which ordinary taxpayers are footing the bill for?"

She held her microphone out to him. He looked at her with distaste.

"As far as I am concerned, people who work for government are entitled to privacy with regard to their personal lives. Of course, the more senior a person is, the more the onus is on them to disclose relationships that could have a bearing on their work performance."

Simone Shaw attempted to interrupt him again, but he refused to yield.

"And if you're going to talk about wasting taxpayers' money, you might want to look a bit closer to home, Ms Shaw. Because it was your newspaper that broke the story. Meaning that you and your colleagues are the reason why I'm having to stand here today talking to the media, as opposed to getting on with what the public pay me to do."

Again, she tried to answer him, but he continued with, "So I would advise you and your editor to think a little bit more about ethics and the bigger picture in future, rather than focussing on the art of titillation and booby traps."

Silence governed for a second. Michael's face twisted. He was trying to control a smirk. It didn't work. Michael put his hand discreetly over his mouth and although Simone Shaw was trying to speak into her microphone, the sound of her voice was drowned out by a loud, collective bray from the other members of the press. A gaggle of schoolboys guffawing at a rude joke. Michael gave up trying to deny the humour now and moved his hand away from his face, joining in with the mirth.

The volume of the laughter finally tailed off, so the viewers were able to hear him saying, "I can't believe I just said that. Oh, God. Wrong word. Sorry. That wasn't meant to happen. I think I'm turning into Sid James."

He had opted for the Boris Johnson dithering mode again, which I had seen in his interaction with the police on Brindleford. All a ruse. Fresh laughter erupted and he shook his head in mock despair, turning away from the crowd and walking back into Eland House.

The camera moved back to Justin, the freakily bespectacled political correspondent. He was trying but failing to disguise his amusement as he told his TV audience, "Well, as you just saw, that was Michael Chiswick, Minister for Communities, addressing the press on behalf of the government. He was scathing about some of the press treatment of Mr Hardy and his family. And as you can see, the minister had a particular point to make about the media laying …" his face broke out into a grin, "into … ah … I mean …"

The journalist started giggling, quickly trying to complete his report.

"Erm, sorry. I mean, the media engaging in what Mr Chiswick referred to as 'titillation and, er … booby traps'." He burst out laughing. We could barely make out his next words. "And now back to Peter in the studio."

Peter in the studio was also grinning like a Cheshire cat. He began with, "Thank you, Justin. So we've just seen Michael Chiswick's take on some of the media attention facing Ben Hardy. But there was also a bit of a bust-up there between a … mmpphhhh!"

He dissolved into hysterics at his own faux pas. We watched as he fought to control his composure. And failed. Several seconds later, he was wiping his eyes, telling his viewers, "I do apologise. That was most unprofessional of me … Oh dear."

I grabbed the TV remote control and held it out to Jade, wittering to myself, "Honestly! What on earth is the matter with people?"

Jade quickly changed the TV channel. "Yeah. So gay!"

I ignored her remark. Not sure if she meant it as an insult or an adjective. Gemma plonked her empty cup of tea down hard, onto the coffee table.

"I know! For fuck's sake. If they think that's funny, they need to get out a bit more. Sad bastards. I mean! Some woman has big plastic tits and all the blokes think it's hilarious. Even the gay ones, like that minister! Bloody men. Anyway. I'm starvin'." She offered a pack of biscuits around. "Who wants a ginger nut?"

"Ha! That minister's hair were a bit red, weren't it? Ginger nuts!" Jade snorted, accompanied by a collective descent into sniggers. I left the room and headed back to my office with Michael and his Sid James reference ringing in my ears. It seemed as though my life was morphing into some kind of *Carry On* farce.

Still, it made a change from violent death, maternal distress and destructive sexual encounters with Shaun.

Chapter 10

PAN HANDLING IT

Back in my office, I commenced with the usual multitasking. Hammering out one-line replies to emails while picking up voicemails. There were six new messages on my phone.

The first was from Brenda at Lancaster House.

"Just to let you know about Mary Simpson. She's fine, so she is. She will insist on trying to brew up by putting tea bags into the electric kettle, so she will, but there's nothing else to worry about. New Banks say it's going to be at least a week before her flat's ready to move back into. So let's hope your Medlock Council lot can shell out a few more pounds to keep her with us until then. Also – I hope you don't mind – but I've given your number to Dawn – the girl with the kids who came in at the same time as Mary. Maybe you can help her. She's still saying that she doesn't want to press charges against that idiot. So help me! I despair of that one – I really do …"

It was a pity that Dawn hadn't wanted to report Vinnie. Not exactly unusual, though. Sometimes, if the violence escalated – perhaps became focussed on the children – a woman might finally decide to report a case to the police. But not always.

I moved on to the next voicemail. My mother. But not an intentional message. Once more, she had called me by mistake. Resulting in an inordinately long message that seemed to centre around her making a request to the local butcher. The conversation was as clear as a bell. Even if she had probably dialled me from her handbag.

"I'll have that shoulder, please, Colin; less fat, though, if you don't mind. Our Terry's got quite enough of that on him already, eh, Anne?" Mother was out shopping with her friend.

"And I'll have one chicken pie please, Colin. And a medium pork. Not that I should really get one for Terry at all, really, Anne. What with his cholesterol and everything. But he deserves a bit of a treat this week after laying that stone flagging all by himself. Because I can't really help him, not with my feet. And our Rachael's never been much use in the DIY department …"

Then a crackle and the call ended. The next message was from Mum again. Now on the subject of Anne's impetigo, followed closely by, "We've been asking the council for a pelican crossing here for fourteen years now." I decided to delete it when we got to "and the price of lamb is just shocking, isn't it?"

Then, hot on the heels of my mother's liaison with Anne and the butcher, came another woman's voice.

"Hiya, it's me, Dawn. I just wanted to say thanks and all that for helpin' to get me into Lancaster House the other day. Brenda said yer could maybe help me with the housin' an' shit. I don't wanna press charges and all that, but I'm not gettin' back with Vinnie. And I just need to get off Brindleford and away. Me sister lives in Medlock not far from your centre place, so maybe you could help me to transfer over there. But I can't be havin' a maisonette thing 'cause of the buggy."

She paused. There was a rustle. And a whining child.

"Will yer just shut it?! I've told yer! I'm on the bleedin' phone and it's important! Here! Just eat yer crisps!" she growled. Then she continued.

"Right. And I can give yer the money back for the … er … vicar bloke at the same time. For all the nappies an' shit. Anyway. Can you call me? 'Cause I've hardly got no credit left on this phone. Ta." She left me her number and I noted it down. I would get one of the caseworkers to give her a call.

Then another message from my mother. A muffled, "Well, Anne, I'm going to get these little skeletons here, because Lydia's already asking for some decent Halloween decorations this year. Yes, I know it's ages away yet but our Rachael hasn't got much of a clue about doing things like that with the kids. It'd be Christmas before she —" I deleted her.

The final message. Not Mother.

Even more ominous than Mother.

I was halfway through attacking a stack of overflowing papers on my desk. But this new voice abruptly halted my shuffling. Causing a paper-cut.

It was a familiar voice. A deep but gravelly Yorkshire accent.

"Rachael. It's me. Shaun. Been ages, I know. Listen, I need to talk to you about something. I'm run off my feet as per usual. But yeah. Call me."

He left his number. I recognised it. Same as it always was. Although I'd deleted it from my contacts last year, I remembered it well. It contained three consecutive sixes.

I sucked my finger, and turned around. Staring out of the office window.

What the hell was going on with my heart rate? Had someone wazzed a bit of speed into my cup of coffee when I wasn't looking?

I focussed on the outside. My little office overlooked the clapped-out local park. Scruffy patches of rhododendrons, drab-looking grey squirrels and the sun-faded children's playground equipment bordered Sisters' Space. Inside the perimeter of the playground was an all too familiar sight. A worn-down mother going head to head with a wilful toddler. The child was refusing to come off the slide and get back into her pushchair. I could faintly hear a one-sided conversation.

"Jordan! Come *on*! We're going to Nanna's!"

Then, "I've told you ten times now. I'm not tellin' you again!"

Followed by, "If you don't hurry up you can't have no fizzy cola bottle sweeties!"

Next: "I'm countin'! One. Two. Three."

And finally, "Right. That's it. I'm goin' without you! You can stay here on yer own!"

I watched her march away, pushing the empty buggy. Jordan wasn't remotely bothered that her mother was now a hundred yards away and outside the playground fence. The woman stopped and bellowed back to her daughter. Something about a new pink tricycle that would now be forfeited to the Gods of Small Child Misbehaviour, no doubt. But the tot didn't flinch. She had zoned out. Continuing up the steps of the slide. Then down the metal chute. Finally, Mum cracked, storming into the playground, snatching the reprobate toddler off the slide, parcelling the now kicking and screaming child under one arm and dumping her back into the pushchair.

Two other mothers with kids in tow arrived at the playground as she steamed past them. The other parents didn't even register the incident, although two elderly ladies sitting on a bench just outside the playground looked up and shook their heads. Whether the gesture was aimed at the behaviour of the mother or of the daughter, I wasn't entirely sure.

("It seems so much easier for you Rachael, to focus on the problems of others. Rather than to feel the discomfort and pain of your own negative emotions...")

Yeah, yeah, yeah. The softly spoken words of Fran On Feelings. She meant well. However, she seemed to think that this strategy of avoidance was something I had chosen to develop since Adam's death. (Nah, Fran. This is a lifelong thing, this is.)

But now Fran's words, the tired mother, awkward offspring, old ladies and mangy squirrels had faded away. And here I was. Still clenching the phone. So ferociously hard that it was making indentations into the flesh on my palm.

The buoyant moment, the buzz of seeing Michael on the telly. That bubble had been burst now. And here was Shaun. With his I'm So Busy And Important and his Give Us A Call.

The good news was that I had been so preoccupied over the last two days, that I had completely forgotten Linda Beveridge's words about Shaun. The bad news was that the mere sound of his voice had tipped me into a tailspin. I continued to stare out of the window. One of the mothers was now pushing the children on the roundabout. Round and round. The kids were screeching happily. It made me feel sick, just watching the damned thing. I wondered if other parents found it amusing to watch their own child lose their balance when disembarking from a roundabout.

Skittering to the left or to the right, and then falling over.

Or perhaps it was just me. Shades of sadism present in my parenting skills?

Either way, there was only so much that anyone, adult or child, could take of the roundabout ride. It was probably the least-used playground equipment in the park. And there was a damned good reason for that.

I moved away from the window. No. I would not be calling Shaun back. That particular little mini-series had been repeated after Adam's death. And there would be no further re-runs in this lifetime. My sister's words were always helpful at a time like this.

"Some people learn lessons the hard way, Rachael. You might be a tough sod in many ways, but I can't see you making it through any more Shaun-induced self-harm. And I'm not looking after your kids when you're locked up in a loony bin and eating your raffia basket weaving while trying to convince people that you're really Joan of Arc..."

Vicky's pearls of wisdom might be hard. Grown from your typical east Manchester grit. But they were usually spot-on.

I sat down at my desk and immersed myself in paperwork. After half an hour my mobile rang. Mother again. This time it was a live call. The specialist subject was 'rude bus drivers'. I tried to shout down the line at her in the hope that she would hear my voice emanating from her handbag. No such luck. Three minutes later the phone rang again. I went through the same ritual. Then after two minutes, another trill. I snatched it up and bellowed, "For God's sake, Mum! Will you please get Dad to show you how to lock your keypad?"

"Blimey, Rachael – you're scary!" came Michael's voice. "What's your poor mother been doing to make you so cross with her?"

"Oh. It's you, Michael! I'm so sorry." I gabbled, "My mum and her inability to use a phone properly..."

He had called to ask if I had seen his TV appearance that morning. And what did I think of it. I was surprised. A vision of Matthew sprang to mind. My youngest, proudly handing me a sticky piece of paper covered in glue, tinfoil and sequins. *"Mummy – do you like my bestest picture ever?"*

Why the hell would someone like Michael Chiswick want to know what I thought of his press conference? I told him this in not so many words (minus the tosh-collage analogy, of course.)

"Yes, I did see it, actually. And have you heard from the prime minister about it yet? What he thought?"

There was a smile in his voice. He was in good spirits.

"Oh, yes. We had words. He seems to think that I'm very clever and very cunning in relation to how I handle the press. 'Well done on throwing the buggers a left-fielder' was his exact turn of phrase."

"That's great, then. And I'm sure that what he thinks … is a little bit more important than my take on your performance."

"Ah, no. I care deeply what you think of my performance. In every sense of the word."

"Fnar Fnar. Get on with it."

"All right. No, I just wondered what the female perspective might be about it. You know, you being a woman with … with …" He was searching for the right word.

I provided him with one.

"With breasts?"

"No!" he chuckled, "I was going to say 'with principles'."

"Right. OK. Well. I watched it here with some of the women. Service users. They were quite impressed that you stood up to 'Big Tits Brainless Bint' as one of them referred to Simone Shaw."

"I like that. Rather un-politically correct for your place, though, I would have thought."

"Well, I do my best, but I can't brainwash people as much as I'd like to. What else? Oh, yes. They liked your anti-homophobia rant. Although that's because you're as 'bent as a nine bob note' yourself."

"Of course. But blimey. They're very gifted with adjectives at your place."

"And overall, we all thought that you handled it really well until you allowed it to degenerate into a bad episode of a Benny Hill show. And then we switched it off, in general disgust at the usual male behaviour." He laughed.

"What a scathing bunch you all are! So I suppose that I've failed miserably in your eyes. I was hoping that my favourite feminist friend could reassure me that I hadn't made too many sexist remarks in one sentence."

"Well, I'm with the prime minister for once, on all of this."

"What do you mean?"

"I don't believe for a minute that you suddenly morphed into Bernard Manning this morning. I've got you sussed out. I think that you employed a few diversionary tactics there."

He began to protest, but there was a knock at my door.

"Hang on a min." I called out.

"Sounds like you're as busy as I am," he replied. "Anyway, I have to scoot. Got a lunch date with Baroness Golding. She might be pushing ninety but she's still hot to trot in high heels. Speak later."

I hung up and headed for the office door, yanking it open and nearly falling into the arms of Jake Bamber.

"Steady on, sweetie!" he grinned, enveloping me in an enormous hug. Jake was as lean, handsome and tanned as ever. Now sporting a very sculpted beard. ("Do you like my wee goatee?") And a couple more earrings than when I had last encountered him.

"You're looking beautiful, Rach! You were so thin and pale the last time I saw you. A scrawny little thing. Plus, you've caught the sun this weekend, by the looks of it. I see your little freckles there … and thank goodness you've grown your lovely boobs back!" He held me at arm's length for inspection. Jake should have known me well enough not to comment on my personal appearance. (And why did every male in the land – gay or straight – seem to be wittering on about breasts today?)

"Thanks. And you're looking far too suave and immaculate for someone in your line of work. I mean, I swear to God that you're turning into some kind of champagne socialist … look at the cuff-links. What's that all about?"

Jake ignored me and upped the ante with his mock-camp voice.

"Well, Marxist or not, some of us are born with an infinite sense of style. Nature, not nurture. And for once, Ms More Shabby Than Chic, you're not doing badly today. OK – wearing a Gypsy Rose Lee elasticated top isn't the best way to place your breasts on display, but if you pull it off each shoulder like this," he tried to fiddle with my blouse, "you'll be getting every hetero bloke from here to Liverpool all hot and bothered. Listen to Gok here!"

I swiped at him to stop it.

"Leave my clothes alone. I'm happy without either style or grace. And pack it in with the Alan Carr act. This is me, remember?"

He held up his hands.

"OK, OK, I'll stop it with the stereotypical gay male stuff. I'll go back to my true Mr Testosterone mode. See, I'm frowning and baring my teeth." He did his best to glower at me as he drifted over to my desk, sitting down on the corner of it. But then cracked me a grin and began to twirl one of his earrings around.

"It's been ages, Rach. I wish I saw more of you. You should never have had those kids. They put a real spoke in the wheel of the Rachael and Jake show, those little varmints did. Or was that Adam? Bless him…"

Jake was one of the few people who could speak freely and easily about Adam. Without having to whip out a qualifier or anticipate me running off into the loos to slash my wrists.

"Well, I wish I saw more of you, too. When was the last time? February, wasn't it? Yeah. I think we said our goodbyes on the Curry Mile in Rusholme. You were throwing up outside The Purple Harem, if I remember correctly."

“Oh, God, was it that long ago? The Manchester Council Survivors Club is always a good night out,” he mused. “Although you had to go home at 9 p.m. to get back to the kiddies, I recall. But, yes. We must sort a night out. You can invite the Manky Posse. Girls are annoyingly good at that staying-in-touch-with-people thing.”

“And men are usually lazy arses. Whether gay or straight.”

“Oh, I do so miss our gender-based bitch-fests … no one quite rises to the challenge like you do, dear.”

He fiddled with his car keys. I noticed that the keyring had a mini-portrait of Steve McQueen, Jake’s favourite pin-up. I could see the Steve attraction for sure and was just grateful that Jake wasn’t into the motorbike side of things, like bad-boy McQueen had been.

Adam used to say that my knowledge of all things car, bike, engine or non-human moving item was so paralysingly bad that I should try to make a claim for disability benefit. That I was the most mechanically challenged person he had ever met.

“Anyway, missy. I’ve popped over to see you because Martyn Pointer reckoned I should check out the party line with you. About this little old lady that you were gallivanting about with on Saturday. And who am I to argue with Martyn about that, now he dwells in the lofty land of senior management? So. Because the bunch of shysters who make up our maintenance team at New Banks can’t get her flat shipshape for another week, it looks like Medlock Council are going to be shelling out another week’s stay for her over in Manchester at Lancaster House. Something that a particular wanker at the Town Hall won’t be happy about.”

I clicked my tongue. Khoisanesque.

“Are you referring to Shaun there, by any chance?” I asked. Jake coughed, “Fucchar!” and covered his mouth with his hand, continuing, “Sorry. My Tourette’s again.”

“Very amusing – and not at all un-politically correct, Jake. But anyway, given the fact that Shaun is the council’s director of … what the hell is the name of it again?”

“Leisure and communities. Or the other way around. Can never remember.”

"Yes, that. Which is probably the biggest job going at Medlock Council after the chief executive's. I can't imagine that someone so important as he is these days would be arsed about whether a flea-ridden and incontinent old lady is costing his temporary rehousing budget a few extra quid."

Jake jangled his keys and then pointed one at me.

"Ah. That's where you're wrong. Mr Shaun Elliot is quite happy to neglect his swimming pools and his community centres if the issue at hand has anything to do with housing. Housing is his first love. And because our lot at New Banks has the contract for delivering Medlock's crappy excuse for a homelessness strategy … and because Martyn Pointer is the big boss at our marvellous housing association … well. It's just too tempting for Shaun not to wade in and have a bit of a cat-fight with his arch-enemy of old."

"Well, yeah. I can see that. But getting Miss Simpson over to Manchester and to Lancaster House was totally justified. She's elderly. She was soaking wet. And she's got dementia. She couldn't afford to wait while you rang round all Medlock's B & Bs. We agreed that on Saturday."

Jake shrugged. "True. But you know and I know that those two won't see it like that. Once they're out there and comparing the size of their dicks."

Martyn and Shaun had worked together at Manchester Housing at the same time as Jake, Linda and me. Shaun thought that Martyn was a smart-arse. Martyn thought that Shaun was a smart-arse. It was that simple. And over two careers spanning various local authorities, associations, boundaries and jobs in the north-west, they had carried a track record of being stupidly obstinate over minor things. And now into their most recent roles. Shaun heading up a huge part of Medlock Council, and Martyn's New Banks Housing Association managing what used to be the Council's housing stock. If Jake was correct in his analysis, Shaun would accuse Martyn and New Banks of riding roughshod over their homelessness contract with the council. And Martyn would want to defend Jake's actions.

And to get up Shaun's nose as best as he could.

It was all quite pathetic, really. Shaun might be slightly superior to

Martyn these days in terms of the overall local authority pecking order, purse strings and pension contributions, but Martyn would still do anything to square up to Shaun. Which was a bit futile really because Shaun had almost a foot in height on Martyn. Ha-bloody-ha.

Jake's smirk had faded by now and he spread his fingers out, beginning to examine his oh-so-manicured nails.

"You know. Martyn can be a pain. A whinge-bag. What with his bible-bashing and all of that Jehovah's Witness 'life on the straight and narrow' stuff. But he's OK in general. And when compared to Shaun … well. Sometimes I really can't believe how Shaun changed. From when we were all working together at Manchester, I mean. He was a good laugh. It's insane, isn't it? That we're fretting about how that wanker will react to helping some old dear out."

I folded my arms and let Jake finish. I didn't want to get into a discussion about Shaun and the past.

"Or did we ever really know him, Rachael? Well, it took me a while to see his true colours. Which I did when I realised how he was messing you about. Way back then …"

I narrowed my eyes at him. Warning. But he waggled his fingers at me.

"Yes, yes. I know that you don't like me even talking about it. And don't worry – I've never mentioned it to anyone else. God knows why it all had to be secret back then. But at least you met Adam a bit after that and got the idiot out of your system."

"Jake!" I snapped. "Move on, please. I have."

He sighed and returned to fiddling with his car keys.

"All right. All right. Don't get your knickers in a twist. But I'm not exaggerating about Shaun. Since he's been heading up stuff in Medlock, it's been redundancies left, right and centre. I'm run ragged with all the union representation that I'm having to do. Trotsky was right when he said that once the proletariat —"

I interrupted him again.

"Yes, but before you try to flog me a copy of *Socialist Worker* – like you usually do, Jake – can we crack on with the stuff about Miss Simpson? It's all fine by me. You can go and tell Martyn that he's got the ammunition he needs. I'm happy for him to say that I was the one who refused to let her sit in a puddle while you rang round all the B & Bs. It was me who took her over to Manchester and to Brindleford, after all. That might shut Shaun up, at any rate."

He considered this for a moment and then nodded. "Nice one. I'll let Martyn know. Cheers."

Moving away from my desk, he was getting ready to leave when he added:

"Anyway, Rach. We still have another ace up our sleeves, don't we? A certain politician that you had there with you. When you called me…"

I shook my head. "That wasn't planned, Jake – that was a total, weird fluke sort of thing."

He held his palms up and out towards me – all innocence.

"I'm not saying that it was planned. I for one know how you have a tendency to attract all kinds of nutters and freaks. It's a Rachael Russell speciality. And I don't see why this wouldn't exclude politician-type tools of the Establishment."

Hands on hips now, I scowled at him.

"Oh, you can huff and puff all you like, Rachael. But you know damned well what your junior management are like. Terrified of the senior managers above them … that lot with their narcissistic personality disorders and their rampant self-obsessions. So, why not make the most of your new friend's heavyweight credentials if we need to?" He stopped and cocked his head to one side. Eyes dancing with mischief. "What were you doing with him anyway, honey-bun? It was a Saturday afternoon! I mean. What on earth were you doing in some filthy maisonette with a Tory boy? The mind boggles…"

"Jake!" I moved over to the office door and closed it again, doing my best not to sound too defensive. I hissed at him, "Look – stop calling him a 'Tory boy', will you? He's not. As you damned well know. And he's hardly a boy. Anyway. The reason I happened to see him on Saturday was to do with this place." I jerked my head towards the corridor. "He's been helping us out with the publicity for Sisters' Space. Our Chocolate and Cafe project. We've had some brilliant press coverage since he visited us. Plus … he's all right, actually. Even if my politics are a little bit left of his."

At this, Jake spluttered out, "Left? Does he know that you were with me at Marxism 2002 and plotting to blow up Parliament?"

I folded my arms and gave him the daggers.

"Hilarious. And that was donkey's years ago. And I only went to your Marxist conference because I managed to get cheap train tickets and we could kip over at one of your boyfriend's in —"

"Ah, yes. Stevie the Slinky Stalinist … I remember him well …"

"So while you were transfixed by your lectures on Revolutionary Workers' Councils in the Baltic States, I spent most of the time in the British Museum looking at King Alfred's jewels."

A wicked smile now.

"And I bet you've been taking an equal interest in King Michael's jewels, eh? Maybe you've always had a secret thing for the Eton boys, Rach."

"He's not an Eton boy! He went to Ampleforth. Even though he's Jewish," I began. And then decided that I was giving away too much.

Far too much.

"Ah – so he's Jewish? He's Jewish. Rachael, please, please tell me that you found this little bit of information out in the way that I am truly hoping you did…"

I was doing my best to keep a straight face but somehow, the laughter began to leak out. I knew that I couldn't pull the wool over this old pal's eyes. Jake took this as license to descend into Camp Minciness. He clasped his hands together, gave a girly-shriek, then seized my hand and commenced trying to waltz me around the room.

"Oh, sweetie pie! I knew that sooner or later you'd be back on the scene, breaking blokes' hearts. And stomping all over the affections of a

Tory boy would be our finest, most anti-Establishment plot to date! Come here and let me ravish you!"

He stopped the prancing and held me by the arms, attempting to kiss my neck with his tickly new beard. I was laughing and trying my best to swipe him away from me, so neither of us heard the knock or noticed the office door opening until Gillian cleared her throat.

"Erm ... Rachael?"

Jake and I paused, looking over to the doorway. Our struggle had involved my blouse being pulled off one shoulder, exposing rather a lot of bra. A file had been knocked off the desk during our tussle, scattering papers across the floor.

Gillian's eyes widened, but then she smiled.

"Oh. It's just you, Jake." She had worked with Jake on various rehousing cases in the past and knew that the two of us were good friends. But her smile quickly vanished and she pulled a face, gesturing behind her. Because the next visitor might not be too tolerant of such manifestations of office friskiness.

And all six foot five inches of Shaun Elliot entered the room, stooping slightly in order to avoid knocking his head on the door frame.

Chapter 11

ENTER HADES

Gillian's normally brash voice sounded slightly on edge. Embarrassed, perhaps, on my account.

"I did explain to Mr Elliot here that we work on an appointment system at Sisters' Space…"

"And I told her that I'm the fella *here* who pays all your wages. So of course you'd make time to see me. Like you've no doubt made time to see Bamber-boy."

That voice. It's hard to describe Shaun's voice. Deep, but hoarse. Reverberating. As though he had been gargling with gravel. (I told him this once. He claimed that Yorkshire males were so well-hard that their mams weaned them on aggregate.)

He was still standing in the doorway. Suited and booted immaculately, with his arms folded. Sizing up the frivolous scene in front of him. Then he shook his head slowly.

"Hope that's not a client's file all over the floor." A quick tut. "I mean, I know that you're a bit last century here. Using paper files. But surely you do your data protection? Proper security and storage. Due diligence. All that shit?"

I tugged my blouse straight again and tried to catch my breath. I was struggling to find sufficient oxygen, and not because of the freakish foxtrot with Jake. My hands moved to my throat. Fingers already cold. I moved my hand to the warmth at the back of my neck. Thawing out the shock.

And then the words came easily enough.

"Nice to see you too, Shaun. And you might be a VIP in the local municipal celeb stakes, but Gillian is right. We do have to be strict about the appointment system. Especially with male visitors. Even if they are dressed in really lovely and expensive designer suits, like you are."

A sneer and a jerk of his head. "So what about Bamber-boy then? Did the cuff-links bleep him through the security system? Have you had him chipped?"

Jake glared back. Having finished with the camp-clown act, he decided to move into more defensive mode, biting back, "Obviously, I don't quite cut the dashing hetero real male presence. So I'm no threat to the ladies in this place. Unlike others."

I gestured for him to help me pick the papers up off the floor, before he came out with anything too close to home.

Shaun turned to Gillian, "Get us a brew, would you?"

Gillian curled her lip and came up trumps.

"Sorry," she said. "We're a bit short-staffed. And we like to empower people here. Kitchen's round the corner. Help yourself."

I grinned at the floor as I fished for the paperwork. Shaun was clearly used to having his own personal tea-maid these days. And Gillian had been untypically restrained, for once. I'd half expected her to tell Shaun to get his own sodding brew.

The Director of Very Important Things in Medlock walked over to the window and looked out onto the playground.

"Depressing view, Rachael. Should see mine, from the Town Hall. Can see to Jodrell Bank on a clear day."

On the floor, putting the file back together, Jake sang under his breath, "Mnnneerr ... Should see mine..." I did my best not to snigger.

Shaun turned away from the window as we both stood up. I placed the file back onto the desk and he addressed Jake again.

"Anyway, what are you doing here?" He looked down at his phone, scanning messages. "What's the betting that Martyn Pointer sent you over? So that Pointless and his New Banks crew can cook up some bullshit story about why I'm paying for some pensioner to be temporarily housed over in Manchester. When she should have been put up in one of our B & Bs in Medlock. You lot at New Banks have tried to pull too many fast ones on us over the last few months."

I was trying not to get too side-tracked by Shaun's accent. Sure, I lived in West Yorkshire these days and I was more than aware that my kids would grow up with that gentle west-Yorkie burr that Adam had possessed. That my offspring had become tiny white-rose traitors to my Lancastrian red-rose upbringing. With their 'Nor' instead of 'No' and their occasional broad-as-beans 'Mummeh' instead of 'Mummy.'

But here was Shaun with that particular patter and pronunciation from the Leeds area. Shaun said 'Arr' instead of 'I'. He said 'Bratfort' instead of Bradford. And maybe I needed to get out a little bit more, but such tiny aberrations of articulation for this Mancunian lass had somehow always represented Exotica.

Sod it. I could always blame my Emily Bronte obsession for that kind of thing.

So I quickly answered him, before Jake could.

"Funny, Shaun. Now that you're in charge of most of the council, I would have thought that the issue of a little old lady needing a bed for the night would have fallen way, way down your list of important local-government golf tournaments to attend."

Jake didn't miss a beat either, looking directly at me.

"Well, Shaun has always had a big heart when it comes to the well-being of vulnerable people, so I'm sure that his interference – sorry – interest here is quite genuine. I guess we'll no doubt have his utmost sympathies when he hears that I'm checking up on a case that I'm working on with the women's centre." He turned back to me. Eyes subtly widened. "So you can tell your client, Rachael, that we've just had a three-bedroom come available in one of her preferred areas. She can call me if she wants to chat about it. OK?"

"Cheers, Jake." Shaun had no doubt rumbled us, but I went along with the fabricated excuse.

Jake ran long fingers through his now elegantly tousled hair and informed me, "Right. I'm off. Unless you don't want to be left on your own with the Big Bad Wolf?"

Shaun had already become bored with the conversation and was now tapping away at his phone. He looked up, though, surprised at the remark. He was probably getting more than his fair share of front-line insubordination this morning. Good. I ignored Jake's words and followed him over to the door, opting for the professional mode again.

"Thanks, Jake. I wish more housing officers would make proper use of Sisters' Space like you do. You're not doing a bad job, you lot at New Banks, you know. I hope that Martyn appreciates you all." Jake nodded.

"He's not a bad 'un. Thank God I don't work for the council, though. It's only my opinion of course, but the senior managers there don't really seem to take it seriously … the subject of tackling domestic violence."

"Jesus!" Shaun's stare was incredulous. He looked up from his phone and then back down at it as he continued. "I am still here, you know. It's like listening to Woman's Hour on Radio 4 with you two. Are you both suffering from PMT this morning or something?" He raised a hand without even looking at Jake. The classic, rude 'I'm too busy to even say goodbye properly' gesture.

Jake was out of the door. But then he stopped and turned around. He'd changed his mind about something.

"So, Rachael, I'm going to be glued to the evening news tonight. Now there aren't many men who are that good-looking and also have screen presence. And real intelligence, too. But he's the lucky one – bagging you, I say! I shall be taping it actually so that I can —"

"Go on! Go!" I called out at him. Half-amused at what he was trying to do, but half-irritated by the reckless but playful attitude.

Shaun rose to Jake's bait as he left us, putting away his phone and wandering over to my desk. Hands in pockets now, he looked out of the window again.

"What's Bamber-Boy on about?"

"Nothing," I answered, under my breath. "Just Jake being Jake."

"Stirring it," Shaun replied, folding his arms. "Never changes. So what does he mean about the evening news? You going out with a newsreader or something?"

"No," I sighed. "Anyway. I only just got your message on the phone. I was going to call you back. When I got a minute …"

"Thought I'd beat you to it. Couple of things I need to sort." He jerked his head at me. Perhaps expecting me to grab a pen and pencil and Take A Letter, Miss Jones. Shaun's time and priorities these days were clearly so much more important than mine.

"Firstly, I've been in post at Medlock for three months now. So I need to have a once-over of this place. And, as the council mostly funds you – what is it we give you? Seventy-five per cent?"

"Sixty-five."

"Whatever. We're keeping you afloat. And secondly, you've been getting lots of publicity about this new so-called business venture of yours. So we need to talk."

"Right, then," I turned on my heel. "You can have a quick tour of the place. We've got a chocolate-creation workshop starting in a minute…"

"Nah, hang on." Something had taken his interest. He picked up a photo of Matthew on my desk. Taken only a few weeks ago. My youngest was in the paddling pool. Holding up a decapitated doll of Lydia's, while shouting with glee at the camera.

"This Matthew?" he looked up at me.

"No. It's some random kid I abducted and tried to drown in a paddling pool. Of course it's bloody Matthew." Shaun ignored me.

"God he's grown. Must be – what – how long? Since I saw them …Look at him! Just like … just like Adam. The image of him …God."

My defences went up. So different to the way that Jake had mentioned Adam. Jake had been warm-hearted and natural in his turn of phrase. Shaun had stumbled over his words. Shaun was acting as though he had nothing to feel guilty about, nothing to even try to conceal from anyone. I twisted the rings on my fingers. Round and round.

Then he picked up the photo of Lydia. A typical Liddy prima donna pose where she had wound several of my mum's colourful silk (well, probably polyester) scarves around herself. She was hanging over the edge of a chair and the camera had captured her with a vivacious, mischievous expression.

"And look at Lydia, now! Wow. She's beautiful." He put the picture down and turned to me, a slight smile playing at the corners of his mouth.

"Just like her mother."

"Oh, give it a rest, Shaun," I turned round again and made as if to leave. He might be the Director of All That He Surveys in Medlock and his council might be key player contributing to the financial survival of Sisters' Space. But he was no boss of mine. And he certainly had no right to start rifling around with personal items on my desk.

"You can either stay here and look at the family album, or you can come and meet some of the women who rely on this place. Or maybe you don't get paid enough to spend time with real people these days. How much do you earn, now? I read that the salary scale that Medlock appointed you on is the highest ever achieved by a person who isn't actually the chief executive of a council."

He put Liddy's photo back onto the desk, and followed me, muttering something along the lines of, "hormonal headquarters of Medlock, this place…"

Sisters' Space was based in a small, 1960s primary-school building on the outskirts of Medlock town centre. The school itself had closed in 1998 and a few years later the council had decided that the premises could be used as a centre for local women who needed support and that there should be a special focus on tackling domestic violence. Funding had always been an issue for the centre – for its staff and for the building itself. The place was looking pretty shabby these days, and I had a list of charitable foundations as long as your arm to apply to. The council had made it quite clear that we couldn't expect any more help from them than we already got.

Shaun followed me down the corridor and, to give him his credit, he seemed genuinely interested in the centre. He even stopped and began chatting to some of the service users, providing Gillian with the opportunity to beckon me away from him.

"Rachael, we need to keep him away from Dee. Bev says that she's been necking the Tammies again this morning. And you know what she's like at the best of times. What the hell is Shaun Elliot doing here, anyway? Will this be to do with the rumours I heard about funding cuts?"

"No," I said. "He's just having a nosey around, after all the publicity that we've been getting. But like I said before, Gillian – chill pill. Temazepam is on tap here today, by the sounds of it. So if he's freaking you out that much, go and ask Dee if she's got any spare."

"I might bloody do that, Rach."

I motioned for Shaun to follow me to the other end of the centre, where our new project was based. The initiative was all uncharted waters for us. A new and exciting opportunity for Sisters' Space. But for me, it represented much more than simply the latest development at work. No one knew this, but the original idea for the Chocolate and Cafe enterprise had been sparked by Adam. We were on a family day out to Hebden Bridge and while we were in a cafe, Adam had told me:

"If there was a way of combining your love of coffee and chocolate with that mad work of yours ... helping women out, I think that we'd be totally redundant in your life. Yeah. Now that'd be the dream Rachael Russell job!"

And I've always liked a challenge.

Adam had – unwittingly – hit upon a great idea. The location of Sisters' Space was perfect. We were practically in the centre of town where there were very few (half-decent) cafes. Certainly no chocolatiers. We saw some heavy footfall to and from the nearby shopping centre. So, all in all, it was a fantastic way to build the women's skills and confidence and ultimately to generate some much-needed income for Sisters' Space.

Shaun and I skirted around the new cafe chairs and tables (donated by an unusually generous local furniture company – I was still a tad concerned that it had fallen off the back of a lorry), and I gestured towards the seating area.

"Right. Here's Charlene's Chocolate Factory and Cafe. Looks pretty unimpressive at the moment, I know, but you won't believe the amount of interest that we've had so far. Come the opening day —"

Shaun interrupted me.

"Who the hell is Charlene, anyway? One of your teenage mums here, or something?" I gave him a best bitter-lemon smile and told him that our project had been named after Charlene Fullham. Charlene had been a young woman from the Manchester area who had died in a house fire, along with her one-year-old son, some eighteen months ago. The fire had been started by her violent partner as an act of revenge when she told him that she was leaving him. After getting drunk, he had beaten her to death and then set fire to the house. The toddler had died of smoke inhalation. Daddy was so smashed out of his face that he hadn't realised his son was asleep upstairs.

I reminded Shaun that it had been all over the national news for days. But Shaun was unabashed. Shaun always was.

"Well, I've never heard of her." I looked him square in the eye.

"Interesting," I replied. "But no wonder, really. Because from my mental calculations, Charlene was killed shortly after Adam died. Meaning that you would have been doing much more important things like choosing table arrangements and sugared almonds for your big posh wedding in Harrogate. The pressure of all that must have affected your memory, Shaun. Post-traumatic stress disorder caused by shade of cravat choice."

Shaun looked at his phone. Not listening. So I carried on.

"Yeah. The pressure of all that must have caused you to forget to tell me that you and Jess were about to get married. While you were still playing the car-park liaison game with muggins, here."

(And if the lemons looked, sounded and tasted bitter. So what? They bloody well were.)

Shaun didn't respond. He never did when I raised the subject of Jess. Which I rarely did.

By now it was time for the workshop. We made our way to the rear of the cafe's kitchen, which we used as the base for the chocolatier side of the project. Shirley, a shy woman in her early seventies, was leading the session. She had been coming to the centre for two years now, having finally got rid of her thug of a husband after forty-five years of being knocked about. Unlike some of the women who came to Sisters' Space, though – the more serious, tough and abrasive characters – Shirley was all sunshine. An air of innocence, like an old-fashioned Sunday School teacher. Andrea, another woman who we had supported to become a fully trained chocolatier, was assisting Shirley.

Three other women, including Bev, were perched on chairs surrounding the preparation area. Shirley had prepared the couveture over the last couple of days, and as Andrea wielded the thermometer her partner in chocolate demonstrated the different types of textures that the heat process could produce. All of this was accompanied by the usual Bev-style comments ("Half the stuff in this place is second hand – so I hope yer thermometer hasn't been shoved up anyone's arse in a former life.")

Shirley explained about the most common spices and flavourings for chocolate, and Andrea – quiet but canny – noticed that Shaun had a low attention threshold. She cast several different types of chocolate in Shaun's direction, and after licking his lips ("not bad at all …") he guided me to one side again, away from the training session. Lots of searching senior managerial questions all ready for me. How much market research had we carried out? What were our expected financial projections? Had we produced a full business plan? What was our approach in terms of volunteers and opening hours? And finally:

"All of your women are more than a bit 'on message', though, aren't they, Rachael? That's got to be your doing, of course. Still, from what you're saying, the figures stack up. Seems pretty much ready to go. So why aren't you open yet?"

"We wanted to take the 'slowly, slowly' approach and get the online ordering system up and running first. With the publicity we've had after the MP's visit, things are moving pretty well on that side of things. But we wanted to do a proper launch. And we don't have the funding for that right now. In fact, I was going to approach Councillor Casey to see if there was any way that we could get a small grant from Medlock to help us with the launch."

Shaun gave a hollow laugh.

"You'd be barking up the wrong tree there, Rachael. Kathleen Casey isn't exactly a fan of yours. She refers to Sisters' Space as 'a Feminist Coven'. Thinks you're brainwashing women with a load of radical ideas."

I considered this.

"Well, it's news to me that the Leader of the Council seems to think that I'm running a Hogwarts for gullible local women. But I guess it makes sense, come to think of it. She's always avoided my phone calls or emails." Two-faced old bag. I carried on. "So Shaun, can you not sort us out with some kind of…"

He held his hand up at me, to shut me up while his phone buzzed and he tapped a one-liner to a faceless bureaucrat somewhere. And then he looked up at me.

"Overall, I like what you're doing here. What gave you the idea? Was it that film *Chocolat* – you know – with the French woman and Johnny Depp? Ha. She was accused of being a witch, too, wasn't she?"

I exhaled, impatiently. I wasn't going to reveal that the initial idea had been inspired by Adam.

"No. Nothing like that. And the film came after the book. It was much better, actually. Darker. But then reading anything halfway intelligent has never been something you're very good at, has it?"

He ignored the insult, pocketing his phone again and changing the subject.

"Anyway, there's a few other things sloshing around in the world of local-government politics that you need to be aware of. Can we go and grab a drink?"

It was more or less lunchtime by now and I didn't have any other appointments. I nodded. No doubt I'd bloody well have to brew up for him after all, even if Gillian had managed to get out of it. We walked back to the main part of the building and I headed for the kitchen.

"Tea, then?" I asked. Shaun's had always been a builder's brew: white, with no sugar. But instead he motioned to the front doors and to the reception area.

"No. I meant go out for a drink. Won't keep you long. I've got loads on today."

You are kidding.

(But, no he wasn't.)

I came very close to inventing an elaborate story involving the need for me to supervise a lunchtime chlamydia-testing session. Talk of yucky women's problems had always been a great way of putting Shaun on the back foot. But then I realised that the earlier, writhing nerves brought on by his arrival had gone. Dissipated.

Perhaps I could deal normally with him now. Without losing the plot completely.

And he clearly had something on his agenda that he wanted to discuss. And Shaun being Shaun, he wasn't going to take no for an answer. Plus, he was director at the place that was keeping the centre afloat. And perhaps I could try to wheedle some funding out of him for the big launch day.

(These were not Excuses. These were Reasons, by the way …)

I shrugged my shoulders, trying to make it clear that I wasn't that keen. But I followed him out of the doors.

We walked through the park and headed towards the A6, which ran through the centre of Medlock. Perhaps through force of habit (because it wasn't the shortest route to reach the main road) we made our way through an area of the park that I always thought of as the 'Secret Glade'. Dense rhododendrons lurked in the shade of oak and ash trees, and this little pocket of privacy was overlooked neither by my workplace, the New Banks (former council-owned) housing estate or the shoppers tottering along the A6. A discreet little meeting place for loved-up Asian couples from the local sixth-form college, who were embarking on early, illicit affairs. Shaun and I had met there ourselves on plenty of occasions until about a year ago. But I wasn't going to remind him of that.

I trotted along, trying to keep up with him. Shaun as always, was unaware that most normal-sized people couldn't keep up with him. I exaggerated my efforts and threw in a dramatic huff, causing him to comment, "Sorry, Stan. Forgot about you being such a short-arse."

(Ignore the 'Stan'. Ignore it.)

"And I can't remember the last time I saw you in shoes with heels. Not that I'm complaining, like. Wouldn't have thought that your flat-footed feminist mates at your centre would have approved, though. Mind you, that Gillian probably likes the look of you in them. So. Have you got a big meeting on this afternoon or something?"

"No."

"Just that you're looking dressier than usual. And I like that top, too. Though it looked even better when it was nearly falling off you. In the office just before …"

"You know what, Shaun?" Giving it back to him, as snottily as I could. "People have been up for sexual harassment charges for saying a lot less than that."

He glanced sideways at me, raising his eyebrows and deliberately slowing his pace. We had arrived at the front gates of the park, on the A6.

"Yeah, well, given our history, I don't think a case of sexual harassment would be that straightforward in a court of law, now, would it?"

I was going to smart-mouth him back, but then my phone began to ring. It was Kate. I took the call, gesturing for Shaun to walk ahead of me. He frowned, putting his hands in his pockets.

"Oh, at long bloody last, Rachael! Sorry about the noise here, petal. In the staff room. But look here, you. Are you avoiding me? I've left you three messages now. I couldn't get hold of you at all on Saturday night to see if me and the kids could pop over to see you all."

"Yeah, sorry, Kate. I was out," I answered abstractly. Shaun wasn't even pretending not to listen. I scowled at him, turning my back.

"Out? Of an evening? That's not like you. You never go out. Where?

Who with?"

"Just out."

"Rachael. Was this a man? Are you seeing someone?"

"Yes to the first. Not sure to the second."

"You cow! And you've not told me yet!" My God … did you …? Was this why no one was home when we dropped by on Sunday morning? I saw that your car wasn't there and the Sunday newspaper was still in the letter box …" I cut her off.

"Well. You're a nosey bugger. And I can't talk right now. Work."

"Oh, sorry. Bad time, mate?"

Shaun was busying himself with his phone again. But still earwigging. I decided to have a dig.

"Yeah. The Big Cheese just dropped in to see us. You know what these people are like. Every second of their precious time is like gold dust …"

He pulled a face at me. Talk about petulant behaviour. I very nearly added an extra dollop of immaturity to the pot by adding, "And he smells like sick!" But I didn't.

"Well. OK. Let's speak later. But don't avoid me, chicken. Or else."

I put my phone back into my bag. Shaun carried on peering at his. "Sounded interesting," he commented.

"Yes," I replied, breezily.

"Clearly something that you didn't want me to overhear."

"Well, you can think what you like, Shaun," I said, dismissively. "So, are we going to the Coffee Wagon?"

"Nah. A proper drink. Thought the Masons' Arms would be better. Nearer, too."

He gestured to the pub, just a few hundred yards away. We walked on, in an awkward silence, for the next couple of minutes. Over the last year,

I had rehearsed in my head so many times what I would say to Shaun if the chance ever arose again. When he had got his big new job at the council, I knew our paths would cross again at some point. But now that the occasion had arisen, all the carefully constructed witticisms and criticisms had vanished. And, after all, Michael had been on my mind for most of that morning. So perhaps this meant that the Shaun Effect no longer existed.

But either way, I stepped along beside him. A small but furious clockwork doll, once again at the beck and call of Shaun Elliot.

Chapter 12

CHAOS, THE TITANS

By now it was the middle of the lunch hour and the Masons' Arms was bustling. Shaun strode purposefully past the punters in the bar area and through to the tap room, finding us an unoccupied table. Tucked away and out of view of everyone else in the pub.

Some things never change.

I perched myself behind the wobbly table and bristled. Shaun went to get the drinks, returning with my mineral water and half a pint of bitter for himself. He sat down, took a sip and then announced, "I like this place. Proper working men's pub. Reminds me of home."

I laughed, cynically.

"Oh, give over, Shaun. You grew up in Harrogate. Not Bradford or Brighouse. And this is me, remember? You don't impress me with the big rough Yorkshire man bravado."

In the past, such a comment from me would have rolled off Shaun like water off a duck's back. But I noticed the tiny twitch of a muscle just under his left eye. Gotcha. He knocked back half of his drink, putting the glass back down on the table. Hard.

"Look – what is your problem, Rachael? I've tried being nice to you for the last couple of hours, but you're just not having it, are you? You're not normally this arsey. What's up?" He seemed genuinely perplexed.

Lacking emotional intelligence, or what? But I didn't want to get into any conversational sparring. And there was no point in being too rude to him, too obstreperous. At the end of the day it was the cash from his council that had been keeping Sisters' Space open. And Shaun was the bloke now in a position to be able to pull strings for people. For us.

"Oh, forget it. Doesn't matter." I took a swig of my water. "Like you said – just me. I'm in a mood, that's all. I'm allowed my off-days you know. Now, what was it that you wanted to talk about?"

My answer seemed to reassure him. He moved slightly closer to me, cocking his head to one side and trying to stare me out with deep-set eyes. Almost irisless pupils. He rubbed his chin, the stubble showing, as always. He had never been one for the clean-shaven look at work.

"Yeah. You definitely don't seem yourself. More uptight."

I shrugged.

"Yeah Stan, maybe you could do with relaxing a bit more. Having a bit of fun every now and then. Can't be a barrel of laughs being surrounded by a load of abused women and man-haters …"

I looked down at my drink. The tiny bubbles fizzed, popped. Bubbled to the surface. Shaun trying to goad me. As of the old days. I declined to reply.

"Tell you what it is Stan. I think that you need to smile more. I miss your smile, Stan. Miss ... well. Miss you, actually." His fingers moved to touch mine.

My toes curled inside their stupid clip-cloppy shoes (which I had decided would be going straight down the charity shop tomorrow.) There it was again. He kept saying the damned word. Stan. There had been none of that of course, while we were in the centre.

Just over a year ago I might have welcomed this kind of conversation. But not now. Not on a Monday lunchtime, in a grotty Medlock public house. Not after everything that had happened. Not after the Michael-weekend.

So I moved my hand away and changed the subject, gazing at my phone instead. Dismissing the attempts at intimacy, "Matthew was a right little rat-bag this morning. Really crabby. I wondered whether he could be coming down with something. I'm half expecting a message from the nursery with a catalogue of woes. Anyway," I nudged my phone to one side again, "what was it you wanted to talk about again?" Brightly and briskly. As if I had had a sudden lapse of hearing only ten seconds ago.

Shaun spread both of his hands out on the table and looked down at them. He'd got the message.

"Okay, Ms Russell. The professional stuff. There's a job vacancy in my senior management team. Policy team leader. You'd be perfect for it."

I took a sip of my drink.

"I've moved away from policy these days, Shaun. In case you hadn't noticed …"

"Oh, frigging hell, Stan!" Shaun leaned back against the seat, stretching his long legs out, clasping his hands behind his head. Doing the Alpha Male without even trying. "You and I both know that you can do the policy stuff in your sleep. And the salary would be nearly double what you're taking home now. Plus, all the other benefits: car, final salary pension, help with childcare costs, flexi-hours, dah-de-dah."

I stood up suddenly. He snapped out of his laid-back, super-confident position, surprised at my movement.

"Don't worry," I opened my eyes wide, exaggerating the expression, "I'm not walking out on you. Not just yet. I need the loo."

Once in the ladies, I checked my reflection in the mirror. I wasn't looking too bad for once. The sun of the last few days had brought my freckles out. Jake had been right. I looked a lot less pale, and healthier than I had done in months. In twenty months, to be precise.

I grinned at my image. It was always flattering to be asked to apply for a job. But there was no question that I would consider it. I loved my work at Sisters' Space. Especially the new chocolatier and cafe side of things. I quickly touched up my make-up, shaking away all thoughts of 'why tart yourself up for a tosser?' There was nothing wrong with taking a bit of pride in my appearance every now and then. Why not let Shaun know what he was missing? He had had his chance. Chances, even. And screwed all of them up, big time.

Back in the corner of the tap room, Shaun was waiting for me.

"So? I'm a very busy and important person. What's the answer? You going to apply for it, or what?"

"Oh, Shaun," I shook my head, "you're about as crap at fake self-effacement as you are at genuine compassion."

"Spare me the insults. What do you think, then? About the job?"

"Sorry, Shaun. You'd have to pay me ten times more than you could afford. Because I'd be bored shitless. Policy isn't for me any more. I love what I'm doing at the centre. Plus, there's the small matter of my kids only having one parent alive these days. The rate you've always expected others to work at is legendary. I couldn't do that. And I wouldn't want to. It's kind of important that Lydia and Matthew get to see their only parent from time to time ..."

"Hey," he put his hand gently on my shoulder, "I know that. I wouldn't expect anything other than the standard hours."

I looked at him pointedly. A man unable to read the subtext. Or unable to decipher social nuances. Or unwilling to take no for an answer from Rachael Russell.

Or maybe all three.

He carried on.

"Of course your circumstances would be taken into account. In fact," he tagged on, "we could even talk about part time, or job-share. If you like?"

I burst out laughing.

"Bleeding hell, Shaun! You, of all people – offering a post as a job-share? Everyone and his dog knows you hate part-timers!"

He stuck his bottom lip out at me, disagreeing.

"Not true, Stan. No. I just need someone I can trust to do a good job. Someone with new ideas. You know. Innovation. And I can trust you."

"Jeez. You're making it sound like you're head-hunting me for MI5! Not for some poxy local authority policy job where I'd no doubt be fudging performance indicators in relation to overdue library books ..."

"Very amusing, Stan."

"And as for trust? Well, you've certainly been able to trust me to keep my mouth shut about us. Both times round, I mean. That's for sure".

"You see! There you go again!" he replied, picking up his glass. "This isn't about the past. This is about now. Going forward. Look," he added, taking several gulps of his drink, "this is going to be a win-win situation for everyone."

"Oh, God, no, Shaun. No. And to hear you coming out with management-speak like that! You used to detest that kind of crap!" I heard a hard edge of air escape from his mouth as he exhaled. The scent of best bitter. He was getting riled now. Good.

"OK, I promise no more management jargon in the presence of Ms Russell. Because it upsets her sensitivities. Bloody hell, Stan, I shouldn't have to try and convince you about such a lucrative job offer – it makes perfect bloody sense!"

I shrugged and moved my empty glass to one side.

"And Stan, to set the record straight, if it makes you feel more comfortable about all of this. I don't fancy you any more. I don't know what you've done to yourself these days, but I actually find you physically repulsive. There. I've said it."

I glowered at him. He drained his glass and put it back down, grinning. Wiped his mouth with the back of his hand, then stabbed his finger at me.

I noticed that Shaun didn't wear a wedding ring. Jess would be the sort that didn't mind. Probably thought that only the married female should have to display the symbol of possession; of property, even. But what would I know? Never met the woman.

"And I'm a crap liar when it comes to you," said Shaun. "Always have been. But if we have to pretend that you remind me of the Elephant Woman in order for you to consider this, so be it."

"Great. You can put that bit in the employment contract then. 'Rachael Russell will be treated like the Elephant Woman and hidden away, as she always was in the past.'"

"Jesus wept!" Shaun muttered. I stood up to go. He followed me out of the door.

Back into the lunchtime sunshine, enhanced by the yellow tinge of carbon monoxide – courtesy of the A6 – we walked back towards the women's centre. I tried to retain some semblance of politeness, making small talk and asking Shaun if he was enjoying his new job.

"Love it. Especially the fact that I've got Martyn Pointer and New Banks delivering the housing contract for us. Having them dancing to my tune. Good fun, that."

I declined to comment.

"But between you and me, things are going to be changing pretty soon. Kath Casey as leader of the council has the biggest say over who gets to step into Roger Wheelan's shoes when he retires as the chief exec in a few months time. And apparently I'm her number one favourite for the post."

"Really? Even though you've only been with Medlock for just a couple of months? Well. That's nice," My voice sounding as flat as it could ever be. Singularly unimpressed.

By now we had yet again subconsciously taken the route through the Secret Glade.

"Yeah, well. I'm telling you, I could do the chief exec's job in my sleep. Roger couldn't run a piss-up in a brewery. I'll sort the place out, all right."

The man was unbelievable. His ego was growing to monstrous proportions. Or had he always been like this? Were the scales finally falling from my eyes?

I turned to him and stopped walking, shaking my head.

"Shaun, I'm racking my brains to try to dredge up whatever it was that I once saw in you. And do you know what? I'm really struggling here."

WHALLEY RANGE COUNCIL HOUSING OFFICE, SOUTH MANCHESTER. AUGUST 1998

Well-meaning sixth-form teachers and their curriculum texts for English literature A level sadly failed to conjugate any ethereal notions of love and romance into the mind of this teenage girl.

It was hard to buy into all that highbrow literary tosh when you lived on the eastern fringes of the Mancunian urban sprawl. When you spent half of your life trailing to college on the 343 Hyde bus route. When your every weekend was devoted to serving pernickety pensioners on the hot roast chicken counter at Morrisons. And when, by the age of sixteen your most exciting romantic encounter to date had been a drunken snog at the Christmas do with greasy Gavin from the Fishmonger's stall next door.

It was even more difficult to believe in any future grand love affairs hurtling towards you when blessed with parents like Patricia and Terry Stanley. Mum and Dad were ever the cynics.

"You'd best not be thinking that relationships are anything like they say they are in the films," Mum used to trot out to her two daughters, if we ever got onto the subject of boys and romance.

Dad would add his two-penn'orth to the pot. "I beg to bloody differ," he would say. "I reckon relationships are exactly like you see in the films. Every time I watch Psycho *or* The Omen *I think of my own marriage."*

Mum's rapid reply, directed at her girls again: "Yes, well. I discovered the truth about romance for myself on our honeymoon, didn't I? When I saw your dad's false teeth in a glass of water next to the bed. And how silly did I feel? Remembering that just before I waltzed up the aisle, I'd been telling our Marjorie that your dad's best asset was his lovely smile with all those pearly whites ..."

Dad would give it back.

"Not my bloody fault I fell off the tram and landed on me face at the Ashton terminal when I were thirteen and my parents took me to a dodgy dentist. Bloke who came from Aberystwyth, he was. Never trusted the

Welsh since then."

But parental relationship disappointments aside, by the age of twenty-three I had managed to amass sufficient romantic and sexual encounters in order to consider myself to be a young adult woman, now quite au fait with the art of grown-up relationships.

Still, by that age, on the grand scale of things I was unimpressed by the hearts and flowers stuff. Because the main thrust of lust in my life was entirely directed at my chosen career.

Housing.

But not just any old housing. Not your high-street estate agency stuff. Not your getting rich through renovation side of things. No. I fell, hook, line and sinker, for social housing. The properties formerly known as 'shitty council estates'. This was the profession that managed to get my juices a-flowing. And here was a vocation with hideously strong similarities to working for the police or serving in the armed forces.

Most days, I certainly saw the military analogies on the estates. During my first week at Whalley Range I witnessed a couple of seven-year-old boys tinkering with some spare concrete sewer pipes that had been left behind after recent road works. It was a couple of weeks before Bonfire Night and the kids had set the pipes up on bricks, creating a pair of rocket-launchers to aim fireworks at elderly ladies who were trundling to and from the local shops. Mocked-up council-estate mortar attacks on the grey-haired enemy definitely fell into your anti-social behaviour category of course, but in some regards it was quite an ingenious little invention, I thought. Almost admirable.

Hanging around on social-housing estates and trying to evict drug dealers meant that the work often possessed a dangerously attractive edginess for some of us housing professionals. But there were plenty more of the more tedious aspects of anti-social behaviour to deal with ('The neighbours are poisoning my plants/dog/toddler', 'The tap water has funny mould in it and it tastes like Blue Stilton'). Not exactly glamorous work, but the vast majority of our residents were decent, honest folk who all too often suffered from societal postcode prejudice.

So with feet placed firmly on the ground (while trying to avoid the dog shit) it took me a while to cotton on to The Subtext. Something was rumbling just beneath the surface.

To begin with, Shaun Elliot was just another name. Just one of a dozen unfamiliar colleagues I had to meet and greet at my new workplace. I was one of the more junior members of staff at the Whalley Range housing office. Shaun was the deputy manager. Five years older than me. Clearly clever. Probably a bit posher, too, because he was from Harrogate or somewhere a bit up-itself like that.

I wasn't initially attracted to him at all. I preferred the long-haired, metal-head, biker types. So with his number-two haircut and his shirt and his tie, he definitely didn't look like my type. And over my twenty-three years I had mastered the art of screening out any uncomfortable feelings that did not compute. So there were no big fanfares or overtures when Linda Beveridge (who had taken it upon herself to mother me) first introduced me to Shaun. Simply a quick handshake and a 'Shaun – this is Rachael Stanley, our new housing assistant. Do be nice to her." And then a gruff "All right?" from Shaun. Always full of the airs and graces.

Shaun was a giant. But he bore his height formidably. No stooping or hunching in the manner that some of the more self-conscious Goliaths in the world tend to adopt. Shaun Elliot was not afraid to use his height. His eyes were just as unnerving as his size. Such a deep shade of brown that they appeared to be pupilless. Framed by thick-set brows that all too often glowered at people, even when he was trying to be friendly. Dark features and dark skin. Maybe some Mediterranean blood? But when he opened his mouth, it was hardly Latino. A strong Yorkshire accent. Shaun was one of the many tykes who had defected from that side of the Pennines for Manchester University and a mistaken belief that life might somehow prove to be more sophisticated in the land made famous by The Smiths and New Order.

"So, you've been here a week already then?" he asked me as he whacked the top of his VDU screen, shaking up particles of dust that glimmered in the fluorescent strip of the office light. I swallowed a sneeze and pointed to his desk.

"Yes. Sorry, though – I've had to put zillions of affidavits in your in-tray. Not a very nice welcome back for you."

"No. But more exciting than a week-long training course on equal opportunities. Complete insult to anyone's intelligence. Total waste of time ..."

Was he trying to provoke the new recruit into a senseless debate on equal opportunities? A sardonic smile played around his lips as he swatted the screen again. Just a wavy yellow line on a green background.

Our first conversation was interrupted by shouting from downstairs. Yelling in the reception was pretty routine in our office, but it was usually the tenant bollocking the staff, rather than the other way round. This time we could hear Eric's – our area manager's – voice reverberating up through the floorboards. It turned out that he was having a go at Jed Crowley, one of the nastier residents on the estate. Pretty bolshy of him, really, as Crowley had had many a stay at Strangeways and had a list of henchmen as long as your arm.

Eric stomped back upstairs and into Shaun's office.

"I'm sick of him and his bloody scumbag lot! Bunch of bastards! They're ruining this estate!"

Eric noticed me – new girl – hovering on the sidelines and shook his head.

"'Scuse my French. Rachael, love. But they drive you to it ..." Eric was a cool character and rarely lost his temper, but when he did, we all knew about it. Even Jed Crowley left the office pretty damned quick that morning, after his encounter with Eric.

A couple of days later, my lunch break coincided with Shaun's. Our office had been converted from two council houses – knocked through – in order to provide a presence on the estate. We had a small kitchen downstairs. It overlooked the back garden. No flowers, decking or bird tables, however. The back yard was a stark strip of mud where staff only ventured for a quick smoke or to disinfect themselves. In fact, at the time when the non-event (otherwise known as The Kitchen Non-Incident) occurred between me and Shaun, Stinky Dave the technical officer was hopping about in the garden. De-lousing himself after a visit to a flea-riddled abandoned property in Fallowfield. I popped the kettle on and could hear his spray can. Hoping to God that he wouldn't wander through the back door and into the kitchen area in his undies.

I parked my bum at the crappy formica table and bit into my ham butty, leafing through The Guardian. *Usually I shared my lunch break with one of the other housing officers – Jake Bamber or Linda – but today, Shaun mooched into the kitchen. He was wearing his navy-blue council coat and had been out onto the estate, to the local sandwich shop. Tossing his paper-bagged purchase onto the table next to me (his favourite, 'cheese salad, no onions, loads of salad cream')*

"Mind if I join you?"

I shook my head and halved the annoyingly large newspaper in order to make some room for him at the tiny table. We made a bit of small talk. Shaun asking me about my postgraduate evening course. Me enquiring about his house-hunting in Chorlton-cum-Hardy and being told, "We're still looking. Prices are coming down a bit, but it's by far the most expensive part of the area. Still, all our mates are in Chorlton and we wouldn't want to live anywhere else in bloody Manchester. The rest of the place is a shithole. No offence, like."

After a few minutes, the conversation petered out. Shaun borrowed the sports section and I tried to focus on the rest of the newspaper. But then an overbearing feeling of claustrophobia seemed to descend upon me. A panic and a need to be somewhere else – anywhere else other than in the poky little kitchen with this Shaun bloke. I stood up suddenly, squashed the rest of my sandwich into a ball and lobbed it into the kitchen bin. Shaun looked up at me, eyebrows raised.

"Crap butty?"

"No. I just forgot. I need some tights. I snagged these. Got to get to the shops, quick."

Looking back, this was a strange and a convoluted excuse to pluck out of thin air. But Shaun nodded slowly, carried on chewing and reading the newspaper. Perhaps he was used to strange female whims. I didn't leave the office to purchase a pack of Pretty Polly, however. I sat in my car, feeling oddly confused. And hungry. And having to listen to Manchester Piccadilly Radio because Radio 4 had gone AWOL for some reason. It wasn't very nice.

The Kitchen Non-Incident only made sense to me some time later. Nearly three years later. This was the length of time that Shaun and Rachael: Round One took to run. Throughout Shaun and Jess splitting up (with her never being told why) and beyond them getting back together. We still continued with it. The inability to stay away from each other. The veneration of one another's bodies, followed by post-coital slump and black despair as Shaun had to sneak out, under the cover of darkness. The new resolve every day. (For God's sake, Rachael, this is doing no one any good!) But then, the agonies of withdrawal.

We were hardcore addicts.

And all this had been kindled during a few minutes of sitting in close proximity to each other. Regaled by the hiss of Stinky Dave's spray can outside as he engaged in flea extermination. And accompanied by greasy squirls of salad cream adorning our Guardian tablecloth.

Shaun and Rachael were simply a cocktail of phenylethylamine, serotonin and dopamine. Straightforward biological and chemical attraction. And reaction (albeit to an extreme degree). Yes, my English literature A-level teacher might have preferred to read about it in more highfaluting literary frills. But at the end of the day, this stuff was as straightforward as a couple of doggies sniffing each other's bottoms.

Over the next few weeks I spent more time with Shaun, thanks to Eric who was a great believer in new recruits 'shadowing' other, more experienced team members. We got on well and we shared the same sense of humour. After a couple of days Shaun took it upon himself to change my name. He did this with other members of staff. Stinky Dave, the technical officer, whose surname was Digbeth, became 'Diggers' (when we weren't calling him Stinky Dave behind his back, that is). The lettings assistant, whose surname was Tidmarsh, was 'Tiddy'. Martyn Pointer was 'Pointless' (of course), Jake Bamber was 'Bamber-boy'. And Shaun derived 'Stan' from my surname, Stanley.

I told Shaun that creating nicknames out of people's surnames was a sign of an archaic, male-dominated upbringing and an aspiration to be upper-class. I said that no doubt his schooling in well-to-do Ilkley or Harrogate or wherever he lived as a kid had been at a well-posh grammar school. I also pointed out that he never referred to Jason, our handyman as anything other than 'Jason'. I told Shaun that he should at least be consistent and not feel at all embarrassed about booming "Mycock!" across the office. (Jason's surname often threw a curveball for many Whalley Range residents when they demanded to know what his last name was.)

Shaun had responded, "All right, smart-arse. So how did you refer to each other at your Manky comprehensive, then? Or did you just settle for your prisoner numbers?"

I told him that in deepest, darkest rough-as-a-bear's-arse Manchester, we preferred to be more lyrical. No silly abbreviations. We opted for alliteration. Meaning that he would have been 'Shaun the Shithead'.

A name that suited him down to the ground, I said.

"And," I added, "I've just realised that you only really christen the men in this office with your nicknames. Why not, say ... Linda Beveridge?"

"'Cause I can only think of the word 'Beaver' in relation to the word 'Beveridge'. And there's no way I want to associate that word with Linda. I can cope with 'Annoying as Fuck Linda'. But I can't be doing with thinking about her and beavers."

"Right. Well, it just struck me that I'm the only woman in this office who's undergone a name-change. Should I feel privileged? Should I be turning cartwheels? Does this mean I'm one of the lads?"

He had replied, "Dunno. Don't care. Anyway, 'Stan' suits you miles better than Rachael. Rachael's a girly name. Especially with the poncey 'a' in the middle of it. Yeah. You're more of a 'Stan', I reckon.")

Shaun had this knack of deciding that he knew best. Even when it came down to imposing a new identity on people.

ROBIN'S WYKE PUB, WADSWORTH MOORS, HAWORTH, WEST YORKSHIRE. DECEMBER 1998.

The wind whipped my hair back, wrapping it around my face and knocking the breath out of my chest. God, but it was cold. I rapped hard on the black, solid oak door. Its paint was peeling and small dark flecks adhered themselves to my knuckles. I tried to turn the brass knob, but it was more decorative than functional. No doorbell. No opening-time signage. Just the usual brewery notice above the door with the proprietor's details. I scurried back again, but the gale was so violent at this end of the car park that it almost knocked me off-balance, whirling my long hair across my eyes, into my mouth. I tried to spit the strands back out, but then stumbled into a deep puddle. Water seeped in through one of my shoes. Back at Shaun's car I flung the door open and collapsed onto the passenger seat, gasping.

"It's horrendous out there – and the door is locked! Seems odd. A pub offering bed and breakfast and not being open after four o'clock in the afternoon."

The Robin's Wyke had advertised a reasonable rate and a cosy, Yorkshire welcome with home-made food and a friendly local atmosphere. Shaun picked up the B & B leaflet, and scowled at it.

"I've never understood what 'home-made' food means. I mean, what's the definition of a 'home' in this context? 'Cause they'll call it 'home cooked' in a pub, in a restaurant ... in a café, for Christ's sake. None of those are someone's home! Bloody stupid."

"I can't get a signal up here to call them," I complained. "Can you?"

He looked at his phone and shook his head. Nah.

"It's freezing! Can you put the heating on?"

"Not unless I keep the engine running. And that's a waste of petrol, that is ..."

"Yorkshire tightwad!"

"So, Stan. Nothing for it but to stay here a bit until they open. Keep ourselves warm, eh?" He put the leaflet down and moved over to me. Taking a handful of my now bedraggled hair and pulling it towards him. He kissed me, softly at first, and very soon his hands were inside my coat. I was shivering from the cold and from the trepidation. In no time at all the car windows had completely steamed up. The wind howled across the moors and over the pub car park. It rocked the car viciously every couple of minutes. Shaun's watch buzzed us out of the stupor of new passion. Five o'clock. He muttered to himself;

"Look. This is bloody crazy. We're snogging in a car like a pair of teenagers. I'm going to be thirty next year. I need my little luxuries in life. Like a bed. I'll go and try."

The rain was slashing at the car in horizontal stabs. It was almost pitch black outside now. I had to flick on the interior light to check my face in the mirror. Chin and cheeks were glowing like a cherry. Red raw from Shaun's stubble. I quickly grabbed my make-up bag and added a dab of concealer. It would have to do.

A few seconds later and Shaun was back at the car.

"It's open. I'll get the bags." We trooped into the pub's hallway and were met by the landlord. A chap with a wire-wool comb-over, who peered at us over wonky reading glasses.

"Were it you two? Sat in your car. In the car park for ages?"

"Yes," I replied, swiping the water off my coat. "We couldn't get anyone to answer the front door."

"Ah, well. The entrance for the B & B'ers is at the back, yer see ..."

We followed him upstairs. The room was ill-matched, chintzy and there was no sign of an IKEA flatpack ensemble anywhere. I was happy. And it was warm. Then he left us, calling over his shoulder,

"Food from six. Stop serving it at eight-thirty."

Shaun closed the door. Locked it.

"Talk about embarrassing!" I said, as I dropped my handbag onto the floor. "It never occurred to me to try the back of the pub."

Shaun dumped our overnight bags into the corner of the room.

"Well, he's the one who should be embarrassed. He must have known we wanted to come in the pub. He should have come and knocked on the window to tell us."

I laughed.

"I don't think so, somehow. We might have been just a random couple who happened to be using his car park for a bit of friskiness. Then he would have looked like a right old perv. Knocking on car windows."

Shaun had escaped into the bathroom "Nice little en suite. A corner bath and a shower. Shame about the wallpaper, but you can't complain for twenty-eight quid each, can you?"

I wandered into the bathroom, too.

"They've got a bit of a mould problem," I noted, looking at the window sill, "but it's condensation rather than damp. Look – you can tell

by way that the —"

"Oi! Stan! Stop it! We're not at work now." He pulled me back through the doorway. "You don't need to try to impress me with your recently acquired postgraduate knowledge of damp versus condensation." He kissed me on the mouth, and moved his hands down and onto my backside, making circular, massaging movements. But I broke away.

"Sorry, but my socks are soaking," I mumbled. "And I'm frozen to the bone."

He looked around the room.

"Right. Always the sign of a half-decent establishment. The mini kettle."

Five minutes later I was lying on the floor with my bare feet propped against the radiator, trying to warm them up a bit. My toes had gradually begun to thaw and the hot cup of tea was doing its job. But my heart was skittering. Nineteen to the dozen. The wind had picked up again, whipped into a whorl down in the Worth Valley, and was now hurtling across the Wadsworth moors. It was pitch black outside, even though it had only just gone 5.30 p.m.

This was the very same moor that my English literature sixth-form teacher had brought our class to see on a day trip to Haworth. Telling us all about Heathcliff and Cathy: two characters cursed with a wild sexual recklessness that tainted their own lives, as well as those of others. "An obsessive and brutal affair," she said. Almost demonic in its darkness and despair. "How had Reverend Brontë's virginal daughter managed to summon up such monstrous creations?" she wondered. (I reckoned that Emily had been having a sneaky pop at Branwell's opium, when he buggered off down to the Black Bull in Haworth of an evening.)

"Did you realise Shaun, when you booked this place, that it's right on the edge of Haworth? Wuthering Heights *is one of my favourite books, actually. Have you read it?"*

"Nah. Saw a film version of it, though. Not my kind of thing. Bit dull."

Toes walked up the radiator. Down the radiator.

Shaun had flicked the TV on and had sprawled himself across the double bed. Arguing with Oprah Winfrey (only Shaun could do that). Oprah wouldn't be drawn into a debate with him, however, so he moved over to the edge of the bed, peering over at me.

"Art tha going to stay down thee'er all day, lass?"

I stretched my legs out against the radiator, called back: "Oh, please. Don't act the Yorkshire bit of rough just because we've crossed the border from Manchester. We all know you're not from the West Riding. You're from the posh Harrogate side."

"Tha'art avoiding the subject, wench. And anyway, I'm from Ilkley. And Ilkley isn't as well-heeled as you might think. Ilkley's got its own problems."

"Yeah. When they run out of fruit scones at Betty's Tea Rooms ... I bet it's like a riot at Strangeways!"

He reached down from the bed and traced his forefinger from the tip of my toe and up to my calf.

"You've got such sexy ankles." But then he looked away, smiling. The rain was still beating against the window. Shocked, irregular pulses.

"I can't believe I just said that to you, Stan. I sound like Victorian Dad. You know. The character in 'Viz.*"*

"I know. So is Viz *as highbrow as your reading matter gets, Shaun? What a waste of a nice, grammar-school education."*

"Yeah, well, that's what my mum would say if she saw me with a slapper like you, from east Manchester."

"Shut up," I reached up. He hoisted me up and onto the bed beside him.

Mouth, neck, earlobes, licking skin. The occasional moan; sweat and saliva. Teeth clashing and too much frenetic action elsewhere to engage in the usual Shaun and Rachael banter. No verbal stuff. Never in bed.

Only one tiny moment of awkwardness, when we remembered to do the sensible thing. A bit of fumbling about in bags, but then back on the bed. Shaun half-joking, "Christ, I can't bloody do this; I haven't used one of these in ages." But lust, the sense of urgency, cancelled out any iota of shyness. There was never any embarrassment again after that. About anything.

And no afterwards. No afterglow. Every time one of us thought that maybe we should rest at this point, the other would begin the slow dance of exploration again.

In nearly three years of encounters after that very first time on the edge of the moors – the time of priming - we only ever managed to catch some twenty or thirty minutes' sleep whenever we shared a bed.

("Sounds like a sex-binge to me," said Kate, when I once confessed how it always was with Shaun and when I asked her whether she thought that this was normal. "Sorry, Rach, but that does sound a bit weird. Houston – I think we have a problem.")

Two hours after that first time together, we took a five minute break. I curled against his chest feeling the texture of his skin, its soft oils against my cheek. He stroked my ear and trailed his finger over my eyebrow. We could talk again now. Shaun spoke first. A dark mutter.

"I've honestly never experienced anything like that before."

The seriousness in his voice made me look up at him. His brow was furrowed. The wind was still lashing jealously against the window, over the bruised moors.

"Me neither. But at least I'm not frowning," I nipped the top of his arm, gently. "You're always frowning, you are."

"Oh, no. I'm not complaining, like." He moved suddenly. Rearranged himself so that I now lay under the crook of his arm. "I'm just thinking. About what I've been missing out on all of these years."

I didn't say anything.

"Because things with Jess have been pretty crap recently. Not just how we get on. But sex, I mean. There's just no comparison with ... with this. But – oh, shit. What am I on about this for? Come here." He pulled my mouth to his again. And we carried on.

An hour later, a knock at the door interrupted us. We were at the other end of the bed now, me pinning Shaun down.

The landlord's wheedling voice. "Just a re-mihn-der! We stop serving t'food at eight-thirty and we're only ten minutes off that now."

"All right, sorry! We're just coming!" Shaun yelled.

I laughed into a pillowcase, giving him a smothered, "Fnar fnar ... you and your Viz *..."*

The pub quietened as we entered. The landlord eyeballed us over his cock-eyed specs. We were the only guests booked there for a freezing cold and wild autumnal night in November 2001. I hoped that the Robin's Wyke pub was as ancient as it claimed to be and that the walls were as sturdy as they looked, after all the bedroom shenanigans. We ordered our food and then found the jukebox, sniggering over the dated music choices. I plumped for the heavy metal. Shaun went for Crowded House.

"Thought you were a biker, Shaun? But your music taste is so bland. Bet you like Joy Division too, don't you? Elevator music for middle-class university graduates."

"Yeah, well, I do like my bikes, but at least I follow my politics with my music. I mean, I don't recall Guns n' Roses ever doing any favours for women's rights..."

I couldn't stop drinking him in, that first evening. His face, his body, his slow but fluid mannerisms. The taste and buzz of him still lingering in my mouth and on my skin even before the hum of the wine that we had ordered began to kick in. I reached over and kissed the bump on his nose. At first, the broken nose had made me wonder if Shaun had been headbutted by one of the Jed Crowley types in Longsight, but it turned out that it had been the result of a rather aggressive grammar-school rugby match. I should have known. Not many of the locals on our estates possessed the height necessary to nut Shaun one.

The tap room was dark, the walls leaching with centuries of tobacco smoke. I wasn't a smoker in those days. That came after. So I sniffed the glass of wine in order to take away the scent of ciggies and ale. We were sharing the pub with about ten others. All locals, nursing their pints and enjoying a game of darts as they sheltered from the battering gale outside. The food arrived and it took Shaun just a couple of minutes to devour it ("I'm bloody ravenous. After all that ...") And then he leaned over to me across the little table as I battled with a rubbery lasagne.

"Hurry up. I want to get you back upstairs. Finish where we left off before the Perv of Robin's Wyke interrupted us. Here. Let me help."

He leaned forward, guiding my forkful away from my mouth and to his, so that I was feeding him. He took the food off the end of the fork with his teeth and swallowed it slowly. His eyes fixed on mine. The edge of his tongue flicking first from his top lip and then to the bottom. I breathed in, filling my lungs with ... whatever this invisible intoxication was.

My appetite had vanished. I dropped the fork back onto the plate. The rattle of cutlery caused a short man aiming at the dartboard to pause and to look over at us. He hoisted droopy trousers further up his waist.

"Get a move on, Gary!" his mates told him. Gary sniffed and resumed his aim. Shaun glanced at the group and whispered, "Can't you see what you're doing to us all here? All these blokes staring at you? I'm getting off knowing that everyone in this room is looking at me. Thinking that I'm the luckiest bastard going."

He was being sweet. In a Shaun sort of way. I told him so.

"I'm not being bloody sweet, Stan. I'm being honest. The blokes over there – they all want to shag your brains out."

I glanced over. Two of them were gawping at Gary's rather pathetic score on the dartboard. The third was examining a wet patch where he had just spilled Guinness onto his Leeds United shirt. The fourth was picking his nose. None of them looked particularly overcome with lust at my own wee feminine form. I tried to point this out.

"Sorry, Shaun, but I think you're living in a parallel universe to the rest of us. I wondered why your eyes are a bit freaky, like an alien's ..."

He dismissed my words, exasperated.

"That's the thing with you, Stan. You don't see it. You once spent an entire twenty minutes waggling your arse at me in the office. You were searching through a load of old house files on the floor of my room,

remember? And I was trying to draft eviction notices. You've no idea how difficult it was, controlling myself."

"Oh, poor Shaun. It's so tough being a man, isn't it?"

"Don't give me the feminist diatribe. It is bloody hard. In every sense of the word. And a lot of women would have been down there, totally aware of the effect they were having on me, but no, not you."

"I can't eat any of this any more," I broke off. He was making me laugh. But turning me on, too. "Let's go back to bed, you weirdo," I said. "Come on."

Oh, Rachael. Did you really buy into all that?

Chapter 13

HERA IS A RIGHT COW

Shaun had stopped walking, too. We were standing next to one of the densest and darkest clods of rhododendron bushes at the far end of the Secret Glade. Stunning when in full bloom. But I still retained a childhood fear of such hulking mounds of horticulture. My sister used to tell me that they were inhabited by scary tramp sorts who would flash their todgers at you if you weren't careful.

Shaun was pretending to look puzzled at my 'what did I ever see in you?' statement. He flicked his head towards the gothic town hall, which loomed as our backdrop behind the perimeter of the park.

"I don't see why I should apologise for having a bit of self-confidence. And I don't get why you've got such a downer on me these days."

My anger piqued. Reaching flashpoint.

"For crying out loud, Shaun! OK, let's cut to the chase. Last time. Shaun and Rachael, Round Two. You lied to me, Shaun. You might say that it was lying by omission. But it was still a barefaced, twatty lie."

He didn't reply.

"Right. There we were. I've been newly widowed. And suddenly, we're back to the old days. Doing the car-park thing. And Idiot here has no idea that while this is going on, you and Jess are planning a wedding. So, I end up finding out about it through the grapevine. The day after an encounter with you in the Arndale car park. Which happened to be just over two weeks *after* you got married. And when we were in the car, you told me that you'd got your tan at the weekend at Bolton Abbey. Not from your honeymoon in frigging Fiji!"

And thank God for that housing-entwined grapevine. Linda Beveridge and her big gob. I'd bumped into her at Sainsbury's in Medlock and she'd told me, "And guess what else? I've just heart that Shaun Elliot's finally done the right thing by his girlfriend after all these years! Proper church wedding – over in Yorkshire!" Then, "and apparently, the little tinker didn't let anyone at work know about it. But then, Shaun always hated a fuss, didn't he?"

Yes. The horror of hearing this little revelation in the frozen-vegetable aisles knocked me out of my grief-lust stupor. Yanked me back to my senses.

Silence. A subtle shrug from Shaun.

"So. Get me! Call me oversensitive and all that … call me Ms Fussy-Knickers. But yeah. I'm still well pissed off about that, Shaun. And you stand here now, with your usual incapacity for understanding the emotions of most normal people, wondering why on earth I wouldn't return your phone calls or emails. Why I was no longer the perfectly reasonable and nice Rachael that I'd always been before …"

I broke off for a second or two. Shaun's hands were in his pockets. Scrabbling for words. *You won't find them in your bloody pockets, Shaun.*

"And even then, you hardly persisted in tracking me down to apologise. You know where I work. You know where I live. And now, eighteen months later, you're back with your swanky new post at the council and you're offering me a job. Regardless of equal opps codes. And while we're sitting in a clandestine corner of the most blue-collar working men's pub in Medlock? What's that all about? Worried that someone from the town hall might see you with me? Might say something to Jess?"

His shoulders slumped slightly at the mention of her name. He kicked at an empty drinks can that some scruffy sod had dropped onto the overgrown path. The word 'Jess' had had its desired, magical effect. His demeanour moving from Mr Cocksure to Mr Cockless. But he wasn't giving up.

"I understand that you're upset, but …" Shaun's attempt at assertive communication with a ranting female was laughable. It was ridiculous. Shaun Elliot had never been one for the management jargon. Until now.

I sniggered, without any real humour, and caught myself standing with my hands on my hips.

Adam used to call it my Fishwife stance. 'A Rachael speciality'. I would always reply, 'Yeah, well. So maybe I married a guppy.'

I quickly put my hands down, moved them away and carried on.

"So let's have it out for once. Don't you ever feel bad about us? Don't you ever feel the odd pang of guilt?"

"Come on. You know I do. Did."

"So why do you carry on with it? With …"

"With what?" He was frowning at me now. With his best Bruce Willis expression. I knew that little trick oh so well. This meant that Shaun was either making a pitiful attempt at acting. Or that was he planning to blow someone up.

"With behaving as though something is still going on between us. It's been eighteen months, Shaun."

He sighed and folded his arms.

"I was just. I can't ..."

He glanced up at the sky. The brightness of the noontime sun rendered the pupils in his dark eyes to pin pricks. I had once told him that he reminded me of a big sexy alien with those eyes. Now I just wished that someone would beam me up, Scotty and take me away from the git.

I waited.

"All right, Stan. It's difficult to talk to you as 'just a colleague'. After everything that happened. I mean – things were so mad between us, weren't they? So … different. Not that I regret it or anything. Even … with the complications."

He unfolded his arms. Gesticulated with his right hand. Trying to explain himself to an imbecile. I kept quiet. Wanting to hear what he had to say. When it came to the subject of 'us', we had never ventured to this level of conversation before; the pheromones had always done the talking. And after hearing the marital headlines, I hadn't stayed around to chat.

"So I'm not sure I would change things if I could," he continued. "Both times round, I mean. Well – the first time – way back when you and I first met, it was a bit traumatic for Jess with me wanting a break. But we'd been together a while then – since university – so 'cause she never knew about you … she just thought it was the seven year itch thing. And the second time round, after … after …"

(Say his name, Shaun – say his name. I dare you to say his name.)

"Well. It was just … complicated. Again. Jess never found out then, either."

Unbelievable. The 'complications' that Shaun was referring to meant him and Jess.

This was all about him and Jess.

A person who I'd never met. Someone I didn't wish any harm upon. Certainly, my ambition in life had never been to morph into the kind of person who screwed another woman's bloke. (Many times. Over a combined total of three years and four months.)

No, that element of the whole situation was definitely something that I wasn't proud of.

But, still.

I looked away from him now, towards the Manchester skies. At a 747 creating a wispy, white trail as it arced round on the flight path towards Ringway. At a newly planted sapling next to me, waving tiny fingertip leaves at us. At the brassy blonde hair of the woman sitting with her back to us on the park bench, her child asleep in its buggy. I hadn't noticed her before. She could probably hear every word of our exchange. But by now I was past caring. I caught a whiff of her cigarette. It made me feel nauseous.

Shaun was still blethering on about a certain female saint and martyr.

“Jess is a really good person. I know that. But the thing is. I can't stop myself when I see you. Wondering. What it would be like again. Wanting to ...” he reached out to touch my arm. I jerked it away.

There was a litter bin not far from where we were standing. Overflowing with rubbish. Several wasps were buzzing with excitement around its contents. One of them darted over and began to harass Shaun. Attracted by his citrus-based, expensive designer cologne, no doubt. Another insect joined his yellow-bellied buddy. Not interested in me. A lady who smells of toddler-wipes and Marmite. Not waspishly attractive enough. Even for the wasps, it seems.

I yanked my hair back into a messy ponytail.

“So, that makes it all right, then? That Jess never knew. For God’s sake, Shaun! I feel bad enough for doing the dirty on Jess, even though I’ve never had the joy of meeting her. Nobody deserves that. But you … you were marrying – no, hang on – you *were* married to her, that last time we were together!”

He curled his lip. “I realise that it doesn’t make sense, Stan. I know I’m with Jess for the long-haul and I always promised her that. But …”

But what, Shaun? What, what, what?

“… I still have these incredible feelings for you. Every time I see you it all comes back. What we have – you and me – I’ve never known anything like it. I probably never will again. I’ll be in some old folk’s home … living off the memories of what we’ve always done to each other.”

His eyes locked onto mine and he smiled, knowingly. Expecting me to mirror it back, as I used to do whenever we talked about growing old and contemplating our lust-driven youthful pastimes. But this face was not cracking a muscle.

His voice was becoming louder. He clearly hadn’t noticed the woman and her pushchair either, otherwise he wouldn’t have carried on.

“Stan. Come on. You and me. We’ll always have this … whatever you want to call it – this sex thing. This mad, potent connection stuff going on for us. I’ll always want you.” He scratched the side of his head in frustration.

I wondered whether he had head lice. Or scabies. Probably not. Shaun and Jess didn't have kids. They had a cat called Ozzy, but as yet they hadn't experienced the delights of children. Maybe it was a flea infestation, then...

He interrupted my increasingly bizarre thoughts. "And you'll always want me. I know that."

I tried to keep the shaking, the tremulous fury, out of my voice when I finally answered him.

"No. It's different now, Shaun. Never mind the first time around when I was stupid enough to believe that we might have a normal out-in-the-open relationship at some point. Yeah, forget your *Fatal Attraction* crap. Think about this … about your complete lack of regard for me, the second time round. When I actually knew better. When I'd found my life with Adam. That's what you should be hanging your head in shame about. Because it was *you* who came knocking on my door, in the middle of the night after he had died."

He held his hand up, abruptly.

"Not fair, Stan. You saw me at the funeral with the rest of the crew from the biker club. You said that I should come over some time, meet the kids …"

I narrowed my eyes. No red mist descending, but the blood was pumping hard and fast in my veins. My head was buzzing as angrily as the nearby stinging-things.

A wasp zipped perilously close to Shaun's ear. They could be vicious little devils at the tail end of summer. He tried to knock it away.

"No, Shaun. Get logical about this. Adam wasn't some complete faceless stranger to you. You'd known him through the bike club. You'd had a few beers with him over the years. And yet, when he was killed, you were back and knocking at my front door. A hell of a lot of people would find that to be morally dubious …"

"That's not how it was …"

"No! You were on my doorstep. Trying to get us to return to the good old days. And then … I was the one, stuck at home with two little kids, wondering when our next 'encounter' would take place. I was the one who had to dump the children to meet you in one of your random car parks after work …"

"I didn't …"

"Shut up! It was me who had to lie to my own family, to sneak around to see you when it suited your schedule. And all in case – God forbid – we upset poor Jess and her delicate religious sensibilities! So if you really want to talk about female victimhood here, take a look at the person standing in front of you!"

He shook his head. At me and at the five or six stripy pests now skirting around him.

"Sorry, Rachael, but you were hardly shy in coming forward —"

I cut him off, hissing, "Don't you dare, Shaun! I was zonked out of my head on medication when you first called round! I didn't know what day of the week it was. I was a total mess. So don't you dare start spooning out the old macho 'she wanted it' crap!"

He swatted at the wasps, trying to muster some dignity as he replied.

"Look, I know it was a really difficult time for you. I know that. I'm not saying — "

But I interrupted him.

"So, your need for secrecy is sick, Shaun. Just sick. Both times round it was. You're just a moral coward. A moral sodding coward who couldn't face up to the thought of what your coupled-up luvvie mates in Chorlton-cum-Hardy would think if you and Jess ever split up. Mess with your dinner party arrangements, no doubt."

An unusual, startled look flitted across his face. That twitching muscle at the corner of his left eye. Yes, I'd finally doled out the truth. Time to go.

"So I won't let you shirk the responsibility for what you did to me after Adam's death. Have you never heard of Jung's theories about the closeness between grief and sex? Why cultures all over the world require women to enter purdah? To stay away from forming sexual relationships when bereaved? Have you never read about the biological and social impact of grief?"

A bit intellectual for the middle of a blazing row. But, hey. He deserved it.

I span on my heel and stalked away from him, leaving him to smack wasps about. Hoping that the little buggers would sting him to death.

"No, I haven't!" I heard him call after me.

"Well, then!" I yelled back. "Go and read a fucking book for once. You ignorant bastard!"

I swiped my security pass through the system and headed back into the building, making straight for the toilets. Funny how the loos are a place of sanctuary for millions of female workers across the world. It isn't quite the same for blokes, though. Men hanging around a workplace toilet don't get the same levels of understanding or sympathy. ("Oh, Barry – has she dumped you again? Come here, petal, and give us a hug! Rotten cow! Oooh, they're all the same, aren't they? Here, borrow some of my aftershave and cheer yourself up.")

Yeah, in the old days when life got difficult and men were being complete and utter cads, us girls would have been able to check ourselves into the nearest convent. But all we have on offer to us in the twenty-first century are the ladies' bogs.

I sat in one of the cubicles, knickers down, bum on seat and with a baleful stare at the toilet door. One of the caseworkers had posted up some positive, reinforcing messages for women to peruse as we go about our business. Chirpy reminders like 'No one can make you feel inferior without your consent' and 'I had no shoes and grumbled until I met a man who had no feet'. Adam would have called it "self-help-manual-inspired tosh."

I would have disagreed with him, of course. Thinking along those lines can be helpful. If you're in a receptive mood. But I wasn't up for counting my blessings right there and then. And while, overall, I was very grateful to have my feet still in working order, the sentimental slosh wasn't cutting the mustard with me at that particular moment in time.

No. It would be more helpful if I could leave my own little scribbled message on the toilet door.

'Shaun Elliot is a tosspot.'

And while I'm regressing back to my comprehensive-school days, why not also tag on, 'Mickey C is 100% Fit'?

But what about Adam? He would need to feature in my missive. I'd have to go for the sixth-form approach. Get a bit more poetic;

'Adam. We love you. Where are you ...?'

My vision began to blur. Shit. I was making myself cry now. No, that wouldn't do. I'd have to scribble another bit below it. A bit more Morriseyesque.

'Because your dinner's in the oven, it's burned to a cinder. And you promised me you'd sort out the funny smell coming from the drains ...'

Maybe more Victoria Wood than Morrisey, in the end.

I started to snigger to myself. But I was laughing with – not at – the dead. Adam would have got it, all right.

And anyway, the whole ridiculous thing had reminded me: that drain-like pong was still coming from the kitchen sink every time I switched the washing machine on. Adam might have been my boy, my love, my children's daddy – dab hand at all things techie and motorbike, but he was bloody useless at practical household tasks. Call a plumber, Rachael.

Oh crap, no. Cost a fortune.

Pity-pot session over, I headed for our team meeting. It passed the time, helping me to dismiss the uncomfortable lunch hour with Shaun. By 3 p.m. the meeting had finished and I headed towards the kitchen and the corned beef sandwich that I had been promising myself for several hours. The room was occupied by a handful of women who had just finished a support-group session. Amidst lots of noise and laughter, I was greeted with a sudden and lairy:

"Wooo-hooo!"

Grabbed in a gruff embrace, a big kiss was planted on my forehead and I was nearly overcome by a heady scent of perfume and fruity chewing gum. A triumphant voice:

"This is her what saved my frigging life on Saturday! Bless yer little cotton socks!"

It was Dawn. Dawn with high spirits and infectious enthusiasm. Despite the black eye and the swollen lip, she wasn't looking too bad. Poppy-Rose was there too, cruising between the knees of the other women, a mushed-up biscuit clenched in one tiny fist, which she was attempting to rub into the fishnet tights of the child-unfriendly Jade. They were all smirking though – enjoying the sight of me being roughed up by the incorrigible Dawn. Bev, who came to the centre most days of the week, already seemed to know my buoyant attacker and called out from the other side of the room.

"Christ, Dawn! I didn't think you meant Rachael! I thought you meant some other volunteer from here. Rachael runs this bleedin' place! What were you doin' draggin' her away from her kids, of a weekend?"

Dawn shook her hair and her oversized hooped earrings, giving me another big smacker on the cheek and then winced. Her lip still hurt. I fought the urge to wipe my face. I've always been funny about being kissed without inviting it.

"Well. I didn't bloody know who she was! She didn't have no kids with her then, did she? Just some posh vicar." A brilliant smile.

"But anyway. I just wanted to come over here and say thanks for everything. I haven't seen that total nobhead since Saturday now. Brenda's good at keepin' him away."

Dawn was buzzing. As opposed to the effect of drugs (which always had to be considered) she was probably riding on a high of being around other women who had gone through similar experiences. She gave me a bone-crushing hug again and tousled my hair.

"Wow! So you're the big boss, then? Ha! I got lucky, did I? You turning up with yer swanky God-freak? Anyways, I couldn't be bothered with waiting for you to call back. So I thought I'd get the bus over and see if you can get me a transfer off of Brindleford as well as seein' me sister at the same time. Can't believe I've just bumped into Bev, here!

She lives next door to our Debs!"

Bev nodded. "An' she's all right, your Debs is. Don't know how she manages to have so many blokes on the go, though. You can see one leaving the back door while she's got another hanging round at the front. Dunno where she gets the energy from, what with four kids an' all. Still. She does all right by 'em. Always turned out nicely, they are."

Dawn winked at Bev. "Yeah – she's a good 'un, is my big sis. Looks out for me. Hates Vinnie's guts. So, yeah," she turned back to me now. "I wanna get transferred off Brindleford and over 'ere. Nearer to Debs. An' me mum is only down the road in Levenshulme, too. So can you help us with that?"

I smiled wanly, not wanting to give her any false hopes.

"It's not always that straightforward, Dawn. First off – it's your current landlord and your new one who'll need persuading. There'll be various criteria you'll need to have met in order to get fast-tracked for a transfer. And if you want to go to a New Banks home in Medlock here, they'll have to take into account things like … if you've got any rent arrears, if you've ever damaged the property, had any other problems during the tenancy on Brindleford."

I stopped for a minute, remembering what Michael had told me about the bailiffs. Or whoever the men who made off with the entire contents of the house were.

She answered me with, "Well, I've never been in debt in me life."

(Lucky you Dawn, lucky you. There was a day not so long ago when I could have said that, too.)

"Benefit pays us full rent. Always has. And the only problems we've ever had were through that nobhead. Nowt to do with me. All him and his bastard family. Plus, I never had him put on the tenancy with me. Just in my name. That'll 'elp, won't it?"

"Usually. Normally a joint tenancy is the best option for partners, but not where there's violence or abuse going on."

"So, d'you reckon we've got a chance then? Getting over near Debs and Bev 'ere?"

"You'd probably have a better chance if you reported it to the police. What Vinnie did to you, I mean. If New Banks think they're going to be faced with Vinnie hanging around you, they might think twice about letting you have one of their properties."

I knew, of course, from Brenda's earlier phone message, what the answer was to all this. Dawn shook her head.

"Nah. I told the pigs when I saw 'em that I don't wanna report it. I don't wanna be bothered with all that shit. 'Cause if Vin gets another conviction – an' if he reckons it's 'cause of me, it'll just make it worse for us all. See?"

I saw, all right. And I tried not to sigh. But it was back to the same old dilemma.

"I do get what you're saying, Dawn, but I really have to recommend that you have a chat with one of the caseworkers here. About the different kinds of legal action available."

She narrowed her eyes. Was this Rachael woman not listening?

"What? Like an injunction, you mean? No one can friggin' ban Vinnie from stuff. He always goes wherever he wants to —"

I interrupted her.

"Well, there are different types of injunction. Non-molestation orders and occupation orders, for example. And there are different legal paths to think about – civil or criminal law. But, for now, let's just get you sorted out with the right caseworker and then we can..."

Dawn, however, had only one thing on her mind. She flapped her hand at me.

"Yeah, but just getting off Brindleford would sort it out. Movin' to somewhere where he don't know where we are. Makin' it nice and doin' it up. Our own place. Without him."

I tried not to sound exasperated. Dawn was coming out with some of the classic lines. She genuinely thought that a new house, a new road, a new sofa would fix her situation.

"Look, let's book you in with Marsha for an appointment. She can talk you through all of this." I cut her short, not wanting to discuss her personal case details in front of the other women. They might start comparing notes or thinking that I was showing favouritism by helping Dawn out during the weekend.

But more importantly, my stomach was grumbling away. Lunch was desperately needed. I yanked open the fridge door and commenced battle with a tower of diet soups, yoghurts and skimmed milk. Locating my lunch box, I opened it and took a bite of a sandwich, walking towards the door with the intention of tackling an overdue report while scoffing my food at my desk. But Dawn persisted.

"So the vicar. What's the score there, then?"

The group of women looked at me.

"What vicar?" asked Gillian, as she sipped her usual cup of rooibos tea.

I casually chewed my sandwich as I reached the kitchen door, disregarding Dawn. Pretending that I either couldn't hear her or had a gobful of butty.

But Dawn just raised her voice and cooed, "Actually, I thought he weren't bad for a God-botherer. Where's his church, then? He's the sort what might get me havin' a bit of a religious reversion."

I couldn't resist calling back over my shoulder.

"I think you mean 'conversion', Dawn. And somehow, I don't think that that would be a genuine 'I've seen the light' moment."

Dawn was playing to the crowd, though.

"Well, whatever. There aren't many men of the cloth what are half decent. Bet I could get him all hot and bothered under his doggy collar …"

Collective cackling from Dawn's new mates and a "You're as bad as your Debs, you are!"

I ignored them, but Bev's voice was now directed at me. "Hey, Rachael! What kind of butty have you got today?"

Here we go.

"Corned beef," I answered. Taking another mouthful and glancing back at her. Bev folded her arms in disgust.

"Bleugh. Can't be doin' with corned beef. Looks like VD scrapings, it does."

I scowled at her. Bev did this every time she saw me having my lunch. Last week she told me that my tuna mayo and sweetcorn sandwich reminded her of cat puke but without the hairy bits. And on another day, that my coronation chicken resembled "our loo, the mornin' after a take-away from the Brindleford Bismillah".

Back at my desk, I tried to invoke my appetite again. No go. I shoved my lunchbox to one side. Bloody Bev. Still, I was glad of her distraction from Dawn's vicar jibes. I knew that Brenda wasn't one for tongue-wagging and that she would be discreet about Michael's identity. But had Dawn guessed? There were rather too many jokes about the priesthood for my liking. And despite the dippy dramatics and her entanglement with Vinnie, I could tell that she was a sharp one.

The phone on my desk jangled, and on answering it I was met with the lilt of a Blackburn accent. Martyn Pointer. It hadn't taken him long to call. He and Shaun had always been career rivals. Always after some dirt on each other. Both men were polar opposites in terms of their looks. Martyn was short and squat with blonde, but now thinning, hair. And they were also at the extreme ends of the spectrum in terms of their manners. Martyn was skilled at charm and compliments. Shaun saw no need for either. Martyn, though, had a tendency to whine and complain if his enchanting etiquette didn't get him his own way in any given situation. But, like most of my old buddies from the world of housing, he was a good egg.

"All right, Martyn? There must be some reason why the director of New Wan – I mean New Banks – himself is calling me. Anything to do with a certain housing officer called Jake? Something in relation to an old lady … who I am totally and utterly responsible for having transported to the dark side of Manchester on Saturday?"

I heard a pause.

"And good afternoon, Rachael. And how on earth are you, too, this fine day?"

"Sorry, Martyn," I laughed. "It's been a long day … but I thought you might get in touch fairly soon. You really don't need to worry about the thing with Miss Simpson. Didn't Jake tell you that I'm happy being blamed as a far-too-helpful passer-by?"

"Yes, he did. And it's nice to hear that some people we work alongside still have principles, Rachael. Obviously I need to try to anticipate anything that Shaun Elliot and his cronies throw at us about helping poor Miss Simpson out. He's the sort to get all political about paying a few more pennies to help a poorly pensioner. But that's not actually what I'm calling about."

"Oh?"

"Yes. The thing is, New Banks have just been allocated rather a lot of money from the Social Enterprise Loans Coalition. We applied to them over a year ago and, to be honest, I'd totally forgotten about it. So now we've got this funding, which we have to act as agent for, to lend to a couple of local social enterprises as soon as possible. There's no interest rate. It's a marvellous package. And I wondered if you might be the lady to help me spend it?"

"Oh, right." I paused for a second. "Well, it's really nice of you to think of us, Martyn, but we're managing OK for now. We're not one hundred per cent grant reliant, as you know, but no … we don't really need a big loan at this point in time."

(Enough of the debt situation at home, thank you very much.)

"Oh. Shame. It would have been nice working with you again. But seriously, things can't be easy for you guys over there. Given the cutbacks that a lot of the non-statutory services are up against. So don't discount my offer straight away, will you? I do need to get it spent as soon as possible … but I want it to go on something worthy. And Jake tells me you've made some brilliant things happen at Sisters' Space. A chocolate enterprise. Sounds very exciting."

"Well, we think so. But anyway, Martyn. Going back to the Miss Simpson situation. If the council start giving you a bollocking over the Lancaster House thing, you don't need to worry. We're all singing from the same song sheet. And I won't be taking any shit about the fact that I decided to get Miss Simpson to somewhere safe and dry as fast as I could. Only a complete arsehole would say that we should have left her in that frigging awful state while we tried to ring round the B & Bs."

And then I remembered that Martyn was a Jehovah's Witness and that I had always done my best not to swear too much around him. Oh, well. Martyn spent most of his Saturdays wearing a dark suit and trying to persuade innocent householders to read copies of *The Watchtower*, so he was probably used to regularly being told to fuck off.

"Oh, I'm not concerned about that, Rachael. We did the right thing. Even if it doesn't fit with Shaun Elliot's dog-eat-dog view of the world. No – I'm more nervy about allocating this loan. I've got three weeks to sort it. Actually, I was thinking of asking Shaun Elliot to apply for it personally. He only seems to be able to afford a new car every other month. Latest Lexus model at the moment…"

"Yeah. Well twatty, or what?" (Whoops, there I go again.)

Despite always giving off that slight whiff of religious sanctimony, Martyn could never resist a dig at Shaun. But I promised to keep the idea of a loan on the back-burner, and hung up.

At 4.30 p.m. I packed up and made a beeline for home and the other side of the Pennines. As I got into my car, my phone buzzed. A message from Shaun. It read:

"Sorry @ all. S x."

I toyed with the idea of texting him back and giving him the usual Jehovah's Witness send-off. But there were two elements here. Firstly, Shaun never apologised. So this was definitely one for the history books. And secondly, I needed to keep on walking that council funding tightrope for the centre. Had to keep Shaun sweet. So I kept the return message brief.

"4get it. Thx."

Ten seconds later, as I was about to pull out of the car park, another message pinged at me. Shaun could never resist the last word.

'Can't 4get. Always @ x.'

As I headed back down the Levenshulme Road, I puzzled over its meaning. Did it mean 'always about'? Or 'always around X' (love) Or 'always at X' (love)? Whatever. I wasn't going to waste any more brain cells on Shaun today. I pressed 'delete'.

As Kate had said to me on many a previous occasion, Shaun is *such* a shithead.

Chapter 14

THE AGE OF IRON(ING)

"Matthew is utterly shattered, and I'm rather pooped, too."

This was Lydia's description of their respective physical conditions after a long day of Early Years learning curriculums. Looking at their weary faces, I felt the usual squeeze of guilt and that feeling of parental failure because I relied so heavily on nursery and wrap-around after-school care. In truth, though, I didn't have much choice in the matter. I had a mortgage to pay. On my salary alone, thanks to The Great Insurance Screw-Up.

After Adam's death, I had once confessed to Jake Bamber my concerns about all the childcare help I relied on. He had replied:

"C'mon, Rach. Do the wealthy sit there fretting about sending their little brats off to boarding school? No. Capitalism wants your average woman to buy into the crap that only the mother can look after the kids best. And that traps women in a vortex of domesticity and political apathy. It takes a village to raise a child, remember? Anyway, if you're keeping someone in a job by paying them to look after your own snotty-nosed offspring, so that you can have a life yourself, then all the better for everyone, I say."

I had answered, "Bloody hell, Jake. I was only fretting about not being there to wipe my own kids' arses. And someone else teaching them how to write. I wasn't worrying about me single-handedly scuppering the rise of the proletariat!"

But Jake The Trot certainly had a point. This lady would never fall foul of a vortex of domesticity, that was for sure. He'd seen the state of my house. And despite the odd pang of remorse, I had none of the feelings of jealousy that some mothers have of their children's carers. In fact, I had nothing but huge regard for them. Pink Trinny, Matthew's favourite nursery nurse, rolled her eyes when I collected Matthew and he told me, "Mummeh, I only eated six baked beans. 'Cause it were pooey food here today."

Pink Trinny confirmed this (well – the six-bean consumption, not the pooey food). Trinny was a gorgeous black girl with neon-pink hair and an admirably laid-back attitude to childcare. She didn't seem in the slightest bit bothered about his lack of appetite ("Oh, you know Matthew; he'll refuse his favourite things one day, and the next he'll be nicking stuff off everyone else's plates.")

Matthew's tiredness meant that I didn't have to pin him down with my knee as I usually did when strapping him into his car seat. Lydia, however, resorted to exhausted peevishness.

"This car is so rubbish. Why can't we have a cool, black car like everyone else? We never have anything nice, do we, Matthew? And this car smells of Edam. Like stinky old socks."

I ignored her and switched on *The Best of Death Thrash Metal*. One of Adam's favourite albums which perversely (and ironically) always took the edge off the kids' grumpiness.

After a neither healthy nor nutritious tea (recipe: open one can of hot dogs, heat in microwave, slap them on cheap white bread and roll them up in an attempt to create 'hot-dog bun') I herded the kids off to my bedroom. They were being treated with a kiddy-film on the old laptop that I had kept for such occasions. For once, I had decided – just for once – I would get to choose the TV channel myself. The News.

I switched on BBC1. The boys at the Beeb were of the opinion that Michael had managed the Ben Hardy situation extremely well that morning. The programme moved from the studio to the waning sunlight at the tail end of Downing Street; to that Justin Jones, the man with the dodgy spectacles (did he never go home?) It seemed that this would be one of those pointless 'twenty-four-hour news reporting' scenarios, where the presenter would have no news to report but would try to convince viewers to keep watching by hanging around Number Ten with an animated look on his face. So I was about to switch the programme off when Lydia appeared, chiming, "Oh. Boring. Grown-up telly. Well dull. Another yoghurt, if you please, Mother. And Matthew says, 'Bring another basket of your finest!' Although poopy-pants has spilled most of his yoghurt over the duvet …"

Would I never learn? Runny substances, small children, laptops and soft furnishings do not mix. I jabbed my finger at the kitchen, indicating that with her second yoghurt, Lydia would be expected to sit at the table. But a sudden wave of excitement projected itself from the TV. A sleek, black car pulled up just behind the reporter at the gates, stopping for the usual security check. Justin Jones pushed the silly specs back up onto the bridge of his nose, held his fingers to the side of his head as he checked his earpiece and then relayed the information to his viewers.

"And I've just been informed that Michael Chiswick, the communities minister – who caused a bit of a stir this morning with his phraseology – has just arrived behind us, here in Downing Street."

The rest of his words were drowned out by Lydia, who had decided to act as co-commentator.

"Downing Street! Mummy – is that where Downy Duckling lives? That man does look a bit like a duck, doesn't he? A bit of a ropey old duck in glasses, though. One getting ready for the slaughter house! The big chop!"

"Ssssh!" I hissed, as I moved closer to the TV. The car glided through the famous black iron gates and stopped only feet away from the cameras. The journalists began to poke their media implements through the railings, accompanied by calls of, "Mr Chiswick! Mr Chiswick?"

Michael emerged from the car, wearing his business best this time. The Ten Downing Street look.

For the second time that day, a sense of nervous anticipation washed over me. Seeing the man I got naked with at the weekend on our TV screen. Lydia appeared to be excited, too, but for very different reasons.

"Hey – it's that bloke off our fridge! The pirates and princesses man!"

"Ssssh!" I spat again, trying to cancel out small-child inane ramblings. Michael turned back towards the iron railings. Doing the cultivation of the media thing. Our man from the BBC seemed to be flavour of the month, though, because Michael directed his attention at Ol' Four Eyes.

"Justin?"

"Mr Chiswick – is it true that you're here because the prime minister has asked Ben Hardy to resign from his ministerial position?"

Michael flashed his politician non-committal smile. It wasn't quite Tony Blair – less of the fake humility and certainly baring fewer teeth. But I was learning that the TV smile belied how he truly felt. It was different to the grin that I had been exposed to when alone with him– the media beam didn't possess the tiny wrinkle at the corner of the eyes, the crinkles that told me when he was truly amused.

"Well, I've just been asked to pop in for a quick meeting with the prime minister and I'm sure if anything is going to happen, you chaps will be the first to know."

More clamour from the rest of the reporters at the gates.

Now Matthew entered the lounge, walking stiffly. Yoghurt smeared across his cheeks. And in his eyelashes, somehow. With a yoghurt pot wedged on each hand. Matthew's best android-style.

"Look, Mummeh! Ah'm a well-cool Wobot!"

I chose to temporarily ignore the sticky mess, and turned back to the TV. Lydia was paying no attention to the yoghurt-robot-sibling either. She was narrowing her eyes at the TV. Michael was heading towards Number Ten now.

"He definitely is!" She crooned. "The fridge man!

That newspaper clipping on the fridge again. It was embarrassing enough before I'd happened to get jiggy with the fella. Now, somehow, it seemed to be exuding a whiff of immorality. Me parading a weekend-shag while my kids scoffed their Coco Pops of a morning. Must bin the damned thing.

Lydia added, "He must be as nearly as famous as you are, Mummy! But Grandad says that that man is a slimeygit. Whatever that means."

"Please! I'm watching this!" I gritted my teeth, shooting her one of my best evil-red-laser-beams-from-the-eyes glances. Great. Another reminder that Dad hated Michael, his local MP. Mind you, there were few famous people or politicians that Dad did admire. He would probably only approve if I was dating Arthur Scargill. Perhaps Dennis Skinner. Or Spike Milligan. Maybe Harry Seacombe. Gobby firebrands or dead comedians. Strange chap, my dad.

Michael had half-turned, consenting to answer a final question. One that resurrected the juvenile theme of the day's news.

"So you won't be making any more 'boobs' today then, Mr Chiswick?"

Michael paused for a moment and turned back with his work smile again.

"Oh, very droll. You lot need a training course in making half-decent jokes, I think!"

I smirked back at Michael. The bugger had nicked my line.

Then Michael was safely deposited behind the sombre black door of Number Ten. And two messy yoghurt pots were deposited by Matthew on my living-room rug. I didn't smirk at my youngest.

"Boobs, boobs, nice boobies … nice and fat!" chanted Matthew, as he tried to squash the yoghurt pots together before I could reach him.

"What did he just say?" I turned to look at Lydia, incredulous.

"You heard him." Lydia's response was a little bit too sassy for my liking. She proceeded to take the remote control off me and attempted to search for one of the more hideous children's cartoon channels.

"Well, where on earth did he learn that from?"

Lydia shook her head. Disinterested. She twirled the remote control.

"I dunno. He's a boy. He's stupid. You know. And anyway, you daft little spanner," she tried to poke Matthew in his stomach, "it's tits. Not boobies. Don't you know anything?"

"Lydia!" But before I could get any further, Matthew began singing:

"Tits tits tits! Nice and chompy!"

"Oh, thanks a lot, Lydia! I can't believe you just said that!" I yelled. The yoghurt-smeared child decided that he wasn't waiting around for the female-dominated drama and headed off upstairs, chanting "tits" to himself. I rounded on Lydia.

"You do not say words like that!"

Lydia had the grace to look sheepish for once.

Two hours later, both children had been parcelled into bed. It was 8 p.m. and the silence engulfed me. The hour when the Ghost of Non-Adult Companionship began its nightly stalk throughout the house.

A quick calculation: It had now been some twenty-one months and two days since Adam had been killed. Before his death, being on my own had never been a problem. I would have welcomed a weekend alone or just an entire evening simply lying on the settee, reading a book. I was a person perfectly at ease with solitude. But not any more. These days, I yearned for evening conversations. Grown-up chats. About anything that offered a bit more levity than a ten-minute soliloquy as to whether the 'old Daphne' or 'new Daphne' from *Scooby Doo* was much prettier ('as purple suits her better – don't you think so, Matthew?')

My gut reaction to losing Adam was to need my own mum. But something between this mother and daughter had always rankled. A default towards misunderstanding one other. During the first few months after Adam's death, attempts at communication between us had led to rather a few flashpoints. Not helped by the fact that Mum got it into her head that my method of grieving was somewhat abnormal.

One day, about eighteen months ago, I overheard her talking to Dad and her friend Anne, from church. In what she thought were hushed tones (but actually, the people in the end terrace could probably hear).

"I'm just worried that she's not doing the stages properly, Terry ... you know. Shock. Then anger. And, oooh. I can't remember what layer of grief comes next. Is it 'denial'?"

I had seen Mum's latest book at the side of her bed: Grandparents

Amidst Tragedy: Helping Your Adult Children and Grandchildren Live Beyond Bereavement. *The thought of this woman – previously choc-full of common sense – now having to read up on how to help her family touched a raw nerve. I stalked into the kitchen, hands on hips.*

"Well, I'm sorry, Mum, if I'm not doing a good job of ticking your boxes for the stages of grieving. But maybe some of us don't need a bloody book to tell us how to cope with bereavement!"

Anne was nibbling at a raspberry bun. She stopped and blinked. Looked at my dad. My mother felt the need to go into semi-scolding mode.

"I wasn't saying that, Rachael. It's just that when someone has ... when someone has ... I mean, after Adam ..."

"Died!" I offered. "And why do people get so het up about the words? What do they matter? 'Passed away', 'died', 'departed', 'moved to the other side', 'croaked it', 'kicked the bucket' – whatever! Who cares? However you say it, it all just means the same thing. Oh, I'm sure that your new, very evangelical minister would have a nicer turn of phrase. And a cheery outline of what heaven and 'the new earth' will be like for us all. But I can't buy into that crap."

A crumb from the raspberry bun lodged in Anne's throat. My mother whacked her on the back and then tried to say something to me along the lines of "So don't you believe in God any more?" But I cut her short.

"Well, I don't buy into religious brainwashing. So-called followers of God who manipulate human weaknesses, persuading us to put 'faith' into something that, quite frankly, our Matthew and Lydia could have invented between them. No. Sorry. I just think that if you're dead, you're dead. Adam is dead. I don't understand why people can't just say that word! Dead!"

When I finally managed to stomp on the verbal brakes, there was a heavy silence. The two older women stared at me. Both speechless for once. But then a high-pitched voice replied:

"Or what about ... as dead as a donut? Or are you supposed to say 'as dead as a dormouse?' 'Cause can donuts really be dead? And anyway. Do dormouses live in doors?"

The happy-go-lucky reply of my daughter, as she sauntered back into the kitchen. Her grandad's reading glasses perched on her tiny nose and sporting an enormous pair of black Y-fronts on her head ("I'm a nun! I'm Julie Andrews, I am!")

I'm not sure if she knew what we were talking about. She was only five after all. But either way, I knew that she wasn't keen on 'That Anne from Grandma's Church'. So she would have been quite happy to freak the poor woman out.

I glanced over to my dad, who was trying to fix the mantelpiece clock (which Lydia had, for some reason, been shoving pipe cleaners into. Dad looked from me, to my mother, to Anne, and back again. The air sizzled. He yanked another pipe cleaner from the inner workings of the clock, and casually commented, "Well, love, that sounded like our Rachael's doing your 'anger' bit pretty well."

A staccato pause. And then my mouth broke into a grin. My dad. Few words. Maximum impact. Dampened the stoked-up atmosphere.

And yet, despite my mother's lack of sophisticated emotional lexicology (the woman was about as subtle as a sledgehammer) I missed having her living just that bit closer to us. For the common sense, for her practical nature, for the fact that she loved Lydia and Matthew every bit as much as Adam had done.

But most days my mum wasn't there, of course. No significant other adult was.

And so, this was the worst time of the day. When my heart ached for Adam. When I couldn't distract myself with other people's crises or concerns. I missed every stupid, annoying little bit of him. Even the pathetic jokes and ridiculously corny double entendres. The Basil Fawlty impersonations. His inability to put the milk or butter back into the fridge. The sheer number of Wagon Wheels and Jaffa Cakes that one man could get through in a day. And, in the old days, the bits of motorbike that would suddenly turn up in the bath. Usually only half an hour after I had finished cleaning it.

But most of all, I missed him. My beautiful bloke. My children's daddy. My best friend and my biggest champion. I craved for that easy affection that had always existed between us. For sure, I had been the less touchy-feely one in the relationship. Half the time I had been too wrapped up in my own stupidly busy world. But I needed someone like Adam: someone who could sense exactly when I needed to be hugged, cuddled or dragged off to bed. He usually knew what I needed, before either my body or my mind realised it.

And now, all of a sudden, I was moving into a new landscape. Here was Michael. Here was sex. So easy; so natural. And so soon. Surely that couldn't be a positive start to a relationship?

Yes, and there he was too. There in That London. Going head to head with the media and the opposition. And here was I. Up north, wiping bottoms and tidying up Lego. There was simply no benchmark for this kind of situation. And now? Enter Shaun Elliot again. With a juicy offer on the table.

No point in leafing through the pages of *Cosmo* for a bit of advice on this one.

I decided to do the ironing. Maybe my mother was right. Maybe I could seek solace and joy in producing nicely-turned-out children. And I could slurp a large glass of red while completing the task in hand.

Halfway through the pile of clothes, Kate called me. I put her on speakerphone so I could carry on with the ironing. The first part of the conversation involved Kate breaking off every now and then to shriek at Bob, her husband ("It's the lazy git's turn to put the twins to bed, but I just caught the three of them sitting on the bed and watching the footie!") And the second part involved her shrieking rather too much and making far too many juvenile comments. This was after she had managed to wangle from me whose bed I had crashed out in on Saturday night.

"I cannot believe this! I just saw the guy on the news … everyone laughing their socks off because he made a joke about breasts! Christ. If only people knew that the minister was on such good form today because on Saturday night he got a good shag!"

"Keep it quiet, Kate. Not even Bob – okay?"

Then it was, "Yeah, yeah. Hang on – I'm just googling him."

"Oh, don't, Kate; I haven't done that sort of thing. It's too intrusive."

"Bollocks, mate. You're so old-fashioned. Everyone googles each other. Hang on ... hmm. His Wiki-entry … it's all a bit limited. Michael Chiswick must be the most boring bloke on the planet. Probably lives with his mother or something. Or else … he's got stuff to hide. Some dirty little secret from the past. Maybe from his time in the army. Probably killed Saddam Hussein or something. And the government are complicit in covering his tracks …"

She screeched with laughter at her own joke, but we were still on speakerphone, so I shushed her. The conversation was becoming raucous. Even the iron was hissing noisily.

Lydia was still awake, as usual. I could hear her singing along to *Jesus Christ Superstar* upstairs. (How many parents have to ban their children from excessive listening to religious musicals? I do.)

I decided to try to distract Kate from the Michael information hunt. Yes, it would be interesting to have a poke around and find out more about Michael's history and former incarnations thanks to the joys of the internet. But I didn't want to do that right now. Things felt too new – too strange, still. And I didn't want to spoil a burgeoning relationship with information overload. Or get all green-eyed about past lady-friends. So I told her about Shaun visiting me at work. About going for a drink with him. About the job that he wanted me to apply for. But I omitted the bit about the barney in the Secret Glade.

My oldest and dearest chum was aghast. She launched into her usual anti-Shaun tirade. How he had reduced me to a "gibbering wreck" in my early twenties; how he had "very inappropriately" turned up to my wedding reception (Adam had invited all his casual acquaintances from the biker club and Shaun had taken him up on the offer, even though Adam had no idea about the fact that Shaun and I had once been involved with each other); how he had "totally taken advantage" of me after Adam's death.

"And the twattiest bit of all – having his end away with you when you were still away with the fairies after losing Adam…and forgetting to tell you that he had got married!"

I managed to shake off my usual stirrings of deep-rooted shame with regard to her latter comment. Only Kate and my sister Vicky knew about the second time around with Shaun. It wasn't my finest moment, that was for sure.

"Thanks for the synopsis, Kate. But all I'm talking about here is a job. A dull job, no doubt … but I'm fretting about money at the moment. And, to be fair, he seemed genuinely interested in what we're doing with the chocolate project …"

"Rachael! 'To be fair'? This is Shaun we're talking about!"

I was quiet. So her voice levelled somewhat.

"Oh, I don't know, chicken. It's just a bit funny, that's all. You start this thing with your swanky politician bloke and then Shaun trucks up just a day later. I mean, maybe he can sniff out when some other dog has pissed over his lamp post. His perceived territory, you know? Maybe he can sort of sense a threat to his manhood …"

"Gee, thanks!" I added, with fake glee. "So here's me. The innocent and hapless lamp post. And there's Shaun and Michael. Both of them trying to pee over me! You make it all sound so terribly romantic!"

"Well. They don't do pistols at dawn any more, you know. But come on, mate. You have to admit that when it comes to Shaun the Shithead, you go into paralysis mode. He's like this big horrible tom cat. Playing about with this wee terrified mouse."

"Oh, please. Don't make me out to be some kind of damsel in distress, Kate! I spend most of my waking hours telling women that they don't have to be passive victims, so I don't need my best friend telling me that I'm powerless to make choices …"

She tutted, as my phone began to beep.

"Look Kate, I've got to go. Got a call. Speak soon, OK?"

It was Michael.

"Just dashing from a vote and over to Bob Porteus's place," he announced. "You know – the Health Secretary – for a spot of supper. But I thought I'd give you a quick call. How's your day been?"

"Interesting. But not as fascinating as yours, I bet. How did things go with the PM?"

"Oh fine, fine," he answered casually. "Nothing to worry about there. Looks like Ben Hardy will have to resign during the next few days.

Shame, but that's the way the cookie crumbles. And the PM is still quite tickled with my press conference. He seems to think that I'm a genius at evasion and distraction. That I deliberately hammed up the 'boob joke' and managed to pull off what could have been quite a risky tactic."

"I kind of thought that, too. So, did you?"

"No comment. You've both got very suspicious minds …"

"But Michael," I began to ask, as I slapped the eighth pair of Matthew-trousers down onto the board, "don't you have to be a bit careful about pissing off someone like Simone Shaw and her crowd? Surely you'd rather stay on the good side of her and her cronies?"

"Oh, God, no. She's one malicious bitch, I'll give her that. So if she's got a bit of egg on her face – or her tits – then it's good all round, I say. They're pond life, her sort. Utter pond life."

"You sound like you detest the gutter press more than the opposition!"

"Well, they're a bunch of scumbags and losers, of course. That goes without saying. But generally speaking, us politicians do abide by a certain set of rules. We have our conventions. Shaw and people of her ilk don't. The whole 'Michael Chiswick is Gay' rumour, which has been running for several years now, was actually created by her and her lot at the *News Of The Nation*."

"Right. Well, don't turn it into a vendetta."

"Rachael, you worry too much. We've got people like Alex … the Twat on side. And I've got my own guy, Marvin, who helps with the spin."

"Well ... I think that you're too blasé about things. Don't forget that I'm not entirely green when it comes to how your political spin and spats can end up. But, anyway, just so long as those gay rumours about you aren't true …"

"Ha. Surely you realised that for yourself after Saturday night … Still, that kind of rumour never bothered me too much. It's nasty, character assassination, of course. But on the other hand it's a nice cover-up for all sorts of other kinds of heterosexual misadventures …"

"Oh, don't tell me. I don't want to know about your sordid sexual past."

"Well, actually. It's been very boring," he sniffed. "My sex life. Until recently, of course … Anyway – what's that funny sound?"

"I'm doing the ironing. I've got you on speakerphone. See? There you are, off for supper with your Cabinet colleague. And here's me ironing Dennis the Menace T-shirts. Height of glamour, eh?"

"Oh. I thought you were either having an angina attack or you were breathing heavily. Shame. I thought you might be getting all hot and bothered while speaking to me ..."

"I am getting all hot and bothered, but it's because of the ironing."

"But seriously, Rachael. I'm desperate to see you again. Craven with lust. Don't you fancy a bit of smut? Go on. Talk smutty to me…"

"How about … sod off you mucky bugger?"

Footsteps on the stairs behind me.

"I have to go, Michael. Small person has left its bed …"

"OK. Tomorrow, then. Night."

Lydia appeared at the living-room door, looking forlorn. She wandered over to me for a cuddle and showed me several holes in her rainbow-coloured stuffed cat ("Matthew tried to crucify him on his Bob the Builder workstation. And I just found him now … all up there on his own and bleeding to death.") I consoled the cat with lots of kisses, pausing to remove fluff from my tongue as Lydia piped up.

"Is that friend of yours and Daddy's – that Shaun – going to give you a nice new job so that you're happy all the time?" she asked.

Lydia had developed a new habit of lying at the top of the stairs at bedtime listening in to my conversations. I wondered just how much she had heard. I did my best to sidestep the question.

"No. Auntie Kate and I were just talking about different jobs we could do. That's all." I touched the tip of her nose. "And the last thing you should be thinking about, poppet, is jobs. You know what? I love my job. It does make me happy. But what makes me most happy in the world is you and your smelly little brother."

"He is smelly, isn't he?"

"Pongy."

She grinned and snuggled into me, trying to buy more time before the inevitable shooing back to bed. But then she asked me, "Mummeh? No one is going to wee all over you, are they? That would be really nasty of them."

"No. Don't be silly."

"And Mum? Why were you talking about Sooty and Sweep to that man? On the phone."

"I don't know what you mean, Liddy."

"Sooty I mean. He said he wanted you to talk about Sooty to him."

Like I said. Small kid, big ears.

After Lydia was safely tucked up in her bed again, I went back downstairs to set out the kitchen for the routine of a Tuesday morning. PE bags, lunchboxes, notes to teachers all ready to go. On my way to put the milk bottles outside the front door I noticed that some ad-hoc artwork had been doodled onto the infamous fridge photo. Lydia's earlier reference to 'princesses and pirates' when she mentioned the news clipping now made sense. Only Liddy had decided that I would be the pirate with the eye patch and black hat. Michael had been awarded the tiara, the jewels and the Cupid's bow lips.

Good job that Simone Shaw or anyone else at *News Of The Nation* couldn't see it. They would have whipped a Michael Chiswick gender-bending story out of it before you could have said 'mammary glands'.

Chapter 15

THE CAP OF INVISIBILITY

The next day was officially the last day of summer. Bands of muggy clouds with an accompanying nip in the air heralded autumn's arrival. Unusually for us, the Russell alarm clock (goes by the name of Matthew) had malfunctioned that morning. Normally it woke us at 6 a.m. on the dot, but for some reason hyper-tot was opting for a lie-in. I managed to get both children toileted, dressed, bagged up and out of the house on time. The only mishap we encountered between bed and bon voyage was Matthew falling head first into the recycling bucket outside the front door. Not hurting himself, but acquiring a rather interesting scent of pickled onions and red wine. I hoped that the nursery wouldn't notice. He was usually a bit of a whiffy child, anyway.

In the car I missed the news headlines. Matthew had been holding us hostage to his musical preferences for several weeks now, so we were forced to listen to what even Lydia was now calling 'The Sodding Wheels on the Bus CD' (my fault, that.) However, after kiddie drop-off I caught the tail end of a news report.

"And another allegation of misbehaviour of government ministers. Directed again at the Department for Communities – but this time involving the senior Cabinet minister himself, Michael Chiswick ..."

In shock, I shot through a red light. Luckily there were no cars turning into my lane. My breath had frozen. Suspended in my lungs. I tried to turn the radio up, but with my addled brain I ended up switching it off by mistake. Shit. But never mind that stuff, I told myself. Concentrate on getting to work without going all dizzy blonde and orphaning the kids completely.

Ten minutes later, while in a standstill at the Woodley traffic lights, I managed to get the radio back on. But Radio 4's 'Today' programme was now wittering on about some kind of crisis in the North Sea due to cod depletion. Sod and bollocks. I realised that I hadn't had time to switch on my mobile phone that morning. I reached over, pressed the button and it buzzed over a dozen times. Lots of missed calls from various unknown numbers, as well as a voicemail. As soon as I could, I pulled over to check it. It was from Michael.

"Have to be quick, Rachael – but have you seen the headlines? If not, get a copy of *News Of The Nation* asap. You'll see what we're up against. I've got to go straight into a meeting with the PR bods. Do some damage limitation. Don't panic. And don't talk to anyone. At all. I'll call you as soon as I'm out. Hope you're OK."

A slippery sense of dread descended into the car. A mackerel sky hung over Medlock. I parked my car at Sisters' Space and then ran over to Singh's newsagent.

And there it was.

Slap bang next to the scratch cards and Maltesers. *News Of The Nation*. With a glorious, technicolour front page that read 'On Yer Bike, Mike!' accompanied by an enormous photograph of Michael riding Vinnie's motorbike through Brindleford.

I tried to swallow, but my throat had turned into sandpaper. I picked up a copy of the newspaper and opened it, nearly dropping the damned thing in horror. There, on page two, was another huge photograph. But this time of me. Well, me from the back. And of Michael. The headline next to it shrieked 'Michael's Biker Chick?' and below it, the blurb read 'After his cheeky ride around the streets of a Manchester estate, Michael Chiswick returned home with his mystery blonde, where they were seen smearing sun-tan lotion on each other. Do you know who Michael's girl is? If so – call us now!'

I closed the newspaper and clutched it to my chest. Unable to move. Staring at the rack of gaudy celeb and lifestyle magazines in front of me. The shellshock must have been obvious, as Mrs Singh, the shop owner (and a lady more used to seeing me purchasing vast quantities of midget gems in her establishment) felt the need to ask, "You OK, lovey? You looking a bit funny. Need some sweeties?"

I shook my head dumbly, paid for the newspaper and headed for work. I swiped myself into the building and gave only a cursory "Morning" to our receptionist. I hid myself in my office, closing the door firmly and only then did I open the newspaper out onto my desk, spilling out the twisted words and dreaded photographs before me.

My spirits lifted slightly. The photograph didn't show my face at all. Just the back of my head and the tops of my shoulders. On Saturday, during the flood saga, I had tied my long hair into a ponytail and wound it into a messy bun at the top of my head. Not the way I normally wore it. I had to admit that the halter-neck had been a good choice; my back looked quite toned and tanned for once. In fact, I thought to myself, I could pass for a woman slightly younger than my thirty-nine years. Perhaps I should always insist on being photographed from behind.

Despite the profound shock and the squirming snakes in my stomach, I allowed myself to smile warily. The newspaper's ramblings made it clear that nobody knew my identity. And the photograph was helpfully mysterious. But then, in the next instant, my hopes thundered back down to earth. No. This would not be the best thing in the world for Michael's reputation; for his career. Bollocks again. The likelihood of anything continuing between us was now minus five and counting.

And then a wave of self-righteousness washed over me (admittedly, this was more about trying to stave off the certainty of romantic disappointment). Last night I'd actually warned Michael not to be too casual, too complacent about Simone Shaw and her shitty excuse for a newspaper! But oh, no: Michael had said that he knew what he was doing. Didn't need the advice of a know-it-all broad from up north. He had Alex the Twat on his side.

What a sodding pig's ear this was turning out to be.

My phone started buzzing. I was going to ignore it, but saw that the number was Kate's.

"So much for secrecy!" she shrieked.

"Kate. Shush!"

"You rotten trollop! Telling me not to say anything to anyone. 'Not even Bob', you said. And bugger me – if you aren't star of the country's leading arse-wipe rag the very next day! We've got it here. In the staff room. And I've been looking at the coverage on my phone too. You're all over the Net, mate!"

I couldn't tell whether she was genuinely annoyed with me or whether she was simply finding the whole thing bloody hilarious.

"Look, I haven't a clue how …"

High-pitched little voices were chattering away in the background.

"Well, we're about to start morning assembly. But I told the Head I've got a bit of a family crisis going on and I needed to make a quick phone call. *Hey!* Hang on a minute, chicken ..." She broke off and nearly deafened me with a bellow of: "Joshua Myers, how *dare* you do that to the Prayer Tree! I can see exactly what you're doing with everyone's prayers and I'll be with you in sixty seconds. Just stand there and don't move!"

I waited.

"Sorry about that, petal. Little shit. It's always the ones with the well-off parents, isn't it? Anyway. Yes. You. How on earth did that happen? And what were you doing in that photo? Were you sniffing the back of his neck?"

"Oh, Kate." I exhaled wearily. I was now sitting down at my desk and trying to clean crud from in between my keyboard's keys. A sign of deep stress. "I know that this sounds ridiculous, but I was actually looking at a flea bite. On his back."

A guttural snigger.

"Oh, yes. From your good samaritan bit with the old lady. Fantastic! Truth is always stranger than fiction! Anyway. What about the photo on the front cover? The golden boy of politics and motorbike thing?"

"Hardly a boy. But yes. He's into his bikes. And he ended up talking to this nutter who shouldn't have been riding a bike because he was off his head on smack. So Michael drove it back home for him. That's all."

"That's all. Bit funny. I mean … it seems like every bloke you've ever been involved with is into his bikes. And …"

"Yeah. It is. It was. A bit strange … obviously."

A small pocket of silence for a minute. Then Kate's clipped, but gentle tones.

"Sorry, chicken. Bikes. I don't mean to make light of it."

I puffed out the air that I had been storing in my lungs.

"Kate. You're the last person who needs to fret about talking about stuff like that with me. But, yeah, you're right. Why is it always bikes with me?"

She chortled. "Perhaps you look like the town bike?"

"Sorry, Kate. I'm having a sense of humour bypass today. But anyway, none of this adds up for me. Who could have taken the photos? Of Michael on the bike? And then of us in the garden later on?"

"Photographers trailing you without you realising?"

A sudden roar from her: "Joshua Myers, will you please stop wiping your bogies on Megan's hair? That is perhaps the most disgusting behaviour that I have ever seen! And don't give me that look! I saw exactly what you did and I can tell you that you're going to be in Time Out before we even get to morning break!"

She came back to the phone.

"Look – I have to go. Spoiled little gits to discipline. Look, try not to stress too much. I only recognised you because I know the whole story. Obviously, I'll be keeping my mouth shut. I shan't be selling my soul to the evil media empires. Even if *News Of The Nation* wanted to pay me ten thousand for it. Yes, pal, I love you that much! And I hope that your Michael friend is chilled about it too. Because, quite frankly, Rachael, if he isn't, you're best off without him."

She blew me several kisses down the phone and then went off to secretly cuff Joshua Myers about the head while Ofsted and social services weren't looking.

I managed to pass the next few hours sitting in on caseworker meetings with some of the women, catching up on paperwork and popping in to the cafe to see how the online orders were progressing. It was beginning to bother me, though, that after the initial voicemail left by Michael, the only contact my mobile phone had logged was from missed numbers that I didn't recognise. Either those bloody annoying sales calls that I'm always getting, or the escalating hassle from the bank. And I didn't want to speak to either of them. For very different reasons.

And I wasn't going to call Michael. Because he had said that he would call me.

I'm old-fashioned like that.

I couldn't concentrate on the online sales system, so I asked Bev to make me a very strong coffee using our new-but-second-hand barista equipment. She could tell that I wasn't in a great mood, so she left me alone and didn't even ask about the contents of my lunchbox or allude to egg mayonnaise and its similarities to vaginal discharge. I pretended to rifle through paperwork as I sat at our empty coffee bar and nursed my cup of caffeine overkill, wishing I had some whisky to add to it. I became extremely morose.

I started thinking about karma and my behaviour on Saturday night. Far too reckless for a widow in purdah. So serves me bloody well right. Mentally, I began to rehearse the coming phone conversation with Michael. The one where he would tell me in a gentle but firm way that getting involved with someone like me was proving to be a little bit too dodgy. Because, after all, I was a female with neither breeding nor connections. Living a life far too close to those of beaten-up women, drug users and demented old ladies. And, no doubt, my connections with Al Qaeda and Idi Amin would go against me, too.

So au revoir, Mad Mancunian Totty.

At noon, with only the sales calls and scary bank account overdraft people to show for missed calls, I went outside for a bit of fresh air. I wandered the few hundred yards to the park and into the Secret Glade. I found a bench and closed my eyes, feeling ridiculously sorry for myself and descending into full-scale victim mentality. Not something I liked to do on a regular basis, but then it wasn't every day that I received the honour of Mystery Bimbo in the national press.

I decided to lie down on the bench. I tried 'Breathing the Power of the Universe into your Centre of Being.' A technique that Marsha, our mindfulness maestro, taught in her body awareness class at Sisters' Space. I tried to remind myself that I had faced worse in my life. Much worse than this trivial media tin-pot tosh.

Much, much worse.

Maybe the twaddle and the self-talk and the extra oxygen worked, although it was more likely that I was utterly shafted through early morning Matthew awakenings. Either way, I drifted off into a semi-snooze. But I was cruelly jolted out of my drowsy state by a deep voice.

"Slacking off, Stan?"

I looked up to see Shaun. Looming above me. Blocking out the sun, so that I didn't even need to shade my eyes. How very symbolic.

Smart, sleek, in what looked to be yet another very expensive suit. I tried to sit up quickly, and he waved a hand at me.

"Oh, carry on with your horizontal posturing. Don't mind me. One of your staff said you'd headed off towards the park. I had a hunch that you might be here."

"Jeez, Shaun, you're like a bloody bus ..."

"Yeah I know, don't see me for ages and then all at once it's non-stop."

"No. Out of date, polluting the atmosphere and a big hit with pensioners because you're cheap." (Lydia would have added "and because you smell like travel-sicky throw-up chunder", but that wouldn't have worked quite as well.)

He did that really annoying eyebrow thing. Raising just the one. Once, when we had been in bed, I told him that I reckoned he must have practised it for years as a teenager. That he would have been the sort to stand in front of his bedroom mirror, trying to perfect the James Bond look.

"How very rude. Especially when I'm here with your welfare as my main concern."

I sat up. About to disembark.

"Well, whatever it is, Shaun, couldn't you have just phoned me or sent me an email like normal people do? I'm sure you have a lot more important things to do with your time than mooching about a women's centre. Or the local park."

"Actually, I do. Got a meeting to discuss our lovely CEO Roger wandering off into the land of retirement," he answered, checking his watch. "But I've got a few minutes. And right now, seeing you is at the top of the list. Although I did *see* you several hours ago. Flashing your booty at the entire country."

I felt the colour drain from my face. I had already jumped off the park bench and was ready to leave. But his words seemed to have turned the cracked and dry cement around the park bench into quicksand. I couldn't move. But I was sinking slowly, resolutely. My tongue felt thick and furry. And, for once, the words wouldn't come.

"So, let's talk jobs, Stan." He gave me a sly wink and with ultimate self-assurance, he neatly perched himself on the bench. "Because after today's little performance in the newspapers, I'm now left wondering whether I should be offering you the head of PR at our place …"

I sat down next to him, with a thump.

"But that ..." I glanced sideways at him. "How did you know it was me?"

He shrugged, and pulled a face. The downward shrug of the mouth. His best Robert De Niro face. (The Robert De Niro face was for when Shaun was being the big man, showing me that he was above caring. The James Bond expression was adopted in order to take the wind out of my sails. And there was that Bruce Willis face, too. The look that said 'I'm trying to be compassionate here, but screw it, I'm still going to blow your Nanna up in sixty seconds flat.')

But right now we had the De Niro gurn.

"Well, Stan, not too many people will be familiar with your bare back. But the mole on your left shoulder was a dead giveaway for me. So after

Jake's little comment about 'your man' and 'the evening news'… and what with Mickey boy showing a bit of interest in your women's centre all of a sudden, it hardly took a genius to work it out …" He cocked his head to one side. "And I have to ask myself, Stan. Where did all your political principles go? Getting mixed up with the likes of him? What happened to the CND? What happened to peace marches and demos? I mean, hardly a red in your bed, is he?"

He moved to Bruce Willis mode. Trying to look concerned for my sake. It narked me. Neither Bruce nor Shaun did empathy very well.

I turned to look directly at him. Slow-burning anger.

"Firstly, that photograph isn't what you think."

He laughed, shaking his head. "Yeah. So you weren't putting sun-tan lotion on him, then?"

"And secondly, even if I was seeing him, or was involved with him in some way, why would you be entitled to an opinion on it?"

He stretched his long frame backwards. The classic hands-behind-head position.

"Oh, come on, Stan. Use your noggin. The taxpayers pay me to do a job where I have to give a shit. Where I have to care about whether locally funded services are being run well. I'm their guardian angel, if you like. So if someone who is supposed to be managing a local service is running around half-naked in the national press … I do have to seriously consider whether Medlock council taxpayers' money is being jeopardised. Don't you think?"

I burst out laughing. It had a slightly hysterical edge to it. I think I accidentally spat on him. Good.

"Don't you give me that crap!" I shot back at him. "You know that we've achieved all of the bloody outcomes that your lot have set for our funding. You know I'm good at what I do – that we help more women in the area than anyone else ever has. So don't you start spinning a load of bollocks about me not running Sisters' Space well!"

"True. And no one's saying you've not done a good job. Until now. But what they will be saying – if they realise who the pin-up girl is – is this: do we really want someone doing this job who's not only flashing her bits all over the national press but who's also shagging the man responsible for all the massive funding cuts? Cuts that are just about to be announced and which will hit the Greater Manchester authorities the hardest. With Medlock Council facing the biggest percentage slash."

I kept quiet. This was news to me.

"But also because I do care about you, Stan. Not just your professional standing but personally, too. I know that you think I don't. I know you think you got the shitty end of the stick with everything that happened. Between us. But I was trying to get it across to you yesterday – when you went off in a hissy fit – that I do. I do care, I mean."

Silence from me. He took a pen that he had fished out of his pocket. Began clicking it, in and out. Clickety click.

"And when I twigged what you were up to with your Chiswick bloke, I mean, sure – there's a part of me that felt a bit, well ... jealous. So. Are you happy that I've admitted that?"

No response.

"Well, you should be. Because it's something I've never fessed up to anyone else before." He clicked the pen again. Irritating me. Big time.

"Still. I can get over all that. But can you? I mean, do you really think that someone like Michael Chiswick is going to stick his neck out for you? Everyone knows he's a man going places. This is nothing personal, like, but why the hell would someone like him jeopardise everything for a fling with a single mother from up north? 'Cause that's exactly the way it's going to look."

No response.

"Some bint from Manchester – from Yorkshire or wherever you claim to lay your hat these days – has been getting the minister a bit giddy. It's a bleeding gift for the opposition, Stan. A gift! You may be bloody sexy and smart and appeal to the likes of me … but no one – not even you – is worth the government coming crashing down. Sorry if it sounds hard. But that's how they'll see it. They won't give a shit about you and yours."

I stayed quiet. Wondering if I could seize the clicking pen off him and stab him in the eye with it.

"Just look at these funding cuts he's presiding over. The guy is on another planet to you when it comes to political values. I mean – he's even ex-army, for Christ's sake!"

I looked at the pavement mottled with chewing gum. Shaun was on a roll.

"So, forget him. Go for the damned job at our place. You're wasted at your bloody women's place. Think of the future. We're talking another twenty thousand pounds on top of what you're already earning. You can hardly refuse that. Come on – think of your kids. Front page of *News Of The Nation* … I mean, Jesus!"

Normally, by now I would have taken up the bait. Mouthed off at Shaun. Delivered a rant and a rave or sidled off somewhere in order to silently fume. The perfection of passive-aggression. But not right now. Something felt different here.

"Your family," he was saying. "Don't you think that you've been through enough?"

Shaun stood up. Dwarfing my five foot two inches. He reached out his hand and smoothed my hair back behind my ear. A peculiar sinking sensation engulfed me as the blood drained from my upper body. And my legs felt on fire. Adrenaline rush. A Shaun-charge.

No words, now. For what seemed an age. And then he spoke – a hoarse, voiced whisper.

"And I know what I'm talking about here, remember? I was that kid without the dad. Without the mum, too. And yeah, I got lucky. Got adopted. Nice, wealthy family, for sure. But …"

He looked away from me. Those oh-so-dark eyes, perhaps recollecting. An IRA bomb. An explosion in a pub. A five-year-old-boy, orphaned.

That was Shaun.

And he never talked about it.

He rubbed that bump on his nose, as if to bring himself back to the present. Here and now, in a crappy Medlock park.

"So, yeah. I know that money can't buy you love, and all that. But it can go a good bloody way to alleviating things. To taking the pressure off. And this job – this money – would certainly do that for you. For all of you. After the … insurance thing."

I steeled my jaw. Regretting that I'd ever let Shaun into that little secret.

The letter addressed to Mrs Rachael Russell told me:

> *"We must regretfully inform you that your husband's life insurance policy did not cover him for motorcycle riding. Although Mr Russell's previous policy of some two years ago did contain cover for accidental death due to collision whilst riding a motorcycle, this aspect of the policy had been changed during the renewal application made seven months ago when Mr Russell informed the company that he was no longer in possession of a motorcycle.*
>
> *All of this detail is held on our records, which we are happy to share with you at any time.*
>
> *We are sorry that we could not be of any further assistance to you at this unfortunate time. As the event of your husband's death occurred during vacation, we suggest that his holiday insurance may be able to offer you further advice with regards to cover and recompense."*

That was me. That was my fault.

Nagging Adam to give up the biking. Just after Matthew had been born. Too dangerous, Adam. You should have stopped all of that as soon as Lydia arrived. Now that we've got the two kids you really should sell the bike. And don't forget to take it off the insurance. It'll keep the premium lower, of course. Call them today. Go on.

And as for holiday insurance? Sure, Adam was covered. But not for 'dangerous sports'. He hadn't thought that he and Jim might decide to hire a bike for a day – on a whim. And on their last day in South Africa they were trying to squeeze every last drop of enjoyment out of the trip without having to be bogged down by run-of-the-mill crap like insurance clauses. So the only help we got from the damned holiday insurance was for 'repatriation of remains in event of death whilst abroad'.

Yeah. Cheers for that.

I stood on my toes. Not trying to gain any height. That would have been a joke. Shaun had a good one foot and three inches on me. So, I was just trying to gather some more oxygen. To clear my head before, I spoke.

"Shaun, it's nice of you to be thinking about me and the kids. But it seems that things are getting a bit confused here. Look. Going back to the newspaper stuff – at the end of the day, you don't need to try and ladle any more pressure onto me. I'm big enough to look after myself. And I promise you that if my name, or Medlock Council's, gets dragged into all this … into the media spotlight, I'll resign immediately."

His chin tipped downwards. He was still perilously close. I could smell his aftershave. Citrus and spice and all things nice. I took a step back from him.

"Now, I've got to get back to the centre. And you've got your meeting."

I turned to go and flicked a little wave over my shoulder at him. His voice drifted after me.

"Right … I'll hold you to that. But on the job offer … you've got until next Friday. That's the deadline for other applicants. Not that you'd need to worry about them, of course. But we need to keep up the appearance of equal opps and all of that bollocks …"

I kept on walking. Nodded. Not looking back.

"And Stan? I'm not going anywhere. See?"

Yeah, Shaun; but could you – would you – ever be seen going anywhere with me? Out in public, I mean?

Due to Matthew falling into the recycling bin that morning, I had forgotten to bring my packed lunch. I headed for Betty's Big Baps, next to the newsagent, and decided on a plain old cheese butty with lashings of salad cream. Staying on the safe side. Although Bev would no doubt still conjure up some allusion to pus or a fungal infection.

I was confident that Shaun was trying to call my bluff. That he would never tell anyone else about my involvement with Michael. All this talk would no doubt prove to be mind games on Shaun's part; there was far too much at stake for him. The liaisons between the two of us had always been kept secret from his own circle of friends and colleagues. So I didn't believe that there would be any mention of Rachael Russell or who she was seeing – just in case Ms Russell herself got bolshy and wanted to spill the beans. I knew Shaun well enough by now. Best keeping little Rachael as his little secret. He might get off on coming across as being Mr Arrogant, Mr Abrasive and Mr Arsey, but he didn't want to be known as Mr Adulterer. Didn't want to hurt Saint Jess. Surely got to give the man a bit of credit for that?

And he had his pride. And his reasons. Despite his shithead accolades.

Maybe having both your parents blown to smithereens at an early age does that to you.

I checked my phone as I trudged back to Sisters' Space. Still nothing from Michael. Just half a dozen missed phone calls from an unknown number. Bank's call centre, no doubt. They could sod off. Let their graduate trainees go and patronise some other, poor frantic widow with psychotic pixies for offspring. I would take a rain check for today.

But maybe Shaun was right. Maybe chasing a Cabinet minister (or, to be more precise, dropping my knickers rather too quickly for one) was chasing moonbeams. Here I was, single mother up north. Barely managing to make the mortgage payments, even though I was doing my best: buying the shop-brand version of whatever crappy cereal the kids were into at the moment, forgoing the luxuries like fancy presents and holidays, pretending that I was getting a buzz from the wee treasures I found in the charity shop at the end of the road.

And this month we had developed a bit of an embarrassing overdraft problem. Thanks to a failed MOT for a certain, much-loved Fiat Panda. Which apparently needed two new tyres and brake pads. And, of course, there was no male around to double-check this garage report out with

(other than my dad telling me, “Sorry, love, I could only help you if you happened to be driving a traction engine.”)

We had gone six hundred and seventy into the red. Hence, me not taking calls from random bank-type people at the moment.

I had always been proud of my ability to make ends meet. But these days, I seemed to be losing that knack. We were fast becoming swamped by overdue bills and incoming demands. And although I loved Sisters’ Space, I had to admit that there was a part of me that desperately wanted to be able to relax about the financial side of things. Not have to constantly fret and stress about every little penny. Not have to worry about paying for the next batch of school uniform or argue with Lydia over whether I could afford to take her to see her latest favourite musical at the Lowry or at the West Yorkshire Playhouse (And God forbid that the kids might ever want to go to university.)

I swiped my way back in to the centre and reached my desk, checking my phone yet again. Nothing. I reached for the sandwich in the paper bag and inadvertently squidged salad cream all down my shirt.

Yes, this was me. This was my life.

The afternoon dragged on, checking case workers’ advice logs and attempting to apply for yet another grant for Sisters’ Space. Usually I enjoyed the group planning sessions for the official launch of Charlene’s Chocolate Factory, some six weeks away, but today the gathering descended into an hour of interaction that should have been named Stupid Meeting Anonymous.

After agreeing the final selection of chocolates that we would have ready for sale come the launch in early November and after ticking off the bookings now made for bouncy castle, magician and the usual ragbag of local fete stallholders, the women decided to have a natter about ‘what’s in the papers’.

Shirley rarely spoke out at meetings unless directly asked, but she suddenly took it upon herself to declare:

“Isn’t it odd? About that Michael Chiswick. He’s been all over the papers for the last couple of days. Yesterday it was some gay affair going on in his government department. And today it was stuff about him riding on a motorbike on Brindleford and some mystery affair he's having! And he seemed so nice and charming when he was here the other week."

I was silent. Not even deliberately quiet. The usual ability to steer the conversation back to the point of the meeting had disappeared. I hoped that my always-reliable deputy, the outspoken Gillian, might be able to take over from my sudden attack of verbal constipation. But then Gobshite Central waded in. Dee (who was loose cannon personified whether she had necked a load of jellies or not) just snickered and pulled the ever present "spazzer face", "Hardly fucking news, that. Fucking politicians. They're always at it with some slapper, somewhere or another."

I should have interrupted her to remind her of our policy in relation to derogatory language – but I was rendered dumb by the fact that the slapper in question was actually, yours truly.

Jade agreed. "And old people shagging ... bleugh. Always makes me feel ill. Shouldn't be allowed."

Shirley cut right in. Unusually for her, she sounded rather tetchy and complained that Jade was "being ageist towards people". Then she took it upon herself to remind everyone that "not all politicians are untrustworthy. Tony Benn, for example."

But Dee got the wrong end of the stick, bellowing, "Tony Benn? He were the one with all those teeth who invaded Iraq! Couldn't stand the wanker!"

And then, after being corrected by Shirley, she declared, "Well, Tony whatever. They're all a bunch of rich lyin' bastards …"

Meanwhile, Bev had been fiddling with her phone.

"I'm googlin' that Michael Chiswick right now. An' actually, I reckon we should invite him back … he'd be good PR for us. Tryin' to get the message across to your usual blokes, I mean. They'd all look up to him round 'ere if he's riding motorbikes all over places like Brindleford and knocking off the odd lass. An' if he's got the power to influence the rest of the dickheads in charge of the whole friggin' country … let's get him back 'ere! Give the man more choccie, I say!"

I groaned. Gillian cast me a strange glance. Bev concluded her googling by informing us, "An' he served in the Armed Forces for many years, apparently. Ooh – I do like a man in uniform!"

Shirley had clearly had one too many cappuccinos that morning, "And I like a nice tall man. Like that Shaun Elliot from the Town Hall who's always in the *Evening News*. He must be – what, six foot three, or something?"

Six foot five, actually ...

"Yes, he'd be very handsome, he would, if only he'd smile a bit more. Miserable swine."

I looked at Gillian, but she seemed as disconcerted as I was. Feeling as though she was trapped in Heterosexual Hell, no doubt.

Shirley carried on. "I always think it's nice when you've got a big bloke towering over you. You sort of feel protected."

Classic, wasn't it? Women who had spent half of their lives getting knocked about by men. Trying to change things and to learn a bit more about why this kind of thing happened. Trying to improve their self-esteem and work towards true independence here at Sisters' Space. And apparently, all we want is a nice tall man to protect us ...

Says little Rachael, who always secretly liked the height difference … ("Keep up with me, Stan!")

Bev was still staring at her phone screen. "Yeah, but the only thing with big blokes is you know that they'll end up with a knackered back. 'Cause it's not natural bein' that tall. So their backs are always gettin' shafted …"

Followed by a horrible pervy cackle from Dee as she rubbed her purple leggings, leering. "Send 'im to me, love! I'll knacker 'is back in no time!" Cue lots of sniggering and shrieks of laughter.

What a bloody nightmare. You spend one afternoon (and night) with a Cabinet minister and before you know it, not only are you flashing acres of your naked flesh to the entire country but you're rendered speechless in your own workplace while your service users pick over the dregs of your most recent sexual encounters.

Sod. Sod. Sod.

But then the meeting room door opened and thankfully I was beckoned out of the meeting by our receptionist. A phone call from someone who was insisting that they needed to speak to me urgently and who wasn't taking no for an answer.

Chapter 16

ARISTOPHANES' ARRIVAL AT NUMBER TEN

I snatched up the landline phone, grateful for the excuse to leave the ridiculous meeting. But my stomach lurched as I heard Michael's voice at the other end of the line.

"Where have you been, Rachael? I've been trying to get hold of you all day!"

I picked up my mobile, which I had left on my desk. "Weird. I haven't had any missed calls from you."

"No," Michael interrupted, speaking quietly and more urgently now. "Sorry – I should have said. As soon as the shit hit the fan this morning, I went out and got a new SIM card for my spare phone. So I could call you. Different number. Different phone. Like I said to you the other day, there are times when it's best not to use my regular number. Let alone my landlines."

"Oh, God – crap. Sorry! I kept getting calls from an unknown number. I just presumed that it would be the usual salespeople. Or the bank. So I ignored them. Oh, God. Is it really so bad that you can't use your own phone to call me?" My spirits slumped. Hitting rock bottom again. I steeled myself. This phone call could well be our last one.

"Yes. Well, no. The situation is nothing like as terrible as it might have felt to you this morning. The PM seems to be on a bit of a positive, upbeat trajectory this week when it comes to certain news items. Most of the Spinny Boys and our Party chairman have decided to take the tack of

'Here's a great example of a red-blooded male in top government post, who hasn't actually done anything wrong and who half the electorate can now really relate to much better'. Has quite a nice PR vibe, apparently. As opposed to the 'Posh Boy Probably Gay' rumour that was doing the rounds up until now."

"Yes. That's what Bev said," I murmured.

"Who's Bev?"

"Oh, just one of the women who uses the centre here. They were discussing you. The newspapers. I kept my mouth shut, of course. But Bev, she reckoned men that … well, the kind of men in her life, unfortunately … would think you're 'one of the lads', as it were."

He laughed. "Fantastic! She's on the same wavelength as the PM and his Spinny Boys. And Marvin too. He's my own Politbureau chap, who's going to try to milk some positive mileage out of it for me in tomorrow's newspapers. So your Bev should make the move down to London. She could be earning a fortune down here."

"No, that'd never work. Bev has this thing about sandwich fillings. And London eateries are notorious for having exotic concoctions. It would cause the nation's capital to grind to a halt if you had Bev as a resident …"

"Sorry, Rachael, but you've lost me now."

"Never mind. So, what next? Are you going to have to do another press conference or something?"

"Oh, no. It's very different to the whole Ben Hardy saga. Nothing in this whatsoever about my ability to do the job. It's just your usual tabloid muck-raking. And because it's *News Of The Nation* – Simone Shaw's rag – it's all coming across as sour grapes. Because of the boob jibe yesterday."

"Right. So you don't respond?"

"No. Other than Marvin doing some positive spin on it all for tomorrow's rival papers. And, of course, the opposition will have a bit of a dig at me in PM's Question Time, but they'll be more focussed on Ben Hardy's screw-up. In fact, the PM seems to think that my manly exploits will help take the edge off all that."

"Well, then. I guess … that's good … isn't it?" I had been taking the phone call standing up, but the relief allowed me to collapse heavily into my office chair.

"It is. But there is an issue that the PM is still quite concerned about."

"Oh, yes?" I asked, the ball of stress forming itself again in my stomach. I picked up the photograph of Lydia on my desk and tried to polish the silver frame with my sleeve.

"You."

"Me?" Horror-struck. "What do you mean, me?" I held no particular regard for the prime minister, or his politics. The man held no interest whatsoever for me. But it was still more than a little disconcerting to hear that the leader of our glorious nation had an opinion on Rachael Russell. The shock of this set my mouth off and running.

"He might well be the prime minister," I began, "but what I do and who I do it with is none of his concern! And you can tell him that I bloody well —"

"Hang on! I think you're getting the wrong end of the stick!"

I caught my breath. Michael sounded vaguely amused.

"Apologies, Rachael. That's my fault. Poor choice of phraseology. What I meant was that the PM expressed concern about – well, in his words, about the lady involved."

"Really?" Unsure of what to think now. Be flattered? Or appalled? But I let Michael continue.

"I agree with you that our private lives are exactly that. But from his point of view he did have to ask a few questions. I guess you'd call it 'relationship risk assessment'."

"Sounds very romantic, that." Runaway gob again.

"He just wanted assurance that I wasn't getting involved in anything stupid or dodgy. Because as you well know, that kind of thing can affect the entire standing of the government. And, of course, I've got ministerial obligations to honour. So I can't afford to get all precious about it."

My anger was ignited. Bad enough with Shaun and his games. Now Michael and his Friends from the Feudal System. Best intentions overruled, I launched – guns a-blazing into a full-on tirade.

"Fantastic! Brilliant! Nice to know that no one gives a shit whether I'm the one getting involved in anything stupid or dodgy. And whether I have obligations myself. Like – parental obligations, or …"

I wanted to say "widowhood obligations", but it wasn't something that you could roll around your tongue. Sounded clumsy in the mouth. And I couldn't think of a better alternative quickly enough.

"Rach," he answered softly. It was the first time he had called me that.

'Rach'. Like Adam used to.

"Don't take it the wrong way. Please."

There was a silence. An emotionally drenched pause.

"I'm sorry. Once again, my words do seem to be coming out in rather the wrong way today. Look. It's the PM's job to cover his own arse first. And then to check out things from my side. But he trusts me. And he knows that I'm not an idiot." He paused, but when I didn't respond, he continued.

"So we had this very brief – but necessary – conversation along the lines of 'Right, Michael. Tell me that you've not dropped any bollocks here that I should know about?' And I said that no, my relationship with you is all squeaky clean. Above board. No hint of a scandal. Obviously he knows I'm single. And I told him that you lost your husband just under two years ago and that you have two small children."

"Oh."

"I hope that that was OK?"

"Sure. Well. Of course. It's a fact, isn't it?"

"And then, perhaps because of your situation, he was quite particular about telling me to watch out for you. You know. 'If you can, don't let her identity get out. Because you know what bastards they'll be. They won't give a toss about what she and her family have all been through.'"

"Oh. Fair enough. If he said that ... that's pretty decent of him, I suppose."

"Well," I heard him chuckle and try to contain it. "Actually, I dressed it up a little more for you. His actual words to start off with were, 'Who's the blonde?'"

"Ha!" Vindication now. "How typical! Just like the tabloids! He judges me by my hair colour!"

"Ah, but I soon set him straight. I said, 'Oh, no – she's not a real blonde; I discovered that for myself'."

"Oi! You better not have!"

Michael laughed dirtily. The mood had changed so quickly between us; the conversation had moved on so fast that my head was having difficulty keeping up with my body. Sudden wave of lust.

"But seriously," he carried on "You're right, of course. We don't have to explain ourselves to people. But it will make life – your life, in particular – a hell of a lot easier if we keep a low profile. I'm a lot more used to this kind of crap than you are."

And now another change in the atmosphere. Dampening my ardour. Jacking up the paranoia levels, instead.

He picked up on my quietness. "I don't mean that we have anything to hide. I mean that we should perhaps be careful about who knows. About us."

(Oh, I'm good at that. I'm very well-practised at all that. The hiding business).

"OK. Well. That side of things is fine," I answered briskly, trying to shake off my ancient superstitions. "The only people who know are Kate and Jake Bamber. You know – my housing buddy. Neither will say anything to anyone. Oh. And ..."

"And?"

"Hmm. Someone else did guess. But I don't think it will be an issue."

"Who?"

"I doesn't matter, Michael."

"Who Rachael?"

"This bloke. Called Shaun"

"Bloke. Called Shaun." He paused. "Would that be the bloke called Shaun that your friends mentioned on Saturday during the phone calls? The Shaun who, when I enquired about him, you gave the classic politician's answer on? Totally avoided my question."

I felt awkward. Rumbled. And dirty shame clawing at the pit of my stomach. But I took a quick breath and answered as quickly as I could.

"Yes. That would be the very same person, I'm afraid. It's a long story. We do have a bit of a history. But I've had nothing to do with him for ages. For good reasons, which I'll tell you about some other time. But the problem at the moment is that he now heads up a lot of Medlock Council, which part-funds Sisters' Space. And he turned up at work this morning when he realised I was the person in the photo with you."

There was a short silence. Then Michael said, "Ah. But how did he know it was you? You had your back to the camera."

"He said he recognised the mole on my shoulder. He knew that you and I had already met, at Sisters' Space. He put two and two together."

"What did he say to you, exactly?"

I exhaled sharply. Not a pleasant memory.

"Words to the effect of … that I shouldn't get involved with a two-faced politician like you. A man who only cares about his career and who likes to slum it on a temporary basis with common-as-muck single mothers. That it will all end in tears. Oh, and that my romping around half-naked in the national press has now compromised my ability to manage Sisters' Space."

"Jesus, Rachael. He sounds like a complete prick."

"Yes. Well."

"So what did you say?"

"You can imagine what I very nearly told him to do. But I've got the centre to think of..."

(And bills to pay.)

"So I was a bit more diplomatic than that. And I think – well, I hope – that I called his bluff. Told him that I would resign instantly if it all led to any work-related issues. He didn't expect that reaction from me. He's a pretty overbearing kind of person. He expected me to cave in."

"Good. So ... and I'm sorry to be asking you this ... but it is important. Do you think that he would tell anyone that you were the lady co-starring in the *News Of The Nation* with me?"

I half-laughed "No. He won't. Not his style at all. But it's all a bit odd. I don't know if you remember from that phone call I had with Linda Beveridge on Saturday? He wanted to speak to me about a job. Working for him. Senior management post at the council."

"Of course I remember. Like I said previously, you avoided my question on that one. But anyway, what's so odd about that? No doubt you'd be good at the job. And no doubt the guy wants to get into your knickers."

"Michael!"

"Just stating facts, Rachael. But the point is, are you tempted?"

"By what?"

"Either. Him, or the job."

I laughed. Trying not to make it sound too hollow. Too fake.

"No, Michael. I've already told you. He's a shithead. And the job is dull. Very dull."

He wasn't stopping there, though.

"So would this job involve lots more money for you?"

"Yes. Lots."

"And isn't that an attraction for you? You just mentioned that the bank were trying to call you …"

Can't fool this fella.

"Michael, I'd be lying if I told you that I've got stashes of the green stuff. Life can be a struggle. As it can be for many people. A bit more cash would be lovely. But we get by. You've seen the state of my nails. And my car. My clothes. I'm hardly a high-maintenance girl. But I've never really cared about all of the trappings. And the three of us… Well. We cope on what we have."

(For now.)

"Right. Well. That's good to hear. Not the bit about you being unable to afford the all-essential weekly manicure and all that. But the fact that the money isn't a huge motivation for you. Still …" he added. I could hear him clicking his tongue. As though he was thinking deeply.

"Rach, it wouldn't surprise me if the guy starts upping the ante on you. Especially if he knows about us. About this. And if he does, there is something that I can do. If he starts making it difficult for you."

"Yes?"

"Well." A long pause. I could hear the sound of London traffic in the background. The whine of a distant ambulance siren.

"We can take him out. 'Little accident' or something. No sweat for me, given my connections. Sorting out that kind of thing…" A cold and detached answer. Not one that I had been expecting to hear.

I suddenly remembered that Michael was an army man. The wars and conflicts that had actively required combat and armed action on his part. My mind spooled back to the weekend. To the scarring that blemished the skin on his back. To those war wounds that he had said he would tell me about, one of these days. Perhaps I had been wrong all along about his character. Perhaps Michael was yet another man on this earth whose preferred solution to a difficult problem was to resort to violence …

"Rachael?"

"What?"

"I'm only joking! Ha! You went all silent on me then. Not like you. Ha! You nearly believed me there, didn't you? You're so gullible sometimes, you know!" He was guffawing so loudly that I had to shout to get him to shut up and listen to me.

"That's not funny, Michael!"

He carried on, chortling away. Very amused by his joke.

"But really," he added, "stay away from him. But then, you being you, you'll probably now go and do the opposite, just because a nice man like me has made a polite request. That's the trouble with you feminists …"

"Oh, just generalise enormously, why don't you? I'm more than happy to respect a polite request. But perhaps a little gesture or two of appreciation would help to see it along."

"Point taken! Mental note to Michael: buy flowers, chocolates and shallow tokens for a woman who claims not to be materialistic and who will probably go and sell her side of the story to *News Of The Nation* tomorrow."

I chuckled. "But that reminds me. I was wondering whether the spin-doctor sorts have been hassling you about that side of things. If I would try to sell my story."

"Oh, yes. I did get a bit of a grilling on that front. From Alex …"

"Alex the Twat?"

"Yes. In fact, he was very rude about you and it ended up with …"

"Why? What did he say?"

"Well. It wasn't very nice. I'd rather …"

"Oh bloody hell, Michael. I'm a big girl. Tell me. Most weeks don't go by without some bloke or another here shouting abuse at me. I'm used to being called a fat ugly slag and a stupid biffer and much worse ..."

"Well, OK. He called you the Merry Widow. I know, I know. He's a total shit."

"Ha. That's all right. That's quite witty, actually …"

Michael was dismissive. "Well, I wasn't happy about it. And I ended up losing my temper with him."

"Really? What did you do?"

"I called him a twat. And I walked out."

"Really? You called him a twat? Is that a word you'd normally use in your office?"

"Wasn't mine. This was the PM's office. And his use of language tends to be a lot fruitier than mine most days, anyway."

"Hang on a minute. You mean all this happened at Number Ten? With the prime minister there?"

"Yes. This morning, in his office. But it's no big deal really. I mean, we all know the guy is a twat. It's just that no one usually says that kind of thing to his face."

"Tell me …"

"Right, well. Just as the conversation turned to who the mystery lady was, Jane – the PM's wife – stormed into the room, carrying their littlest. Toby, their toddler. Now Jane … she's a little bit highly strung. Flips every now and then. She strode past the rest of the staff, saw me, and said, 'Oh, Michael. Nice to see you. Glad we didn't get to see any *more* of you, though, in the paper this morning. Would have quite put me off my breakfast.' Then she plonked the baby on the PM's desk and said, 'Toby. Meet Daddy. Daddy. Meet Toby. Daddy – time for Toby's nappy change. The first that Daddy will have done in a fortnight!' And then she charged out again."

"Crikey!" I sniggered. "Bit embarrassing for the prime minister ..."

"Yes. But the worst thing was the stink. From the kid. It – sorry, he – had a dirty nappy, so the entire room … well. You're a mother; you know. And Alex, he was trying to ignore the whole baby-on-PM's-desk situation and was using the opportunity to round on me and say stuff like, 'So, Michael. This woman you've been at it with – how long have you known her and does she have a habit of sleeping with people and then appearing in the newspapers?' And meanwhile, the PM was bellowing "Jane! Don't just bloody leave him here! I'll do his bedtime nappy!" He tried to pick Toby up, who then started having a tantrum because he wanted to stay on the desk …"

"Ha! I love it!"

"…And then he bit the PM. The kid did, I mean – not Alex. And in between all this, Alex called you the Merry Widow. And I told him that he was a twat."

He paused for a minute. "And that's your fault, Rachael. Because ever since you thought up a new label for Alex, I haven't been able to think of him in any other way …"

"Oh great. Blame me for my gobshite ways!"

I heard a deep chiming in the background. Brass tones. The sound of Big Ben, drifting above the never-ending roar of traffic.

"Well, actually, the PM didn't seem to disagree with me. Once he had managed to offload Toby onto some poor aide, he turned to Alex and said, "Yes, Michael was right, Alex. That was twattish behaviour. Sort yourself out, for fuck's sake."

"Interesting morning all round, then."

"For sure. But the only thing that none of us can figure out is who took the photographs – you know, me on the bike, and you and me in my garden."

"Yes, it is odd. I mean, no one on Brindleford recognised you. Apart from Brenda. And your cottage in Mottram … I mean, it's not exactly a village that attracts members of the national press. Nothing ever happens there."

"Other than Doctor Shipman and the Moors Murderers having been previous residents, of course …"

"You just had to go and mention that, didn't you? Us locals try to put that kind of thing behind us. But if you London-centric lot had your way, you'd be running ghost walks or creating some sicko sort of theme park about it all."

"Actually, you've got some good ideas there. And the area could do with a bit of a boost in the tourist figures ..."

"I won't even dignify that with a response."

"So does your rampant anti-London obsession mean that you won't come and visit me here? I was thinking … we've got the party conference in Brighton all next week —"

I interrupted him.

"You know, it never ceases to amaze me. You lot are back in Parliament for what – two weeks' sitting after your extremely long summer break? And then you're all off on your jollies again to the seaside. For your so-called conferences."

"Last year's was in Manchester, Rachael. Hardly the seaside! And we work damned hard at conference."

"Oh, please. We've had this kind of conversation before, Michael. I've been to party conferences, remember …"

"Yes, yes. Anyway. Stop changing the subject … London. After next weekend and the conference has finished, why don't you come and spend a few days with me in the Big Smoke?"

A jolt. I hadn't been expecting that. I managed to keep the surprise out of my voice, though.

"Well, that'd be nice. I could try to get over my latent prejudices maybe. But the kids …"

"I know. I thought they would be an issue. But isn't your sister in London? Wouldn't she have them?"

I thought for a second. Vicky's flat was the least child-friendly place that I had ever encountered. Matthew would end up breaking all my sister's art deco pieces and maybe even torching the place. And perish the thought of such a long train journey with the little critter.

"No."

"Oh. Really? Shame."

"No, sorry; I mean, no to Matthew. But Vicky would probably cope OK with Lydia. And, I wonder ... whether my in-laws in Reading would take Matthew for a couple of days?"

"That would be excellent. I know it's not easy with kids. Well, I can imagine. But let's see what we can manage between us. My schedule often has to change at the last minute, but we can but try, hey?"

I agreed. We can but try.

After we hung up, I realised that I had forgotten to ask him about the funding cuts that Shaun was accusing him of having masterminded.

Chapter 17

TANTALISING APOLLO AND ARTEMIS

I spent the rest of the afternoon working on the same old (probably futile) funding application for the centre. By 4.15, I was thinking about packing up and leaving for home when I heard a timid knock on my office door. It was ajar, so when I looked up from my desk I was surprised to see two children standing there. Two familiar-looking children. Tyler and Tia.

I rose from my seat and gestured for them to come in properly, rather than hang around the doorway. Tyler was scuffing its frame with the toe of his shoes. They were both dressed in school uniform.

They moved hesitantly forward, not knowing where to stand; what to do. Looking as though they had been summoned to the head teacher's office. I motioned for them to sit down on the easy chairs next to the desk.

"To what do I owe this pleasure? So, did you come all the way from Mottram on your own?"

Tyler rubbed his eye with the palm of one hand and began to jiggle his leg, and Tia just shrugged and slouched, looking over at her brother.

After an uncomfortable silence, she said, "Well, we had to get two buses to get here. An' we got lost when we got off the second one. We hadn't got a clue where we were. His GPS app froze." She nodded towards Tyler, who was still limbs-a-jiggling.

"An' when we found that crap park outside," Tia continued, "we went in there for a bit to figure out where we were exactly. An' a dog tried to bite me. We've never been to Medlock before. It were, like, right stressy."

Her brother mumbled in agreement. "Yeah, and I'm not coming to Medlock again. It's shit, it is. It's even shitter than Oldham."

"But, anyway. What we've come for, like, is to say we're sorry. An' to give you this."

Tia's voice grew smaller and she looked sheepishly up at me from beneath her pale eyelashes. She handed me a grease-spotted brown envelope.

"Can I open it?"

They both nodded. It contained two twenty-pound notes and a piece of torn paper, from a school textbook by the looks of it. Untidy handwriting read: 'Where reelly sorry'.

I shook my head. "I don't understand." I frowned and looked back up at them. "What are you saying sorry for?"

"For the photo. Obviously ... Like, durr!" Tyler burst out of his fidgeting mode and leaned forward. "We had these photos on Tia's mobile of you and thingy Chisswickson. An' we knew you stayed at his house, anyway. 'Cause we're not stupid, like."

I held my hand up.

"Wait a minute. You're saying that Tia also had a mobile? That she took photos of Michael Chiswick?"

Tyler looked at me. With an expression that clearly read 'moronic bint.' Of course they both had their own mobiles. What planet was I from, eh?

Tia bit her lip and nodded, wrapping her pudgy arms around herself, a hug for comfort. She carried on with the story, screwing up her pink and freckly face.

"An' yeah, so I took a couple of photos. But we didn't really know who he was. Proper, like, yer Cheesywick bloke. Well, we knew he 'ad a bit of money or whatever, 'cause of his car and bouncer blokes hangin' round 'im. But then, yesterday – like, Monday mornin' – we saw 'im on Sky News. About that queer poofter fingy bloke workin' for 'im down in London. An' some people were sayin' that it were really bad to be a queer poofter an' doin' what he were doin'. But I fink it's bang out of order havin' a go at 'im for that innit?"

I nodded.

"So, yeah – the telly were on like, before we got off to school and us mum … well. Me an' Tyler were gettin' all psyched up when we realised it were 'im! Yer Cheesehead bloke. So, yeah, she were askin' us what the frig we knew about 'im. An' we were sayin' that we, like, knew 'im. An' that we'd helped 'im out with the mad old lady at her flat. And, er …"

I looked at them both. I had a feeling that I knew what was coming next. Tyler sniffed and wiped his nose on his sleeve, taking up the tale. I was right.

The twins' mother had seized the phone and contacted *News Of The Nation*, selling the photographs to the newspaper. At first the kids had been "well chuffed". Until mum said she'd put it in a bank account for us till we're like, sixteen. And we're, like, 'Yeah, right – bullshit – we all know she'll blow it on the gee-gees'."

The twins had managed to track me down, thanks to them having had a good nosey in my "crap car" and seeing all the leaflets about "your violent place here". And I tried to do the stern and disappointed headmistress act, but it was difficult not to crack a smile when Tia revealed one of their real motivations for wanting to find me.

"Well. We were finkin' about how people kill themselves. When they've had a bad story written about them in the papers … like … they go a bit mentalist. An' that."

They were both gazing at me, all frog-eyes. Clearly trying to gauge my emotional or psychological wellbeing.

"Mmm," I said.

"So, er ... so yer not going to go and kill yerself, are you?"

I shook my head. "No, Tyler. I won't lie and say it's been a good day for me today. But no, I'm not at that point. Yet." I smiled grimly.

"And what about 'im?" Tia asked, referring to Michael. "Yer boyfriend. Is the prime minister gonna go all Alan Sugar on 'im and start on with the 'You're fired!'"

"Or," Tyler added, "is yer Cheese-maestro bloke gonna go and jump off of Big Ben or summat and kill 'imself?"

Tyler's comment brought a very vivid picture to my mind of the Right Honourable Michael Chiswick about to launch himself off the Houses of Parliament and into the Thames. I had to stifle a giggle with a mug of lukewarm tea.

"Well," I replied, "for starters, I wouldn't really know what Mr Chiswick thinks about all this. Because, despite what you think – he isn't my boyfriend."

I caught Tia smirking at her brother.

"But I do appreciate the fact that you came all the way here to apologise. Still … doesn't your mum know where you are?"

Tyler laughed now. Stupid question, lady, "Nah, she never knows where we are."

I pointed at them now. Glowering.

"But you'll have to explain this bit to me. The money." I handed the open envelope back to them.

Tia did her best. "Well, politicians are always doin' stuff for people or sayin' they're sorry with money in brown envelopes. Bit like the Mafia."

"And?"

Tyler continued the explanation. "An' we were finkin'," Here, Tyler became very animated, "right, about your own kids. Right – if we've, like, ruined your life and turned you into a total freaky basket-case and you ended up locked up in the loony bin, so that you couldn't even have a crap without someone watchin' you, what if, like, your kids one day want to try and find out why you went all mentalist? What if, like, they come looking for the people what did it to you? An' that's us! And what if they, like, take us out and torture us really slowly by pouring lighter fluid on different parts of our body and settin' it alight and then they get these pliers an' ..."

Now Tia took up the tale.

"So – what we were finkin' was – if we do the brown envelope fing with you now. It might stop yer kids comin' and findin' us and puttin' some Regatta on us or whatever they call it. An endin' up with us being decapitated an' that in, like, ten years' time."

Here were two youngsters who spent a bit too much time watching rather unsavoury films and TV programmes. Perhaps similar to Vinnie and Dawn's two boys. I thought of Lydia. A girl who would cry for hours if she found a dead daddy-long-legs in the shower. I couldn't see Lydia wanting to behead Tyler or Tia at any point in the future. Matthew, on the other hand, had been worrying me of late. He had developed a rather disturbing interest in eating garden snails (live). And in stringing up Lydia's Barbies with her skipping rope. Plus, the crucifixion that took place last night on the Bob the Builder workstation. And this morning I found him pulling the stuffing out of his toy sheep and shrieking "I killed LambyWamby! I ripped his guts out! He's really dying badly!"

Thankfully, the twosome interrupted my darkening thoughts.

"So, 'cause we're not stupid," Tia chipped in, "an' we know that us mum is never gonna give us any of that money … we found her bingo money. When she went down the pub at lunchtime … Well. There you go." She nodded towards the envelope.

"OK," I snapped out of my oh-so familiar ruminations as to The Future Of Matthew. "If you did steal this money from your mum then there's no way I can accept it from you. But I can see that you're really sorry about it all."

Wide-eyed nods.

"Yeah. We are. But what was well weird," Tia added, "was that there was another photo. One of yer Cheesemonger bloke ridin' that motorbike. An' we never went there with you to Brindleford, did we? So we never took that bike photo what got onto the front page!"

Tyler was genuinely puzzled, too. "An' I'd never go to Brindleford anyway, 'cause it's full of Man City scuzzers. We're Liverpool FC in our house, we are."

That thought had already occurred to me too (about who took the other photograph – not about the Man City scuzzers or whether the twins were Scouse-loyalists).

I glanced at the clock. Half past four. Let's wrap this up.

"So, have either of you, or your mum ..." I gave them a steely look "had any more journalists visit? Or speak to you at all? Or the other grown-ups in your life?" Finishing my glance in Tia's direction.

"Not what we know of. Not since yesterday when Mum were on the phone to them. And Dad moved over to Rochdale with his new girlfriend, a few months ago. Though she wants them to move to that Hebden Bridge place, now. She's like, into her crystals and her dragons and all of that. She's like, so well up herself, she is. So anyway, he doesn't know nowt. And after today … well. We're not sayin' nowt to no one. No way."

She folded her arms again with a flourishing emphasis. Tyler unconsciously mirrored his sister. They seemed to be batting for my side now. But they needed a bit more to shore them up.

"Good. But you might come under a bit of pressure … from your mum. Or another grown-up. You wouldn't believe what nutters adults can be when it comes to the lure of money. Like … vultures around an animal carcass. Ripping it to shreds ." Tyler's eyes lit up at that little analogy.

"So maybe. If you two can be brave enough to stand up to the grown-ups in your life – you know, a bit like the kids in *ET* or … *The Goonies*?" My knowledge of children's films made in the twenty-first century was proving to be a bit embarrassing. Either that, or these two had never seen any of the classic kids' films. Both were looking a bit clueless now.

"Erm. *Home Alone*?" I asked. They nodded. At least they'd heard of that one.

"OK. So. Maybe in a few years' time you might end up having a book written about you. Or even a film made about the kind of kids you two are. You know. Really tough kids. Well hard. Taking a stand."

I wasn't sure if my film idea sounded really flaky or just crappy and transparent. So I decided to throw in a monetary benefit. Despite what I'd just told them about the greed of grown-ups.

"And obviously, if a well-cool film was made, you could have a lot of cash yourselves. When you turn sixteen, I mean. Without your mum taking it off you like she'd have to right now."

I thought a bit more and then tried to sound less like a capitalist, mercenary scumbag. "But you'll have to be resolute about all this. Stay strong."

Both children nodded eagerly. Tia looked as if she was going to rock her head off with agreement. "Yeah. No way. They won't crack us. They'll never break us! Will they, Ty?"

Oh good. The film analogy had worked, after all.

And the hyperactive imagination of Tyler had been spiked.

"Yeah! No ways! We'll take it to the grave! Even if they, like, try and erase our memories with some weirdy injection shit. Or even if they, like, try and slice our ears off and pour acid in our eyes!"

I interrupted his gruesome meanderings and moved to the back of Tia's chair. I leaned on it in a subtle yet dominating teacher sort of way.

"So, if you two are really genuine about your gesture today," I pointed at the brown envelope in Tia's hands, "then I think that the very least you can do – no, the best that you can do – is write a little letter of apology to a certain man."

"But I'm shit at writing," said Tia.

"Doesn't matter. Most politicians are, too. And he happens to be a fella who holds a lot of power in this country. He may even know a filmmaker or two. You need to tell him how sorry you are."

I grabbed a pad of writing paper and two ballpoint pens from my desk drawer and handed them to the twins.

"Write to him," I urged, tilting my head. Doing the Don Corleone. Wishing I had some cotton wool to stuff in my cheeks for dramatic effect. "Show the man a bit of respect, eh?"

Chapter 18

TABLOID TITANS

On Wednesday morning, after dropping the children off and arriving at work, I visited Mrs Singh's newsagent to see what the *News Of The Nation* had to offer today. Michael and I had had a long conversation the night before. I had told him about the twins' confession. ("Don't bother sending me their letter of apology, Rachael," he laughed, "the less paper trail on this whole thing, the better.") He had tried to reassure me that any news stories the following day would be much more favourable, thanks to the efforts of his own PR bloke, Marvin.

But despite his upbeat attitude, my early morning had been filled with anxiety and distraction. I had been "in la-la-land", according to Lydia. My stomach clenched with icy dread as I entered Mrs Singh's shop but I shored myself up with the purchase of a large quantity of midget gems – as well as the newspaper – and then headed back to my car for a bit of a perusal. But Michael had been right. In *News Of The Nation* the story had been relegated to page seven, where the newspaper claimed that Michael Chiswick was "furious" about the allegations regarding his private life. And I was pleased to see that no one had come forward offering a story about The Bimbo's identity.

But the *News Of The Nation*'s coverage still contained an interesting element for me. An interview with one Michelle Murray of Lapwing Road in Brindleford. Shelley 'I'll Kneecap The Bastards Myself' Murray was a woman I knew all too well from my time way back when, managing the Brindleford estate. It seemed that she had been canny enough to spot Michael in motion, telling the newspaper, "I just thought it was some bloke trying to nick our Vinnie's bike." Hence, her scrabbling to take a photo of him with her phone.

Mystery over.

I'd already noted Vinnie's surname during our encounter with him. And it turned out that Shelley was Vinnie's aunt. And that she thought it would be a nice thing to sell the photo to the newspaper and let the whole world know about her vigilance. Shallow gene pool sharing equally depthless moral values.

She was full of self-righteous anger about people tearing around the estate on motorbikes. It was people like Michael who put the lives of Brindleford's children in danger. She had some very forthright and interesting opinions. Such as:

> *And now that I know it was the minister in charge of communities himself, I'm even angrier. Because instead of riding bikes around, why isn't he sorting out the problems on our estate?*

I snorted in disbelief. Very much doubting that Shelley ever could have strung together such an eloquent sentence. Every interaction I had ever had with her on Brindleford had consisted of her either grunting in a Neanderthal fashion or attempting to smack in the face whoever was "givin' me the agro". She had even gone for me once. A proper, old-fashioned attempt at a headbutt when I'd refused her a transfer to a different street. Thankfully I'd managed to side-step her in time. I wondered if the *News Of The Nation* had any idea of the kind of tenancy and police record that their interviewee had. Probably not. Probably didn't care.

But another newspaper was taking a different approach. Hailing Michael as some kind of national hero. The *Daily UK*, the *News Of The Nation*'s main rival, had a front-page headline that sang "Minister Saves Elderly Woman ... In Shorts!" Badly written, I told myself. Was it the minister wearing the shorts? Or was it Miss Simpson?

But somehow or another – and it was probably down to that Marvin – the *Daily UK* had unearthed a little more about Michael's Saturday afternoon. Pages three to five consisted of interviews with Mr Bridges and his daughter. Plus photographs of the damage to the two maisonettes, shots of some of the more salubrious streets (graffiti, etc.) on Brindleford, and an attempted interview with Miss Simpson. I bought a copy of both newspapers ("You're looking better today, lovey!" Mrs Singh told me. "So pale yesterday!") and once the initial writhing had dissipated, I almost enjoyed sitting in my car and perusing the articles. There was a rather unflattering photograph of Mr Bridges, standing barefoot in his living room as he attempted to demonstrate the sogginess of his abode. Because he was dressed in a shirt and tie (being of the generation that tended to dress up for photographs) and because the photographer had no doubt told him to look serious, he had ended up with rather a constipated expression And giving off the distinct impression that he had only recently escaped a lunatic asylum (sans shoes).

James Bridges, aged 72, told the Daily UK*: "It was the worst day of my life. I had just come back from the market in Ashton and I saw all this water pouring underneath the front door. I nearly died of shock. And when I went inside, it was just heartbreaking to see it all. Someone fetched the local MP. Well, I didn't know he was the local MP then. He had these daft shorts on, and you don't expect your local MP to turn up in purple shorts with a mucky T-shirt on, now, do you?"*

Mr Bridges told the Daily *that Michael Chiswick located the stopcock, turned off the electricity, called the housing association for assistance and rescued the elderly lady and her cat from the flooded flat above. Then he began to bail out water from Mr Bridges' flat using kitchen utensils. Diane Adamson, Mr Bridges' daughter, told the* Daily*: "Michael Chiswick was an absolute godsend and I'm only sorry that we didn't have the foresight to thank him there and then. If it wasn't for him, I think the damage would have been a lot worse and my dad wouldn't have had help from the housing association as quickly as he did. And even though Dad is still a bit cross with the old lady upstairs about the flood, we are grateful that Michael Chiswick managed to persuade her to leave and to take her to somewhere safe. He's a lovely man. He's not my local MP and I don't always agree with his government on things, but if I lived in this area he'd get my vote. I think it's very sad that anyone would try to muckrake about his private life. The* News Of The Nation *should find more positive stories to write about, rather than inventing a load of rubbish!"*

I remembered Mr Bridges' horror – his panic – when he had realised that he might not have the insurance to cover him for the flood damage. I had thought of this several times over the last few days. But it seemed to me now that he had been covered after all. Otherwise I couldn't imagine him or his daughter sounding so upbeat about the situation. Although, of course, the *Daily UK* would have paid them for the interview. Or perhaps even Michael's people had contributed …

Either way, I was pleased for them. For Mr Bridges, after so recently having lost his wife. Nothing worse than having an enormous dose of misery injected into your life and then even more piling itself on top of it all. I continued to read on, smiling to myself now.

> *The* Daily UK *attempted to speak to Miss Mary Simpson about the incident, but as she is now resident at a local hostel we were unable to contact her directly. The hostel's warden, Brenda Kray, told the* Daily*: "Miss Simpson is a very fragile elderly lady so she can't give you an interview. But I can tell you this for nothing - that she is now Michael Chiswick's biggest fan!"*

Bless that Brenda Kray.

I wondered if Alex the Twat and the prime minister would be pleased with the coverage, even though it had been Michael's very own PR guy, Marvin who had generated the counter-story to the original tabloid story. I was relieved that there was no mention of my presence throughout the soggy situation. If Mr Bridges or his daughter had talked about me, in all likelihood the powers that be would have wanted my involvement kept out of it. Suited me just fine. My phone buzzed. It was a text message. From Kate:

"U shd c wot MC put on twitr @ u!"

I texted her back:

"Don't do twitr. Sum of us hav a life.. Dont txt me. MI5 watchin ..."

I knew that my comment would feed into her very own peculiarly paranoid whims – usually about Big Brother and satellites in outer space watching her while she was exfoliating herself in her super-duper jet-stream shower cubicle. She watched far too much TV, did our Kate, despite her protestations about the overkill out of school hours lesson-preparation for primary school teachers. But no go, as per the freaking our Kate out. I immediately got one back from her:

"Miseryguts. U reali want 2 no tho don't u?"

Yes, she did know me too well. I texted her a curt "Go on" back.

"Sum1 askd him wot 'that foto' was all @. He sd 'classy lady inspects my war wounds'."

I did the LOL thing. It hadn't occurred to me that Michael 'did Twitter'. Still, most politicians probably did. Had to, to keep ahead in politics. Boost your following. In fact, Twitter was probably the geriatrics' choice of social networking these days. I LOL'd in real time at Michael's tweet. Me. Classy indeed. I sniggered again, shaking my head. My car window was open and an old man trundled past on a disability scooter, casting a strange glance at a woman giggling away, alone in her car. I texted Kate back.

"Every word true."

The car radio was wittering away and I heard Michael's name mentioned. Radio 4's morning news. The headlines.

"Junior Minister for Communities, Ben Hardy has announced his resignation following the revelation of his homosexual affair. The prime minister has just issued a statement outlining his regret at the departure of Mr Hardy and containing a request that the press respect the privacy of both families involved."

I postponed locking up the car and entering Sisters' Space for a few minutes, in order to hear the rest of the news. After the headlines, the Radio 4 newsreader continued: "And as the press, the government and the opposition continue to disagree over whether the Ben Hardy affair is a noteworthy scandal or not, Michael Chiswick, Minister for Communities told us earlier that some of the recent reporting focussing on him was a pretty pathetic attempt to tarnish his character and that he was sure they could have created a juicier story if they'd tried a bit harder. So, next in the studio we'll be asking ourselves whether the media is making much ado about nothing."

Blah blah blah, as Lydia would have said

I switched the radio off. I was sick of hearing about it all. Although I felt better about the fact that the latest coverage had a pro-Michael angle, my sudden news obsession was getting me down. And my kids, too. Before leaving the house that very morning, Lydia had whined at me. "All you ever do is listen to the boring old news!" And then she moved on to tell me (in her best northern dialect) that I was a "bobbins mum who doesn't even know what's cool in footwear". Apparently my cardinal sin was referring to an expensive brand of shoes (that she did not and would not be owning) as Footsie Wootsies when their real name is Tootsie Wootsies. I was in no mood for a reasoned discussion about this, however, because Matthew was fighting with me like a wild cat as I sought to remove the socks that he had been wearing for forty-eight hours. Doomed to losing both footwear battles in equally childish measures, I scornfully replied to my eldest.

"Oh, I'm so sorry, Lydia! I'm so sorry that I don't know the latest designer tosh brands for shallow families! Maybe it's because I have my mind on more important things. Like the war in outer Mongolia or northern Azerbaijan, or wherever!"

Lydia stuck her tongue out at me. Hiccupped a half-sob and flounced out of the house, into the car. Slamming its door, hard. When I managed to persuade Matthew to follow us (luring him with a promise that he could wear his sister's tiara), Lydia was sitting fiercely upright in her booster seat and scowling at me.

"You're a prize grump this morning," I said to her. "Did you get out of bed on the wrong side, or what?" As if to a twelve-year-old. Always the verbal level that I had to pitch things at with Liddy. Until she turned seven in a few weeks, when I would have to up the stakes a bit and make the language more suitable for a fourteen-year-old.

"Says you!" came her reply "You're just one big blimmin' pain in the ulterior!"

I burst out laughing. Not helpful. Petrol to the flames.

"It's not funny! Don't you dare laugh at me!"

I decided not to reply and to give her a chance to regain her temper. Soon, we had reached the second track on 'The Wheels On The Sodding Bus' CD (it being 'Five Little Frigging Annoying Fish Went Swimming') and out of the blue, Lydia snarled at me in full-on teen sulk mode.

"Just because you know about wars and things, you think you're *so* clever. But people who listen to horrible things like that are just horrible themselves! And your head must be like just one big war, war, war all the time!"

At the mention of the word "war" Matthew began a series of machine-gun noises. Followed by something that sounded like a ground to air missile attack. And then several landmine explosions.

"Oh, do shut up, you stupid little beast!" Lydia snapped at her brother, borrowing a favourite phrase courtesy of Enid Blyton.

Matthew impressed me by yelling back, "You stink like Timmy the dog!" (his own language skills were clearly coming on), but in the end I stopped the row by growling at Lydia to stop crying and then shrieking at Matthew to "pack in the explosion noises, or you're in Time Out!" Both children were subsequently dropped off and I set off for work. Feeling worn out before the day had even begun. No. It had not been a good start.

I vowed to myself that there would have to be less listening time for all things political and media while the kids were in earshot.

But I swiped my way into Sisters' Space feeling a whole lot better now, thanks to that wonderful Marvin chap. And Michael's invitation the previous day – the London lure – had made me wonder whether a break would do the whole family some good. Despite the usual early morning bickering and arguments, I had been enjoying the company of the children more in recent weeks. Feeling less desperate; less suffocated, somehow. As I switched my computer on, I frowned at how closed in, how drained by their own little needs I had felt during the first year after Adam died.

Things had been bad back then. Really bad. The hardball horror. Strike One – the accident. Losing him. The unfairness of Adam's life being cut off in such a pointless, stupid and illogical way. It Should've Been The Holiday of a Lifetime. And he hadn't even made it to the age of forty. Strike Two – the shock of being catapulted into single motherhood. (Yeah, that particular bit hadn't been in the marital or child-rearing contracts.)

A hard ball of fury and resentment had lodged itself in my heart. A canker of a curveball. Leaving me with painful, shameful deliberations. Those thoughts and fantasies about abandoning my children. About buggering off and letting someone else deal with all the hard work and decision-making.

And Strike Three, of course. The Great Life Insurance Fuck-Up.

Oh. And not to mention Strike Four. An entanglement with a certain Shaun Elliot again. Shaun and the car parks. Talk about stress overload. Talk about an insane, horrific year.

But that was last year.

This is now, I told myself. And now is time to develop a new, positive attitude to life. All the blokes I seemed to know had this unshakeable confidence thing going on. Michael, Shaun, Jake, Martyn Pointer, my dad; hell, even the sodding postman and the way he'll happily flout Post Office regulations to sign for my parcels when I'm not at home.

What is it about women's inability to throw caution to the wind – to take a risk every now and then?

So, to hell with it. Maybe Michael will have to cancel at the last minute. But so what? Getting ditched for a three-line whip would hardly be worse than what I've been through in the last year or so.

Plan for a bit of spontaneity, I thought. (I'm good at contradictions in terms).

Chapter 19

PLANNING FOR THE PARTHENON?

After our usual Wednesday morning team meeting I met with Andrea and Shirley. We had an extremely dull chat about health and safety in preparation for the launch of the cafe and shop. Opening your premises and serving hot drinks and snacks always requires another mound of paperwork to be carried out and half a dozen action plans to be written. Not my forte, that's for sure.

And then I went back to my office to make the phone call. My in-laws, Julia and Malcolm, had remained close to Adam despite their move to Reading just before our wedding. Adam had been their only child. The physical distance between us meant that they had kept most of their grief and horror at arm's length from me – perhaps deliberately. Perhaps they thought I had enough to deal with. But I suspected that Adam's side of the family were even more dysfunctional than mine when it came to any revelations about vulnerability, when it came to the whole talking about feelings thing.

I knew, though, from the odd confidential chat I had had over the phone with Malcolm, that Julia had been battling hard with depression since Adam's death. Several months ago Malcolm had told me, "I'll never come to terms with losing our Adam. Never." But even he was struggling to understand the depth of Julia's despair. He would urge me to "send the kids to come and stay with us – it's the only time I see her as her old self!" But with Lydia being at school full time, and Matthew being a child version of Jack the Ripper, I had been reluctant to. Or perhaps I hadn't felt there was a viable enough reason to do it. Until now.

Malcolm answered the phone in his best circa 1956 telephone exchange manner.

"Russells!"

A booming voice. Like Adam's. Or, Adam's – like his.

Sending me off on one. Scrabbling sorrow at the pit of my stomach. Most days I managed to cruise along, to blank it all out, but it still never ceased to amaze me how the grief-addled brain could suddenly experience that feeling. Of being slammed around the head with a sledgehammer. Just hearing those echoes of Adam's sent my subconscious catapulting into the past.

Adam, shortly after our honeymoon:

"Don't think so, Rach. It won't ever be me running off with a younger model. If anyone's going to be doing the 'leaving' in our relationship, it'll be you. You're the flighty one. You're the one needing the high emotional maintenance."

You were wrong about that one, Adam. And it was even worse for your parents than it was for me.

Because being widowed while your children are still very young is horrendous. It's shocking. It's a vortex of asking 'What If?' and 'Why Me?' Of waking up in the middle of the night from the most terrible nightmare you ever had and finding out it was true.

But. At the end of the day you can always find another love. Someone else. You have that choice, after all. And if you lose a parent you might well get lucky, be blessed to gain a brilliant step-parent. To find a parent-substitute. Or possess a set of incredible grandparents, or something.

But if you lose a child, there is nothing remotely like a form of replacement. You're left with a child shaped chunk missing from your life. Whether you're grieving over a tiny baby or a grown man.

I clenched my jaw, shaking my head. Hard. This was just another sideways swipe of sorrow. It still happened every week or so. Whether it was a photograph, a letter addressed to him, the way that Lydia blew her nose … It used to feel like every hour – on the hour. So maybe things were progressing for me. Maybe life was moving on. Perhaps too fast, though, come to think of it. And not at a speed – or in a direction – that Julia or Malcolm would approve of. So there would be no mention of any men on the scene during this little conversation. That's for sure.

So I outlined my thoughts on 'a little tourist trip' to London for Lydia and I. And asked him whether he thought they could cope with Matthew for a whole weekend. Malcolm sounded enthusiastic.

"Sounds great. But let's check with the boss, eh?"

He passed the phone to Julia, who gushed, "Oh, we've never had Matthew to ourselves – that would be lovely!"

"You sure that you can handle him? He's a bit …"

Julia brushed my fretting aside.

"Rachael – I've told you so many times what a crabby little boy Adam was …" she trailed off for a few seconds. Lost in sadness. But managed to collect herself and added, brightly, "And these days we have more TV and DVDs. And those soft-play places to go if we start to have any problems. So don't you worry!"

I wanted to tell her that gadget and experience overload was a sure-fire way to get Matthew to kick off big time, but whenever I offered any such advice to either my parents or Adam's, I was always met with the same response: "We have had children ourselves, you know!"

So I didn't bother.

Next, I called my little sister. Vicky was rather different from me. She was all-aesthetics and a science-obsessive, as opposed to her clothes-clueless and bleeding-heart liberal elder sibling. But we were close and she had always been a huge fan of Adam. She had moved to south London five years ago for her career, and had no intention of settling down and "feeling smug about the fact that I managed to carry out a bit of basic biology", as she liked to refer to the act of having a family. Even at the age of fifteen she had been determined never to have any children.

Still, she sounded chipper at the prospect of having Lydia to herself for the weekend. But suspicious about my reasons for wanting to be in the capital of Blighty.

"You hate London!" she said. Followed closely by, "It all sounds a bit odd … you dumping Liddy on me and not staying here …" And then: "Hey … this better not be some weirdy Shaun sordid liaison thing rearing its head again. Because if it is … I'm finally going to tell Mum and Dad all about …"

"Bloody hell, Vicky!" I burst out laughing. "Just listen to you! 'Go and tell Mum and Dad'? I thought you were the director of some highbrow international electronics techie multinational. Not my kid sister threatening to grass me up for nicking her Easter eggs!"

"Well, I don't care …"

She carried on with her petulant response, so I interrupted her before she could engage any more deeply into her usual character assassination of Shaun. I gabbled my excuses.

"Got to go – things are mental around here. Bye for now."

After talking to my in-laws and to Vicky, I'd been on a bit of a high. I called Michael to tell him that it was looking like a trip to London was on the cards. I was hoping that he would be as pleased as I was about it all, but he answered his mobile with a rather clipped, "Sorry … bit too busy to speak right now." He called over to someone else in the room with him: "Yes, we'll be there in a minute, Marv."

I put the phone down and ruminated on this for a bit. Perhaps all the publicity folk – the spin doctors like Marvin and Alex the Twat – were playing a longer game with Michael. Working on him slowly so he would ultimately run like the wind from me, my cursed personal life and my limpid social concerns.

(Probably letting your imagination run away with itself, Rachael.)

I rapped myself on the head, with my knuckles. Hard. Yes, here I was, forgetting that only a couple of hours ago I had decided to steam ahead with life from now on. Plan for me and for my small family and not focus on needing anyone else in our lives apart from each other. And if life decided to chuck the odd chance at us to have a bit of fun, presented a light moment or two along the way … or a significant new person in our lives – then all the better.

But a new distraction now presented itself. One of our receptionists, bearing a huge bouquet of flowers, entered my room. She had a tight little smile on her face. She might have seen me rapping myself on the head, but it was just as likely that she was pleased for me. Wondering whether the poor wee widow was back in the game.

After she left I tore open the envelope, expecting them to be from Michael after our jokey chat about me being the type of woman to demand flowers and chocolates.

But no. The card had just one word.

'Stan.'

I stared across my desk. In shock. I focussed on the vision outside the office windows. The pathetic park and the faded playground. In all of our not-time together, Shaun had only ever given me two things: a pair of socks (which he once left at my bedsit in Trafford by mistake) and an old copy of *Housing Studies and Research Methodology*.

This was strange. Everyone and his dog knew that Shaun didn't do gifts. Didn't do gestures.

My thoughts were interrupted by the sound of a baby's squawk, and I looked up to see Dawn at my office door. Clad in a clingy purple and green striped mini-dress and with the latest celeb-style sunglasses. They helped to hide the bruises, at least. New nails and new hair extensions, by the look of it. Chewing a wad of gum and looking souped-up; cooking on gas.

"Awright, missus?" she chirruped as she sashayed into the room. "Ooh, nice. Someone's popular," she added, as she noticed the flowers. I flicked my hand towards a seat and she plonked herself down, letting Poppy-Rose freewheel herself around the office.

"Just come to let you know that it's lookin' like you was wrong!" she sang victoriously.

"Story of my life," I smiled. "So what was I wrong about this time?"

"Well – actually, I'm exaggeratin', really. You were right in one way. 'Cause they said I'd have somethin' like a ten-year wait to get a house in the places I really want – nearer me sister. But ..."

She gave me a second's pause for dramatic effect and mimicked a fanfare.

"Ta-da!! There's one just come free in Steppin' Vale. Which is an all right place, innit?"

I nodded, answering, "Yes, but blimey, Dawn. It doesn't normally happen that fast. Especially if you're moving over from Manchester to Medlock."

"Well," she said, as she examined her nails, "Brenda Kray gets on right well with the Brindleford housing officer. Who knows me. Well, knows Vinnie dead well. What he's like. And they called up this bloke they used to work with at Medlock – who's at New Banks now. Who put 'em through to this Jake Bamber, what they also know. And then – just this mornin' – this Jake Bamber rang me up and asked me if I knew you. An' I said yeah – course – and you'd helped me out. And next thing I know, I've got a viewin' lined up for this three-bed house on Friday!"

If I had a fiver for every time I had either heard or thought 'Housing: it's so incestuous'…

No one was playing the system here. We were just trusting each other's judgement. And Dawn's case – because of the violence and the children – would get priority consideration. She realised this.

"So, yeah. I were a bit gobsmacked myself, actually. But I go straight to the top of the list 'cause of all the grief what that nobhead has caused me an' the kids."

She lifted the sunglasses to show me.

"Purple and green. Matches your frock."

"I know." She popped her gum at me. "Bloody corker this time, eh? Bastard. Anyway. I just saw Bev goin' into her relaxation class and she says the house is only a ten-minute walk from hers – an' from our Debs'. An' social services can sort the lads out with their new school there. So it's looking well good. Yay!"

She leant over to the toddler and urged her to join her in arm-waving merriment. Poppy-Rose just stared at her mother, looked befuddled and farted. Dawn roared with laughter.

"Just like yer brothers, you dirty little sod!"

She turned back to me.

“An’ I know I said it already. But I just wanted to say thanks again.”

I shrugged. “It's what they pay me for.”

She disagreed. “Not on a Saturday, they don’t. I’m not daft. I know you didn't have to help me out. An’ there was something else I wanted to say, too.” She looked away suddenly. Slight embarrassment.

“I knew that Vinnie and most other people on Brindleford wouldn’t have twigged it. An’ that fat cow Shelley Murray didn’t, either. Til it were in the papers, I mean. But I did. Straight off.”

“Twigged what?” I asked, caution in my voice now.

“I mean, who he was – the minister bloke. They’re all a bit behind the door in Vinnie’s family. Total thickos. I think they’ve got problems up there, actually.” She tapped her forehead, her initial bashfulness disappearing now that she was into her story. “Like, for example, Shelly’s married to Vinnie’s Uncle Denzel, though he’s banged up again now. An’ his nickname is SFB. Ha!”

“SFB. I don’t get it.”

“SFB – Shit For Brains. Cause he’s as thick as pig shit. They all are. Anyway. It took ’em all till first thing Monday morning to work it out. When they saw the headlines on the news. That story about that gay bloke what worked for him. I mean, yer minister bloke were all over the telly, weren’t he? You couldn’t bloody miss him. So then Shelley and all her lot were all, like, ‘Hey, let’s make some dosh out of all of this with me photo of him on our Vin’s bike!”

I held my hand up.

“Whoa. You’re going too fast for me here, Dawn. I saw Shelly Murray in the papers this morning. She reckoned she’d taken the photo of … of him, Michael. Because she thought he was stealing Vinnie’s bike. So is that true?”

She crossed her legs, giving me a flash of a tattoo at the top of her thigh.

“Yeah. Shelley had been sat in her front garden. Havin’ some beers when yer bloke came past. She knew it were Vinnie's bike. Says she thought summat weird were goin' on. She thought someone might be nickin' it. An' she's always up for an excuse to go and get someone's head kicked in. So she took a photo with her phone. An' she's always photo-in' everythin'. Makes quite a bit out of insurance stuff. Car accidents. Spillages in the supermarket aisles and that."

Sounded about right.

"But anyway. I realised it all after you'd left us in the hostel. Seen him before on the telly, y'see."

I nodded and chose my words carefully.

"Well, yes. He is in the media a lot."

"Zactly." She fished into her large shoulder bag and brought out a bottle of milk for the baby.

"An' some of us," she commented more to the baby now than to me, "Unlike Shit For Brains an' your daddy, like to watch stuff other than boxin' or the footie. Don't we? Some of us might not be as stupid as her teachers thought she was when she were at school …"

Her daughter had moved over to my bookshelves, where she had embarked upon yanking out the books one by one. She saw the drink and toddled back to her mother. But Dawn's mind was now elsewhere. She barely seemed to notice Poppy-Rose's attempt to grab the milk as she continued to swing the bottle by the teat. Perhaps lost in ancient battles with GCSEs and unimaginative teachers.

"Stupid is the last thing that I'd call you, Dawn. But I don't understand how you know all this. Haven't you been living at the hostel since Saturday?"

"Oh, yeah. But didn't you used to work on Brindleford yerself?"

"Yes."

"Well, then. You know what it's like for news spreadin' like wild-fuckin'-fire. My cousin Katrina is shacked up with one of Vinnie's brothers. She's a right mug, she is. Always has been. So the poor cow has had Shelley Murray's arse stuck to her sofa the last few weeks. Shelley's a lazy bitch an' she hangs out anywhere where she can get free tinnies or pizza."

I knew Shelley. I knew what she was like, of course, but I didn't tell Dawn this. Dawn finally noticed the child's attempt to snatch the bottle, and passed it down to her.

"So, yeah. Our Katrina was textin' me all of this on Monday. Sayin' how they'd all been sat there goin' on about all the money they were gonna make from them lot talkin' to *News Of The Nation*. But the thing is, none of them could figure out why the 'ell your minister bloke was on the estate. Who he was with. Meanin' you. Vinnie was shitfaced at the time. Wouldn't have noticed you if you'd been prancing round with yer tits hangin' out."

I nodded. Wishing she would stop referring to Michael as 'your'. I knew it was just a local dialect thing, but it was grating on me. She could read my mind.

"So, Michael Fingy. Whatever his name is …"

I looked at her, pointedly. Michael Fingy was fine by me.

"I knew it were Michael Fingy. I were noseyin' out of the window at Lancaster House at the time. When the pigs were there. When they were crappin' themselves for pullin' 'im over on Vinnie's bike! Fuckin' priceless, that was!" She gave out a sudden, very masculine belly laugh. "But, yeah. I asked Brenda on Sunday about you. 'Cause I wanted to say thanks to you at any rate, so I bobbed down here on Monday to do that. As yer know. An' then bloody yesterday – the papers were all, like, 'Who is the mystery blonde?' stuff. So. I …"

I waited for her to finish. She looked down at her bejewelled sandals. She seemed to be embarrassed again.

"Well. I've been thinking about it. Quite a bit. An' I just wanted to let you know that I'm not saying 'owt to no one. No one. Not me mates. No journalists, neither. They can all piss off."

I wanted to hug her. And the grin on my face probably didn't disguise the fact. Sheer relief. Dawn's story could have fetched her the kind of money that she desperately needed.

"Oh, Dawn. God. I really ... really appreciate that, thanks. Wow. Thank you …"

She inclined her head. "S'all right."

"No, no. Look. I'll be straight with you. You know you could sell your story to the papers for quite a bit. Well, knowing my identity and all that crap, I mean."

"Oh, yeah. I know that. An' it'd come in friggin' useful, the mess Vinnie's left us in. All our furniture. Everything. Even Poppy-Rose's baby toys are gone, for fuck's sake …"

I swallowed. My tongue felt tacky. This wasn't an empty gesture. This was a big deal for Dawn.

"But," she carried on, reaching for a tissue from the box on my desk and spitting her gum into it, "some of us have got standards. Or whatever the frig you wanna call it. And you helped me. So I'm helpin' you back."

And now I could feel my face flushing.

"Right … but Dawn. I really should explain to you about that photo in the newspaper – it didn't come across well. What I was actually doing was ..."

She held her hand up and started chuckling;

"Look, hun, you don't have to explain to me. Of all people! An' if nowt is going on between you and yer minister bloke, well. Don't burst me bubble. Don't make me life any more borin' than it already is. I've never known anyone famous before. It's well funny. It's well romantic, actually." She nodded at the bouquet. I looked away. She added, "Even if I can't go round talkin' about it …"

"Dawn, the last thing I would call your life is boring. But all right, if it makes you happy, I'll stop all of the denials!" I beamed at her. Poppy-Rose stopped sucking for a second and gave out an enormous burp. Dawn rolled her eyes. "Pig!"

"Right. But there is one more thing that I wanted to say to yer." She started fiddling with one of her hair extensions.

"Go on."

"On Monday, when I came over here to say thanks to you, an' to see if you could help me with lookin' for a house, I was gonna tell yer then that I'd clocked you an' him on Saturday. Michael Fingy. I could tell that you had summat goin' on between yer."

"We didn't."

Her mouth twisted into a smirk.

"Yeah. All right. At that point. Or whatever. But in the end I didn't say anythin' properly to yer about it 'cause …"

She rifled through her handbag and brought out some more chewing gum. Offered me a piece. I took a stick. Fruity. She popped a white piece into her mouth and nibbled it between her front teeth. I waited.

"Cause it turned out you 'ad enough problems on yer plate that day".

She looked uncomfortable again now. Less embarrassed; more troubled. She chewed. Her lips puckered into wrinkled slick of glittery lip-gloss. I stared. The baby was sucking the bottle at breakneck speed. There was a short silence. All that we could hear was the bottle being drained.

"Thing is," she popped another piece of gum into her mouth, "I was havin' a ciggie in the park outside while Poppy-Rose were havin' a kip. The lady on yer reception said you were out on yer lunch break. So I went and sat in the park, waitin' till you were back at work again. And then this couple turned up just behind where I were sittin' in the park. An' they were talkin'. Well, more like arguin'. An' I suddenly realised it were you."

I nodded slowly. Bloody hell. Yes. The woman sitting on the bench just feet away from me and Shaun on Monday, after the drink in the pub. I had been more than a bit distracted. Not realised that it was Dawn. Even though she had trotted into the centre afterwards and accosted me. I simply hadn't put two and two together. Silly Rachael.

"An' I also knew him. The big bloke with yer. 'Cause he's always in the local papers or telly. Gobbin' off about whatever."

I dipped my head, looked hard at her and replied. "And?"

"And I honestly weren't tryin' to earwig. But madam 'ere," she nodded at Poppy-Rose, "were bloody quiet for once. Asleep. So I heard most of what you were sayin' ..."

"And?" I had run out of conversational skills.

"And, well, it were well weird. Listening to someone like you. Getting drawn into all of his shit."

I stared at her, dumbfounded. Words still wouldn't come.

She sighed. Stopped biting her nail for a minute.

"So alls I wanted to say was, don't take any crap from anyone. Not from your Frankenstein bloke. Or your minister man. Sounds to me like you've had your own fair share of shit in life. Might well be best stickin' with a fella who's in London half the time, though. Best to have a man at the other end of the country. One that you don't have to see too often! Me and Vin got on great when he was in the army and never around …"

My frozen-moment thawed. Ending with laughter. "Dawn, I like your assessment of the situation. Very insightful advice there …"

She beamed at me.

"Nice one. That'll be a three-hundred-quid psychiatrist fee for that. Ha! But really," she turned to go, "glad you're not pissed off with me. I think you're well sound. An' it would be well shitty if you got into trouble over all of this stuff. When alls you've been doin' is trying to help people."

Dawn hoisted Poppy-Rose up onto her hip. Moving towards the door, she directed her words at the baby: "Jesus, though. Talk about people havin' complicated lives! Thought mine was bad!"

I followed and tapped her on the back, trying to convey my gratitude.

"I really appreciate this, Dawn. I know you're struggling for money. That you could have done what Shelley and her lot did. It means a lot to me, this does."

She turned back to me with raised eyebrows.

"Hey – don't be thinkin' that I'm … Let's be straight. I mean, at the end of the day, if I pissed you off – you might well have ended up stoppin' me from gettin' moved off Brindleford to somewhere better. I know you say that you don't have owt to do with who gets a house and where. But I'm not a blood relative of Shit For Brains … remember? I know you lot. How these things work …"

She gave me a wicked grin. I smiled back at her, trying not to mind her lumping Sisters' Space and our independent advocacy approach with the statutory authority figures at the council and those at the housing association. Call me self-obsessed, but I could happily overlook such assumptions when my own arse was in the firing line of the national press.

"Well," I said, "be that as it may, I still want you talking to our solicitor properly about whether you should be going for a non-molestation order or an occupation order against Vinnie, as otherwise ..."

She left the office, and flapped her hand over her shoulder – dismissing me.

"Yeah, yeah, whatever. But yeah, yer secret's safe with me. So long as you keep away from that nob. The other one. Him trying to get back into your knickers. I mean it: steer clear!"

After she had left I mused on how many times all of us – service users, staff and volunteers – would say exactly that kind of thing to another woman who was involved in a destructive relationship.

And yet the chances of her going back to him?

They were far too high to disregard.

Chapter 20

HADES SETS THE LABYRINTH

I had been hoping for some time at the local park at the weekend to let the kids run off some steam, perhaps allowing me to slump on a bench with a book while they went mad on the monkey bars. But the weather conspired against us. Thunderstorms and downpours, crowning most of the country with slate-grey rain and pinched, overcast skies.

On the Sunday afternoon the three of us were all going a little bit stir-crazy. After various squabbles over board games ("Matthew can't even figure out how to play Ker-Plunk! He is such a durr-brain stinky-pants brat!") and who had made the nicest painting of a rainbow (Matthew won this battle when he poured his jar of slurry paint-water over Lydia's hair) I had finally given up trying to carry out even small meaningful and memorable activities with them.

I had rammed some earplugs into my ears. I was lying on the sofa with a cushion over my face. I was letting the kids look at various children's cartoons on YouTube – good old-fashioned Tweetie Pie and Bugs Bunny. And I was hoping that Lydia wouldn't end up downloading hardcore porn or something (making a mental note to myself to sort an internet filter out). I was about to drift off into a nice, drooling sleep when I heard a distant and muffled but mouthy Matthew.

"Turn it off, Liddy! Turn it off! That stupid noise!"

I took my earplugs out. Lydia was peering quizzically at my tablet.

"It's making a funny bee-bop sound, Mummy! Have I done something bad?"

I sat up and moved round to them both. Matthew was licking the edge of the tablet. Strange boy. I swiped him away. Someone was calling me on Skype. It was Michael. I had forgotten that he had added me as a contact a few days ago.

"Budge up," I said to the kids and after a moment's hesitation (to wipe away the saliva and to shove my wild hair in a pony tail) I clicked to accept the call. The video camera started up, and Lydia shrieked.

"It's the man on the fridge! Hey! How did you get onto Mummy's tablet?"

Michael looked taken aback to see Rachael plus two, but he smiled widely.

"The three musketeers! And one of you looks very bad-tempered indeed!"

Matthew growled his best Chewbacca impersonation and ran off to try to find my phone to play with. He clearly preferred Bugs Bunny to the Fridge Man.

Michael was in Brighton and sitting in one of rooms apparently earmarked for Cabinet members. It looked suspiciously like a bar. But then that was probably the desired effect, knowing the whims of politicians and conference organisers. We had hardly had a chance to speak during the last few days, due to the fact that Michael was ensconced in all things party conference. I had texted him a couple of times and there had been a couple of emails. But I didn't want to come across too much like a needy saddo single mum, trailing after a man who might well (despite his protestations) be quite happy with just a 'showing in Mottram for one night only' fumble. And I didn't want to drone on about the complex logistics involved with parking small children with relatives on the off-chance that he might be able to spend a weekend with me. The guy didn't have kids. Hell, he probably thought you could drop them off at the kennels at the last minute or something.

The decision I made a few days ago – to think positively, to take risks – had crumbled quite quickly. Instead, the evening before, I had decided to opt for the default to negative thinking. That way you can never feel too let down or embittered about anything in life. And it had always worked for me in the past. So it came as a surprise when Michael told me that he had noticed that I was online and wanted to say hello. It was all a little surreal. Not just because Lydia was stilting the conversation, thanks to her pint-sized but overbearing presence – but because every now and then the odd familiar face from the TV would appear behind him. At one point, the deputy prime minister materialised, performing some bizarre kind of R & B dance to the background music. He appeared to be slightly drunk, confirmed by Michael's "Yes, the silly old sod's well on his way."

Was it far too early to expose Lydia to some random bloke who may or may not be involved in a burgeoning relationship with her mother? Perhaps it wouldn't have been the right course of action for many single mothers – for many widows with young children. But I knew my daughter best. She wasn't the sensitive type when it came to Mummy sharing her affections. So long as Liddy got lashings of attention from anyone and everyone she came across in the normal course of the day, I could be shagging the boy who delivered our milk, for all she cared.

Michael, though, clearly wasn't used to Skyping with such a verbally-gifted near-seven-year-old.

"So, Lydia," he said. "Do you go to school?"

"No," said Lydia. "I go to a circus. I'm the star acrobat and I nearly broke my neck last week because I did the flying trapeze thing without a safety net."

Man on the fridge paused for a minute and then scratched his head, directing his next comment to me.

"Has she inherited your sarcasm? Or does she have a very unusual imagination?"

I tried not to laugh. Lydia huffed.

"It's rude to say 'she' about people. And anyway. Who are you and why can I hear seagulls?"

"I'm Michael."

"Right. Can I call you 'Mickey boy', then?"

"No. Michael's just fine. Thank you very much."

I'd seen this before with Tia and Tyler. Either Michael wasn't the sort to even try to play the kid-friendly game. Or he didn't know how to.

"So, how do you know my mum, then?"

"From ..."

"From work," I stepped in, quickly.

"Yes, from work," Michael agreed. "And I'm working right now, actually. In Brighton."

"Neverurdofit," replied Liddy, deliberately adopting her thickest Yorkshire accent.

"Not heard of Brighton? Good grief. What do they teach you children at school these days? It's a famous seaside resort. Look – there's the sea." Trying a little bit harder to accommodate Lydia's presence now, he moved his tablet away and pointed it towards a window. The deputy prime minister reappeared. Whirling his arms strangely.

"Who's the fat man – the one that's dancing there?" asked Lydia. "Has he eaten all of the seagulls? 'Cause I can't see any."

"Lydia!" I was appalled. "It's rude to call people 'fat'! You know much better than that!"

Michael started sniggering. This immediately irritated Lydia. Thinking that someone is amused at her expense always gets her back up.

"And it's rude to laugh at people!" Lydia now added. "And anyway, why would you be at the seaside and working? If I were there I'd be on a million donkeys and eating ice cream. You must be bored out of your head sat in that room with all those old men, when you could be doing pirate boat rides and amusement arcades like we always do at Scarborough …"

Michael agreed with her. "It is a bit boring, actually, Lydia. Maybe playing the Penny Falls or whatever they have in amusement arcades these days would be more entertaining."

I cut in again.

"Lydia – why don't you go and see what your brother's up to?"

Lydia ignored me.

"I know what would be dead good," she told Michael. "You could just leave your boring old friends in the room there, and go and find a Punch and Judy show or something – on the pier. Or we could just talk about Sooty if you want? Because …"

Lydia cocked her head to one side. Little cogs and wheels firing up there.

"... because I'm thinking … that you're the person who I was talking to the other day. About mad women who make their boobies bigger. When I had just had that bath where Matthew had nearly weed all over my hair …"

I stared at Michael's image on the screen. He was rubbing his forehead. Perhaps developing a headache. He looked tired. Unsure of his reply. Liddy was presenting a more troublesome challenge than Dimbleby or Paxman did, by the looks of it. Lydia continued with her disturbingly mature and photographically-gifted vernacular, however.

"And I'm thinking … that you've got the exactly same posh voice as the man who wanted to talk about Sooty. About trying to be Sooty. With my mummy the other night. You're him, aren't you?"

I nudged her sharply. "Liddy – I think that I can hear Matthew in your bedroom. Maybe he's going through your box of precious things. If I were you, I'd …"

But Lydia knew when her presence wasn't wanted. So Liddy was staying put. I decided to make things easier all round.

"Michael – it's a bit tricky, all this. I don't like to mix my – work – and small children. And I did promise Liddy that I would let her help me make the tea. And they're both starving. So, speak later, OK?"

He nodded "No problem, ladies. Go and make Yorkshire pudding, or whatever you subsist on in Holme." And he then gave us a little wave. Lydia gave him a casual flick of the wrist and then gallivanted off upstairs. Ready to break Matthew's arm after several prolonged minutes of delving in her shoe-box for shitty plastic gems, no doubt.

Michael and I managed to have a phone chat later on in the evening. He didn't exactly tell me that my daughter was a precocious little brat, but he didn't need to. I got in there first with that particular acknowledgement, making him guffaw.

"Well, I hate to say it, Rachael, but she really is exactly how I imagine you must have been as a child. And look how nicely you've turned out …"

And we ended that conversation with him mentioning the London jaunt.

"Look, it's all a bit crazy at the moment. The Chancellor and all the budget stuff has really put my back against the wall. So I won't be able to say until … about midweek … whether they'll let me have next weekend to myself. That OK?"

(Sure is, Michael. Didn't you know that the Kiddy Kennels can be booked at five minutes' notice?)

The next few days passed quickly. Shaun had been in the regional newspapers and on the TV for three days running. All in relation to the government's funding cuts, which Mr Big at Medlock Council and all his other pals in authorities across Greater Manchester were up in arms about. Cue lots of pictures of Shaun in the *Manchester Evening News* looking cross, mighty and self-righteous in a slick-looking Hugo Boss. A winning combination when you want to sell a news story.

I tried not to dwell on Shaun's words. About Michael not wanting to jeopardise his career for a fling with a bint from up north. And I tried not to think about the fact that by Wednesday there still had only been a couple of quick chats with Michael in between his conference activities, with no mention of me heading to London at all. So in order to counteract such default to negativity thinking, I decided to take the kids to Reading, regardless. Seeing their grandparents would be something for all of us to look forward to. It would be a welcome distraction for me, too, from the mounting bills. I'd had two more final demands that week.

On Wednesday lunchtime there was a charity event at the local community centre in Medlock. Representatives from Sisters' Space had been invited along, so Gillian and I popped over for half an hour. I caught a glimpse of Shaun, towering above the rest of the usual councillor cronies. Gillian left me for a few minutes to pick over the buffet and have a little grumble to herself about the lack of vegan and gluten-free products. And then Shaun appeared at my side.

With a new haircut. A number two. Not many men of forty-four years old could carry that off and still look …

Whatever.

"All right, Stan," he nodded. "Still waiting for your job application to come through … Been run ragged this week, thanks to all the shit that your new buddy in London has been creating for us."

I ignored his comment and instead opted for, "Thanks for the flowers, Shaun. I take it they were from you?"

And I swear to God, that for the first time ever, in sixteen years of knowing him, I saw the hint of a flush glowing underneath the Shaun-stubble.

But he shook it away with his usual ambivalence.

"Yeah well, unless someone else calls you 'Stan' these days…"

Gillian returned with a plate packed high with food. She nodded churlishly at Shaun, but offered us both her pickings. Shaun refused, telling her that a diet of something that looked like dog biscuits wasn't really up his street. And then he left us, mouthing "deadline – don't forget," at me.

Gillian called after him.

"Well, I know you fancy me, like – but you didn't have to go and copy my haircut, now, did you? Like you're stalking me or something!"

I elbowed Gillian, causing her to drop several of her gluten-free soya dog biscuits.

"Don't piss him off, Gillian. He pays our wages."

"Yeah; for now. More funding cuts to face, so they're saying…"

I watched him take another turn of the room, switching on his special brand of disgruntled charm for Medlock's finest. When he left the building I found myself wondering what it would be like, working in the same offices as him. Again.

On Thursday afternoon I had heard nothing more from Michael other than a couple of texts that said things along the lines of "Sorry, it's been crazy!" and "Sick of meetings". I was sitting at my desk, sipping coffee and tackling last-minute paperwork, trying to get everything shipshape for my next day – that long-awaited Friday away from work – when I noticed the email.

Marked 'urgent'. From the Rottweiler. Not that the email address stated this, of course. Her real name was Renee, but when out of earshot, everyone referred to her as the Rottweiler. She was Shaun's PA at Medlock and fiercely guarded his time, keeping the mere mortals from obtaining access to him. I had never met her, but had previously been the recipient of her clipped and cursory worded emails and phone calls:

Dear Rachael Russell

(Renee McCauley - On behalf of Shaun Elliot, Director of Communities and Leisure, Medlock Metropolitan Council):

I am writing to you to let you know that due to the unexpected severity of the government's recent funding reductions affecting Greater Manchester authorities, Medlock Council has been forced to make some difficult decisions as to where the essential cutbacks in our services will be located.

Unfortunately, because the provision of advice and support for women fleeing from domestic violence is not a statutory obligation of any local authority in England or Wales, the Council will no longer be able to contribute towards the funding of the Sisters' Space Centre. This will take place with effect from the new financial year.

Similarly, the increased pressure on the Council as a result of central government's funding reductions means that the authority will be undertaking an Emergency Asset Review of all its capital assets. As you are aware, the former Hartshill School, which has been leased for use by Sisters' Space, is owned by the Council. We, therefore, wanted you to be aware that the ownership of this building will also be under review with the possibility of sale to a third party.

We will let you know the outcome of this Emergency Asset Review decision by the end of November, once Medlock's Councillors and Executive involved have had sufficient time to carry out the review.

Regards, Shaun Elliot

I slopped half of my coffee across my desk in horror.

I re-read the email.

What the hell?

How could they – Shaun – have dictated this to his PA? To tell me this in an email? He was quite happy to turn up twice to see me last week. To send me flowers, remind me yesterday about the job offer. And forget to mention this? Relying instead on an officious – out of the blue – email?

This would be a disaster. This would mean redundancies. This would mean Sisters' Space closing – us becoming penniless and homeless. This would mean me losing my job. This would mean …

I grabbed my phone and dialled his mobile. No answer. Straight to voicemail. I tried again. Same result. And again.

Sod it. Call The Rottweiler.

She must have been sitting on her phone. No doubt getting a cheapie because I had responded almost immediately to her doom-ridden email.

"Renee. This is Rachael Russell. I'm the manager of Sisters' Space in Medlock. The support service for women dealing with domestic violence. You just sent me an email …"

"Yes."

"I need to speak to Shaun Elliot straight away. This is dreadful news."

"Yes. But you're not the only service who has to face this kind of news."

"I'm sure. But, I just need to speak to Shaun."

"Well, Mr Elliot is a very busy man."

"I know he is. Aren't they all, eh? But this is pretty desperate stuff, you know? I'm being informed about closure of our services – via email – which, incidentally, is a nasty way of dropping a bombshell on people …"

"Are you questioning Mr Elliot's judgement on this matter?"

"Yes, actually. I am. Yes to the judgement about what I've just been informed of. And Yes to how I've just been informed of it."

"I see."

"Is that a big issue for you, then? Do you have a problem with people who question Shaun Elliot's judgement? Or is he the kind of person who never screws up?"

An icy silence. She clearly wasn't used to being tackled in this manner.

"OK. Look. Whatever. Can you just put me through to speak to him about this?"

"I'm afraid not. He's busy at the moment. He's —"

I interrupted her now.

"A very busy man. I know. You said before. But I'm a very busy woman, so if you don't mind, I must speak to him."

"I'm afraid you can't. I can make you an appointment to see him, though."

"Fine. When is he free?"

"Well. I've got a half-hour slot. Afternoon of twenty-ninth of September."

"But that's nearly two weeks away!"

"I'm sorry if you feel you can't wait that long, but as I said before, lots of services are facing similar issues as yourselves and ..."

“I don’t care what lots of others are facing! I care about our centre and our staff! And I bloody well can’t wait until then!”

I could hear her getting riled now. Swearing at people has that effect on the faceless bureaucratic sorts.

“Well, there’s no need to be abusive. If you have a problem with waiting to meet with him, you could send him an email back. And I can forward it to him.”

“Well, thanks for that – it would never have occurred to me!” I replied and banged the phone down.

I looked at my desk and began to mentally compose the email back to Shaun.

No.

Don’t get into an email war of words. Tackle the bugger, as my dad would say.

I switched off my computer and stormed out of my room, informing my colleagues that I was going over to Medlock town hall before I went home for the day and that I would see them next week after my long weekend. After cutting across a chocca-busy A6 and skirting a couple of streets at the back of the Town Hall, I was lucky to find a parking space. Grabbing the ever-present sheaf of papers from my passenger seat, I tucked my head down and made fast strides past a council security guard and the reception desk. Luckily for me, they were both struggling with a translation issue – West African refugees, by the looks of it.

I didn’t bother with the lift. I ran the three flights of stairs up to the Communities and Leisure Directorate’s floor. I had never visited this part of the town hall before and I was taking a bit of a risk. Renee hadn’t given anything away in terms of Shaun’s whereabouts. He could well be at some Convention for Tosspot Senior Managers in St Ives or wherever the nearest golf course might happen to be conveniently located. But screw it. I was going to track him down one way or another.

After a bored-looking official pointed me towards Shaun’s office, I halted my stride just in time. There she was. The Rottweiler. Early fifties.

Small, dark and wiry. Scary-looking with school-maam specs (the peer-down-your-nose-to-intimidate-others sort.) Her desk was right outside an office that displayed Shaun's name on the obligatory brass-effect plate. I kept away from her line of sight and hovered next to some filing cabinets, leaning on them and pretending that I was casually doing some paperwork. Fido's kennel was on quite a busy thoroughfare, with local authority officer-types scurrying to and fro. I was pretty sure that she didn't know what I looked like. I stared at my pretend paperwork and strained to listen. The door to Shaun's office was slightly ajar and I could hear his voice from inside. Nice one. I couldn't hear anyone responding to his voice. He must be on the phone. I waited for the right time to make my move.

The Rottweiler was rattling away at her keyboard, glaring at her screen. Even her typing sounded aggressive. Probably firing off an equally insidious email to some other poor sod who worked in the voluntary sector. After two minutes she got up and moved away from the desk, heading to a room marked 'Kitchen' just along the corridor. Probably off to find a bone to chew on. I seized the moment, stalking past her desk and straight into Shaun's office.

There he was. Size twelves propped up on the desk and leaning back in his enormous chair. Shaun's employers always had to purchase special equipment in order to accommodate his height. In fact, everything in his room – desk, chair, plants, window – were large. To fit the Shaun scale. As though he was constructing the whole local authority around his own personal requirements. Maybe he was.

Empire-building.

He looked up, mid phone conversation. Surprised to see me. Gesturing for me to sit down, he took his feet off the desk and tilted his head to one side, looking out of the door. Wondering how I had dodged the Rottweiler.

I shook my head to the offer of a seat and instead, walked back to the office door, closing it. He tried to wrap up the conversation.

"Yep. No problem. Will do. Fine. So, it'll be next week at Preston. We can catch up properly then. Bye."

Chapter 21

ATLANTA RETURNS TO THE HUNT

He put the phone down and took his feet off the desk. Gazing at the small but mad-as-a-hen woman standing on the other side of his desk. Arms folded over the paperwork now clenched to her chest. Tapping her foot.

"How did you get past …?"

"The Rottweiler? I brought a tin of Pedigree Chum with me."

"Right. Like that top, Stan. Colour really matches your eyes."

My shirt was red. So was my mood.

I stayed quiet. He stood up. Mirroring Body Language with the Purpose of Calming Down Hysterical Female Employees was probably a module at Senior Local Authority Managers' Finishing School. He flicked his thumb over his shoulder at a stunning stained-glass window set in the original stone framework of the town hall. It depicted St George stabbing a dragon to death or something.

"Don't believe you've visited me in my office before. That window's one hundred and fifty-one years old. And never mind that – check out the view. Panoramic, or what? You can see Jodrell Bank on a clear day. Better than the vista from Roger's office, actually. Of course, our cerebrally challenged CEO prefers to have the view of the shopping centre. Probably leering over the lasses."

I stared at him, though, not the view. He nodded his head towards the leaded glass, continuing.

"And there's good old St George, of course. Couldn't ask for a more inspiring English role model on the shittier days that I have here …"

"Shaun, did you not know that St George was actually Palestinian?" I sneered. "And I can't believe you buy into all that St George for England crap. Anyway. Don't start trying to get all chatty with me. I'm here about the email I just got from you."

He cocked his head to one side, listening.

"You're pulling the funding on us? You're looking to sell off our building? And I'm informed by email? A snotty, officious email not even from you – from your pet dog?"

He pulled a face. The Robert De Niro one.

"I called her up straight away," I continued. "And what an absolute cow that woman is! I tried to speak to you and she says that you've got no appointments free for two weeks!"

"Well, things are mad. Thanks to your little pal in Whitehall …"

"Yeah yeah – blame someone else, Shaun. But I'll be the one sitting with members of staff and giving them their marching orders. Because you're way above and beyond that these days …"

"Your choice, Stan. You're more than capable of a much more senior job where you don't have to dirty your hands with that kind of —"

"But some of us have a soul, Shaun, and some of us want to sleep at night."

"Yeah well, your principles are all very nice, but —"

"Oh, don't change the subject. Are you saying that I've also got to look at us losing our building? Renee tells me this in some twatty email?"

"We have to focus on non-statutory services. And as for Renee, she's probably going through the menopause or whatever. So I would have thought that you of all people would be sympathetic to the crosses that women have to bear in life …"

Provocation. Courting controversy. This was just how Shaun Elliot's mind worked. Whipping out a semi-offensive remark designed to wrong-foot the opposition. Marking them out as the illogical and overly emotional participant in the debate. I was aware of this kind of thing now. So, I swallowed my fury and tried to speak calmly.

"OK. So let's not talk about the insensitivity of it all. About the fact that it was hardly 'best practice' dropping that little bombshell on me via email. Let's speak the truth here. Last week you seemed quite impressed with what we've been doing, so why all of a sudden …?"

He shook his head. "Come on, Stan. I could hardly predict this one. But someone else who *you* seem to know pretty intimately could have forewarned you. Your man's gone and chopped our revenue streams here at Medlock by some twenty per cent. I've got no other alternative than to find some serious savings here. Get rid of the non-essential services. Sell off some assets."

I cut him off.

"Just because you don't have a legal obligation to fund a domestic violence service doesn't mean that we're non-essential! You've heard about the kind of stuff our service users have to live with. They've got no one else to go to. They can't trust the police. Won't trust social services. They need independent support …"

He held his hand up.

"Rude to interrupt people, Stan. It's not a decision that was taken lightly, I can assure you. And it wasn't down to me, either. Whatever you think. It was the main Communities and Leisure Committee who had to carry out the emergency reviews and make some fast decisions. The politicians here."

"Yeah, I know. Headed up by a certain Councillor Kath Casey. Not our biggest fan. Even you said that the leader of the council can't stand Sisters' Space."

"Yes." He leaned back on his heels. I was tempted to poke a finger in his chest and topple him over. But I resisted the urge. "And as I said, Stan, we've also had to lose other services. Some of the mobile libraries, the free summer sports schools for kids, the welfare benefits advisors …"

"You cut the welfare benefits advice service? Are you frigging mad?"

"See – there you go. Being rude again." He shook his head at me, trying to disguise the twist of a smile. "So, as you can see, other – very important – services like yours won't get council funding. But don't be having a pop at me. At the end of the day, I'm the one tasked with finding where the cuts could be. Not should be, though. The councillors are the ones who make the decisions. I'm not the politician. I'm the executive. Just carrying out the orders ..."

"Bollocks. Don't insult my intelligence."

I was so angry now that I had bitten the inside of my cheek without even realising it. I could taste the blood. It grounded me. What was I doing? Getting into an argument with Shaun had always been an utterly futile endeavour. I looked at the floor and, taking a deep breath, I put the palms of my hands together and pointed the tips of my fingers at him. An almost prayerful appeal.

"Look, Shaun. Just level with me here. Is there no way back from this? Do I seriously need to tell people about redundancies? We've got Christmas only a few months away and it's the worst possible …"

He folded his arms and shook his head.

"Typical, Stan. Thinking about your colleagues and not your own career. I mean, this whole thing could actually turn out to be a positive change for you. I still find it bizarre that a clever, talented woman is stuck in a dead end job when, given the chance, she could be making an enormous difference at the centre of things. Where it really matters. Affecting people's lives en masse. A lot of people. That's what you always wanted to do, isn't it?"

(Michael and Shaun. Singing from the same song sheet. Great).

I set my jaw and stared out of the window behind him. I could just about make out Jodrell Bank, a tiny dark bump on the watery horizon of Cheshire. So it must have been a clear day.

He carried on. "You forget how long you and I go back, Stan. You had jobs like this ages ago. Doing the bog-standard managerial stuff. Helping the poor, mostly undeserving and definitely ungrateful members of the public."

I tried to interrupt him, but he shook his head, raising his voice.

"No, all right. Let me finish. You're way too good for that kind of thing. You're the visionary type. Not so long ago, you were advising the government on those steering groups in Whitehall. You had all those bloody top civil servants ringing you up, asking your opinions about stuff."

I kept quiet, letting him talk. It's always nice to have someone say pleasant things about you. But this was getting silly. Visionary type, my arse. And interestingly, the more silent I became, the more I noticed a change in his demeanour. He was growing frustrated. Animated. Not the chilled-out, couldn't-give-a-shit Shaun that most people got to see.

"I mean, if it wasn't for you, half of the women in centres like yours across the country wouldn't be getting all the legal help. Or the welfare benefits that they're now entitled to. Thanks to the stuff that you – you, personally – have achieved for them. They might not know that. But I do. And I know how you work. You quietly shake things up. You influence people. And that's why I want you here, working with me. If I'm going to be the one stepping up to the CEO post, I'll need a damned good team. People I can trust."

He turned back to the window, looking out. A 747 droned past us, on the descent towards Ringway, leaving a trail of fluffy pollutants across an almost cloudless sky.

"And I'd pay you twice as bloody much as you're on at the moment. You know that. And you need the money," he muttered.

I tried to collect my thoughts before I began.

"Shaun. We're going round in circles here. I'm not interested. Even if I lose my job at Sisters' Space thanks to your stupid – sorry, *necessary* – funding cuts ..."

"Not mine. Your man at the Ministry."

"It's rude to interrupt, Shaun," I said, pointedly. "So, even if I was going to be made redundant, I wouldn't want to be doing a policy job again. And I'm managing financially. Not that it's any of your business."

(Liar).

"Well, let's change the damned job, then!" he threw his arms up in despair. "Maybe there was too much bloody focus on the policy, anyway. We can shift responsibilities a bit. You can go out and visit homeless old ladies and prison inmates. Disabled lesbian refugees from eastern Europe who have TB. Whatever fallen on hard times group of people takes your fancy."

I shook my head."No. And as I've said to you before, Shaun, you can't just go offering jobs like that to people. What happened to equal opps?"

He snorted. Getting narked with me now. Bristling, even.

"Yeah, right – when was there a time I couldn't get around equal opps? We just go through the motions with interviewing the others. I know who I want here – and will you stop doing that?" he pointed his pen at me.

"What?"

"Looking heavenward. Rolling your eyes. You know it drives me mad!"

I was about to tell him where to shove his pen and his complaints about my eye-rolling, but we were interrupted by a light tap at the door. As the Rottweiler waltzed in, a look of surprise contorted itself upon her face. Almost physical disgust at my presence in the Omniscient Office of Her Great Giant.

"So sorry, Shaun. Is this someone you made an appointment to see, without telling me?" She looked directly at him, disregarding me. But I'd heard plenty about her and was aware that her modus operandi was to belittle people. So, before he could answer, I jumped right in.

"No, this someone just turned up right out of the blue because *that* someone," I pointed my finger at Shaun, "needs to consult with me over something. Urgently. In private."

The pet pooch was taken aback. Had probably never seen anyone speak to her Mr Elliot in such a way. Her presence in the room meant that Shaun had returned to his usual, unruffled manner, though. He reached over to the wall next to him and altered the angle of a painting of Medlock market in Victorian times. It didn't need straightening.

"Ladies – please. Yeah, Rachael should have made an appointment and all that. But give us ten minutes, Renee, and I'll go through those minutes with you. Promise." He nodded at his PA.

She realised that she was dismissed. Setting her jaw in place (thinking of gnawing a bone again, no doubt), she flung me a filthy look as she left the room.

(Get in your bed, Rover…)

As soon as she had gone, I closed the door with a good hard push and then sat down on the two-seater sofa next to Shaun's desk.

"I just want to know, Shaun. Are we talking a double whammy here? In addition to us losing our sixty-five per cent funding? When you've got to submit your recommendations to this so-called emergency asset review … will you be pushing for the sale of the building as well?"

He stood still, with his hands on his hips. Shaking his head, smiling warily at me.

"Look. Even if I did recommend that, Sisters' Space is still an entity in its own right. It seems to me that the whole concept of enterprise can't be working at your place, if you can't sell enough chocolate rabbits to pay people's wages there. Rudimentary principles of social enterprise – I would have thought that you …"

I glowered at him.

"You know we're not at that stage yet! I went over the business model and the plan in plenty of depth with you the other week. It would be another six months before we're breaking even. Which makes it even more stupid that you would do this to us now!"

He shrugged.

"Nowt that I can do about that, Stan."

I paused again. This was getting me nowhere.

Now was the time to up the ante. Play dirty.

"You know what? I wonder if your HR department or the *Manchester Evening News* maybe, would be interested in a story about some poor grieving widow. About her being bullied by one of the most senior men in local government in the north-west … due to the fact that they had an aborted love affair. Quite recently, actually. And all because he wants her to take a job that she doesn't want. A job that he seems to be making up as he goes along … and because he's a complete nobhead."

Nobhead. I was sure that I hadn't used that word since high school. Must be Dawn's influence.

Shaun was quiet for a few seconds. Reflecting. And then:

"Ooh, you're good, Rachael. You're really bloody good." He tapped his pen on the desk. "You're accusing me of blackmail now. Jesus! See what I mean? That's why I want you on the team here. You see so many other angles and avenues in any given situation. We need someone like you here. Someone who, clearly, can still impress the suits in London ..."

And now I quickly thought of something else. A complementary tactic.

"Funny you should mention London. I'm off there tomorrow."

"Yeah?" He was interested now. Glad of the change of subject, no doubt. "Work or pleasure?" he asked, standing up and walking towards me around his desk. Closer.

"Pleasure. Long weekend. Going to see my in-laws. May go to see my sister ..."

"She still in London?"

"Yes."

"Funny, that."

"What?"

"You wanting to go to London all of a sudden. You've always tried to avoid it. You hate the place."

"Well, perhaps I've changed my mind. Some of us have to change our opinions, don't we? A sign of maturity, apparently." I stood up.

He folded his arms and perched on the edge of his desk.

"One guess. Why you're going to London."

"Oh, Shaun. Will you just bloody leave it? Am I not allowed to go and check out a few paintings at the Tate Modern or have a gang bang with the Household Frigging Cavalry without you spouting your views at me? What do you care?"

I was getting desperate now, but this was good stuff, actually. I was getting under his skin. He shifted his weight and looked at his feet. At mine. Jet-dark eyes began to move up my body. A slow crawl.

"Well, that's just it," the gravelly Yorkshire intonations had softened now, sounded hoarser. "I do care. I think you're getting yourself into something that'll really hurt you. Someone has to tell you that."

(No one else about to, is there?)

His words and the change in his disposition were stirring that emotional melting pot once more. A slow spin; a laborious whirl with ribbons of sorrow, frustration – and fury.

Time to leave. This wasn't working after all. Shaun wasn't giving me the story I wanted to hear. No offers of a lifeline for Sisters' Space. So no point in staying. But I wasn't going to ignore his last remark.

"Shaun. Don't be such a hypocrite. Acting like the expert on what I should be doing in order not to get hurt ..." But I couldn't disguise the sudden change in my voice. Wobbling, faltering. I looked away quickly, hoping that he wouldn't notice the oncoming tsunami.

But he had.

"Hey," he called faintly, reaching over and touching me on the arm. "Hey. Sorry." Keeping his hand there. He stood up now and moved towards me, brushing his hand lightly against my back and beginning to stroke it gently. Up. And then down.

"Come here; come on." Pulling me closer to him. I resisted at first. Sulky-child seconds. But I let him lead me towards him. So that my face rested against his chest. I could feel the heat of his skin through the shirt. The scent of soap and fabric conditioner, the citrus and spiced notes of his aftershave. And then underneath that, I was breathing in the more personal and biological chemical properties …

Every nerve end in my body was jangling a warning.

Cattle-prodded. Painfully, jolted alive.

That's how it had always felt.

But this time, a real spike of fear in the pit of my stomach. That adrenaline again. Coursing through my veins. Spurred on by the legendary pheromones of Shaun and Rachael.

So much truth contained in legends. So many tough lessons to be learned.

And I didn't want history to repeat itself. I didn't want the ruinous agonies that being involved with Shaun always brought. But I wanted to stay here, too. It was familiar and oh-so-sweet territory. Getting doped to the eyeballs on dopamine. Seconds ticked by. Shaun placed his palm on the back of my head, stroking it gently. Slowly, deliberately, he moved his lips to mine. Just for a split second. Just so I felt the taste of him. Just so I was reminded of how it could be. How it would be?

Then he moved an inch or two away. Saying softly under his breath, "I don't know why you make life so complicated, Stan. I know I'm the last person that you'll take advice from. But I just think that you could be doing so much better for yourself. With your career. And in terms of men."

And then the town hall clock struck the half hour. A deep, brassy clang. But it wasn't the bell that knocked me back into my senses, deflecting me away from that moment of odd and unplanned intimacy. It was the fact that for a split second I had read Shaun's words as a reference to Adam. My imagination, perhaps. But jarring me, nonetheless.

I looked up at Shaun, caught a quick glance of his towards the door. Slight anxiety, a small frown in case the Rottweiler might walk in. See him holding me.

And then I glimpsed something on his desk. A discreetly placed photograph of a pretty, dark-haired woman clad in khaki colours, her image surrounded by greenery. Jungle vines, by the looks of it. Probably saving some gorillas in Uganda. Single-handedly re-foresting the Amazon.

Jess, no doubt.

Reminding me. I'd always be that dirty little secret.

I moved backwards, gathering more lucidity of thought. Hoping that the words would follow.

"Well. This is all very friendly, Shaun," I gave a quick blink, "but some of us have got kids to collect right now."

He nodded. Hands in pockets now.

I turned on my heel. Headed for the door.

"Stan?"

"What?"

"I mean it about the job. Closing date is tomorrow. I can't see that you've got any other options. Even if we don't sell off your building."

"Right."

"So just get the application in – 5 p.m. tomorrow."

I looked at my watch. Terribly important things to do, Shaun.

"Yeah, 5 p.m. tomorrow. I'll think about it."

He took a couple of steps towards me. My fingers were resting on the door handle, a slow push downwards. I-need-to-go.

Holding my gaze for a minute, he smiled grimly. Reached out and swept the tip of my chin with his fingers. Tracing his hand across my throat. Testing my reaction. Then he said, quietly, "You're still one real mindfuck, you know."

I pushed the handle down hard. Moved away from his touch and opened the door.

"See you, Shaun. I'll guess I'll be hearing from you. One way or another. Or from Fido in the foyer here."

"Yeah. And Stan?"

"What?"

"On London. I wouldn't take the risk. If I were you. Call me if you need me."

"Right."

"You know that some of us will always be here for you ..."

I glanced back over my shoulder. But he had turned around. Drinking in the panorama of urban Manchester through the prism of a slain, glass-eyed dragon.

Ignoring the venomous stare of the Rottweiler, I made my way down the municipal stairways and back into the council car park. I opened the car door and plonked myself onto the driver's seat. I reached for Matthew's emergency day-glow lollipop stash in the glove compartment, although a triple G and T would have been more welcome. But sugar would have to do.

Think, Rachael. Think.

I glanced at my phone. Four messages on my voicemail. The first was from the mortgage people, querying why I hadn't been able to make this month's minimum payment. The second was from Matthew's nursery, asking me to pick him up as soon as I could because he had "bitten another child on the head" and had to be sent home due to their safeguarding policy.

How the hell do you manage to bite someone on the head?

The third voicemail was from my mother. Not meant for me, apparently. The phone-in-handbag trick. Today she was asking her local pharmacist "for your most effective pile treatment. He's suffering terribly with them at the moment. Of course, sitting in his shed on that damp allotment for half the weekend so he can avoid his grandchildren didn't help. They're a bit … hyperactive."

I deleted all three messages.

Because that said it all, really. No amount of thinking was ever going to change the state of affairs, which Shaun had just related to me in his usual blunt fashion. The bleeding obvious, quite frankly.

Michael and Me? Could never be. Our lives were poles apart. Were great big ruddy socio-economic, political and several hundred miles of railway tracks apart. Never mind the motorbike thing. And the army thing. And God knows how many more reminders that it could never work.

I sucked at Matthew's lollipop. Bubblegum flavour. Hideous. And then I listened to the final message.

It was from Martyn Pointer.

Martyn had heard all about the cuts at Sisters' Space. He wanted to let me know that there was still time available to take out the social enterprise loan that he had previously offered me. And that there was a separate loan facility that allowed an organisation to pay for the acquisition of a property. "So perhaps Ms Russell would like to have a further chat about this, with a view to moving entirely away from the parochial tendencies of a certain Mr Elliot."

So. Go on, Rachael. Call him.

But I rubbed the back of my neck, instead. Nerves and muscles a-jangling from Shaun-sex endorphins had morphed into a dull ache now. Unsure what to do.

That was the thing about an encounter with Shaun. The charge was so forceful, so power-packed, that as soon as it began to wear off you found yourself wondering when the next bolt would come – not looking for it, exactly, but perhaps anticipating …

I shrugged as I chucked the phone back onto the passenger seat and then opened my car window, spitting out the sickly lollipop. Generating a look of disgust from an elderly black woman trudging past the car with her two heavy shopping bags.

What to do? Jobs, money and men. Lethal sodding combination.

At least with Shaun I knew the score. Was on home turf.

What would Adam want for me? For us? Anyone's guess. We'd been living life too much to ever really talk about the What Ifs. And anyway, who the hell could have pre-empted this particular little geometrical combination of What If Corner?

I started the engine. The car radio boomed into life, causing me to jump and to clutch the steering wheel.

And there it was.

AC/DC's 'Highway To Hell'.

(Cheers for that, Adam.)

And I laughed and I cried.

I laughed and I cried.

"A wicked and adulterous generation asks for a sign."
(Matthew 12:39, Bible NIV)

EPILOGUE

So here I was again.

Sitting on a park bench with stretched-out legs. Toe-tapping. Wondering if Mr Very Big and Important Person in These Parts would arrive on time.

The pigeons were getting a bit too friendly for my liking. Pecking perilously close to my shoes. Yes, I was wearing heels again. Not stupidly lascivious loved-up heels. These were pretty but prudent. The sort that a lady in waiting would choose to meet a man who didn't want to draw too much attention to the both of them while in public.

I crossed my legs, startling the pigeons. They flapped off drunkenly, towards the rhododendrons. I squinted at the face of the clock in the distance. Fifteen minutes late.

A rubbish bin, a dozen or so yards away, was attracting wasps. This year, they were hardy little critters. We were heading for nippier days and there were still no signs of them buzzing off to the great nest in the sky. Best to stay away from the stripy flying things at this time of year. They would be in a rather foul mood.

As I would be, too, if he didn't turn up soon. I'd arranged a lot of stuff, re-jigged quite a few schedules, and woven some elaborate stories in order to be here. To see him.

I jumped suddenly – nearly knocking my handbag off the edge of the seat – as a pair of hands reached from behind the park bench, covering my eyes. Holding my head firmly. Not yielding.

"Oh, very funny," I muttered.

Met with silence.

"So – am I supposed to … guess who? It's going to be a tricky one, this …"

I heard a sigh, partly muffled by the floating chimes that came to us across the lawns. The big clock striking quarter past five. A clipped response.

"Like I said before. You'd be dreadful in the army, Rachael. All too easy to ambush."

"Yeah, well. Some of us have read *War and Peace* and understood what the subtext was all about, without being so mindless as to think it might be a great and glorious thing to do. To join the military …"

He dropped his hands from my eyes. And I craned my neck back, meeting those grey eyes at last. He reached for me. All upside down. Mouth on mine.

And there was a definite charge there. Perhaps even rivalling that of the Light Brigade.

Michael pulled me up from the park bench and nodded towards Westminster station.

"Welcome to my stomping ground, Ms Russell. Sorry it's all been a bit last-minute for you. Now. Only say nice things about our chaps in the army, if you don't mind. I've got ministerial obligations here, remember?"

I let him kiss me again. Five o'clock shadow in the shade of Big Ben.

"And hand me that annoying little suitcase-on-wheels thing of yours. I'm taking you right back to my barracks." I got up from the bench and frowned at him.

"Speaking of all things military, Michael – isn't it time that you told me about those war wounds of yours? You were happy enough to joke about them on Twitter, but you did say that there was a story behind it all and I for one still don't know how you —"

"Yes, yes. All in good time, though. All in good time." Accompanied by a sharp nod and that blinding grin – dimples dancing in the waning light. His fingers reached for mine as he told me:

"And now, my lovely northern broad – quick march!"

I rolled my eyes.

But for once, I did as I was told.

THE END

KEY TO CHAPTER TITLES:

Prologue1 – 'FRIGG IN HELL' – **Frigg*** (also known as 'Freya') was viewed as the goddess of motherhood and the weaver of fate.

Prologue 2 – 'KERES ON THE ROOF' – **Keres** were spirits (female) of violent death.

1.'PANDORA ON THE DOORSTEP: REAL TIME' – **Pandora** was the first woman, created by Zeus, king of the gods. Pandora opened 'that box' and unleashed every woe and evil into the world. The only thing remaining in the box was Hope.

2.'PANDORA PROPS UP POSEIDON' – **Poseidon** was the god of the sea, and watery things in general.

3.'ERIS AND ARES – GOING AT IT' – **Eris** was the goddess of strife, discord and war. **Ares** was another war god, and a lover of violence.

4.'POOR OLD PEGASUS' – **Pegasus** was a beautiful, immortal winged horse.

5.'SANCTUARY OF DELOS (OR THE DOSSHOUSE)' – **Delos** is a sacred island for the Greeks. It is said to be the birthplace of Apollo and Artemis (see 19).

6.'DIONYSUS, THE AMPHORA AND A CRAP FROZEN PIZZA' – **Dionysus** was the god of wine and enjoyment.

7.‘TWO TALES OF THANATOS’ – **Thanatos** was the god of non-violent death.

8.‘POST-HIMERUS, AND BATHTIME’ – **Himerus** was the god of sexual desire.

9.‘AMAZONS IN AGREEMENT’ – The **Amazons** were a race of female warriors.

10.‘PAN HANDLING IT’ – The god **Pan** was half-goat and half-man; a musician with a sense of mischief.

11.‘ENTER HADES’ – **Hades** was the dour god of the underworld: head honcho of the dead.

12.‘CHAOS, THE TITANS’ – **‘Chaos’** was the voidless state referred to by the Greeks before the creation of the world. **The Titans** were perceived to be the ‘elder gods’, who ruled before the Olympian gods (such as Zeus).

13.‘HERA IS A RIGHT COW’ – **Hera** was Zeus’ wife and the quarrelsome goddess of marriage.

14.‘THE AGE OF IRON(ING)’ – The Greeks believed that they were living in **The Age Of Iron** – a time of relentless toil and hardship.

15.‘THE CAP OF INVISIBILITY’ – The **cap** was Hades’ favourite article of clothing. Helped him to carry on being a sneaky bugger.

16.‘ARISTOPHANES’ ARRIVAL AT NUMBER TEN’ – **Aristophanes** was a Greek writer of comedy plays; he often poked fun at the Establishment in Greek society.

17.‘TANTALISING APOLLO AND ARTEMIS’ – **Apollo** and **Artemis** were twin gods (brother and sister). Apollo was said to be god of the sun, of light and of the truth. Artemis was the goddess of wildlife and was not particularly fond of men.

18.‘TABLOID TITANS’ – See 12.

19.‘PLANNING FOR THE PARTHENON?’ – The **Parthenon** was a magnificent temple built on the Acropolis, Athens in honour of the gods.

20. ‘HADES SETS THE LABYRINTH’ – The **Labyrinth** was home to the child-chomping Minotaur. We don’t know if Hades had any hand in creating the Labyrinth, but you can bet your bottom dollar that he thought that it was a marvellous idea.

21.‘ATLANTA RETURNS TO THE HUNT’ – **Atlanta** was the goddess of the hunt. And of running.

**Frigg is the only non-Greek included in the chapter titles. Always nice to have a bit of cultural diversity, I think.*

Coming Soon.

Get ready for the next book in the Rachael Russell series!

34

Find out more about the words, world and wonderings of Chris L. Longden at:

www.funnylass.wordpress.com